"WHEELER IS A MAST...
TERS—A STAND-OUT ...

*El Paso Herald-Post*

"Richard Wheeler's novels of the Old West transport the reader straight back to that fabled era: you intimately know the territory, the people, the times. If you haven't yet traveled into the past with Wheeler, do so now!"

—Marcia Muller,
author of *WHERE ECHOES LIVE*

"WHEELER NOW JOINS THE RANKS OF LARRY McMURTRY, GLENDON SWARTHOUT, TONY HILLERMAN AND DOROTHY JOHNSON."

—*Billings Gazette*

"From the moment I read his first novel, *WINTER GRASS*, I've been a fan of Richard Wheeler's writing. What he does better than most is consistently, book after exciting book, draw his memorable characters with bold, bigger-than-life strokes. Already a master at pacing and story, Wheeler lends his magic touch to exploring the little-known dynamics of an entire era with sensitivity rarely seen in today's writing on the opening of the West."

—Terry C. Johnston,
author of THE PLAINSMEN series

"WHEELER HAS DONE FOR THE WESTERN WHAT C. S. FORRESTER DID FOR THE SEA STORY."

—*Rocky Mountain News*

Tor books by Richard S. Wheeler

*Forthcoming

# SKYE'S WEST: WIND RIVER

## RICHARD S. WHEELER

TOR

A TOM DOHERTY ASSOCIATES BOOK
NEW YORK

WIND RIVER

Copyright © 1993 by Richard S. Wheeler

Cover art by Royo

A Tor Book
Published by Tom Doherty Associates, Inc.
175 Fifth Avenue
New York, N.Y. 10010

Tor ® is a registered trademark of Tom Doherty Associates, Inc.

ISBN: 0-812-52142-0

First edition: October 1993

Printed in the United States of America

0  9  8  7  6  5  4  3  2  1

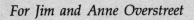

*For Jim and Anne Overstreet*

# Chapter 1

The winter of 1853 opened old wounds. While the biting winds of the Hunger Moon shivered Barnaby Skye's buffalo-hide lodge, something shivered his soul. Day after day he slumped before his lodgefire, scarcely aware of his patient wives, old Victoria of the Crows and lovely Mary of the Shoshones. His chunky little boy, Dirk, crawled into his lap only to be ignored.

In times like this, Skye would saddle his yellow-eyed terror, Jawbone, and ride down the Platte River to purchase a jug of salvation from the Fort Laramie sutler, his friend and agent Colonel Augustus Bullock. But no jug of spirits could cure what lay in him now.

He knew from the quiet glances of his women that they worried about him. Old Victoria understood him so well they rarely needed to speak., She chose not to speak now but sometimes pressed her brown hand to his unshaven cheek, a gesture that said she loved him and would wait for him to conquer the demons that had wrestled his heart to the ground.

Young Mary had snuggled close to him under the thick buffalo robes in the blackness of the winter nights but he had not responded. He saw her worried glances but didn't care.

There are times that leap upon every man when he is stricken by the panorama of his own life. He suddenly sees himself through all the years of his struggle, the victories and failures, the waste and disillusionment. Sometimes that evokes pain; less often, pride. Occasionally joy. But this bleak winter of the soul Barnaby Skye felt no pride in what he'd achieved because he'd accomplished nothing. Not since the age of fifteen, when he'd been pressed into the Royal Navy right off the banks of the Thames, had he had a life of his own.

He'd been a prisoner of the Queen in frigates and men-of-war for more years and months and days and hours than he cared to remember, until he had jumped ship one foggy night when the Royal Navy had come to visit Fort Vancouver on the Columbia River in the wild wastes of the New World. He would never see England again.

Now, in this bitter season of 1853, he could make no sense of his life. He slouched before the cheery fire, drawing no heat from it while blizzards chucked snow down the smoke hole and his wives busied themselves with their endless tasks—and worried about him.

Gone were the Cambridge schooling, the hearty life in Victorian London, the company of bright learned men, and all the rest. Gone and dead. Now he was a border ruffian, a guide, a coarse squawman, a beached schooner.

The spring thaw came but his spirit remained dark and frozen. The patience of his women had frayed. They stared stonily at him as he slumped in the gloom of his lodge, and fled outdoors to bathe in the coy sun and sniff the racing whippets of warm air. They embraced the goodness of life even if he could not. He scarcely noticed when the first meadowlarks arrived.

One day an Oglala boy handed him a note from Colonel Bullock requesting that Skye ride in to the fort. Skye gave the boy a tobacco twist and stepped outside into a glaring April morning, saying nothing to his curious women. He hunted for Jawbone, intending to make peace. The battered blue roan, insulted by Skye's neglect, had taken to sulking in cottonwood groves a mile distant, gnawing bark to stay alive. Skye sighed, lifted his battered silk top hat, ran a gnarled hand through his gray-shot hair, and wished he hadn't been bothered.

Jawbone sprang at him from a copse of greening cottonwoods like a war party of Sioux, and screeched a whole winter of complaints. Mister Skye stood stock-still. Jawbone bit him on the shoulder, nipped his hand, and snarled in his ear. Then he lifted Skye's top hat off his head—an act deserving the death sentence—and stomped it in the mud.

"I know, mate, I know," Skye muttered, straightening out the dents in the hat.

After that Jawbone butted him and permitted him to run a hand under the tangled mane. Ten minutes later, their friendship patched and tentative, Barnaby Skye rode toward Fort Laramie, Jawbone strangely happy.

The Army post snoozed in the white light of April. Skye rode across the muddy parade seeing not a soul. He cascaded stiffly from Jawbone before the cavernous sutler's emporium. At once the horse swung around, rump to store, ready to commit mayhem upon man or beast.

Colonel Bullock, as usual, worked at his rolltop desk in a pool of stunted light at the rear. The old Virginian stood, surveyed Skye, and sighed. "You didn't winter well, suh," he said through his Vandyke.

"I discovered I have no reason to exist," Skye said.

"I'd advise a bath," said Bullock. "Until then—you're right."

"You want me?"

"Your summer's been preempted."

Skye could make no sense of that. "You found a client so soon?"

"The client found you, suh. Against my better judgment."

"Well, turn them down. I don't want any clients this year."

His agent laughed thinly. "You don't just turn down the United States Government, Mister Skye."

"I do. Have you something in that decanter?"

"Always. But we've nothing to toast. Here's the straight of it. Colonel Hoffman got word by courier yesterday. The Indian Bureau's planning a big pow-wow with several tribes on the Wind River. A peace conference like the one in eighteen and fifty-one, but up at the old rendezvous site at the confluence of the Wind and the Little Wind.

"You know what those peace conferences are—getting 'em to quit pickin' on white men. Our esteemed commanding officer's been requested to send runners out to the Crows, Eastern Shoshones, Northern 'Rapahoes, and Northern Cheyenne to meet the big cheeses from Washington City round about the fifteenth of July. Hoffman's instructions are to hire you and your ladies as guides and translators. The Army'll pay you sixty dollars—thirty a month and chow for two months of guiding; the Bureau'll pay two hundred the summer for translating."

"That's for all of us?"

Bullock chuckled. "Mister Skye, that's not how the government thinks. It's not inclined to pay women even for scrubbin' shirts. Our friend the colonel said he had no choice—that's the price, take it or leave it. I'd say take it."

Skye pondered it. "I'm done with guiding. Tell them no."

Bullock arched a brow. "You don't mean that."

"I do."

"You're into my pocket, Mister Skye. Two hundred eighty at the moment. Mostly to fuel your bad habits. You'll need a payin' client—unless you have . . . other plans."

Skye sighed. "What do they want, Colonel Bullock?"

"Guide the Indian Bureau party—that's the superintendent, Cummings; the assistant, his brother; a chief clerk, and a dozen flunkies. They'd attach you to a troop of dragoons out from Fort Leavenworth, comin' along to protect the big mucketymucks. On the Wind River your ladies'd translate to the Crow and Shoshones; you to the rest. And then you'd bring 'em all back here safely afterward."

"No."

"Hoffman says you're the man for the job. Every warrior on the Plains respects you. You're a legend. You're big medicine. You've got that old-time religion. If they're going to listen to anyone they're going to listen to Mister Skye."

"I'm sick of it. I'm sick of the wilderness. I'm thinking of going east."

"You, suh! You? Mister Skye, I've known you for years. There's never been a cross word betwixt us. You're an honorable man, suh. You pay your debts. I can't fathom what's eating you. Something is."

Skye sighed, feeling trapped. "Tell me about Cummings," he muttered.

"A fine Virginia family, Mister Skye. Victorious Bonaparte Cummings. His younger brother is the Reverend Wellington Waterloo Cummings. Sons of Jericho Trumpet Cummings, a Norfolk planter. Victorious is running the Indian Bureau with a good firm hand. He's fair to the tribes; better than the War Department ever was when they ran it. And his brother Wellington—why, suh, he's got a vision of what's good for the Red Man. He thinks maybe the Noble Savage should be given religion."

"Indians don't need white religion."

"Superintendent Cummings wants to remove them far from settlers and then show 'em how to farm. The Reverend Mister Cummings sees an idyllic future for them, guided by the Bureau, learnin' their ABCs and gospels and living like white men, plowin' prairie. They're relying on the good offices of your ladies to convey the cast-iron future to the Shoshones and Crows. They're well aware that the younger Mrs. Skye's a clan-sister of Chief Washakie."

"That's it, Bullock? We're to retail the Indian Bureau's plans to the tribes?"

"For two hundred sixty dollars. And maybe you can pick up some other coin."

"Tell Colonel Hoffman no."

Bullock cocked a brow. "I feared you'd say that. I told the old honker so. Workin' for the government, Mister Skye, is a basket of snakes. You want me to convey your everlasting esteem and sincere best wishes and your unspeakable delight in the flatterin' offer?"

"Just tell him I'm no longer guiding," said Skye.

# Chapter 2

The rivers foamed with winter's burdens but Barnaby Skye's melancholia didn't melt. He sat in his own arctic circle while all around him nature rioted and rejoiced. Sometimes he ventured out to visit Jawbone. But the ugly old roan didn't cotton to it and knew that Skye was not himself. Whenever Skye approached, Jawbone clacked his yellow teeth and snapped, as if Skye were a horsefly.

His wives no longer stared at him patiently. Now they peered solemnly at him, hard-eyed, and talked between themselves just out of earshot. The Skye lodge was disintegrating. He didn't care. One day under a cottonwood whose budding leaves made a misty veil above him, he remembered Margaret, the girl he'd been sweet on in London before the Royal Navy snatched him. He'd thought he might marry her after he finished his schooling. He liked her freckles and sausage curls and pink bows; but mostly he liked her because she was serious and talked about the Corn Law, and the Luddite riots, and the depression.

He thought of all the things he could not talk about to Victoria or Mary. Like the books he'd read or the plays he'd seen or the debate he'd heard or the latest folly on the Continent. Except for a book or journal he begged from travelers, he'd enjoyed none of that. And through all the years of exile in the New World—first as a trapper with the fur brigades, then as a top man with American Fur, and finally as a guide—he had never stopped starving for the pleasures of civilization. When had he enjoyed a witty lecture? A trenchant debate? A musicale? A friendly pub, an inn, a game of Charades with laughing girls? He sighed, riven by memories, and stared blankly into an empty land.

Victoria and Mary had not asked him about his business with Colonel Bullock, and Mister Skye hadn't told them. They eyed him sadly each day, enduring his suffering and telling themselves that the Planting Moon would bring a change. But when Sun overpowered Cold Maker and Mister Skye didn't change they took to staring at him stonily.

"Don't you like me anymore, papa?" Dirk had asked one day after Skye had brushed him aside. The women paused, waiting for an answer, the moment pregnant. But Mister Skye just patted the child absently and stared into the emptiness around him.

After that things changed. The women vanished for long periods, wandering along the Platte River, talking to each other. They didn't want to be in a lodge made gloomy by Skye's melancholia. Jawbone remained sulky, barely tolerating Skye, who bestirred himself once a day to wander out to the meadows and stare at the ugly brute. Jawbone began to flesh out on the lush buffalo grass after nearly starving to death because of Skye's neglect, but Skye barely noticed.

Much of the time Skye scarcely knew where he was;

the wilderness he had loved and fought, his refuge and enemy for a quarter of a century, mocked him. He sighed occasionally, wanting to be somewhere else, even on the teak deck of a British frigate, hearing its sails snap in the shifting breeze. Rule, Britannia! The vagrant thought amazed him. He'd been a miserable wretch in the Royal Navy. But it had all been better than this. He peered about him, finding no solace anywhere. The New World seemed loathsome to him. Ah, for one mug of Guinness ale with some good men at some hearty pub!

Late in the spring—Skye had lost track of time—Victoria approached him.

"We are going back to our people," she said without preamble. "You don't like us no more. You ain't gonna be happy until you go back to your own people."

"Victoria—"

"Leave me alone, smelly dog. We're going."

He stared listlessly as Mary and Victoria loaded their packhorses, emptied the Skye lodge of their robes and parfleches, and saddled their little mares. Then they rode off. Victoria looked back once, her cheeks wet. Dirk, in Mary's lap, sobbed. Skye watched them weave through cottonwoods and around a canebrake, and then they vanished.

Jawbone, frantic at the separation, raced after the women, whickering piteously, but they shooed him away. He edged back to Skye, snorted angrily, and then trotted in crazed circles, helpless to stop the sundering of the only world he'd known since he was a mean little colt. Skye watched somberly. Jawbone looked uglier than ever. Skye remembered the silky thoroughbreds dancing through the cobbled streets of London and the disciplined drays responding to the delicate touch of coachmen. None of them were grotesque outlaw nags.

A chapter of his life had ended. He barely bestirred himself to eat or hunt. He stared despondently at the waters of the North Platte, flowing steadily toward civilization. As spring advanced, the legend and the terror of the Plains shrank into a shell of his former self.

An Oglala boy sent by Colonel Bullock found him lolling before his tattered lodge. The sutler wanted to see Skye, the boy announced. Skye blinked, barely hearing, but at last he nodded. It took him an hour to catch Jawbone, who bit and butted before letting Skye throw a pad saddle over his back. Then Skye rode through a velvety green spring to Fort Laramie.

The post sutler peered up from his office chair, shocked. "Mister Skye, suh, something is plainly wrong."

Skye nodded.

"Are you ill? Should I summon the post surgeon?"

Skye lifted his silk topper and settled it into the rat's nest of graying hair. "Victoria and Mary left me. Took my boy."

Colonel Bullock, U.S.A., Ret., absorbed that, dismayed. "Are they coming back?"

"No."

"May I—would you forgive my asking what happened?"

"Let it alone. I'm going home."

"Home?"

"London. All this"—he waved a weary arm—"is empty. Only I can't. Deserters can't."

"That was nearly three decades ago; you were pressed in anyway."

"Someone'll remember."

"That's the past, Mister Skye. You're just having a bout of phantasms. A plague o' might-have-beens. Lost your bearings for a spell. Let me tell you, suh; no life's been better lived or happier out here on the borders than yours. You're the envy of every border man."

"Borders!" Skye roared. "When do I get to read a

paper or sit in a coffeehouse? Or talk? The women . . ." He wanted to say that his Indian wives could never be companions of the mind. There was nothing here; he had come face-to-face with a sea of emptiness.

Colonel Bullock's nose wrinkled. "Mister Skye, it's nothing that a bath won't cure. You build yourself a sweatlodge and steam it out of you . . . No. Give your duds to some Oglala woman for fixing and cleaning. No, better yet, I'll have the farrier sergeant turn over a horse trough. I'll fetch some hot water. Watch out for ladies. I've a ball of yellow lye soap here. You get, ah, sweetened up and I'll send for your ladies."

"Why'd you call me in?"

"Oh, that. The Indian Bureau still wants you and your ladies. They've upped the ante. Now they're sayin', what'll you do it for? Colonel Hoffman told me they'd settle for your usual five hundred. They're getting plumb desperate; there're guides aplenty to take them to the Wind River but not a soul with your reputation among the tribes, your abilities . . . I'll tell 'em you're indisposed and your ladies are—no longer available."

Barnaby Skye peered out the grimy window at soldiers doing rifle drill on the parade; at canvas-clad troopers grooming their mounts at the stables; at a military post alive with the approaching summer. In a few days the first of the California emigrants would roll in. The mob kept getting bigger ever since the forty-niners raced pell-mell for Sutter's Mill across the continent.

His hair hung in greasy ropes; his face lay under a lawn of stubble. His burly, scarred body stank. He didn't care.

"When do they want me?"

"They wanted all of you—the woman to translate. They're en route now out the Platte Road. A dragoon troop, some ambulances for personnel, and a couple of light carriages for the Indian Bureau superintendents."

"I'll take it."

"Mister Skye, suh. I knew you'd come to your senses."

"Summon the farrier sergeant. Tell Colonel Hoffman that five hundred is acceptable."

Augustus Bullock smiled thinly. "I'll put your usual kit together and credit your account—after a little talk with the colonel." He led Skye along the gloomy aisles and handed him a ball of yellow soap.

"It'll pay you off and give me cash to get out of here," Skye said.

# Chapter 3

The Superintendent of Indian Affairs, Victorious Bonaparte Cummings, preferred not to think of his person
as obese. Big, rather. A man of his girth was a weighty
man; a man of substance. Furthermore, none of his
three hundred and sixty-odd pounds was soft; his
flesh was granite through and through as befitted a
gentleman of military caste. The outward appearance
was but the manifestation of his inward greatness. He
wore a black worsted suit tailored to dignify his formidable person. He was not to be seen in public without
a cravat and freshly starched white collar; nor did he
much go abroad without a glossy silk top hat and his
gold-knobbed walking stick, both of which added to
the impression he made upon others. He carried his
bulk fittingly, with slow, dignified steps that bespoke a
measured man with a measuring mind.

The trip out the Platte River Road had been capital.
Lieutenant Truscott's 2nd Dragoons had proceeded
just ahead of the great mob of immigrants heading for

California or Oregon; the Army's grain-fed mounts trotted across the Plains with scarcely a halt. Those few westering emigrants the government train did pass were impressed by the sight of Truscott's troop escorting several Army ambulances drawn by big Missouri mules, and Cummings's own conveyance, a light carriage with tandem seats. His Army driver occupied a portion of the first; Cummings filled the whole of the plush leather seat just behind it. The second part of the expedition, the freight wagons carrying the annuities to be given to the tribes on completion of the treaty, were a few days behind.

On the whole, Cummings couldn't complain. There'd been a few spring squalls, at which time he'd repaired to the covered ambulance and whiled away the downpour in the company of his brother, the Reverend Wellington Waterloo Cummings, and the Bureau's dimwitted chief clerk, Alphonse McGinty. The ambulance benches were naked pine, which wrought some discomfort on Cummings's person and aggravated his hemorrhoids. Thus he always returned to his light buggy the instant the rain stopped, to the consternation of his driver, who wiped the leather seat dry and worried about exhausting the two trotters when the burdened carriage plowed deep furrows in the mud.

It was all going to be just fine.

Lieutenant Truscott's splendid dragoons, F Troop, the bay-horse pride of Fort Leavenworth, maintained their sprightly pace and raised Fort Laramie, some seven hundred miles later, on the very June day the treaty party was scheduled to arrive. Cummings reminded himself to commend the young officer. The fellow was a dashing sort, with neck-long blond hair and a face so angular it looked to be whittled of birch. Unlike Cummings, whose eyes were black and manly, Truscott's gray eyes conveyed something delicate and disdainful, as if he could condemn gladiators with a downward turn of his thumb.

Cummings approved. As a Virginian of good family he knew there were only two classes on earth: those born to command and those born to obey. In this little party he and Wellington commanded; McGinty and the rest obeyed. Thus it would be at the treaty councils, he thought.

The terrain interested him. The blue bulk of Laramie Peak loomed beyond, and closer at hand, the darkly forested hills that begrudged the Platte. The decrepit fort interested him more. This farthest outpost of American military power had been scoured by wind and hunkered on a naked flat where no mortal ought to abide.

Truscott halted his command and ordered that the colors be broken out. His men wiped their sleek horses, shook dust out of their tunics, and rubbed their boots clean. Then the treaty party marched into Fort Laramie on a trumpeter's trill, a dazzling contrast to the sullen laxity of the post. Soldiers haphazardly emerged from barracks and stables to watch Truscott's smart progress across the parade. The lieutenant was clearly showing these frontier regulars what the United States Army could and should be. Cummings saw Colonel Hoffman, the commanding officer, emerge from the headquarters and stare with his arms folded across his bosom.

Truscott halted his column and saluted. "Lieutenant Truscott, F Troop, Second Dragoons, reporting on schedule, sir. We have the Indian Bureau party with us."

Hoffman nodded. "See to the comfort of your troops," he said.

That struck Cummings as virtually an insult. The CO might be difficult. But they wouldn't be here long. Cummings swung slowly to the ground, as befit a man of his bulk and station, and proceeded toward

Hoffman, intending to bite the hand that would feed him.

"Welcome, Superintendent. Let's repair to my office and we'll cut the dust," Hoffman said.

"Pleased to join you, ah—what did you say your name is?"

"Yours is Victorious Bonaparte Cummings."

An ill wind was blowing, Cummings thought as he mounted the ten steps with dignity. Not an officer of the day, not a sergeant major, not an aide-de-camp lurked in the homely place. Within, the colonel ushered him to a hard seat and settled into a swivel chair behind his battered desk. Cummings decided to stand. Height and bulk gave a man an advantage.

"You had a pleasant journey?" Hoffman inquired.

"Quite perfect. The lieutenant should be commended."

Hoffman reached toward a decanter on a sideboard and poured amber fluid into two tumblers. "Water?" he asked.

"Neat."

The colonel added a splash of water to his own glass and they drank.

"We're short-handed. All but a garrison are out patrolling. Some packmule trains heading for California came through even before grass was up. Carrying oats, I suppose. I'm sure the lieutenant will see to your comforts."

Cummings let the good corn spirits settle and then got down to business. "Well, sir. Where do we stand? Did your runners go out on schedule? And what about that guide, Skye?"

"The runners went out. We sent three reliable men, mostly mixed-bloods, children of the fur-trade days. They'll bring in the bands to the Wind River in early July."

"Have we the support of your command?"

"Absolutely."

"We'll put the tribes on reserves and keep them well away from the road. It'll be best for them. We'll have no trouble with the Snakes and Crows—they've always been friendly—but the northern Arapaho may be more difficult. And we know little about the Bannocks. Did you hire Skye?"

"Yes. He prefers to be called *Mister* Skye, Superintendent."

"Of course, of course. We've an inch-thick file in Washington City on the man. Some sort of lord of the prairies, he and his cutthroats. You got him at last, eh? What a price."

"A third of him, anyway, sir. His wives have left him. Probably to their own bands."

The news irritated Cummings. "Who'll translate? We counted on those women to influence—"

"Mister Skye speaks Shoshone and Crow fluently; he can talk to the Bannocks because their tongue's close to the Shoshone; he'll be comfortable with the Arapaho but may need some help with the Cheyenne. As for Mister Skye's influence, sir, with or without his women, don't underestimate—"

"I've heard the stories. Most of them invented by Skye himself, I imagine. I know the type."

Hoffman shook his head. "What you've heard is what the tribesmen say about him."

Cummings laughed easily. "Well, you got him, anyway."

"Maybe. His terms are five hundred in advance. And he'll place himself under you alone, not Truscott. He won't place himself under a military command— and if you knew his story, sir, you'd understand."

"In advance? Impossible. The accountants won't permit—"

Hoffman sighed. "You'd better look for another man. I've no one to recommend. There's only one Skye in all the West."

"Surely he's not irreplaceable. No man's irreplaceable."

Hoffman smiled wryly. "If you want your treaty you'll accommodate Mister Skye."

"Colonel Hoffman, that's a novelty," said Cummings, wheezing out his amusement.

# Chapter 4

It felt strange to Victoria to be traveling without Mister Skye. Ever since her father had given her to him long ago when she was blossoming into lithe womanhood she'd ridden at his side. But that had passed, like all things on the breast of Mother Earth.

Through the Planting Moon she led Mary and Dirk ever westward toward the roots of the Wind River mountains, where the Shoshones nestled. Victoria was as wary as ever, sliding ahead to study the desert country from the protection of faint gulches. This was a land roamed by the fierce Arapaho and Northern Cheyenne, and sometimes the Lakota, too.

Mary wept as each step of her pony carried her farther from the great, boisterous, impossible man she loved. But Victoria understood. The Sky Chiefs had spoken. Mister Skye needed his white people now; it was as simple as that. But profound, too. Victoria knew she could never give her man the magic he craved; she could not talk to him about the things in books, the mysteries of white people, the amazing music from brass and stringed instruments she'd heard once or twice, and all the other strange things.

She would keep some good memories and live her life as best she could. She was getting old and letting go wasn't so hard. For Mary it would not be easy. Every glance at her son would open her wound. Mary would never grasp that a Shoshone woman would never again be good enough for Mister Skye.

Victoria wondered what Mister Skye would be like among the white men, living the way white men did in one of the great cities. He would probably wear cloth instead of leather. He'd put away his bearclaw necklace, the symbol of his medicine, and wear a white shirt and cravat like the traders. He'd cut his long hair, shave more, and set aside his belt knife and rifle. He'd bathe more often and not smell so terrible.

He'd entrance pale women in skirts and many petticoats who'd find him huge and masculine and ugly, intelligent and exciting. He'd talk to them about all those things she'd heard him talk to other whites about, like Congress and Whigs and Millard Fillmore; Elizabeth Barrett Browning and Nathaniel Hawthorne; David Livingstone and Isaac Singer and chloroform. He would take a woman who knew of these mysteries and never speak of his red women again. His pale and beautiful wife in her many skirts would never know of Mister Skye's red family.

She'd seen many a white man abandon his Indian family and go east, never to be seen again. It all seemed natural enough: if she were to live with him in those frightening places she'd pine and slowly die until the moment of her release came and she could return here to the lands of the Many Peoples or walk the trail of the Many Stars.

She'd watched it unfold in him, a loneliness and need he couldn't resist. Mary had thought Mister Skye was angry with all of them. But that wasn't it. Mister

Skye had drifted back to the people of his childhood. It had torn him to bits.

Resolutely Victoria set her coppery face westward through a glorious spring day. Puffball clouds shot shadows across the open country. Behind her rode Mary and her solemn child on one pony. Three pack ponies followed, bearing the contents of Mister Skye's lodge. They'd left him the lodge and his own few things; all the rest was theirs. It would help them create a new home. He'd be on his own for food, clothing, and comforts: the thousand things his women had joyously done for him. Let him find a white woman who'd give half as much.

So fond were the two women of each other and the little boy they'd jointly raised, that they planned to stay together: Mister Skye's family—without Mister Skye. This they would do among Mary's Snake people but Victoria planned to visit her own Absaroka now and then and renew old kinships. And Victoria would help Mary understand that no Indian woman could ever again fill the needs of the man they'd shared.

Behind them, stamped in the moist sands, lay an indelible trail that any hunting band or war party could follow. Victoria had cut several such trails herself, one of them the northbound passage of about thirty horses less than a day earlier. With the coming of the grass came the moons of war. She squinted from behind some greasewood, surveying distant horizons with eyes that could see a sparrow on a distant stalk. She found no trouble, but that didn't mean trouble wouldn't find her. Many were the warriors who'd enjoy doing their worst to the wives and child of Mister Skye.

Some intuitive sense, honed on a lifetime of danger beside Mister Skye, urged caution upon her. She motioned to Mary and they turned their ponies into a dry gulch, following a game trail into a walled gully that paralleled their route.

"I wish Mister Skye was here," Mary whispered.

Victoria glared at her. "We ain't gonna see him again."

"He'll come for us," Mary whispered.

"No, this time he's gone."

Mary sighed. "I don't know what I did . . ."

"He's no damn good. Forget him. We're going to make a lodge now."

"How can you say that? He was like an eagle and when I saw him I trembled."

"He's a white man. They never stay with us long."

She saw Mary shrink into herself and turn her face away. Good, Victoria thought. Let her learn about white men. She waited in the quiet while the ponies ripped the grudging grass. They all were winter-gaunted. She and Mary were as winter-gaunted as the ponies and even more starved for the most needful foods.

Angrily, she slid her old percussion lock from its saddle scabbard and padded up an incline until she could peer out upon the cloud-decked world. She studied the vibrating country, seeing it seethe under the passage of the puffy clouds, but she saw no danger. Still she waited, cursing her instincts. Without Skye she'd become too cautious.

She'd been his eyes and ears, gliding invisibly through alien country, the advantage he and Mary and the child had over a menacing world. It seemed odd that she could not turn, nod to him below, and see him lift his old top hat and settle it again, her message received and understood. She slid back down into the gulch.

"We'll go now. Not a living thing out there."

"Are you sure, Victoria?" Mary's cautions reflected her own. Mister Skye's absence had bled them of their boldness.

Victoria nodded crossly and mounted her slat-ribbed mare.

"Where is papa?" the boy asked.

"In his lodge," Mary replied.

"I want him."

"We're going to live with the Snake people. Maybe he will find us there."

"He won't find us there," Victoria said.

Mary stared at her, eyes brimming, but she turned her pony and followed once again behind Skye's older wife.

Victoria hawked and spat.

All that dancing-sun day they pushed westward across a harsh land of greasewood and prickly pear. To the south lay the arid Rattlesnake range; to the north the dying convulsions of the Bighorns, a twisted fortress where malign men gathered to dream of plunder.

But they passed safely and Victoria allowed herself to focus on things other than their passage. She would never have a man again; she knew that. Not after Mister Skye. But she would encourage Mary to welcome a man. There'd be many Snakes who would play the flute outside her lodge. In a while, after Mary had found a new lodge among Chief Washakie's people, Victoria thought she might drift north and winter along the Elk River with her Kicked-in-the-Bellies people. Oh, she would have wild stories to tell the children around a winter lodgefire! She'd sing songs of Mister Skye's victories, her own coups, and the moments they hid from armies and fought for their lives. She'd tell them about white men and all their wonders; and maybe she could prepare her Absaroka people for the things that she knew, in her darkest moments, would happen to the People when white men wanted their lands and shot away their buffalo and herded them onto starve-out patches of bad ground. Thus would a spurned old woman still find purpose in her life.

"Sonofabitch!" she muttered, mad at Mister Skye all over again.

# Chapter 5

Skye stood quietly in the mess hall, undergoing scrutiny. Before him sat several august officials of the United States Government, their foolscap spread before them on a dining table.

Skye had endured the scrutiny of his prospective clients many times while he in turn evaluated the people he might take into the wilderness. He always tried to weed out the foolish because his life depended on the good sense of those he escorted. The men before him looked sensible enough and the presence of a cavalry troop would probably make the trip safe.

Their gazes were focusing on his nose. That was understandable. His nose was a continental divide separating oceanic watersheds. It had started life an ordinary nose, but years of brawling on Royal Navy ships had broken and pulped it until it had inflated to the size of a banana. While they admired his nose he took the measure of the fattest man he'd ever seen, encased in black like a globe in mourning. He'd never seen such an equator on a mortal.

That would be Victorious Bonaparte Cummings. Just to the right of him sat the assistant superintendent, a man of normal proportion wearing an Anglican clerical collar. To his left perched a delicately hewn lieutenant in dress blues and gold buttons, sporting long yellow tresses and a silky goatee. A problematical man, Skye supposed. Off to one side sprawled the Indian Bureau clerk, bald and red-faced Alphonse McGinty.

Nothing else about Skye attracted their attention. He wore a ready-made flannel shirt that Bullock had supplied him, buckskin leggins and an elkskin vest the post laundresses had renovated. He stood before them clean, shaved, sweet-smelling, and in rare possession of his decaying faculties. About his neck he wore his grizzly bearclaw medicine, the hallmark of his prowess among all the tribes of the northern Plains. Only the battered silk top hat in his gnarled hand was unusual for a scout on the borders.

"Well, Skye, you come highly recommended. Hoffman here, the Chouteaus of St. Louis—all the rest," said the superintendent.

"It's *Mister* Skye, sir."

"Ah, yes, so we've heard. We've a folder in Washington City on you." The Honorable Victorious Cummings's brown eyes surveyed him intelligently.

Skye thought he might like the man. "I take my clients to wherever they wish to go, avoid trouble, and get them there alive and safe."

"You're an Englishman."

"Born in London."

"What are you now?"

"A man in the wilderness."

"That brings up a point," said the lieutenant with the wounded look in his eyes.

"Mister Skye, this is Lieutenant Truscott, Second

Dragoons. He'll be commanding a troop of dragoons for our comfort."

"Skye, it says here you jumped ship—deserted from the Royal Navy," Truscott said.

"It's Mister Skye, sir. I did that. At Fort Vancouver in twenty and five. I was pressed in. A press-gang nipped me on the banks of the Thames when I was fifteen. I was a slave after that, never setting foot on dry land except for the kaffir war."

"But you deserted your post. Would you desert us?"

Skye sighed. "The bonds I forge of my free will— such as an agreement with the Indian Bureau—are bonds that I consider inviolate. The Royal Navy bonds, sir, lacked my consent. They ripped me from my family—I never saw my parents or sisters again."

"Nonetheless you deserted, Skye."

"It's Mister Skye, sir . . . If I place myself in service it will be to the Indian Bureau. I won't place myself under the direction of any military officer. You understand, surely."

"No, I don't. We can't have draftees deserting. By military law you could have been shot."

Skye smiled and turned away. His guiding career was over.

"Wait—Skye." This time is was the reverend assistant superintendent, Wellington Cummings.

Skye paused.

"We know you're a good man with the aborigines. Well respected. We need you."

"I'm not your man, sir."

"We think you are. The success of our negotiations depends on you and your wives."

"I'm alone, Reverend."

"You can translate?"

"Shoshone—and Bannock, which is close to it; Crow fluently; I understand the Cheyenne. Get along with the Arapaho."

"We'd hoped your wives would help—they're so influential."

"Help with what, Reverend?"

The superintendent himself chose to reply. "Why, Skye, our purposes are to settle each of the tribes on a generous homeland guaranteed by treaty; stop their incessant warfare; teach them farming and herding; and secure for white men the right of passage along this California Road. That's the gist of it."

"Some of it's workable," said Skye.

"Not all of it?"

"Perhaps I can help you understand the Indians while we travel, sir—if I choose to accept this employment."

"We've put a lot into this. May we count on your absolute obedience, assistance, and loyalty?"

"No. I take the Indians' part on many matters. But I'll tell you what I think'll be acceptable to them—and what won't be."

"That's exactly why we need you. You must bring them around to our view. They say you're the one man for it."

Truscott intervened. "Skye has ducked the matter of loyalty, Superintendent. I think that's the most important of all, given his history."

"You heard my answer a moment ago, Lieutenant," said Skye, squinting squarely at the officer. "My loyalties are divided. I will tell you what's possible, what's feasible in a treaty."

"Well, Skye, loyalty is everything. Will you be loyal and obedient in government service?"

"My sympathies lie with the tribes, sir."

"You haven't answered me!" Truscott's voice lifted a notch and crackled with willfulness.

"I'm a man without a country," Skye said.

"Victorious, that's exactly why we must have him," said Wellington. "A perfect man for the job."

The superintendent addressed the unhappy lieutenant. "Mister Truscott, no one could be better for our purposes. Skye's liked and trusted by the Indians. What you see as a defect is his greatest asset for us. He has big medicine among them. No employee of ours could be half so effective."

Truscott pursed his lips.

Victorious Bonaparte Cummings turned again to Skye. "Our wagons with the annuities and camp supplies are due within the fortnight. After that we'll proceed directly to the Wind River. You'll guide, determine our campgrounds, deal with passing tribesmen. When the treaty council convenes, translate diligently and persuade the chiefs to accept. You'll also inform us of their tribal customs so we can deal wisely with them. Now then, Skye, this matter of cash in advance—"

"Mister Skye, sir."

"Yes, yes. It's most unusual. The federal government pays for services rendered. Submit a bill after—"

"I'm not your man," said Skye. "I've guided a long time. It's been my experience that clients don't want to pay at the end of the trip. They think they could have gotten there without my costly help—or they lack cash and never intended to pay in the first place."

"But we're the government—"

"From what I've heard about the way your Treasury rejects bills properly submitted, sir, I'd be even less willing—"

Superintendent Cummings sighed, which had the effect of an earthquake rattling mountains and shaking valleys. "Very well. We must have you. I've asked our chief clerk, Mister McGinty, to prepare the bills. Now then, we'll excuse ourselves. We must see Colonel Hoffman."

Skye watched them rise and file out the door into a bright sun, leaving only the clerk.

"Here you be," said McGinty. He handed Skye a draft.

Skye studied the figures, which came to $375. "I agreed to a fee of five hundred, Mister McGinty."

"Oh, yes, five hundred it is, friend. You've made a voluntary contribution to Young Democracy, a friendly society devoted to fostering the administration of Franklin Pierce. That was a hundred. And there's a wee little fee for clerical assistance—expediting things, you know."

"I don't think I'll volunteer the gift to President Pierce's society."

"Oh, you'll volunteer it, friend. Lots of other competent lads eager to volunteer."

Skye pondered it, tempted badly. Even three seventy-five would pay off Colonel Bullock and stake Skye to a new life.

"Find one," said Skye, slapping the draft into the clerk's hands.

# Chapter 6

Skye studied the new draft that his agent, Colonel Bullock, handed him. It was made to the order of Barnaby Skye for the sum of $450.

"You may as well take it, Mister Skye. You won't do better this season," urged the sutler.

"It's not what I asked. What's the fifty-dollar chop for this time?"

"Why, suh, the nobby little clerk—McGinty—had to write it a second time seein' as how you rejected the first. He'll call it expediting. He sticks government contractors—you, Mister Skye—with a little expediting fee . . . twice now for you. He's not getting poorer in government sarvice."

"Is this the way the United States Government works?"

"The government is its clerks, Mister Skye. The bureaucrats run the show. They're a slippery lot."

Skye sighed. "I want to get out of here and go east. Would you carry me on your books for a while?"

Bullock shrugged. "I won't, suh. Not in the frame of mind you're in. You're like a man with cooties. All I can say is, here's a sure thing, a draft on the Treasury. I'll put it on your account, deduct your current balance, outfit you, and you'll still have a tolerable nest egg to drink away all winter. I doubt you'll go east, Mister Skye."

Skye pondered it. "Am I going to have trouble with McGinty out on the trail?"

"I imagine. Never cross a chief clerk; that's a rule of survival. In our Army, sir, it's the same: never cross a paymaster or a quartermaster. Never cross a sergeant major."

"Who overruled him?"

"Himself. Cummings."

"When do they want me?"

"Their wagons are in, Mister Skye. They're shoving off at dawn."

Skye surrendered. "All right. Make up a kit. And add a duckcloth tarpaulin."

"A tarp? Any size?"

"Tent size. Bedroll size. I'm not taking the lodge. Don't have any way to—now that . . ." He couldn't say the rest.

"I see. I could store it for you, Mister Skye."

Skye nodded, not wanting to talk about that. His wives' well-crafted eleven-skin lodge, which had compassed so much of his past happiness, sagged dark and empty, with nothing in it but a parfleche containing his few possessions and a bedroll.

All the years he'd roamed with the fur brigades he'd been a man without a roof making rude shelters with ax and knife, blankets and robes. He didn't want that again, but he could endure a summer of it before he left the country for good.

"I'll get the lodge. Make up my kit and don't forget the jug."

"Mister Skye, suh, if I ever forgot the jug you'd take

your trade elsewhere." The colonel hee-hawed into his mustache.

"I will anyway," Skye muttered. He lumbered through the cavernous store and into the bright shade of its veranda. There he spotted Jawbone, ears laid back, teeth clacking, whoofing and snorting and ready to slay. Surrounding him were a dozen Fort Leavenworth men, all of them looking amused. And edging toward Jawbone, a tight smirk on his face, was Lieutenant Anthony Wayne Truscott.

"Stand back!" Skye roared, racing between Jawbone and the lieutenant.

The officer paused only slightly and edged forward again, intent on snatching Jawbone's hackamore.

Skye sprang again, this time catching Jawbone's rein and yanking the horse's head just as Jawbone screeched something so demonic that it raised the hackles of the men. They edged backward.

"Don't ever, ever get within a dozen feet of this horse," Skye bellowed.

Truscott stopped, his lips pressed white. "I suppose he'll kick, is that it?"

"No, he'll kill," Skye roared.

Something compressed the pupils of Truscott's eyes. He cocked his head, measuring Jawbone. "Ugliest horse I ever did see, Skye."

"Say, fella, would ye take two bits for 'im?" asked a dragoon.

"Don't offer so much; you'd git took," said another.

"How come he's got all them scars and holes? Where's the rest of his ear? You eat it for food when you was shy of a meal?"

"That there thing ain't a horse; it's a horned cyclops."

Jawbone shrieked again, his corded muscles rippling and shivering, his yellow eyes mad.

Skye loomed over Truscott and spoke with a quiet urgency that would carry to every man. "This horse's trained for war. He can kill. If I'm going to be guiding this outfit you'd better get used to him. You respect him and I'll teach him to respect you. You mess with him and he'll kill you."

"An outlaw horse, is that it, Skye? He ought to be shot. We can't have him around cavalry mounts."

"Lieutenant Truscott, he won't go anywhere near the cavalry mounts. He stays with me. See to it that your Army horses are kept well away from him."

"Skye, I'll handle the dragoon horses any way I choose."

"It's Mister Skye, mate."

Jawbone screeched, a howl so terrible it shot a visible shudder through the lieutenant. Skye stared unblinking, and at last the lieutenant backed off.

"Keep him away from my mounts, Skye. If that stud wrecks my geldings—he's dead. I'll shoot him myself."

"I'll take that under consideration, Lieutenant."

Truscott smiled. "Actually, Skye, you ought to resign the job. You're not the man for it. And that's not the horse. The government needs animals it can trust." He permitted himself a brittle laugh and walked off, followed by his men.

Skye watched them go, a sick worry spreading through his gut. "Whoa, boy," he muttered, running a gnarled hand through Jawbone's mane. "I don't know about this. Sixty dragoons looking to put a bullet in you."

Jawbone snorted and bit Skye's shoulder. Skye snarled and Jawbone wheeled and reared. Moments later Skye rode the snorty horse up the Platte, wondering whether things would ease along the trail. They usually did. Truscott would relax. The dragoons would come around. It'd be all right.

Skye rode back to his camp steeped in thought. He needed the money; he wanted to pay off Bullock and get out. But not at the cost of Jawbone's life. He de-

cided to try two or three days on the trail with the
peace party. If the dragoons didn't settle down he
would quit on the spot, although he hated the thought
of it. He would return to Laramie, refund the government pay, and take Jawbone far away. He would head
for some city where a man could conquer a loneliness
he could no longer endure. He would still owe Bullock
but it couldn't be helped. He grimaced, not liking his
options.

Skye had always known what he would do if Jawbone were lamed or injured, or if he could no longer
guide. Up in the Pryor Mountains in the heart of Victoria's country ran a herd of mustangs that had supplied the Crow Indians with horses for generations. In
the summers the mustangs spread out upon the surrounding prairies; in the winters they hunkered in the
sheltered canyons and peeled green cottonwood bark
for a living. It was horse heaven, with salt licks and a
few springs, shelter and freedom. There would he take
the old reprobate and set him loose among the mares
to enjoy his last days and rear up a generation of colts
with Jawbone's blood racing through them.

Skye reached his camp, rode through brush until he
found his three remaining packhorses, and herded
them to the lodge. There he haltered and picketed
them, swung fleeces and packsaddles over their backs
and faced the forlorn lodge, which glowered its rebuke
at him.

Dismantling lodges wasn't familiar work. Skye proceeded mechanically, his mind hating what his fingers
were doing. He pulled out the willow pins that held
the cone of leather together and let it slide to the grass
like a woman's skirt, revealing the nakedness of a
household. He lifted the poles one by one and carried
them to the first packhorse, arranging them into two
bundles tied at the upper ends. Then he added the
three bound poles that made the basic tripod, folded
up the heavy lodgecover and its lining, and heaped

them on a second packhorse. He loaded his personal duffel onto the third while Jawbone paced and snorted, sensing the badness of this.

"It's all over, mate," Skye muttered.

The horse pressed close, nudging his chest.

"Times change," Skye said. He peered at Jawbone, whose head hung low. He swore there were tears in the animal's eyes, but that was ridiculous.

Skye looked at his handiwork, unsatisfied. Much remained of the camp; Victoria's brush arbor, Mary's squash garden, a brush-and-stick corral, a heap of squaw wood, meat-drying racks, a pile of antlers and horns, and the rusted barrel of a longrifle that Victoria used sometimes as a spit.

It looked like a cemetery. Nothing remained of the little family drawn together by Skye's design to live in freedom and wander the unfenced world far from laws and prisons, far from armies and politicians and city streets. It hit Skye hard.

He clambered slowly aboard Jawbone and turned the horse toward the fort, tugging the packhorses along on a picket line. Not until this moment had Skye fully grasped that he was letting go of everything he'd drawn to him for a quarter of a century, for the sake of walking into the unknown. Slowly he lifted his battered silk top hat as a last salute and settled it again, feeling lost.

# Chapter 7

The snow-crowned Wind River Mountains loomed large in the west, mysterious and awesome in their grandeur. They lifted Mary's heart. She could see the country of her people. It would be easy to find them. In the winter they would be down on the Green River far to the south; now they would be anywhere from the roots of the mountains to the Yellowstone Country, gathering for the great summer buffalo hunt.

She had only to find one of the five bands of her Eastern Shoshones to learn the whereabouts of her own village, led by Chief Washakie, her clan-brother. There would her mother and father be and all her sisters and brothers.

Of the Eastern Shoshones there were twelve hundred and she did not know most of them. But every one of them knew her, little clan-sister of their greatest chief and younger wife of the white man whose name evoked respect everywhere. The thought of being instantly recognized by the warriors of whatever band she found swelled something within her and made her immediate future seem as glistening as the bold mountains.

Each day she and Victoria had ridden ever westward through a hateful land, across sandy wastes, past poison springs and naked rock where nothing lived but snakes. But ahead, rich with promise, lay the foothills and shady glades where her people summered. The Eastern Shoshones lived a life of sweetness along the eastern slopes of the Rocky Mountains, enjoying abundant game, laughing creeks, cool summer camps, and safety from their worst enemies, the Utes.

She rode much of the time with Dirk on her lap and when he became too heavy she put him behind her and let him cling. She and Victoria had slid into silence, the reality of life without Mister Skye steeping their souls like tea leaves. Mary had choked back the hurt when it became unbearable. Victoria had told her over and over that Indian women were not good enough for Mister Skye anymore; he needed his own kind now.

"We'll make a damn good life; maybe you'll find a good Snake man," Victoria had said with more cheer than Mary could understand.

Mary remembered when Mister Skye had visited her people in her eighteenth summer and how she had caught his eye. He'd caught hers, too: she'd never seen a face so rough and menacing and yet so warm. She'd averted her eyes when he had kept looking at her. Then the Absaroka woman had looked at her, too, and she didn't know what to make of it. She was Blue Dawn then, ripe with the need for a man and lodge of her own.

She'd smiled at him for several days and shyly listened when he talked to Chief Washakie. He had a voice that rolled like thunder down a mountain chasm and a laugh that made the whole world laugh, too, like some sky creature above the world.

Then her father, Rising Crow, had asked her if she'd like to be Mister Skye's woman. She could scarcely grasp what he was proposing. Woman of the great white man? How could such an honor come upon her? She had nodded dumbly, more frightened than pleased by the prospect. How would the white man's sits-beside-him wife treat her? Would they speak her tongue? Her two mothers had beamed at her. Her real mother, Lodge Maker, glowed with the honor. Her almost-mother, Pretty Doe, had nodded and said it was good to be a second wife of a great man.

Mister Skye had offered a heap of things: a rifle and powder and shot; blankets, knives, an ax, and kettles. Enough to enrich the whole lodge of Rising Crow. They had dressed her in the softest antelope-skin dress, fringed at the hem and sleeves, and bound her feet in dyed moccasins, parted and braided her hair, and bound the braids in mink pelts.

"The white man will be very proud. You are the fairest of all the Shoshone people," her mother had exclaimed. Then her brother Strong Horse had carried her to the little lodge of the white man and set her down there before the thick, scarred giant with the strange hat and his thin, hard-faced wife.

"Ah, Blue Dawn!" rumbled the white man. "I hope you'll be happy with us. I'm going to name you after a revered lady of my people, Mary; and you'll enjoy the company of this handsome woman of the Absaroka whose name from me is Victoria."

And thus was her life reborn. The older woman couldn't speak Shoshone but Mister Skye translated at first. Mary learned that Victoria was delighted to have a new woman in the lodge to talk to; she loved being with Mister Skye but the long stretches away from her people had made her lonely. Soon the women were friends.

All her days and many of her nights with Skye had been filled with wonder and joy—until now. She'd known so little, and learned so swiftly. Everything Skye did seemed new and strange. She and Victoria had evolved their own language, mostly English laced with Shoshone and Crow words. They had made Mister Skye's lodge glow with laughter and quick smiles and jokes they played on their strange winter-faced man.

But now each of the thousand memories of her life with Mister Skye was wreathed in pain. Nothing hurt more than the remembrance of those moments when they'd fought together, sharing blood and death; she, Victoria, Jawbone, and Skye against terrible enemies. Somehow they'd survived. Mister Skye and Victoria had taught her war skills. She could shoot and hunt, stalk and hide, subsist on almost nothing, decoy and trap. And the legend that at first encompassed only Mister Skye and his grizzly-claw medicine swiftly expanded across the northern Plains to include his women and his terrible horse. The small lodge of Mister Skye was a medicine army.

"We're almost to your people. See how high we are above the desert. You've got to change your face," said Victoria.

Mary nodded. Every thought that filled her mind had etched itself upon her smooth face until Victoria and Skye could read her just from the lines around her lips and the cant of her head.

"I cannot make my sadness go away."

"When you see your brothers and sisters you won't even be thinking about that sonofabitch Skye."

Victoria shocked her. How could the old woman be so hard? Hadn't she loved Mister Skye longer than anyone?

They camped on a swift cold creek with foam riding it, and Mary tasted snow and high country in the biting water. Spring storms growled over the crags, threatening to drench the women and the child. Victoria plunged deep into a box elder grove and hewed down saplings, which she bent into a wickerwork frame and covered with her best smoked cowhides salvaged from the lodge. They'd turn water and stop wind. But the growling of the Sky Chiefs subsided and the great columns of black cloud raced north instead of east. They settled into chill spring night marked by the sounds of animals.

Mary did not have to find her people; the next morning they found her. A hunting party of three young men on ponies patched with winter hair edged down the creek looking for cow elk on the meadows. And found the women dismantling their shelter.

"What is this? Strangers!" said one in Mary's tongue.

"Aiee! See who I am!" she cried in their language while Victoria muttered curses and reached for her flintlock.

"Who is this who speaks the tongue of the Shoshone? You don't look like one of us," said a solemn young man, surveying dresses and moccasins that looked as much Crow as Shoshone.

"I was called Blue Dawn, daughter of Rising Crow. Younger sister of Strong Horse. And this is a woman of the Absaroka people. We are the lodge of Mister Skye."

"Mister Skye! Aiee!" At that the young men peered about eagerly, wanting a glimpse of the great medicine man.

"We do not see the one you talk of."

"He's not here," she retorted crossly. "What people are you? We want to find my people—Chief Washakie's people."

"They are half a day's walk north. We'll take you.

Here is news to sing about. When will the white man come?"

"Dammit, let's go," said Victoria, irritated. She understood Shoshone as well as her Crow tongue, but rarely spoke it.

All that morning the young men led them north across drainages, up and down grassy slopes purple with pasqueflowers, while Mary asked questions about her people as fast as they crowded into her mind. Victoria rode apart, ever alert, as careful to study horizons and forest edges as ever, scorning the carelessness of the Shoshones. But Mary scarcely noticed. The sweet words of her people tasted like honey in her mouth and she chattered happily until suddenly she noticed one of these young men gazing at her solemnly.

"Is something wrong, Rabbit Catcher?"

"No. It was said among us that you were the most beautiful of all the Shoshone women, brighter than Morning Star—and now I have seen it with my own eyes. Many played the love flute but the white man had more gifts for your father."

She met his gaze and found both yearning and reserve there. Suddenly Rabbit Catcher seemed more than a young man she'd met by chance. But she pushed that disloyal thought out of mind. She was Mister Skye's woman!

"Yes, Mister Skye gave me a good life with many pleasures," she said. "But I am glad that I please you, Rabbit Catcher."

He said no more.

A while later they rode down a long slope, their horses jarring under them, and into the grassy valley that cupped Washakie's village. Many fine lodges dotted the meadow, each the hearth of a family: children, busy women, old men basking in the rioting spring breezes, tied horses, trotting dogs. Something sweet swelled in Mary's heart. Even as the village discovered the visitors and raced out to meet them, her spirits soared. There, at the far side of the green meadow, stood the familiar, beloved home of her parents. For the first time in many moons she felt no unhappiness within her.

"Is this the place, mama?" asked Dirk.

"This is our home now," she said.

# Chapter 8

The hilly country west of Fort Laramie annoyed Victorious Bonaparte Cummings. It slowed the party. Army mule skinners driving the heavy wagons loaded with annuity goods for the tribes whipped their big Missouri mules upslope and then hung on to the brake levers when the wagons rumbled downhill, pushing into the breeching of the wheelers. The Indian Bureau party was making only ten or twelve miles a day.

Cummings, who was himself a retired major, could not fault the young West Pointer and his dragoons. Truscott had posted a vedette well ahead of the body; he had flankers out half a mile and a rear guard well behind the wagons. Perhaps the California Road didn't require such caution but the lieutenant was taking no chances.

Cummings had learned that they'd follow the well-worn road along the Sweetwater almost to South Pass. Well east of the Wind River Mountains they would head north toward the confluence of the Popo Agie,

Little Wind, and Wind River, following a route used by the fur companies for years. They scarcely needed a guide; not when all but fifty miles would be the national road.

He felt his carriage sway under him, tipping his massive person one way and another like whiskey sloshing in a jug. It wasn't unpleasant except when they bounced over a rut or rock. And then he quaked. His only complaint was that his girth prevented company. He occupied a double seat. Just behind, in the ambulances, his colleagues and clerks engaged in a lively if ribald commentary about the Wild West, not in the least inhibited by Wellington's clerical collar.

Skye seemed lost, now riding beside the Indian Bureau conveyances, then sliding back to the wagons, and sometimes pushing forward or out to a flank. But he always steered clear of Truscott and his command knotted up front. The man was used to leading, Cummings supposed. He had nothing to lead nor were his services as a guide needed—not as long as they traversed a rutted trace twenty yards wide, grooved into the clay and earth by the passage of countless iron tires.

Very well, then. He'd find a use for Skye.

"Private, send word up the line that I should like to consult with our guide," said Cummings.

In short order, the black carriage closed on Skye, who sat Jawbone to one side.

"Come along beside and we'll talk, sir."

Skye nodded and steered that appalling horse close to the carriage, aggravating the big mules.

"You're used to leading but this time you're a man who's just tagging along."

Skye eyed him cheerfully. "It takes some getting used to. Usually my wives—ah, we're out running the ridges."

"The lieutenant has things under a tight rein."

"By day."

"He posts night guards, Mister Skye. He did last night."

"Nothing that would stop the summer fun."

"Summer fun, Mister Skye?"

"Horse stealing."

"We're at peace with the tribes, are we not?"

"Horse stealing doesn't count."

"What would you recommend to the lieutenant?"

"I wouldn't; he'd not take it kindly from me."

"What would you do instead?"

"I'd graze the horses morning and evening—noon, too—and then hobble them within the camp."

"Have your clients ever lost horses, Mister Skye?"

"More'n I like to think about."

"Is that what you did—hobble them in camp?"

"I have Jawbone, sir."

Puzzled, the superintendent waited for more but Skye said nothing. "That's a remarkable horse, a hellfire and damnation horse, sir. Take it from a Virginian who knows the best horseflesh. Give me a Jawbone over some pretty horse any day."

"I don't think Lieutenant Truscott agrees with you," said Skye, a rare smile building in his melancholic face.

"He's a pretty-horse man. In war, sir—which is the natural estate of you people out here—in war, prettiness isn't worth a lick."

Something bright crept into the guide's face. He ran his hand under the monster's mane. Jawbone clacked his teeth and snorted, terrorizing the mules. "He's a war-horse—a sentry, a charge of grapeshot, a snapping banner, a bugle call, and a line of riflemen, sir. He's also crazy—a biting, kicking, whirling fool. A word from me'll turn him into a killer. He'll stand all night over us ready to screech. You're right, sir—pretty isn't worth a lick. Not in a horse. Maybe in a woman, though I debate it."

"He's an outlaw?"

Skye turned somber. "Truscott thinks so. But not yet. Maybe someday I'll lose control."

Cummings liked the man. They rode quietly awhile, eating the dust of those ahead.

"Would it be any disrespect if I asked you about your name? Yours and your brother's?" Skye asked.

"Not at all. My father and grandfather named their children in ways that would remind them of life's possibilities. He is Jericho Trumpet Cummings, aware every moment of his life that the walls came tumbling down. He named me, the older boy, for the moment of Napoleon's ascendancy. He named Wellington Waterloo for the moment of Wellington's triumph. It's all consistent when you look at it right."

"Do you live by it?"

"I do. I'm a force to be reckoned with. Apart from gnats and fleas, nothing—nothing—has stayed my progress. Mister Skye, if you were named Victorious what would you do with your mortal life? Now you just watch me these next fortnights. I'll have my treaties. I think I know what's good for the tribes and they'll get it. I know what's good for the republic and we'll have it."

"What's good for the tribes, mate?"

"First, you must understand they're footnotes in the history books. Once you grasp that, you grasp the nature of true kindness. My proposition is—the future belongs to the white race. Some of the tribes—the New England ones—are almost extinct. The best we can do is put the aborigines far away from white men somewhere and leave them alone. Put them into their zoological gardens, so to speak. Feed them but don't expect anything from them. Now Wellington disagrees; he thinks they can be turned into farmers and servants. But that's a minister for you!"

"I'd hate to think of my—of people like the Crows and Shoshones living in a kind of prison."

"Ah! You're seeing the particular. The white men are

coming. We're riding in the ruts of thousands and thousands of wagons; this trace has seen hundreds of thousands of boots and shoes. Who knows where the flow will head next, eh? Wherever gold is or good land or dreams. Best to remove the savages to their own obscure preserves before they're, ah, rendered extinct."

"They'll die away, Mister Cummings. Of broken hearts and shame. Boredom and vice."

"Well, have you a better plan, Mister Skye?"

"Shoot them."

The guide's horse, acting on some invisible signal, broke into a jog, putting distance between them.

"Skye!"

The horse paused. "It's Mister Skye, mate."

"You're a difficult fellow. Why do you insist on Mister?"

"It's a term of respect."

"Well, I explained my inherited name to you; perhaps you'll oblige me with a larger answer."

"I suppose it's an English quirk in me, sir. It gives a man station. Like Mister Truscott. Like my father."

"Your father?"

Skye didn't answer. Nor did he have to. It explained everything. Absolutely everything, the superintendent mused.

"At Fort Laramie you volunteered to instruct me about the ways of the Indians, Mister Skye. I'm willing to listen. You ventured that my plan was only partly workable, wasn't that it?"

"I was wrong."

"It's workable, then?"

"If workable means a slow death rather than a fast one."

Cummings felt the bite in the man's voice and the grim set of his face. "Sometime, as we progress west, sir, I'd welcome your counsel. I care about the red people. It's not only my bound duty but my humane choice. Congress wrenched the Indian Bureau from the Army to see to it that the tribes had a protector and a voice among white men. Now, you see? I wish to fulfill my sworn duty."

Skye stared at horizons as if deciding whether or not to cooperate. "Later, mate. Let's talk a few days down the trail. Meanwhile you might ask yourself why you're alive and what gives you will and purpose—and breath."

The strange man on the strange horse, an apparition from some other world, glided ahead again and Cummings didn't stay him. Skye had things to teach and Cummings meant to learn.

# Chapter 9

The second night out Lieutenant Truscott chose to stop at Horseshoe Creek, a grassy flat that was a favorite resort of emigrants. The column halted in the bright light of the June evening and Truscott's troopers began to care for their horses.

Skye watched the Honorable Victorious Cummings stand, stretch, grasp his gold-knobbed walking stick, and step down from the groaning carriage, which seemed to breathe a sigh of relief. Safely on earth, he drew a finger across a fender, exposing the glossy black lacquer.

"Dust," he said.

"Yassir!" said his driver, a private. The man produced a feather duster from the floorboards and dusted the black broadcloth of Superintendent Cummings and then the black lacquer of the carriage.

Skye watched quietly, his arm over Jawbone's neck. All day he'd kept clear of the cavalry, especially Truscott. He intended to keep it that way the whole trip. He'd do his work for the Indian Bureau and head east. Perhaps Philadelphia. He'd heard it was civilized and literate. Boston was more so, but too puritanical for a man reared in London. But all that was the future.

It was a novelty to guide a party and have nothing to do. But in his present mood that suited him fine. The less visible he was, the better. He slid the pad saddle off Jawbone and let him graze freely. The ugly brute peered malevolently at the distant cavalry horses and the nearer harness mules, as if studying ways to murder the lot. Then he yanked up bunchgrass, rotating in circles to keep the whole world under observation. Jawbone didn't like this arrangement any better than Skye.

A private approached on foot. "The lieutenant wishes to confer with you at once, sir."

Skye sighed. "Very well, mate. I'll be along."

He walked over to Jawbone, who was grazing with his ears flattened back. "Stay," he said. Jawbone lifted his black snout and bit Skye with grass-stained teeth.

"Avast!" Skye roared.

He found the lieutenant at a command center a hundred yards ahead, beside the creek, cutting a handsome figure. He'd thrown his blue cape over his shoulders as if to highlight his blond goatee and shining hair. An aide was grooming his gelding. The trumpeter and another man were erecting his tent.

"Skye, we've been on the road two days and we've had nine incidents involving your horse. Mister Cummings's driver, here, Private Glad, reports that your horse upset the dray mules so much the carriage went out of control."

"It's Mister Skye, sir."

"Skye! This isn't Laramie. I'm here with sixty armed dragoons and they're the law you'll heed from now on. I'll call you any way I choose. What are you going to do about that horse?"

"Perhaps you'd better train yours, Lieutenant."

Truscott pursed his lips, as if scarcely believing the insolence he was hearing from a civilian. "Those happen to be some of the best-trained mounts in the world, Skye. The cavalry knows how to discipline horses."

"Trained on a parade ground, I imagine. They're mighty pretty, Lieutenant. I'm sure they please the ladies." Skye was sorry at once that he'd said it.

Something dilated in the officer's eyes. "Don't test me, Skye. I'm a patient man but don't try me."

Skye thought about Jawbone and their entwined lives; the sweet bunchgrasses and sheltered coulees and fair winds high in the Pryor Mountains; and all the hot, snorting mares Jawbone would herd and mate, and a hundred little Jawbones thundering across his high and mighty world. And the wet little thing he'd been a moment after birth, and how his great mustang mother licked him dry and nudged him until he wobbled up and began to suck. And all the patient hours welding a bond between horse colt and man, and all the times he'd encouraged Jawbone's bad habits. And how he could take the old devil to the Pryors when this last guiding trip was done, and cry hot tears in the cold wind, and tell Jawbone to stay, *stay*, and turn his back and walk away.

A fear crept into him along with the ancient love. "I'll watch him, Lieutenant."

"You'll do more than watch him. You'll keep him tied. You're letting him wander free over there. That's going to stop. You're going to keep him away from my mounts. I've warned you once; I'll warn you again. If that stud causes trouble we're going to shoot him. We've got a few mares over there and if that horse messes with them—he's dead."

"He can't be tied. No one on earth can throw a rope over him. I trained him that way."

"You trained him—?"

"I did. Saved my life more'n I can count, mate."

"All the worse for your outlaw horse. I'll instruct the guards to shoot him on sight if he gets in among our mounts."

"He won't. And your sentries won't."

"You understand me?" The lieutenant sounded shrill.

Skye intuited that this meeting had to do with a lot more than Jawbone. He smiled quietly. "We're two days out. We've a month or two to get along and get the job done right and the treaty made."

"I don't follow you, Skye."

Skye lifted his top hat and grinned. "Jawbone's a story to tell the ladies back home. Nothing more than that. We'll get along, you and I."

The conciliatory tone served only to harden Truscott. "You'll get along with me whether you like it or not, Skye. Now you're going to find some way to tie up that horse."

"He'll be under my thumb, mate. He obeys me."

"Skye: I'm in command here and that's an order—and don't tell me you're a civilian."

Skye chose his words carefully and spoke with unaccustomed softness. "I'm employed by the Indian Bureau, Lieutenant. You'll want to talk to the superintendent. Perhaps Major Cummings will pass your instructions along. Meanwhile, we've a task to do together, like it or not. If my horse—and I—aren't acceptable to you, why, ask for my bloody resignation. There's no need for all this trouble. You ask me to, mate, and I'll resign the post. You can square it with the Indian Bureau. I'll return to the fort and refund the advance. You'll have to explain it to Cummings, of course. I don't know what I've done to give offense."

"No, no no—they want you. I'd just as soon see you pack out of here this minute but I won't permit it."

"Well, Lieutenant, you can do a man a favor by letting him know how he offends. How've I offended you?"

"As if you don't know."

Skye knew. It wasn't really Jawbone. "Well, Mister Truscott, you make the decision. I can stay and we'll get along as men do when they must. Or I can take my leave if you can't get along."

Around them Truscott's command stood watching and waiting.

The lieutenant seemed vexed. He frowned and squinted, threw his cape about and posed.

"I'll make the decision for you, Mister Truscott."

Skye turned to leave. He'd have to tell Cummings and put some distance between himself and this boy-officer.

"Stop! I haven't dismissed you."

"Tut, tut, Mister Truscott," said Victorious Bonaparte Cummings, penetrating the circle of men like a stately galleon. "Tut now. Lieutenant, what is my rank?"

"Major—retired—sir."

"Ah! Ah! We are going to talk about horses. Now, Lieutenant, there are all sorts of quadrupeds just like there are all sorts of men, each suited to a different task. Now you have some very pretty horses in your command; sound, too. Not a splint or anything else for seven hundred miles. Very pretty. Very obedient. Very military. Very well conformed. Very well shod and groomed. Oh, my, you have horses to quicken a politician's heart.

"Now, young man, let's examine the common mustang, the Indian pony—little misshapen things with high withers, spots, ugly noses, crooked legs, ewe necks, hair falling over the eyes, hard little feet—that happen to be so tough they don't need shoes. Oh, your pretty horses can outrun them for a while. But what happens to your dragoon horses after a few days of the chase, Lieutenant? Why, those ugly little mustangs pull ahead; your Army horses get tired.

"Now, I'm a student of horseflesh and this horse of Mister Skye's is a study. I've been two days observing this singular horse. I'd like to suggest, Mister Truscott, that if the United States Cavalry were mounted on Jawbones the Army would win its wars, terrorize its opponents, frighten dogs, cats, and children, and drive spit-and-polish generals and by-the-book lieutenants out of the service.

"Jawbone, sir, is a *horse*. Not your regular stupid dull obedient nag, but a hot-brained, crafty, bone-headed, mean-spirited devil horse! Jawbone is a trained killer, a saint, a friend, and a lunatic. Jawbone is the king of all the world's horses. Jawbone is an army. Jawbone's bled like a stuck shoat but he's never run from a fight. Jawbone's a creature of this wild land, as native as a cougar, as crafty as the coyote. Jawbone's what first got conjured up in the mind of God when God was sculpting horses. If I feel perfectly secure on this voyage through wild Indian country, Mister Truscott, it's because of Jawbone."

Truscott flushed and clenched a fist.

Mister Skye wished the superintendent had stopped short of deadly insult.

# Chapter 10

As Mary rode into her village her joy was alloyed with dread. She would have to tell her father and mother that she was no longer Mister Skye's woman. She wondered how they'd take that. Her father had a keen sense of honor—and shame. Her mother and her clan-mothers would probably understand.

Familiar faces crowded around her as the village rushed to greet its visitors. That made her heart sing. Forgotten names burst into her mind. Little Boy! Runner! Sings at Night! Golden faces as wide as the moon! Clan-brothers and -sisters, clan-parents and -grandparents, all welded into a great family encompassing the rich village. And there was Lodge Maker! And Rising Crow! She peered about, looking for her brother Strong Horse, but didn't see him. But she saw Pretty Doe, her father's fine fat second wife, thrusting through the crowd.

"Blue Dawn!"

Her Shoshone name. It sang sweetly in her ears and

she knew she'd use it again, soft on her tongue as butterfly down.

"You have come to visit us," said her mother, beaming up at Mary. "It is good. We honor our daughter."

"Come to the lodge," said her father. "We will take you to Washakie. He will want to know that Mister Skye's women are here. Will your man be with us, too?"

"No!" she cried.

"Ah, only the wives of Mister Skye visit," he said. "We will give a feast and invite everyone. No one will give a bigger feast. We will give away everything we have. Tell the Crow woman how pleased we are to welcome her to our Snake village. Both wives of Mister Skye."

"Sonofabitch!" said Victoria, who needed no translating.

"And this is Mister Skye's son; our blood and the blood of the warrior white man are in him," her father continued, peering at the shy, silent boy clinging to Mary's waist behind her.

"He is welcoming you, Dirk," she said. "He is your grandfather."

The boy stared at a man he scarcely remembered and then at the other babbling people crowding around. "Is this my new father?" he asked solemnly.

"He is like a father," she told her son.

Mary stared at her parents, seeing gray in their iron hair. But both looked as hale as ever, hawk-lean and proud. And young, plump Pretty Doe beamed at her lodge-daughter just as if she'd borne Mary herself. Her father and mothers had made a proud lodge.

Shyly she permitted her father to lead her mare through the cheerful throng, past lodges whose dyed symbols of sun and moon and stars and spirit-helpers she adored, each of the lodge owners springing up in her mind like grasses after the snow had melted.

Home again. If they would have her. Beaming boys

helped her off her mare and unloaded the packhorses and led the horses away to the common herd grazing among distant cottonwoods. The joy and sadness of being here overflowed in her. She listened gravely to the village people while barely containing the tears that brimmed in her dark eyes. Her parents eyed her curiously, their faces filled with questions. But that would wait. Sometimes they gazed contemplatively at Victoria, who seemed out of sorts and ill at ease.

Then Washakie came, summoned by some imp who had scurried out to the herd with the news of visitors.

Mary felt shy in the presence of her older clan-brother. Young Washakie had become the head chief of the Eastern Shoshones thirteen years earlier in the white men's year of 1840. She beheld an august man just beginning to gray, like her parents; big and raw-boned, with a strange presence about him that reminded her of Mister Skye. Some natural lordship gave him possession of all around him. But she beheld, too, the suffering of leadership. No man could lead the People without knowing sadness and failure; disagreement and strife; war and burials. It showed in his patient eyes. He wore a white man's blue shirt tucked into his leggins.

"It is my little clan-sister Blue Dawn," he said. "And the older wife of Mister Skye. And the child whose mother is a Snake woman. And where is your man, my friend Mister Skye?"

"Oh—he is not with us."

"Will he come soon?"

"No—not now."

"Soon, I hope. I wish to see him. It is important. Where can I find him?"

"Chief Washakie—we won't see him . . . not now."

"He is ill?"

"Yes! No. In a way. He wishes to—be with himself."

The chief peered at Mary. "We'll talk of these things

later. Now, Blue Dawn, you must visit with Lodge Maker and Pretty Doe and Rising Crow, and maybe Strong Horse will soon be back with fresh antelope for you. He's a good hunter. He's taken a woman— perhaps you didn't know that."

"A woman?"

"That is for your people to tell you," said Washakie. "I will expect you in my lodge when the sun dies. I have many questions." He turned to Victoria, and in English he said, "I want you to come also."

He left them. It was a signal to all the spectators. They drifted away, except for a few children who gawked at Victoria, the Crow woman in their midst. She glared back. Mary had rarely seen Skye's older woman so irritable.

As swiftly as the Shoshones melted away, her father ushered her into the lodge. He would be direct, she knew. The mountain-bred Shoshones did not have the elaborate belief and ritual of their Plains neighbors, which gave them a directness that surprised even white men.

No sooner had Rising Crow seated himself at the rear of the lodge than he voiced his suspicions: "Something has torn Mister Skye's lodge apart. The women of Mister Skye come here and do not know what he is doing or where he is. Has my daughter offended her man?"

She could not answer. She felt she had. She didn't respond and sat with her eyes averted.

"A woman should not offend her man. We did not raise a woman to offend her man."

"Sonofabitch!"

Victoria's explosion halted Rising Crow.

"Mister Skye—he gets tired of red women. He sits in his lodge all winter and stares and looks sick. Bad spirit in him." She waited for Mary to translate into the Shoshone, even though Victoria could do it herself.

"Mister Skye, he wanna go back to his own people, to white women, with all them skirts. He wanna talk to white women in English. He get tired of us; we don't know all that stuff. I see it in him. He sits, don't eat, don't wash, gets Jawbone mad, and then gets me mad. I tell Mary we gotta go—he no good for us no more. He need his own kind. He gonna go east and read the books and listen to the music and all that stuff; he's mighty damn sick of all this." She waved a hand. "White men call it wilderness, which means they gotta do something to it to fix it. They don't like wilderness."

Mary translated automatically, afraid of her father's wrath.

"It ain't Mary's fault. It ain't my fault. We take care of Mister Skye. Mary, she give herself to him but he pushes her away. We come here; she wants to be with her people. We maybe join you if you want. Maybe we go to my people if you don't. We gotta go someplace."

Mary found herself crying, and didn't know why. But then it came to her as she converted Victoria's rough English into her own tongue; the break with Mister Skye had become real now. There was no hope. He was gone forever.

Rising Crow sat contemplatively, absorbing all that, while his two wives watched and waited. "A man needs his people. I never knew why Mister Skye didn't go back to his people," he said at last. "I am glad you have come back, Blue Dawn. We are honored. We are glad that the Crow woman joins us. We have room in our lodge, and the wives of Mister Skye bring us honor and power. We will tell the village that you have come to live with us. Our lodge will be full again. Strong Horse has his woman—Little Mink. Soon they will have a baby. The clan women made a new lodge for Strong Horse and Little Mink so we have much room. We will give a feast and pay the town crier to sing the news to all ears. We will see if Mister Skye comes for you. And if not—" He shrugged. "It is not good for a young woman with a good boy to be alone. I will find someone for you."

Mary nodded mutely. She did not want a Snake man.

# Chapter 11

The whole company wanted to explore Independence Rock, so Truscott called a halt. Superintendent Victorious Bonaparte Cummings was as eager as the rest to study the tens of thousands of names inscribed in the brown granite landmark, which rose like a whale's back out of the valley of the Sweetwater—a visible sign of American empire. He had himself driven right to the foot of the hump.

"My good Mister Skye, would you do me the service of telling about the landmark? I see my brother's here. Perhaps you'll oblige us both."

Delight lit the craggy face of the guide. "I can do that, mate. I can show you some of the early signatures from the trapping days: Tom Fitzpatrick; Milt Sublette. But you won't find Old Gabe—ah, Bridger there. He can't write."

"Are the names chiseled in?"

"A few. Mostly painted with tar from the buckets

the wagons carry; some are house paint. Some made from gunpowder and grease."

Victorious lumbered to earth from his carriage and peered augustly at the tens of thousands of signatures decorating the most famous landmark and message board on the California Trail. His sense of history told him he was witnessing the conquest of a continent and it suffused him with joy.

"A lot of white men have come west," Superintendent Cummings said. "It is a sign of the times."

"So far, over a hundred thousand, mate. And a million animals. The Army keeps count at Kearny and Laramie."

"Look there—signatures fifty and sixty feet up that granite. How did they get there? One thing white men can't do is fly." He laughed.

The fractured and cleft granite vaulted smoothly upward, covered with names painted much higher than any mortal could reach. Everywhere, often obscuring the older Oregon Trail contributions, was the roll call of the California gold rush, the building blocks of what the politicians in Washington City were calling Manifest Destiny.

Skye led them toward the southeast corner of the humped hill, where the oldest names remained, many of them dating back to the caravans taking supplies out to the rendezvous of the mountain men in the twenties and thirties. "I knew them all," said Skye. "Most've gone under."

"It's like a great graveyard," said Wellington, "a list of the dead who've passed through and left their mark. Each soul en route to a better life somewhere in this golden land."

"John C. Frémont thought so, too, Reverend. See that big black cross painted there? He did it. It's made of india rubber and grease. He saw the rock as a giant gravestone—and wanted to honor the dead who passed by."

"How do you know that?"

"I was one of his guides—back in forty-two."

"I see the cross as the holy sign of the future, Mister Skye. Here we are, Christianizing the wilderness, bringing the sweetness of civilization to the savages."

Skye studied them pensively. "Maybe now's the time to talk about that," he said with a curious quietness. "You wanted me to."

"Yes, do, Mister Skye," said the superintendent, who leaned heavily into his walking stick. "Permit me to find a place of repose," he added, beginning a stately promenade toward a slab of granite that would afford a seat.

Skye turned toward him. "First, tell me what your intentions are. Then I'll tell you how the tribes'll react—what's feasible and what's just white men's presumption."

Victorious Bonaparte peered about, wanting no eavesdroppers, and found none. The dragoons and Indian Bureau personnel were reading names written on rock, or daubing their own.

"The tribes, sir, are the past; white men are the present and future, given our natural gifts and superiorities. It's my duty as head of the Bureau to give the past a decent burial. Put them into safe refuges before they're all run to the ground by soldiers or settlers. In their national homes they can either take to our ways and assimilate—or wither away. I'm their legal protector.

"We're going to insist upon a peace among them; define boundaries; guarantee safe passage along this road; acquire the right to build forts and railroads and pikes and telegraph lines. As for the rest, we'll build them some model farms, teach them farming, and school them through the sixth grade. We'll supply annuities for twenty years to keep them alive after the buffalo are shot away. That's as much as civilized men can do for them. Beyond that, it's up to them."

Skye nodded bleakly and turned to the reverend.

"Victorious is a bit pessimistic, Mister Skye. If men of the cloth will go among them—like the Whitmans in Oregon, or Father De Smet—why, the tribesmen'll be eager converts. They'll learn the moral and spiritual lessons they'll need and be weaned from their nomadic hunting and warring life into good citizens. This is a good thing: these poor innocents in these wilds will be settled around the agencies and their minds opened to the faith. Quite apart from God's harvest—the fruit of baptism and regular instruction—there'll be a harvest for the republic. So—the Cummings brothers are somewhat at odds, eh?"

The guide nodded. "You see it the way most white men would."

"Well? Well? For a fortnight now, you've intimated that we've things to learn, Skye. Be about it!" urged Victorious.

"It's Mister Skye, sir."

Victorious Cummings quaked with mirth. He'd taken a liking to the border ruffian. Noblesse oblige, he thought.

Skye peered at the stout brown rock that bore mute testimony to history's greatest spontaneous migration—testimony to the howling need for the treaty parley.

"Hardly know where to start," he muttered. "But let's take the homelands. Home, for them, is whatever land they control at the time. The Crow've been here a long time. But the Sioux and Cheyenne arrived recently, pushed here from the East. All the world's their home—no fixed place. In their view, nobody owns the land. What it boils down to is, you're going to have a tough time keeping tribes inside of the cages you're planning for them. It's not in their way of thinking."

"Well, Skye, they're going to have to get used to it because that's what we'll insist on. We're the ones imposing the treaty; to be frank about it, we do it by right of conquest."

Skye sighed, as if he'd anticipated the response. "All right. Just don't expect them to stay in their cages."

Skye got no answer and plowed on. "Now, a treaty has to be made with all the chiefs. A head chief like Washakie of the Shoshones can't make a treaty for all his bands even if he's their top man. And worse, the next generation doesn't feel bound by those agreements. Their notion of a treaty isn't like yours."

Victorious Cummings was feeling dismissive, sitting at that rock of empire. "Well, they'll have to deal with it."

Skye turned to Wellington. "When you ask a warrior to stop hunting and warring and start farming or herding cattle, you're asking him to become a woman. That's all woman's work. He won't do it. He'd die first. You know how a boy gets ahead? Wins a wife? Becomes a chief? With war honors—stealing horses, counting coups. You're taking his manhood from him. It's a matter of shame. You want to turn them into farmers? Keep them from collecting horses? That's really the same as turning them into drunks and beggars panhandling at every outpost. Is that your Christian vision?"

"Why, Mister Skye . . . Of course the change'll be difficult—from neolithic savage to civilized citizen. I'm sure you're right, my good man. But it can't be helped."

Skye lifted his top hat and ran a rough hand through his graying hair. "It's slow death, is all. Waiting and despairing and dying. Their ways rule them. Look at it in reverse, Reverend. What if they conquered you and made you give up your faith and learn their ways—or die? Would you surrender your Christian faith, mate?"

Wellington smiled. "I would not surrender my faith. Tell me, Mister Skye—have you any better plan?"

Skye's response smacked Victorious Cummings like a war club. "You could all get out."

"You're dreaming, Skye. Whites are flooding in, no matter whether the government approves. The redskins have no say in it. It's not planned; nothing can stop it, including the Army. Land and gold. Dreams like opium. My task is to help the savages pick up the pieces and you ought to thank me for it."

"Superintendent Cummings," said Skye edgily, "you'll have it your own bloody way."

"Suppose we make no treaties. Suppose we leave the savages to their devices, to sink or swim. Then what, Mister Skye?"

The crumpling of Skye's visage was terrible to behold, like the desolation of a widower at the fresh grave of his wife. "I don't know," Skye muttered. "There's no answer."

# Chapter 12

No bitterness had ever pierced the soul of Alphonse McGinty, not even when he discovered signs in Boston shop windows saying that Irish Need Not Apply. He'd seen lots of signs like that in the United States, and was perfectly familiar with the attitude, having spent the first forty years of his life under the imperial British thumb.

Instead of brooding or drinking away the last of his shillings, he had bought passage on stagecoaches and railroads that deposited him in Washington City. There he had sought his fortune in a place where any warm body counted. Politics was the refuge of the oppressed: he would find a politician and make a living. In the Old Country his father and uncles were knackers: they had acquired the rendering charter from the English and had the sole right to buy a dead animal in County Clare at whatever price they chose to pay. It had been a trade the lordly British scorned. Thus had the lesson been learned: there was always wealth in political connections.

He had arrived in the capital at that propitious moment in 1849 when the Bureau of Indian Affairs was being transferred from the War Department, where it had treated the savages shabbily, to the Department of the Interior, where it could treat the Indians even more shabbily. Alphonse McGinty's worldly ways, cast-iron smiles, oleaginous cheer, and familiarity with accounting immediately won him a clerking job, and a year later the prized position of chief clerk. He staffed his office with kindred Hibernians. In return he had been an invaluable supporter of Zachary Taylor and Millard Fillmore, and now Franklin Pierce. With unfailing good cheer he had dominated the Bureau the way sergeants major ran the Army—that is, with brute power, tempered only by obsequious nods toward his superiors.

His effusions of joy had much to do with his mounting wealth, only some of which was the fruit of his salary. He treated his clerks well. In turn they had offered him their implacable loyalty. As for the wealth, it was extracted from various sources, such as a fee for any service, whether required by his job or not. While those expediting fees, as he called them, added up, they barely accounted for his growing fortune, or the affluence of the Indian Bureau clerking staff.

Much more important to Chief Clerk McGinty's purse was the control of annuities, those goods given the tribes for a period of years, usually in exchange for land the tribes surrendered by treaty. The annuities were essentially a bribe to induce the savages to take up reservation life, though they were rationalized by politicians and officials as humane assistance during the transition from a hunting life to farming and stock growing. The goods given to various tribes were much the same as the products they got from the Indian traders in exchange for buffalo robes and peltries:

knives, axheads, pots and pans, bolts of flannel and calico, blankets, rifles and powder, hoop iron for arrowheads, beads, vermilion, needles and thread, as well as flour, sugar, coffee, and rice.

It had been McGinty's duty to purchase all of these goods from private contractors. He was all in favor of treaties. The more treaties with the savages, the more goods and transportation he and his staff purchased. He admitted to himself that he had a real flair for it; he could skin lucre out of anything, one way or another. As the years passed he had needed more and more of it, largely because he kept a costly mistress on Dupont Circle, the titian-haired Eloise. How he missed her. It would be two months before he rested in her ivory arms once again.

A lot of his wealth simply derived from permitting suppliers to overcharge the government in exchange for a small consideration in greenbacks. But much of it came from other little arrangements. Who would ever know that the axheads given the savages were cast iron rather than steel, and would barely cut down a tree before dulling or breaking? Or that the knives given the aborigines would bend at the slightest excuse? Or that the calico was so shoddy it would scarcely last a month? Or that the blankets were so thin they could not warm the body in cold weather? Or that the coffee beans were a bitter Brazilian variety that had languished unsold? Or that the flour from the Memphis warehouse had mealybugs in it? Or that the rifles had shoddy locks, bad springs and hammers? Or that the casks of gunpowder had been salvaged from a flooded warehouse? Or that freight outfits shipped less tonnage than they had contracted for, helped themselves to whatever caught their fancy and called it breakage? It was, after all, only the heathen savages who suffered, and God knows, they deserved to suffer, given their habit of massacring innocent white men.

Surely the savages would say nothing. On rare occa-

sions an Indian agent had complained—and found
himself unemployed, courtesy of Alphonse McGinty.
Ministers gave him the most trouble. Reformers
wanted ministers as Indian agents, and two adminis-
trations had complied. But not even ministers were
equal to McGinty's blarney and sleight of hand.

The chief clerk correctly surmised that the only possible danger to his happiness was for the treaty parley
to fail. If that happened he'd be forced to ship all those
goods back to federal warehouses at Fort Leavenworth, where an occasional inspector would show up
to tally boxes and barrels, audit bills of lading, poke
and probe. But that had not happened. Every one of
these great parleys had resulted in an agreement with
the savages and the distribution of the goods to the
eager tribesmen. Still, McGinty thought, it never hurt
to be cautious.

He had become an adept listener. He was wont to sit
silently while Major Cummings and the other great
men conferred. He had, in addition, a dozen ears, his
loyal staff, all listening on his behalf, often reporting
news to him even before the Cummings brothers
heard it. In this fashion he had learned that the guide,
Skye, would be critical to this parley; that the man's
influence among these particular savages could sway
them one way or another.

McGinty hadn't much stomach for Skye. A man
who lived so far from civilization would be a difficult
man to control. Still, Skye had something to commend
him: he'd deserted the Queen's Royal Navy and that
made him an honorary Irishman. It was time, McGinty
thought, to butter up the fellow. If this parley depended so much on Skye, then so did Alphonse
McGinty.

In camp that evening he found the big guide off by
himself, as usual, fooling with that dangerous horse.
Skye kept himself and Jawbone as far from the cavalry

as possible, and it pleased McGinty that he knew exactly why.

"Ah, lad, there's a bloomin' war-horse. I never saw the like in the Old Country, but me boss, Major Cummings, he says that's a Devil-forged horse, a wild beast for a wild land. I come to tell you, lad, I admire the ugly thing. Jawbone reminds me of me late brother Patrick, who died in a pub fracas."

"Better stay clear, mate. Any man he doesn't know he's likely to hurt."

"Well, you can teach him I'm a friend."

Skye paused. "You come for something, Mister McGinty?"

"I did at that. Me boys, me poor underpaid clerks, they hobnob with the troopers and teamsters, you know. They're telling me those troopers don't much like your nag there and they're making a lot of brag about it. You know the kind of talk, boy—daring each other to fix that horse of yours, one mean way or t'other. I heard of it and thought I'd pass a quiet word along, as a friend—and for the sake of the Bureau. They'd kill it if they dared, even with the lieutenant saying they got to behave themselves—for now."

"Jawbone won't let them come within ten feet, mate."

"They know it, Master Skye. Oh, they do! Not a man of them's willing to lay down his life just to hurt a mean old horse. But they've got among 'em knife-throwers and fancy sharpshooters and lead-tassel bullwhip artistes—any of them capable of cutting a tendon or nicking a pastern, eh?"

"They're signing their death warrants." The look in Skye's face assured McGinty the man meant every word.

"I believe you, me friend. I see it in you. But what if you don't know who did it?"

"The horse'll tell me."

"Well, me friend, I'll keep my ears and eyes open for

you. I keep on top of things. If this gets beyond the talking and bragging I'll slip you the word."

"Why?"

"It's in me, friend. I'm for the underdog on principle. And another thing: in the back of the clerk's ambulance is liquid refreshment. Now I know you're a man who needs refreshing sometimes. Look for some corked Glennybrook, a blessed product of Celtic Scotland, as pure and smoky as me mother's heart. Just have a nip anytime, me friend, courtesy of the Bureau."

"Thanks, mate."

The man was difficult to know, McGinty thought. But he'd keep on trying. Skye was the joker in the deck.

# Chapter 13

The prospect of a parley with the grandfathers did not displease Chief Washakie. Ever since the tall young man had become head chief of the Eastern Snakes he had been forced to deal with the pale strangers flooding into his people's traditional lands.

In 1841 the first of the wagon trains rolled through the southern reaches of his people's country en route to Oregon. Their numbers were tolerable, they didn't tarry, and they didn't slaughter all the game. But things had swiftly gotten worse. In 1849 a new flood of them arrived, tens of thousands of wagons bound for California goldfields. Their iron wheels cut terrible trenches in the earth. They slaughtered every buffalo that wandered near the trail, leaving his people hungry and desperate.

The flood seemed only to grow each summer. Some red men didn't believe that whites were as numerous as leaves in a forest. Others, watching the parade, said that surely no more white men remained in the East.

But he knew better. Once, Mister Skye had told him that all the white men he'd seen on the Big Road were the smallest part of the nation of them in the East. He had always believed his friend Mister Skye.

Surely this talk with the wives of Mister Skye would give him a good eye! The chief welcomed the women at sundown and his wives fed them elk meat for supper. For a long while they talked about other things. Skye's older wife, deciding to use her halting Snake tongue in honor of her host, talked about her Absaroka people. Blue Dawn talked about her gladness to be among them again.

The tall chief smoked quietly and listened, waiting for the appropriate moment—which came at the time of the evening star. He had many things to ask them.

"Where is Mister Skye?"

Blue Dawn—Mary—didn't reply, deferring to the Crow woman.

"He's left us. He got tired of red women. I don't know where he went. Maybe back to his people across the waters. Maybe to the big villages where white men are."

He turned to Blue Dawn. "Did you make him unhappy?"

"No! I was good to him. I made him happy. We laughed. He played with our son. He had no cares. I took care of our boy. I tanned antelope and elk and I made beautiful shirts—"

She couldn't continue and he saw tears brim in her soft brown eyes. She could not lift her gaze from the ground.

"Perhaps he will come back someday. Maybe he will go to his people and find he is not like them anymore. Maybe he needs to make this trip to find out. I think you should wait."

"He's gone for good. Like all the trappers," said the older wife. "I saw them come and go in the beaver-trapping times."

"Maybe this is good," Washakie said. "Now we have our beautiful clan-sister back and a new child for our people. Wait a while, Blue Dawn. Enjoy your son. When the time comes we will find another man for you. Many would be honored to have the wife of Mister Skye."

"I don't want a Shoshone man!" she cried.

"But why, sister?"

She looked frightened. "I like the way white men treat women."

Victoria cackled but Blue Dawn held her ground. "White men are kind to women," the young woman said.

Washakie knew it was true. Over the winters he had observed the white trappers with their red wives, and after that the wagon people on the road. A white man's woman had more status, honor, and freedom than her red sisters. She was less bound to drudge and obey. Many white men were friendly to their women and spent time with them. Among the Snakes and other tribes the men usually stayed together and ignored the women. Many warriors treated their women harshly; few white men seemed to.

"Maybe white men have better ways than we do," he said slowly. "We have much to learn from them."

"I will wait for Mister Skye," his clan-sister said resolutely.

"Ha! you'll wait forever for that sonofabitch," the older wife said in English.

Washakie caught the sour gist of her English. He addressed her slowly so that she could understand his Snake tongue. "I think the whites have much to teach us," he said gently. "I have thought about this for many seasons—ever since I was a boy. If we learn how to scratch the earth and plant seed we will have grain and greens. If we raise cattle instead of hunting the buffalo we will always have meat. I've talked with their medicine seers in black robes; they are wise and kind. I've talked with the wagon people. They are all chiefs. We have much to learn."

Victoria sat sullenly.

"Mister Skye gave you freedoms and treated you well, and you liked it. Blue Dawn says she does not want to become the woman of a Snake man now. Crow Woman, I think you do not want to become a Crow's wife now. You would not like the way a Crow man would treat you."

Victoria snarled. Then she rubbed her eyes. But she didn't reply. Washakie sensed he had made a point.

"I want these talks with the white grandfathers. I am different from many Snake chiefs—and the chiefs of the other tribes. I know that what white men have is good for the Snake people. I think someday I will try to farm—if they will teach me. It would be good for a chief to give corn to his hungry people."

Victoria sighed. "Chief Washakie. I love the old ways. But you are right. After Skye I would not want an Absaroka man."

It would be harder, he thought, for the Eastern Shoshones to deal with all the changes wrought by white men without Mister Skye. Many had been the time when Washakie and Skye had smoked a pipe and talked of the future, especially the things his people faced with the migration of the whites. Mister Skye had said it couldn't be stopped; the buffalo and deer would be shot away; the best hope was for the Snakes to become like the whites and scratch the earth with their plows. Or fade into the earth, forgotten. Skye had said it sadly, as if something precious was being destroyed. And the sadness had resonated autumnally in Washakie himself.

"Two days ago a runner came from the white fathers at Fort Laramie. Do you know anything about that, Blue Dawn?"

"A little."

"The white grandfathers want us to come to a great

meeting on the Wind River to talk about peace," he said. "Like the Big Talk at Fort Laramie two summers ago. The grandfathers from the big city in the East are coming. They want to meet with ourselves, the Crow, the Arapaho, the Bannocks, and the Cheyenne at the great plain where the Little Wind meets the Wind River. In the next moon. The grandfathers wish to make a treaty with us. Do you know about this?"

"They asked Mister Skye to guide them and translate," said the Crow Woman.

"Will he come?"

She shrugged. "We don't know. Maybe he will."

"What do the white grandfathers want?"

The older woman grinned cynically. "What do you think?"

"The Snakes are at peace with them—but maybe we shouldn't be. We starve because they shoot away the buffalo. Our children are often hungry. Our hunters ride long distances and see no buffalo—or any game. I will tell the grandfathers we must be paid—we must have food or we'll starve."

"When they come it's because they want something."

"Well, so do we want something. What else, Crow Woman?"

Victoria seemed to gain confidence. "First they'll tell you, don't war with any other tribe, not even take horses. Next they'll tell you to leave the whites on the Big Road alone—don't take horses, don't kill one of their oxen for food, don't ask for anything, don't even come close. Then they'll say they got a place to put all your people—lots of room, far from the Big Road. It'll be all yours. If you say you don't want that place they'll say you've got to go there anyway."

He turned to Blue Dawn. "What would Mister Skye tell me?"

"My chief, Mister Skye would go to the grandfathers and make our case for us and be very strong among them," Mary said. "But not even Mister Skye could do any good. He told us that no one can stop it; there are too many coming."

"Thank you, little clan-sister. We will listen to what they are offering us. Maybe it will be good, even though it doesn't seem good for us now. Maybe we will have to give up the old ways and become like them. I am eager to go to the Big Talk. I want you to come and translate for us."

"Maybe we'll see Mister Skye," said Blue Dawn.

Maybe so, Washakie thought.

# Chapter 14

Anthony Truscott hated to rely on the guide for anything, but the moment was fast approaching when he would have to. Soon they'd leave the California Trail and strike overland to the Wind River. And they'd need Skye to show the way.

"Sergeant Pope!"

The noncom spurred his gray horse forward to receive instructions. "Sah?"

"Bring Skye."

"Yes, sah. Get a tight grip on your reins, sah."

Truscott tolerated the impudence. The Big Pope, as the dragoons called him, was a leader of men and Truscott's nemesis. Truscott was afraid of the old sergeant and couldn't bear his own fear. The sergeant halted to one side of the column, and waited.

Day after day, Skye had stayed close to the Indian Bureau ambulances and kept clear of the troops. The man was afraid of what the cavalry might do to that outlaw horse he was so fond of.

Truscott would shoot that devil in an instant were it not for Cummings, whose word among the officials in Washington would blot Truscott's career or advance it. So it was a stalemate, and the best Truscott could hope for was to keep the guide away from his dragoons and mounts. He'd ordered them not to fraternize with Skye, and so far Skye hadn't tried to talk to any of them. But now things would change.

He felt his bay gelding sidle to the right and knew Skye and Jawbone were pulling up. The gelding shivered, and fought the bit.

"You summoned me, mate?"

"I'll thank you to call me anything but mate."

Skye looked at Truscott quizzically. "Sorry. It's an expression from my sailing days. I was a common seaman, sir."

"So I know. Skye, somewhere ahead we turn off for the Wind River. I require your knowledge of the country."

"It's Mister Skye, sir."

A rush of impatience flooded Truscott. "I'll call you what I choose."

"Calling me mister is a common form of civility among English people, sir."

"Maybe you don't deserve civility."

"I'm puzzled, sir. For a fortnight now I've met a wall of coldness from you. No, that's too mild a word. You've scorned me from the moment you laid eyes on me at Laramie. I'd like to know the nature of my offense. What is it, Mister Truscott? Let's have it out in the open." The big man's question hung between them and the lieutenant didn't like it.

Truscott chose to say nothing. Skye was being crude.

"A man's entitled to know the nature of the offenses he is guilty of, if only to make an apology."

"That horse, for one thing."

Skye digested that. "Not the horse," he said quietly.

"I could be riding one of your mounts and you'd treat me the same."

That was true, though Truscott hated to admit it. "Are you questioning my word, Skye?"

"Oh, Jawbone's some of it. But there's more, Mister Truscott. It has to do with my person. Something in me antagonizes you."

Skye was a civilian. For an itching moment Truscott thought to discipline the man anyway: put irons on him and confiscate that horse and shoot it. But the formidable person of Major Victorious Cummings inhibited him.

"Where do we turn off?"

"I'll show you when we get there. We've things to settle, Mister Truscott, and now's the time."

Truscott turned. "Sergeant, please escort Skye back to his place in the line."

"Yes, sah."

But Skye didn't budge and rode that vicious horse alongside the lieutenant as if he hadn't heard.

"You're dismissed, Skye. We have maps that'll get us there."

"The place is ahead four or five miles. There's a nameless branch flows in from the north. You can take wagons up it, and over a divide to a branch of the Popo Agie. Milt Sublette brought ten wagons to the rendezvous of 1830 that way—first wagons into this country. No trouble at all."

"Dismissed, Skye. You may return now."

But Skye didn't. He rode along beside the lieutenant, while that yellow-eyed horse clacked its teeth, glared at the lieutenant's terrified mount, lifted its snout and sniffed the hot air, and veered this way and that like a drunk.

"Not until you give me your answer, Mister Truscott."

Truscott rode silently, fear and loathing building in him. Skye said nothing for the better part of an hour, doggedly staying right beside the officer. Skye was a lout. His feet stank along with the rest of him. His kind populated penal colonies. He should have been shipped to Australia with the rest of the British scum. He wore the clothing of savages, as if skin garments were a badge of wilderness aristocracy. And that grizzly bearclaw necklace—redskin medicine.

"You're looking at my grizzly claws. They're big medicine. A man that wears the claws of the grizzly, he's a man to be reckoned with. It's one way I stay alive. I got mine the only way that counts, by killing a silvertip grizzly and taking the claws."

Truscott said nothing.

"Out here, Mister Truscott, a man undergoes constant testing, and if he fails he dies. Back in the beaver days, the trappers lived in endless hardship: bad horse, rattlesnake, bear, rifle blowing up, poison water, cold, floods, starving, sickness, thirst, drunk, fistfight, drowning trying to get across an icy river . . . But especially the Indians. Bug's Boys, the Blackfeet! I reckon a third went under. Friends I knew, lads I trapped with. Faces at my cookfire, shared my booze. Under the ground. Some just vanished. We called it the Rocky Mountain College and we passed the courses—or died. Sometimes we passed all the courses—and still died."

They topped a ridge and started down a long grade toward a green line of cottonwoods along a bottom.

"Is that the turnoff, Skye?"

"That's it, mate."

"I asked you not to call me mate."

Skye had a way of grinning that was as cold as the North Pole.

"A man wants seasoning. Some horses don't cut the mustard here; fancy blues that turn the eyes of the ladies won't stop an arrow. A spit-and-polish command doesn't win fights. The boys that led the fur brigades were veterans and they commanded respect of all the

pork-eaters and pilgrims just because they'd survived.
Out here, in two years they learned more about sur-
viving than a man did in twenty back in the cities.
They had a way about them. I respected anyone I met
who'd survived longer than I had. They'd sit around a
fire and talk about the scrapes they'd been in, and lie
a little, too. A young man just naturally respected
them because they'd earned it. The trouble is, you're
asking something of your men that you haven't
earned yet. There's no sense hating a man just because
he's an old coon who's been over the hill and back."

"Are you done, Skye?"

"No, I don't reckon. Bloody lot to talk about."

"I don't need lectures."

"Not giving any. There's something bad betwixt us
and I'm giving you some notions to think about. The
truth is, you don't like me because I'm me. I've been
around the corner and up in the trees and across the
river. In a pinch, your command would listen to me,
not to you. Your sergeant there, Pope, he's an old Indian fighter and so's half your troop. Now I saw the
lads come out of Sandhurst—that's the English military academy—a lot like you. The best of them faced
up to it: they let their sergeants run the show for a
while. The others resented their superior officers,
hated their old noncoms who'd fought in the kaffir
wars, or the wars of your rebellion, or against Napoleon. Those boys, they wanted the power and authority, and took it—and ruined themselves." He paused.
"Now then, how do I give offense?"

"If it's not obvious, then you'll never know."

"Well, then, I'll never know—if that's what you
want."

A blind rage boiled through Truscott. The preaching
idiot! The ignorant backwoods brute! He jammed a
hand toward his revolver, murder erupting through
him, and then jerked it away. Here he was, commanding sixty breech-loading carbines, and he couldn't do a

thing about Skye because of that tub of lard Cummings. For now. Not until the peace conference with the savages was done. After that, not even Cummings would give a damn about Skye's fate. Going back, when it was over, he'd find damned good military grounds to do anything.

# Chapter 15

Loneliness weighed on Skye like an anvil. He rode alone, with only Jawbone for a friend. His melancholia had not lifted: for six months he'd wondered who he was and why he'd been put on earth. It'd been a useless life as far as he could see: barren, mean, poverty-stricken, cruel, imprisoning, and empty. This trip had only made it worse: he had nothing to do.

He sighed, as he had every little while, while Jawbone snapped at horseflies. When this was over he'd go somewhere. God only knew where. To sea, maybe on a merchant ship. What else was there? There were Yank cities to the east but he'd never been in one and lacked so much as one friend in any of them. He sighed again, like a man who was facing his ruin.

The Indian Bureau's ambulance rattled as close as its nervous mules permitted. Skye spotted the Reverend Mister Wellington Waterloo Cummings driving.

"Ho, Mister Skye. Would you join me for a spell? I'm weary of driving and all the clerks've abandoned me. They're back exchanging bawdy stories with the teamsters. Mister McGinty likes to talk about his female conquests, but I inhibit him."

Skye nodded. The reverend tugged the mules to a halt. In a moment Skye settled himself beside the divine and took the four sets of lines, leaving Jawbone to his own devices. His horse peered suspiciously into the covered ambulance, looking for live flesh to massacre, and then settled into a shuffle beside the wagon while the nervous mules snorted and whoofed.

"You're too much alone, Mister Skye. I've been watching you. I think you need a little friendship."

Skye hoped the reverend wasn't about to perform some act of Christian charity on him. He wasn't in the mood for charity. "You think too much. I'm doing fine."

The reverend glanced at him occasionally. Skye pretended not to notice.

"Victorious says that's the grandest horse that ever was born. He said that to see such a horse as Jawbone comes but once in a lifetime."

The compliment pleased Skye but didn't penetrate his darkness.

"What're your plans, Mister Skye?"

"I have none. Go east, maybe."

"Then what?"

"I don't know."

"Virginia is a green land with a piedmont and forested uplands. Little villages built of brick, and gentlefolk who'd enjoy you."

"I doubt that I'd enjoy them."

"They tend to be conservative—homebodies, you know. They've never met anyone who's been all over the world, sailed the seven seas, and dealt with the wild Indians. You'd be a curiosity."

"They would find out soon enough I was a squawman."

"You could, ah, remarry. Many a white woman'd find a good mate in you."

Skye laughed harshly and settled his battered top hat onto his greasy hair. "I'll probably go down the river—go to sea from New Orleans."

"Is it what you wish?"

"No; it's what's possible. I don't delude myself."

"Ah, but you do. We're all set upon this earth for some purpose. And given a chance to do our best. And given all we need—if we've the faith and courage to take it."

"Look, mate, I don't need a bloody sermon." Skye nearly shouted it because of the pain inside him like a roaring ulcer, and the fear that he'd begin leaking tears if he didn't roar and keep on roaring.

The man subsided into silence and sat amiably beside Skye in the rocking ambulance. A raucous magpie followed the caravan, a flash of iridescent black and white, staking ground like some dark guidon.

"I like to think each person on earth is given a chance to do something with his life," the man said. "Otherwise, it's all madness, senseless as an asylum."

"The Indian Bureau's about to put the free tribes into an asylum and call it a chance for them to do something with their lives." Skye snapped it out.

"We'll talk about that some other time, Mister Skye. We're talking about your future now. I'm thinking you'd be an asset to the Indian Bureau. Like David Mitchell, a few superintendents back. He was an American Fur Company man, like you; he knew all the tribes and worked to help them. You could, too."

"I'm not interested."

"I think you'd like to throw it away. You'd like Truscott to try something, anything, to hurt that horse just so you can strike back and get yourself killed."

"You don't know that." Sour hatred squirreled up Skye's throat like vomit.

"I was named for the Duke of Wellington—the

Great Duke—and for Waterloo, a messy battle fought against a better general with a smaller force—Napoleon. But the better man lost and abdicated. It gives me a jaundiced view of excellence, and a respect for Fate. I call it the finger of God. The threads of life are tangled and obscure but if we follow that gossamer strand, it'll lead us to . . . our own beauty."

"There you go again."

"You're a better man than Truscott and always will be, but you could get yourself killed. You should join the Bureau. I can arrange it. We shall create a position. Victorious would be enchanted. And, friend, Washington City's full of eager widows."

"And bloodsuckers like—" Skye behaved himself, at great cost to his fevered mind and tongue.

"Well, if rich widows and virtuous maidens and a smart salary don't raise your sap, the chance to help the tribes ought to. That passion, at least, remains in you."

"It's only justice. When you've been pressed into a frigate and made a powder monkey with the sea as your iron cage and death your only escape, you side with the monkeys. I don't know what love means."

"I had it from Colonel Bullock that you do." The reverend said it softly.

"Avast!" Skye roared.

The reverend said nothing for a time as Skye negotiated a series of rocky terraces that set the wagon to creaking. Steering a wagon overland required concentration.

"Mister Skye, I've been a close observer of people for most of my life. I've a large parish, meet all sorts, and catch glimpses of soul and spirit in my good folk. I've been observing you. An impudence, I'm sure; a habit with me.

"I can tell when a man's struggling. And—forgive me—I can tell you're struggling. Worse than that, Mister Skye. You're falling apart. You're not really going east after this and you're not going to sea—your real destination is six feet under."

He waited, but Skye didn't respond.

"I've seen these things in men your age—like the Devil's last wrestle. Get a grip on yourself, Mister Skye. You're bent on destruction. You can do it; you can raise your sails and run down the wind again. I don't suppose you're an Anglican."

"I was."

"Well, I'm a priest of the rebel branch. We're pretty much over to Protestant forms in Virginia but sometimes I yearn for a whiff of incense. It lifts the soul clear up to the choir loft. I'm always open for business, if business you want to do, Mister Skye. But for heaven's sake don't quit now."

"Who's quitting?" Skye mumbled.

"You are."

"It's my life."

"You have it wrong, Mister Skye. It's your death. I'd be sorry to pray over your remains."

"You mind naming one good thing in my life? And one good idea what to do with the rest of it?"

"Here are four: Victoria, Mary, Dirk, and Jawbone. Here are more: rising to a brigade leader with American Fur. Taking people where they want to go through a dangerous land. Dealing with everyone on the up-and-up. Fighting beside your wives' people. I had quite a talk with old Bullock. He's worried about you and frets like an old nanny. Want more?"

Barnaby Skye didn't hear. He hurt too much.

# Chapter 16

The worldly eyes of Victorious Bonaparte Cummings had seen many a sad sight but this was one of the saddest. He beheld the man he admired, Skye, hunched into the roots of a box elder, stinking drunk. The guide clutched a gray jug in his big paw and lifted it to his lips, sucking noisily while some dribbled down his chin. Skye muttered now and then or mangled a bawdy sailor's ditty, and stared sightlessly at the rest of the camp.

Standing directly over him was the brute horse, ears laid back, teeth clacking, tail massacring flies, ready to commit murder. Jawbone was obviously put out with his master. Occasionally he burrowed his ugly snout into Skye's face, and nipped Skye's majestic beak. Which occasioned a roar from the man followed by several yards of billingsgate, subsiding into sighs and sobs. Skye looked filthy. Dirt caked his face and grimed his arms and fingers.

A great pity filled Victorious Cummings as he

leaned into his gold-knobbed walking stick. He'd heard that the guide had the weakness but he hadn't realized how it took Skye over, consumed him, and rendered him less handy than a used corncob.

"It's a sad sight," he said to his reverend brother as they beheld the man's ruination. "Here the man wants to go east and enter polite society—he was born into it, apparently—and look at him. Loose him in a Virginia town and every man of the house would bar the door, every woman would cross to the other side of the street, and every hound-dawg would lift a leg."

"It's my doing, Victorious. This afternoon I braced him with his problems; I told him he was a man falling to pieces; he needed to get a grip on life. I even told him to apply to the Indian Bureau and I'd see to it that he got a job. I told him he could be another David Mitchell."

Victorious wheezed. "I don't think Washington City'd welcome him to its bosom, Wellington."

"One can hope, Victorious."

Skye lifted the jug, guzzled, squinted at them through small blue eyes. "Evening, gentlemen," he said. "Welcome to my parlor."

"Mister Skye—get ahold of yourself. You'll ruin your reputation."

Skye yawned, belched, and scratched his private parts. "Never trust a bloody sailor," he said. "A storm in every port."

Jawbone seemed ready to slaughter them. "I think his noble steed has designs on our persons, Wellington. It is not a horse to respect rank or the clerical collar. Let's retreat."

They did, just as Jawbone sidled around, head lowered and teeth clacking, and screeched something so unholy that Victorious swore it would have opened graves. But at ten yards' distance the horse subsided. Superintendent Cummings supposed that thirty feet was the Jawbone perimeter. The horse settled down, lifted its master's battered top hat, and fanned it in Skye's face. After that sacrilege Jawbone attacked the jug with his yellow teeth, somehow knowing that its juices were the evil he fought.

"Avast!" roared Skye, guarding his ambrosia with both paws. The horse bit Skye's ear and Skye pawed the air.

"He's worse than a temperance society," Skye muttered.

These strange events soon attracted happy onlookers drawn from the ranks of the dragoons. Even Lieutenant Truscott appeared, smirked, and backed away without saying a thing.

Knots of troopers gathered around Jawbone's perimeter to gaze at the spectacle of the drunken guide and the crazy horse. Superintendent Cummings watched them warily, leaning into his walking stick.

"Lookit that crazy horse. Didja ever see such an outlaw?" said one.

"He needs hamstringing. Maybe we should hamstring the guide while we're about it."

"That nag'll kill ye if ye sneak too close."

"There ain't a hoss alive I can't humble," said a blond corporal.

The blue roan trembled, turning sullenly from man to man, his head low and his ears laid back so flat he looked as if he had none. Cummings swore the horse was calculating murder, glaring at the troopers from mad eyes set too close together.

"You'd better stand back, young man," he said. "The guide trained that horse to kill. You're about to get yourself into big trouble—with it and with me."

The dragoon smirked.

One of them pitched a pebble at Jawbone. It bounced off his hip. Jawbone screeched and whirled and then stood trembling, his four legs spread, ready to catapult into his tormentors. Other pebbles sailed into the circle, hitting Jawbone's flank, his neck, and his left foreleg. Jawbone screeched.

"Arrguph," muttered Skye.

Soldiers laughed. This was sport. More pebbles sailed toward Jawbone, some of them thrown hard. One cracked off Jawbone's skull. Jawbone shrieked, bucked and twisted, his hooves murderous. He sallied toward one knot of troopers, scattering them like ten-pins, and then whirled back to resume his station over Skye.

Cummings had seen enough. "You're on report, soldier," he said to the one who'd thrown a rock the size of an egg at the horse. "Go to your bivouac at once and don't come here again. That goes for all of you."

"Aw, who're you to say?"

"I command this expedition."

"And what're you going to do about it?" The question came from the grinning corporal beyond Jawbone, almost hidden in the evening gloom. "Put a nasty note in the looie's personnel file?"

"What's your name, Corporal?"

"I forgot it."

Cummings walked a wide arc around Jawbone's turf, progressing with his innate dignity. Jawbone pawed the ground and clacked stained teeth again. The stoning hadn't stopped. Dragoons whistled and cheered every time a rock bounced off the horse. Jawbone stood like an army poised to erupt from its trenches at dawn.

The corporal had a fistful of bills in his hand and was collecting more. "I'm going to hamstring him. Their money says I can't," the corporal said.

"You're committing suicide. I forbid it. Report to Lieutenant Truscott and wait for my instructions. Do not provoke or injure that horse. Am I clear?"

The corporal grinned and continued collecting the bills slapped into his hand. He had accumulated an amazing number of greenbacks from eight-dollar-a-month soldiers.

"Superintendent, ain't it true you're a civilian?" he said. "Ain't it a pity? Retired majors and Injun superintendents don't cut mustard in the U.S. dragoons." He addressed the rest of the troopers. "Any more betting?"

None made another bet. They peered at each other in an odd silence. Even Jawbone stopped his braying and whirling, and settled quietly beside the stuporous Skye. Tears oozed from the horse's eyes.

Victorious Cummings didn't wait: he cracked his walking stick hard upon a certain spot on the outside of the corporal's knee. A proper blow there could topple a man. It was one of the most painful known. But the blond giant only grinned. "I been hit there so much I don't feel it, Super."

Darkness descended, plunging the wilderness into eerie gloom.

Wellington tried: "I have no authority over you except as your conscience. For God's sake, don't."

A dragoon snickered.

The corporal unsheathed a wicked knife that glinted orangely in the hellish light of distant fires.

"What's the bet?" yelled a soldier.

"That I can hamstring a foot," the corporal replied calmly. He worked his thick black belt free and swung the massive U.S. Cavalry buckle in a lazy arc before him. The brass could cut the horse to ribbons. Someone handed him a rope.

"He'll kill you, matey," slurred Skye.

Dragoons laughed nervously.

The corporal slid into the circle Jawbone had defended, mocking the horse: "Watch the buckle, hoss. Just watch 'er swing back and forth. Gonna put your eyes out with this buckle; gonna pound your tender nose. Watch the buckle—it's coming to bite ya. Don't watch nothing else. You're gonna feel this sticker along the back of your little old foot and it'll be too late."

Jawbone stood quietly until the corporal was ten feet from Skye. Then the horse whirled. Cummings saw the flash of forehooves and then the arc of rear hooves. He heard a terrible thump, the crack of breaking bone. Then a pop like a melon caving in. The corporal toppled to earth and never even twitched. There wasn't much left of the man's head. And his left leg stuck out at an odd angle. The man was dead before he'd hit the ground. Greenbacks filtered down and caught in the grass.

Cumming sighed, filled with pity for the dead. He'd witnessed horror. The man had committed suicide for sport. Cummings wondered if he could bear to watch the forthcoming summary execution of Jawbone, and maybe Skye.

# Chapter 17

They had tormented a great horse beyond endur-
ance—and a man had died. Superintendent Cummings sighed, an oppression as heavy as his body
welling through him. The world was mad.

The dragoons stared at the shattered form, digesting
death, and wondering what to do. No one dared enter
Jawbone's domain and drag the blood-soaked body
away. The horse stood calmly, alert and menacing in
the darkness.

"They'll shoot it," Victorious said to Wellington.
"After tormenting it to madness, they'll shoot it."

"A man's dead," said Wellington, reproachfully. "A
mortal life, may I remind you. Violence ought not to
exist in a domestic animal. Maybe Skye's horse de-
serves his fate."

"No." The word exploded from Victorious Cummings like a cannon shot. He pointed at one of the
stunned soldiers. "You. Get the lieutenant."

The trooper recovered his senses and raced toward

the cavalry bivouac. In a moment he returned with Lieutenant Truscott at his side.

A gibbous moon hung low in the bleak sky, casting grudging light on the tragic scene. Truscott stared at the body and at the horse looming over Skye and at the knots of troopers stationed around the rim of a fatal circle. Sergeant Pope edged into the circle, intending to drag the body away, but Jawbone screeched, a bone-chilling howl that shattered the young night.

"He's a mankiller," the officer said. "No mankiller horse can live."

"The men tormented him with rocks. He endured it to the end and didn't attack them," the superintendent replied quietly.

"A mankiller will kill again. He has the taste of it. He's an outlaw."

"That horse has killed men since about the age of three. He was trained to it. He's a lifesaver."

"I'm going to destroy him, Skye or no Skye."

"Lieutenant, the corporal took bets. He bet he could hamstring that horse. See his belt there? He was swinging the buckle at the horse to divert it. I don't know what he had in mind but he was going to slash a foot somehow. He declared war on Jawbone; not the other way around."

"He's a mankiller." Truscott's voice came flat and hard.

"Have it out with Skye. It's Skye's horse. He'll come around in the morning."

"Sorry, Cummings. A good soldier's dead. This is an Army matter. I'm going to get that body and that means killing the horse first."

Skye muttered something and rolled over. Jawbone nickered at him and pushed his muzzle into Skye's face. "Avast!" Skye rumbled, pawing at the horse.

Cummings saw something he could scarcely bear. Man and horse loved each other and forgave each other's trespasses. "Truscott. I'm the senior man here. Let that horse live. If you injure that horse—or any of your troop does—you'll find yourself in trouble."

Truscott retorted in a voice low and intense. "Corporal Hogg left a wife behind and a child. He was a career soldier, slotted for sergeant when the next opening came. He was the best man with horses in my company. You're talking about a horse that widowed a woman and orphaned a boy. Sorry, Cummings. I'm running my troop the way I want to."

Truscott undid the flap of his holster and plucked at the revolver nestled there. Jawbone screeched. The horse's intelligence seemed uncanny. Victorious Cummings, agile for a man of three hundred fifty pounds, cracked his walking stick against the lieutenant's outer knee. This time he was on the dime: Truscott gasped, screamed, and toppled to earth, pawing at his knee. The revolver exploded as he fell. Jawbone charged, rearing up over the lieutenant, about to pound him to death. Adroitly Cummings banged the horse on his nose. Jawbone whined—the noise reminded Cummings of a child's sob—and retreated. On the dark and bloody ground Truscott gasped and sobbed. Cummings felt sorry: he hated to use that blow on an officer.

"Mister Skye," Cummings called. "Call off that horse. We've trouble here. He's killed a man."

Skye slowly sat up, peered about him, and stood. He leaned into Jawbone. Then he whispered something into the horse's ear and the horse seemed to melt before Cummings's eyes. The twitching subsided into calm.

"All right, you bloody fools," Skye muttered as he settled into the roots of the box elder.

But no one dared to drag away the body. Cummings decided to do it himself: something in him trusted Skye. He edged into the fated circle. Jawbone did nothing. Ponderously, Cummings tucked his walking stick under his arm and dragged the corporal away by his feet, depositing the dead man beside the groaning lieutenant. Cummings ventured onto the dangerous ground again and retrieved the lieutenant's revolver.

He noticed Alphonse McGinty working around the rim of the circle, whispering to troopers. One by one, the dragoons drifted toward their bivouac. By the time the stocky Irishman had bantered his way around, not a trooper remained.

"What did you tell them, Mister McGinty?"

"That I'd give them a gill of spirits if they left the bloody horse alone and went off to their bedrolls to dream about wives and lovers and lasses."

"Spirits? Mister McGinty, ardent spirits are illegal in Indian Country—and the law is enforced by the Indian Bureau."

"We've a small cask for personal use, sir. Not on the cargo list, of course. Courtesy of your clerks. Now, sir, not a boy in the Bureau wants to see us fail at the Wind River just because our hired savage, Mister Skye, is ruint and his skull-busting horse, too. A gill of spirits, sir, dissolves troubles and lights the night."

"You're invading Truscott's command. You haven't his permission."

"Ah, Superintendent, trust an old boy. One lad, he says he's a friend of Hogg and he's going to see that mankiller dead just as soon as you're not around to finger him. Another one or two declined me generous offer, all in bloomin' rage. They'll be sneakin' through the dark. I think you'd best get our boozy boy on his killer nag and out of sight."

Cummings sighed. "You've a sneaking way about you, Mister McGinty."

"And a lot more than that about me, sir." McGinty beamed in the moonlight.

"Mister McGinty, bring me my chair."

"Gonna keep an eye on the rogues, are you," the chief clerk said. "I'll have it brought."

A moment later a junior clerk, Filbert, appeared,

dragging a folding hickory-and-canvas chair especially
constructed to bear the formidable burden of Cummings's person during the negotiations with the tribes.
The superintendent settled into its ample bosom, withdrew a small-caliber revolver he carried in a cranny of
his suitcoat and waited in the cool night. He'd miss
some sleep, but that was a trifle. He had all the time
in the world.

He watched Truscott limp back to his tent silently,
probably planning revenge of some sort. The whole
camp settled into a taut quiet as if waiting for more
trouble. Some of Hogg's friends came for the body,
gazed hard at Cummings, and carried Hogg away.
Cummings could hear the harsh scrape of a spade
back at the cavalry bivouac. In a few days they'd be
singing a new ballad about a devil horse and a devil
corporal and the Devil owning them both. They'd
have Wellington over at dawn to say some words over
the fresh-turned clay.

Off to the west and north towered the Wind River
range, its snowy peaks ghostly in the moonlight—a
land as savage, mysterious, and barbarous as the people who wandered it. This was a mad, violent, uncertain land, and the only thing one could count on was
that sooner or later it would strike down those who
weren't prepared. Like poor Hogg, God rest his soul.

Those creatures bred to the wild could flourish in
it—like that strange, magnificent horse of Skye's. Like
Skye himself, no matter what his origins. Take that
wild horse east into towns or villages or farms and
he'd be an outlaw. Here he was king, a horse to inspire
fear and song in all who beheld him. Man and horse
were alike: put a wild man, bred to this savage country, in the East and they'd jail or hang him sooner or
later. Poor Skye. The man yearned to slip back to civilization, but he wouldn't last a fortnight there.

"Who'd he kill, mate?" Skye's tone suggested
awareness.

"Corporal Hogg, Mister Skye."

"Why didn't they shoot him?"

"I forbade it—and our Mister McGinty bribed them with the promise of spirits."

Skye sat up and hiccoughed. "It's a bad business. The Yank Army'll come hunting Jawbone and get him sooner or later."

"It'll die away, Mister Skye."

"Not in the minds of some. What'd Hogg do?"

"Came after Jawbone with a knife, swinging a dragoon belt with a mean brass buckle to keep Jawbone's teeth away. He had bets that he could hamstring Jawbone."

"I bloody well warned them."

"They did it on a lark, Mister Skye. When they saw you were, ah, incapacitated, they threw rocks at the horse. Drove it crazy. Jawbone trembled but he didn't attack them."

"I didn't tell him to ... Good horse. Too late, though."

"Not if you slip away."

"You think I should?"

"Immediately."

Skye pondered that. "I'm sick," he muttered.

"Get out! While I'm here to guard you. Meet me at the treaty grounds later."

Skye stood shakily and then collapsed to his hands and knees, surrendering to the heaves that convulsed his frame. He humped and splattered the earth with moon-gilded slime. He wept and heaved up nothing at all, his body wrenching nothing more out of his gut. He groaned and spat and wiped away the treacle. He stood dizzily, settled his top hat, spat, shuffled to the wagons, fumbled around for his gear, and slowly saddled Jawbone.

"You'll be safe at the council. Be there, Mister Skye."

Skye nodded, his eyes leaking. He steered Jawbone across the creek and vanished into the wild.

# Chapter 18

Skye rode a mile or two and dismounted, still a prisoner of booze. He felt sick. He didn't know where he'd ridden; it didn't matter. He rode a fugitive, which made him a fugitive, too. There would have been an execution. He drew Jawbone close to him until the horse's massive jaw rested heavily on his shoulder. His hands found the hot, corded muscle under Jawbone's mane and stroked the animal just as he had always done, especially in bad moments. Jawbone snorted softly and pressed a massive cheek into Skye's ear, knocking the battered top hat cockeyed.

"I made you what you are," Skye said to his horse. "So we're both guilty." Then he took that back. "No. You're a dumb animal. You did what you've been trained to do from the time I dried you off and put you on your mare's teat."

He steadied himself as a new wave of nausea roiled through him. He didn't know why he drank. He knew he wouldn't stop. The need pounced on him sometimes and it ruined weeks and months of his life. His women had suffered it because they had to. He'd have to control it when he went east or get in trouble with the constables. The thought of his two red women deepened his melancholy. Gone forever. He might see them at the peace council but it wouldn't matter. Nothing would change. He needed the company of his own kind of women now. . . .

He felt his sweat dry in the night breeze and knew he could ride again soon. But he decided to walk, hoping the steady pacing would drive the rest of the spirits out of him. He was near the southeastern tip of the Wind River range, but knowing that didn't help him because he didn't know where to go. The sense of being utterly alone sifted through him. He'd often been alone in the wilds but usually he'd had a place to go, an end of a trail. This trail had no end.

He had lived so long in the wilderness that it didn't frighten him the way it frightened most white men, who hurried through it afraid. Skye eyed the open country around him as an Indian would: wherever he roamed, that was home. On a warm night in late June the wilderness wouldn't bite him. The moon-lantern lit the way and the bulk of the Wind Rivers told him where he was going.

At first he felt relief: he was once again a master of himself and his domain, safe from arrogant military officers. That vast and engaging man Victorious Cummings had made the trip bearable and then had saved Jawbone's life. Skye felt a debt and knew he would pay it somehow.

He peered about him into a lovely night. An owl cooed from some distant treetop. For half a year a melancholia had gripped him so badly he scarcely knew why he was alive. But now, at least for this moment, he felt a rush of joy as an epiphany. Here he was a lord of his world, beholden to no one, free of bureaucrats, advice-givers, tax collectors, rulers, and armies.

"Haw!" he bellowed. "Har!" This strange fruit of his vocal chords shot into the night and vanished. "Haw, har. That's how the stick floats." He tried a string of gibberish just to hear the sound of his bellowing. He bawled like a bull moose, whistled like a mule deer, and roared like an angry grizzly. His roaring subdued the wilds of his soul. Jawbone nipped him on the shoulder.

"You don't approve. You're an old maid. Now if you'll just bellow like me, we'll chase away our troubles."

Jawbone didn't bellow; he nickered and lifted Skye's top hat from his head and flapped it. This was getting to be a bad habit among the hundred other bad habits.

"A gentleman doffs his hat to a lady," Skye said. "We've no ladies here and doffing my hat to catamounts and owls won't win us any friends."

He extracted his old topper from Jawbone's grass-stained teeth and screwed it down on his greasy locks.

"The bastard was going to cripple you. Doom you to hobble around, unable to get to fresh pasture and water. It was the same as killing you, mate. Only you got him first. They're calling you an outlaw; funny they don't call that corporal an outlaw. Cummings told me they pelted you with rocks and you just stood there guarding me while I was stinking drunk. Ah, Jawbone . . ."

A flood of raw love poured through Skye, love so wild and sweet and tender that he fought back wetness in his eyes.

"Haw! Har!" he bellowed.

Jawbone butted Skye. Jawbone was not one for vulgar displays of emotion.

"All right, mate, all right," Skye muttered, and mounted the evil horse again. He turned Jawbone toward the confluence of the Wind River, the Little Wind, and the Popo Agie, where the peace council would be. He'd go there and think. Cummings believed it'd blow over and Jawbone would be safe after a few days. Skye doubted it. Truscott or one of those dragoons would bide his time, and then one day Skye would find Jawbone sprawled on the ground in a pool of blood, his throat slit or a bullet hole in him.

To think it was to know what he had to do. But the thought evoked a pain in him. It was one thing to think about setting the great stallion free in the Pryor Mountains to chase mares and breed a hundred little Jawbones. It was another thing altogether to do it. The fantasy he could bear because it would be a good thing for the horse; the reality he couldn't stand. And yet he had to do it, now, before the council.

"You're an outlaw, mate. We'll ride an owlhoot trail and put you in a robber's roost and I don't think the Army'll ever find you. We can't underestimate Truscott. The man has it in for both of us. He might come looking. He might hire some scouts, since he doesn't know bear grass from buffalo grass. He's a strange one. If there's one thing I'll do before leaving the country, it's take you to a safe place."

Jawbone cocked an ear. Skye swore the horse understood everything he said.

It would be a bad moment up there, one that would require all his courage and will. He'd pull off Jawbone's shoes, say good-bye to the old warrior, tell him to stay, and then walk away. He didn't know what he'd do if Jawbone refused to stay. There'd be only one way to deal with it: find a harem of mustang mares and let Jawbone fight it out with the stallion. Nature would take over and Skye could slip away unnoticed. He sighed. It was like marrying off a son. More than a son. Marrying off his best friend.

He'd miss the opening of the council. Five days of steady riding would take him to the Pryors and more than a week of walking would bring him to the treaty grounds a few days late. Walking back would be tough; he'd be carrying his gear on his back, and his Sharps, too.

Cummings would think he'd deserted after all. Truscott would gloat. But it couldn't be helped—unless he could find another horse to take him back.

Gently, Skye ran a hand under Jawbone's mane and let the horse pick his way north.

# Chapter 19

Anthony Truscott lay in his tent that night rubbing his sore right knee. He'd never known such pain and he intended neither to forget nor to forgive.

But there were more important things on his mind than pain. Well before dawn he intended to collect a six-man firing squad and execute that horse before Cummings or Skye had a chance to protest. If Skye objected or fought they'd arrest him, no matter what Cummings said. And if Skye would no longer help the Indian Bureau get the treaty it wanted, too bad for the Indian Bureau. He'd just as soon shoot Skye, too.

There'd be some big trouble for Cummings as well. The fatman had struck a fellow officer in front of enlisted men. He'd file a complaint and it would go into Cummings's Army file and the official records of the treaty expedition. Truscott had a friend or two in Washington City and a lot of West Point friends in the Army, and he intended to employ them all until the fatman was driven out of his appointment.

When the day was only a faint promise on the northeastern horizon Truscott slipped into his boots and stalked through the slumbering bivouac, quietly waking Sergeant Pope and others. Ten minutes later they were dressed, armed, and ready. This was going to be an execution, not a trial, so Truscott instructed them to shoot and keep shooting if the horse bolted away. No mankiller horse would be permitted to live in this outfit.

They fanned out, crept between the Indian Bureau wagons, past sleeping forms in bedrolls—and found nothing. No Jawbone. A quiet survey of the sleeping parties revealed no Skye, either. The guide had fled. Truscott iced his rage and chose to wake Cummings, who slumbered upon a specially constructed cot within his wall tent.

Truscott poked his head inside: "Cummings. Get up."

The superintendent awakened with a start and sat up. "Truscott?"

"Skye's gone. Deserted, just as I said he would."

Cummings yawned, swung massive legs over the side of his cot, and crawled into the gray predawn. He wore an amazing blue-striped nightshirt that resembled the Pyramid of Cheops.

The superintendent peered about serenely. "Of course he's gone. I sent him off."

The rage built in Truscott again. "You sent him off! A mankiller horse and a drunken lout of a guide."

Cummings didn't reply; he ducked into his tent and emerged again with his gold-headed walking stick. He leaned into it, quietly surveying the armed squad standing behind Truscott.

"I thought you'd do something like this," Cummings said. He yawned. "There are some who must murder greatness. That's why I sent Skye away. Start some coffee, Truscott. Call off your dogs."

"Where'd Skye go?"

"Into the night, Mister Truscott, into the night."

"Will he be back?"

Cummings paused. "I asked him to be at the council grounds in time to do his translating. I trust that you'll be more prudent by then."

Truscott gloated. "I'm going to shoot that horse and line up every man, woman, and child of every tribe to watch it happen. Teach 'em about the cavalry. And if Skye resists—he'll face trouble also. I use the word politely. Trouble with me, Cummings, can mean anything I want it to mean. Anything sixty armed dragoons can do to a man."

Cummings absorbed all that. "I am quite at a loss, my young friend: what are Skye's crimes?"

Truscott didn't answer. The case against Skye was so plain it didn't need an answer. The man wasn't a citizen. He ought to be sent in irons to British Possessions for a taste of cold British justice. But it would probably end up as a flogging. His noncoms could give Skye something to remember the rest of his life. Maybe Big Pope could show the man what a top sergeant in the U.S. Army can do with a whip.

Cummings began to chortle, and the merry eruption quaked his gigantic person until it heaved and buckled, and the great tent of his nightshirt danced. "Oh, my, Lieutenant. You go draft your bill of goods, and study the military code, or articles of war, or Caesar's Commentaries, or whatever, and make yourself a dandy airtight case. A nice, gold-plated, iron-clad, fact-studded, footnoted, irrefutable case." He wheezed happily. "A wicked steed. Be sure to note his evil temper, his inferiority, his utterly unprovoked attacks. Now, you just set down at your field desk and write it up. I'll help you with the fine points."

Truscott turned icy: "There'll be a full report filed with my superiors and with Congress and the President. I am officially protesting your conduct and your protection of this blackguard Skye and his criminal horse."

"You do that, Tony boy," said the superintendent. He made his stately way back into his wall tent, leaving Truscott to stare at the flaps.

Around him the camp stirred, awakened by the contretemps. Truscott led his firing squad out of earshot beside the creek.

"I'm putting you on special detail," he said to his picked men. "Big Pope, you draw field rations for these men and saddle up immediately. I want you to head north toward the treaty grounds as fast as possible. If you pick up Skye's trail, fine—catch him if you can. He's drunk and probably poking along without a care in the world. If you find him, shoot the horse and take him prisoner. Don't talk, don't parley, just shoot that horse. If you give chase, shoot the horse until it drops. If Skye draws a weapon on you, shoot Skye. If he's not at the treaty ground, wait for him there. He may show up ahead of the Indians. Same orders apply: shoot that horse on sight. Take him prisoner. If he resists—take any measure at all." He paused. "Any questions?"

Big Pope had one: "What if he shoots back?"

"Do what's necessary. Consider it a police action against a fugitive."

"Sah, you mind giving us papers saying he's a fugitive?"

"Yes, I do. No papers. You heard my orders." The men seemed reluctant. "If you fail, you'll face discipline."

Big Pope persisted. "Seems to me it's against the code to be destroying civilian property like a horse or taking a man that ain't got charges on him."

"Pope. This is Indian Country and that means Army country. We run it."

"Yassir."

"On the double!"

The men trotted toward the picket lines to saddle their mounts and load pack animals. Pope raced to the supply wagons. Truscott watched them, pleasure building in him. When it came to a fight with the Indian Bureau he had the edge—sixty armed dragoons. Pope's men would catch Skye easily enough and it'd be over, far out in a wilderness that hid things from the curious. He could count on them: those six were veterans, each a match for a drunken scout.

Off in the dawn murk he saw McGinty skitter out to the men. He handed a sack to Big Pope as the pair exchanged a few words and laughed. The sergeant tucked the bundle into his bedroll before tying it behind the cantle of his saddle.

Truscott thought he'd better have a look. He stalked in that direction while the men loaded their kits.

"Pope, what did McGinty want?"

Pope looked up, edgy. "Wishin' us well, sir."

"What'd he give you—in your bedroll?"

"Spirits, sir." Big Pope looked flustered.

The lieutenant held his hand out. Reluctantly, Pope undid the bedroll and handed Truscott a corked crock.

"Sergeant, have you heard of something called regulations?"

Pope nodded. The others watched.

"You don't drink on duty. And—Sergeant . . ."

"Sir?"

"You don't take bribes."

"It wasn't like that, sir. McGinty, he just said, 'Compliments of the old Bureau. The boys want you to be happy.' "

"Pope: bring back that horse's ears—and maybe I'll give you the jug."

A moment later the six rode into a grim dawn. Truscott intended to have words with McGinty—and Cummings—about a lot of things.

# Chapter 20

Jawbone nudged Skye hard with his cold muzzle, awakening him instantly. The horse nickered softly so that the sound wouldn't carry. Dawn sun lanced across the ridges but Skye and Jawbone remained in deep shadow in a copse of cottonwoods. Skye understood Jawbone's warning: these would be humans. Skye edged up from his blanket and peered down the creek valley. Not far off, blazoned by the low sun, six blue dots rode quietly north. There were packhorses, too.

Skye sighed. He'd underestimated Truscott's rage. Skye peered about him, studying the ridges, and saw no more soldiers. Chances were the six had not seen him yet because he stood in the purple shadow of the ridge. But they soon would. And he didn't doubt that these were Truscott's best dragoons.

He rolled out of his blanket and anchored it to his cantle, pondering his dilemma. Those fancy horses could outrun Jawbone—on the flat. But Jawbone could endure longer and could climb hills and slopes like a goat.

He tightened the saddle girth, trying to make sense of things. His slant-breech Sharps had a much longer reach than their cavalry carbines—if that's what they had. He could fend them off and they couldn't touch him—until they flanked him and drove in from all sides. He would be dealing with shrewd veterans who knew how to take advantage of their numbers.

But if he killed or injured some dragoons, or if he shot their horses from under them, he'd be a fugitive the rest of his life. He could never go east and settle. He couldn't return to Fort Laramie. He couldn't even escape to British Possessions. His old friend Colonel Hoffman at Laramie would be handed federal warrants and orders. His agent the sutler, Colonel Bullock, would disown him. He'd have to flee to the West and board any ship as a common seaman, where no questions were ever asked. And Jawbone would die . . .

He didn't like his options at all. He mounted, knowing they probably would spot him even in the deep shadow. They did: he saw them pause, consult, and then spread out into a wide line and begin a trot up the creek valley along open grassy bottoms, warming up their horses for a run.

That was the trouble with this country: it was open, and only the ridges concealed a man. Maybe he and Jawbone were about to die. Jawbone for sure; and they'd probably take him prisoner if they could. But Jawbone, Jawbone . . . He reached forward under the big brute's mane and ran a hand down the corded muscle of the horse's neck, an ancient act of love. It would do no good to run straight up the creek along the flat bottoms; the faster dragoon mounts would overtake Jawbone in a few minutes. They had another advantage, too: their mounts would be carrying less weight—maybe even a hundred pounds less. The cavalry recruited small men for just that reason.

He headed straight across the creek valley, down into the bottoms and up the bluffs on the west side, where the sun caught him like a black fly on a white tablecloth. Jawbone subdued the rough slope with great bounds, spraying gravel behind him. Skye could feel the horse's muscles gather for each leap. Down the valley the pursuers swung west. None fired. From the ridgetop Skye could see the sheltering bulk of the Wind River Mountains twenty miles distant, the timbered foothills much closer. Dawn sun dazzled brilliantly off the snowy peaks. But Skye didn't have time to enjoy the breathtaking view. Timber and mountains would be his refuge, slopes and ridges Jawbone's advantage over the flatland cavalry mounts.

Jawbone enjoyed the sport, his big lungs pumping the thin air, his gait surefooted as he rocked down a sickening grade that would slow the dragoons. Skye angled northwest toward a gaping coulee that would give him cover on the upgrade. As he raced across the bottom of this dry valley the dragoons topped the ridge behind him, and this time they fired. He heard the pops and knew he was briefly in range. They were shooting straight downslope. Lead scattered gravel beside him. Jawbone swerved and lead whanged stone where the great horse would have gone.

"Go!" Skye cried.

The giant horse burst ahead even as a round burned past and buried itself in grass beyond. Jawbone shrieked, the ancient war-sound chilling and berserk, the madness upon him once again. Skye glanced back: Jawbone's wild shriek had terrified the dragoon mounts, which were rearing and fighting their bits, spoiling the carbine shots of the riders. Skye let his horse thunder straight up the dry valley and then swung left into the coulee. For the moment at least the dragoons were out of sight. He slowed Jawbone but the horse didn't like it and scrambled up the coulee toward a ridge, where they'd be exposed once again.

Jawbone's flanks were heaving and a thick white foam built along his withers and around his stifles.

At the next ridge he spotted the dragoons again, doggedly pursuing. They didn't fire this time but concentrated on gaining ground. Those flatland horses would tire of this soon enough, Skye thought. But it was far from over. If Jawbone went lame or stumbled . . . it'd all be for nothing.

"All right, all right, mate," he muttered. From that ridge he could see across others to the Little Popo Agie, five miles distant, and beyond the creek the forested foothills of the Wind Rivers. The range ran northwest for endless distances, its snowy peaks orange now, a trick of the rising sun. "We'll go for the woods where a horse can hide," he said. Jawbone rotated his ears and listened. In some uncanny way the great horse understood and would go that way without direction.

"Bloody dragoons," Skye muttered. "Truscott's doing. He'll be waiting at the treaty grounds, waiting to kill. This is just the first skirmish. Don't know what gravels the man."

Jawbone sailed downslope again, the most dangerous and injury-prone part of up-and-down country. His leaps as he sailed downslope jarred Skye's bones. But the giant horse never slowed. Skye hung on, a big gnarled hand shamelessly clamped on the pommel.

Jawbone scambled up the next ridge, over shattered rock that lay underfoot, threatening to lacerate a pastern or twist a muscle. Halfway up Skye heard those terrible pops again and saw the dragoons along the ridge behind, close now because of the steep sides of the valley Jawbone was negotiating. Easy target.

"Dodge, boy!"

Jawbone leapt, and as he sailed sideways a bullet creased his rump, missing Skye by inches. Jawbone screeched and Skye felt the horse limping when he hit the earth again. Now the shots came thick, a deadly rain snarling past, plucking at Skye himself, buzzing like rattlers past Jawbone, hissing and smacking. With one final plunge Jawbone topped the next rise and dropped to safety beyond—straight into a juniper thicket. The horse seemed almost to sob with the pain of the furrow through his croup, but he never slowed. He dodged the junipers, snaking through them recklessly as branches of tough needles stabbed at Skye's legs.

Jawbone's breaths came in great gulps and the horse blackened with sweat. Skye felt the limp and knew it would slow Jawbone even more. "Take it easy, boy. We'll use the juniper," he whispered. The horse responded, skirting the thickest groves of the dark shrub. The far slope looked to be as thickly forested with juniper as the one they descended, offering spotty cover.

"Whoa up," Skye muttered. Jawbone needed breath. Crossly, Jawbone worked his way to the open bottoms and Skye glanced back fearfully. He saw nothing. Then Jawbone plunged into the junipers on the upslope, working toward the next ridge, a low one not far up. Behind, Skye spotted three dragoons topping the ridge on winded mounts. That was all. The rough country had worn out the other horses. Pretty horses, Cummings had called them. Pretty horses that limped along behind somewhere.

Jawbone turned briefly to glare down his ugly, Roman-nosed snout at the pursuers and sprang at the hillside as if he were trying to kill it. He ran a blue-streak dash toward the rounded crest. Skye heard only a few desultory shots from the rear, none of which came close. The dragoons were shooting from winded, heaving horses.

The next downslope would take them clear to the Little Popo Agie, and beyond the river into scattered ponderosas that gave way to lodgepole forest. Intuitively Skye steered north rather than heading directly toward the river and cover, choosing the angle along the downslope well protected by the juniper. He was glad he did: one of the missing dragoons bloomed into sight off to the south, trying to flank Skye. Skye's new vector put the dragoon far out of range. A joy built in Skye. He hurried Jawbone into mixed vegetation, pines and juniper and box elder and willow, and crossed the Little Popo Agie where it ran between three-foot banks, which didn't faze his great horse.

They were still coming and they wouldn't quit, but Skye halted Jawbone and dismounted. He led the horse quietly through dappled shade and into the great pine forest at the roots of the Wind River Mountains. He stopped, ran a hand over the sweat-soaked trembling beast, eyed the furrow—which had stopped bleeding—and weighed his next move. Jawbone butted him and snatched Skye's topper from his matted hair.

"Avast, mate," Skye roared, retrieving the battered hat he'd worn so long it was shaped to his skull. "We've still got to dodge them. Dragoons don't quit."

# Chapter 21

Skye led Jawbone up a steep wooded slope until a thick curtain of trees concealed him from the dragoons down on the Little Popo Agie. He struggled upward until he came to a rocky ridgetop, which he scaled. From there he was afforded a good view of the river valley. Far below were the dragoons, reduced again to blue dots on antlike horses. Four were mounted. A man on foot led a horse whose limp was visible even from Skye's vantage point. The other cavalryman had no horse at all and was loading his gear onto a pack-horse.

Skye watched the dragoons head up the river, no doubt toward the treaty grounds, a place called the Meeting of the Waters. They'd abandoned the chase—at least for the moment. Skye sat on the sunny promontory wondering about ruses. But the six dragoons continued north and disappeared behind a hill. He watched awhile longer but saw no more of Truscott's men.

He clambered off the ridge to Jawbone and quietly ran a hand over Jawbone's pasterns, hocks, and knees, feeling for heat. Jawbone seemed indestructible but he knew it wasn't true. Horses were fragile creatures, and their legs were more fragile than the rest of them. He found no sign of inflammation. That's what made Jawbone unique among horses: he could run full-barrel through country that would pulverize other horses. It was the mustang in him, Skye thought.

Jawbone chewed on Skye's matted hair and sighed.

Skye studied his backtrail through the needle-carpeted forest floor and found nothing a dragoon could follow. He led Jawbone up a valley and into a cupped park, scaring off a cow elk with a calf. He loosened the cinch and let Jawbone graze loose-saddled while he curled up in the warm sun, listening carefully for any changes in the rhythms of nature that would signal danger. All that afternoon he dozed and Jawbone grazed. Skye had no food but the area was carpeted with a mountain carrot whose midsummer bloom resembled Queen Anne's lace. Often Victoria had made a meal of them when they lacked anything else. Late in the day he plucked up scores of the plants and washed their inch-long carrots in cold water from a seep. Jawbone stole a few, leering at Skye all the while.

"You bloody beast," Skye said. "You're ugly as sin and mean. Who do you think you are?"

Jawbone paused, bared his yellow teeth, peered down his ugly muzzle with his devil eyes, and nudged Skye hard, toppling his master.

"Blasted miserable no-good nag."

Jawbone pawed the earth and snorted. A deerfly buzzed around Jawbone's wound and he snapped at it.

"Why've I just come fifty miles to save your rotten neck?"

Jawbone yawned.

"I wouldn't do this for any other horse. You're the worst of the lot. You've got a foul mouth."

Jawbone snorted and squealed.

Dusk was approaching and Skye wanted to get out of the forest before it turned into an inky prison. He cinched up the saddle but led Jawbone on foot down-slope, past whipping branches and deadfall, and reached the river bottoms just as blackness engulfed the wild land.

He turned downriver and let Jawbone pick the way. For now he would follow the dragoons. When he reached open country he'd cross ridges to the Popo Agie, and then begin a wide arc around the future treaty ground.

All that night he rode quietly under the surly glow of a quarter-moon, heading north until he struck the Wind River at about dawn. He holed up in dense bottom brush beside the swift river and dozed through the day, guarded by the horse.

Sometime that afternoon a village passed by on the other side of the river. Probably Shoshone, he thought. Probably friends. Maybe even Mary's people. But he didn't want to be seen. Not just yet. Not until he'd hidden Jawbone in the Pryor Mountains. He didn't want some warrior, enjoying a friendly cup with a dragoon at the treaty council, to spill even a word about Jawbone. So he gave Jawbone the command to stay quiet while he lay behind a thicket of chokecherry hoping the wind wouldn't take their scent to the passing horses. Twice Jawbone lifted his snout and bleated. Horses in the passing village whinnied back. But the episodes didn't spin Shoshone warriors into the river to find him.

Skye eyed his traitorous, unreliable, stupid nag angrily. Never had the brute betrayed him before. Jawbone showed no sign of remorse. He obviously wanted to chase after the village. Skye intuited that it

had been Washakie's own village. He had come within
a few hundred yards of Mary and his boy.

No wonder Jawbone seemed cross.

That evening Skye rode Jawbone across vast
stretches of grass until he reached the Owl Creek
Mountains and then climbed easy grades along a worn
path. East of him the Wind River hurried into a brooding canyon with thousand-foot walls, only to emerge
at the north end with a new name, the Bighorn River.
Skye never knew why: probably some trapper's joke.
Mountain men had penetrated it only with bullboats
because the sheer cliffs prevented land passage. Old
Gabe Bridger swore that water ran uphill through it,
but that was just another of Bridger's tall tales to paper over their fear as the mountain men floated
through that mysterious slot in the Owl Creek range.

Jawbone, who was in fine fettle, trotted along all
night, straight over the mountains and down into the
red-rock-and-cedar country of the Bighorn basin. Skye
turned right with a destination in mind if Jawbone
was up to a few more miles of travel. Off to the east
there rose a magnificent hot spring, a wide fall of
steaming water cascading into pools that grew pro-
gressively cooler. Eventually the water drained into
the Bighorn River just below the dark canyon. It was
a famous trappers' and Indians' resort. He intended to
have himself a hot soak and sweat out the last juices
of his big binge while Jawbone stood guard.

Sullenly Jawbone negotiated the last stretch—he'd
come fifty miles this time, some of it at a hard run.

"Keep on walking, you miserable mutt," Skye said.
"You're more trouble than a wagonload of pork-
eaters."

Skye stopped at a patch of dry bunchgrass to let
Jawbone nibble. There was never much grass around
the hot spring because every passing village paused
there. He blinked. The summer sun blinded him and
he pulled his topper lower over his eyes.

He approached the hot spring cautiously, riding through brush to hide his passage. But he saw no one. He would bathe until his grimy flesh was properly parboiled, and then siesta. After that he had to make tracks to the Pryors and leave Jawbone.

He dismounted and stooped at pool after pool, testing the waters with his fingers until he found one that would cook his flesh like a lobster in a pot and another about body temperature where he could relax and dwell vindictively upon Jawbone's sins.

"Stand guard, you miserable beast," Skye commanded.

The horse sagged sullenly, lacking so much as locoweed to munch. He would have nothing to do but murder flies for an hour.

Skye peered around him and then shucked his clothing: the venerable hat first, and then his boots, which released noisome scents that would pollute a square mile of air. Then his grizzly-claw necklace, elk-hide vest, ready-made flannel shirt, and fringed britches. He stood there, a stocky white torso with sun-blackened appendages, and lowered himself into the hotter pool. It bit his toes and seared his rump but eventually he settled into water that smelled of brimstone shot up from hell.

"Ah . . . Ah!"

Jawbone yawned and muttered.

Skye lacked soap but knew the heat itself would cleanse his greasy hair, so he ducked clear under and let the flow pluck at it until he ran out of breath. This he did until his hair hung in separate strands, silky to the touch. He yanked his shirt from the rock and washed it and then his buckskin britches as well, letting the ruthless heat peel thick layers of grease and dirt out of his clothing. Then he erupted from the hotter pond, spread his duds on the rock for the summer sun's blessing, and eased himself into a cooler one. A rock dam had raised the depth a foot or so. There he leaned back into a mineralized crust and dozed into the afternoon—until Jawbone shrieked.

Skye pivoted up with a start and beheld the advancing column of a village approaching him.

"Why didn't you warn me earlier?" he snarled at Jawbone. The horse usually snorted his warnings long before a mortal could see or hear the approach of an enemy. But once again Jawbone had failed him. Maybe it was a good thing to say *adiós* to the bloody rotten horse if he couldn't rely on him anymore.

He eased his head over the rim of rock and beheld a phalanx of warriors approaching cautiously. They had obviously recognized Jawbone.

"Crow, by gawd," Skye said, starting to stand up. Then he remembered he was not attired to stand up, and sank into the water again. At least the Crow wouldn't scalp him as he sat there.

Behind the approaching headmen came a whole village, men, women, and children. He edged up again until he could see who it was. Many Coups! This was Victoria's Kicked-in-the-Bellies! No wonder Jawbone hadn't sounded any alarms. The horse bleated and a dozen village horses neighed their greetings.

Gingerly Chief Many Coups, head of all the Mountain Crows, dismounted, followed by his headmen, who were followed by men and children, old men and grannies—and many headmen and chiefs from other bands. Skye realized that this was a mixed delegation from all the Crow bands and not the whole tribe. Solemnly they gathered around Skye, wave after wave of them, nearly three hundred in all. Skye withered under their benign gazes.

"It's Mister Skye," said Many Coups.

"Give me my hat."

"We didn't know you were so white in the middle. We thought you were tinted like us."

"Give me my hat."

No one did. They gazed solemnly at Skye and Jawbone.

"Mister Skye, my old friend, you don't look right without your grizzly-claw necklace. Where has your big medicine gone?"

"Give me my hat."

"We're going to the treaty council. Where are you going?"

"There—after an errand," muttered Skye, resigned to his fate. "You mind lending me a horse? I need a good horse. And some pemmican. I'll return it with tobacco later."

"Why, I can give you one of mine, Mister Skye. Would you like a good fat woman, too?"

"No, just a horse."

"I understood you would translate for the Absaroka."

"I'll be there," Skye replied.

"Where are your women?"

"I think with the Shoshones."

"But you don't know?"

"With the Shoshones," he replied desperately. "I'll have a smoke with you—later."

"Ah, Skye. A bath is a good thing even in summer. Especially for you. Everyone knows when you are coming even before they see you if the wind is right."

"Give me my hat."

No one did.

Several women began doffing their dresses.

That did it. He erupted from the water, clamped his hat over his silky hair, and stepped from the pool. They watched solemnly as he restored his wet clothing to his carcass, which he finished doing just about the time the other pools were filling up with tawny bodies.

"Now then, Mister Skye," said Chief Many Coups, "we will go out into the herd and look for a horse, and you will tell me why you need it."

# Chapter 22

Over a long life Mister Skye had learned never to duck hard things; it was easier in the end to face them. But now he faced the hardest thing of all. One sad whinny and it would all come apart.

All that day he and Jawbone had progressed through mustang country. The Bighorn range loomed to the right, blue and forbidding. Ahead lay the dreary table of the Pryor Mountains, a refuge and fortress of wild horses from time immemorial. The bleak Pryors had been cleaved from the Bighorns by an awesome canyon cut through thousands of feet of stone by the Bighorn River. In the arid lonely Pryors the bunch-grasses grew scant and tough, silvered by sagebrush. But the mustangs thrived there, protected by the sheer desolation of the surrounding country.

Jawbone danced along with ears cupped forward, seductions reaching his wide nostrils on the vagrant breezes, his stallion juices building in him. The big buckskin stallion that Skye pulled along behind him

reacted the same way, his brown eyes alert, his muzzle
swinging this way and that to see things that sent
shivers through him.

They pushed up Crooked Creek, a scant yard-wide
flow that rose high on East Pryor Mountain, produc-
ing a narrow band of emerald brush in a harsh world
of red-and-yellow rock and purple sage. It was the liquid artery of the mustang country, water in a land
without any. There were few trees. These were bald
mountains where a horse could run forever on the
winds. Ahead lay giant box canyons where mustangs
sheltered from the blasts of winter, and high naked
country that formed a natural horse redoubt against
the Crows who tried to catch them. No one came to
this barren corner, far from travel routes, except the
Crows; no one ever would.

He rounded a bend and beheld a grazing herd, perhaps a dozen horses. But no sooner had he discovered
mustangs than the herd exploded to life, streaking
smoothly toward the sage-silvered slopes. These were
bright mares, mostly buckskins and chestnuts with unkempt tales that dragged the ground. They were led
by a dominant gray mare while a black stallion nipped
them forward, pausing now and then to survey Skye
and snort his defiance at the intruders. The mares vanished around a slope but the stallion stood on a hog-
back, his tail lifted, his head high, waiting for
whatever would come.

Skye felt Jawbone tremble beneath him. Jawbone
fought the rein, and that was a good sign. He reared
slightly and then stood stock-still. He trumpeted
louder than Skye had ever heard him: a challenge and
invitation that sailed out to the wild bunch. Then he
paced crazily. The stallion blood coursed his veins
now, the mares seducing him, the need to fight and
possess building up while Skye's training diminished.
Skye felt Jawbone's need and knew it was good. Jawbone wanted that harem. He lowered his ugly snout,

curled his lips, and snorted murder and mayhem and sheer male joy.

The time had come. It didn't seem so hard now but Skye knew that later it would slide over him like London fog. He was saying good-bye to his boon companion of many years. Jawbone was more than friend; he was brother at arms, confessor, protector, sentry—and Skye's own creation.

There was nothing to do but get on with it. He dismounted awkwardly, wondering why his legs misbehaved. He undid the cinch and pulled off his saddle and set it on the grass. Jawbone's blue roan hair lay slick and wet where the saddle blanket had rested. The horse trembled and peered back at Skye, studying his master with those narrow-set evil eyes, his mind aflame.

Skye withdrew his belt knife, lifted the left forefoot, and pried the clinched horseshoe nails up, one by one, until he could pull the shoe. Then he slid the knife between the hoof and the worn shoe, loosening it. He twisted the knife, slowly freeing the shoe until the nails vanished from sight around the rim of the hoof and the shoe fell free. Then he pulled the shoe from the right forefoot and tackled the rear hooves. That was harder because Jawbone had always resisted the shoeing and unshoeing of his murderous rear feet. Skye sweated in the boiling sun, patiently working up the clinches and then prying the shoes off. When he was done he collected the precious shoes and nails and slid them into his saddlebag. Jawbone's feet were naked now, free to grow like great fingernails. They would be abraded by rock and sand into some kind of balance between growth and wear.

Removing the shoes had exhausted Skye. He felt parched. His shirt was soaked. He returned his knife to its sheath, wondering why his hand trembled. He fumbled at the hackamore that encased Jawbone's snout, and freed it. The ugly roan horse, scarred and knotted, mean and magnificent, stood free, disconnected from Skye's world and will.

Slowly Skye pitched the blanket and saddle over the back of the buckskin. He knotted the hackamore in place, and shifted his bedroll and kit.

Far off on the ridge the black stallion watched motionless, tail lifted, ready to bolt. His harem was probably miles distant.

Skye needed to issue commands, and couldn't. The words were glued to his parched throat.

"Go!" he croaked. "Go get him! Go chase him! Go claim your mares! Don't come back. You're free. Here's water and grass and mares. Make little colts. Forget me. Don't ever think of me again, you damned bloody beast. Forget my voice. Forget my commands. Forget everything I taught you." The words tumbled out in a rush.

"You can whip him. He's a big one, and he's got a big harem. He's waiting to see what happens. Go get him! Just chase him away. Chase him a hundred miles. Then go get your mares and enjoy them. Pick a favorite and love her. Nibble on her ears." His voice cracked in two and he quit talking.

Jawbone stood trembling—torn. He peered at Skye and peered at the distant black stallion. He squealed and snorted. He bellowed a trumpet call to war, and then turned morosely toward Skye, his ugly snout held low, desperation in his yellow eyes.

"Go!" Skye cried. "Go, or the Devil take ye!"

Jawbone stepped tentatively away, turned and returned, a horse cleaved in two.

"Go, ye damned bloody beast!"

Skye did what he had to: he slipped off his belt and lashed Jawbone's croup.

Jawbone shrieked and for an instant Skye thought the horse would murder him. But then Jawbone trotted away a few steps, paused, studied Skye, trotted a few steps farther, and finally began his fateful journey.

The wild stallion on the distant rise shrieked but didn't move. Jawbone bugled and broke into a canter. The black stallion whirled around and vanished behind the rise, Jawbone hot behind.

Skye stared into the emptiness, finding it hard to breathe. A great stillness lay over the land. The hot sun pierced his clothing. A vagrant breeze with the scent of sage upon it eddied around him. The buckskin settled into watchfulness. Jawbone shrank into a dot roiling up distant dust. He reached the top of the rise where the stallion had been but never slowed, racing recklessly down the far side—and out of sight. Skye wished he had paused one last moment at that ridge, stood there like the king of all horses for one blinding moment before he slid from sight. But it hadn't happened.

Skye was alone.

Wearily he clambered up on the big buckskin, feeling him sidle and settle under the unusual weight. The day lay still and hot and sad. Skye turned the horse south and put him into a trot, needing to get away from there as fast as he could.

All that empty aching day he rode south, refusing to think about anything.

Jawbone was safe from the soldiers. That gladdened Skye in a day filled with desolation.

Now he'd translate for Cummings, take them all back to Fort Laramie, and begin a new life—somewhere.

# Chapter 23

When the Shoshone people reached the treaty ground they found only six soldiers, white men with bushy hair on their faces. Chief Washakie's village was the first of the bands to arrive because the great council would be held in the heart of Shoshone country.

"We will welcome them to our land. I will find out where the grandfathers want us to raise our lodges," Chief Washakie said to Mary. "And you will translate. And you"—he nodded to Victoria—"will help also. It is hard to make thoughts in one tongue clear in another tongue. A treaty is an important thing that will be upon our people forever, so we must know everything."

He led his three hundred villagers in a great phalanx toward the blue-shirted soldiers who had camped beside the Little Wind, half a mile southwest of its confluence with the Wind River. Washakie raised his hands in a gesture universally understood. He would welcome these white men to the lands of his people.

A soldier reached for a carbine but a three-stripes chief rebuked him and the soldier set it down. That was good, Mary thought. This would be a time of peace and hope. She and Victoria walked in a place of great honor just behind the headmen of the village for the important office of translating.

Washakie was obviously in a fine mood, beaming at the distant soldiers. He had grievances aplenty against the white men but not against the soldiers. Mary, who knew white men better, dreaded the blue-shirts.

At last the great crowd stood only yards away from the six soldiers. Chief Washakie beckoned to Mary, who stepped forward.

"Welcome to the land of the Snake people," he said, and Mary translated. "This is a good place for long talks. The rivers meet here. There is grass for many days, good water, firewood, and peace." He waved at the vast plain, rimmed on three sides by distant mountains. "The horses will not starve. We welcome the white soldiers. Who do I talk to?"

"Sergeant Pope. We're ahead of the rest a few days," said the three-stripes chief.

Mary translated that. She didn't like the way the soldiers stared at her. She knew she was pleasing to the eyes of males but these blue-shirts stared too long at her, their gaze on her calico blouse and doeskin skirt.

"Where do the grandfathers wish us to camp?" Chief Washakie asked genially.

"Suit yourself," Pope replied. "This here is for the soldiers and the Injun Bureau. We'll pasture our horses here, too."

Chief Wasakie nodded. "Tell him the Shoshones will camp along the Wind River west of the Meeting of the Waters."

She conveyed that.

"How come ye to know English?" the three-stripes asked her.

"I—am the wife of—"

Victoria elbowed her.

"You got a man in the village?"

"No."

Washakie looked puzzled; Mary briefly translated.

"We're lookin' for a big white man with a mean blue horse. Name's Skye. You seen him anywheres?"

Mary's heartbeat lifted. "No."

Chief Washakie intervened. "There is no better friend of our people than Mister Skye. He has helped us many times. He is known to everyone and has great power. Is he coming? We heard that he will be here to help us understand."

Mary translated fearfully—and added a question of her own: "Why are you looking for him?"

The three-stripes chief spat, raising dust. "He's supposed to be here."

"He didn't come with the soldiers and grandfathers?" she asked, and translated to Chief Washakie.

"If he comes in, you just tell me—Sergeant Pope—real quick, and I'll see that you get a little gift for it."

"He went away? Why is this?"

"That horse, we were fixing—" Pope halted. "Who'd you say you was squawed up with?" He stared sharply at her. "Skye, he's got a Crow squaw and a Shoshone one, real pretty. You her?"

She didn't reply but translated to Chief Washakie, suddenly afraid.

"Mister Skye was married to our clan-sister," Washakie said. "Is he not coming here?"

"Cummings—he's the big shot—says he'll come. So does the looie, Truscott. After things quiet down a little." He chuckled. "After he sobers up."

Mary translated that.

"Dammit, he ain't your man no more. Let the sonofabitch go," Victoria muttered. "We got nothing to do with him now."

Mary considered that nervously, and addressed the three-stripes. "I was his woman—but he does not want me now." It hurt her to say it to the white soldiers.

The soldiers grinned.

"You're Skye's squaw, eh? That's real interesting. The big man don't want you, eh? Missy squaw, you just tell us if he comes around. We got a score to settle with him."

"What does it mean, a score to settle?"

"Get even. His bronc killed a good man. Skye was drunk as a skunk. We'll get it."

The news froze her. "What will you do?"

"Shoot it."

"Sonofabitch!" Victoria snapped.

Chief Washakie looked puzzled. Reluctantly Mary translated.

The chief smiled blandly. "Tell the soldiers we will look," he said. "We will see about this horse."

Mary translated. Pope nodded. "There'll be a little firewater for you, Chief, if you find Skye or that hoss."

Chief Washakie nodded gravely, ignoring the offense. Mary saw the iron in his face. "We will make our camp and wait for the others."

Pope agreed to that. "Hey, little squaw, you pop over and have yourself a visit. We got lots of ribbons and a few plugs of tobaccy to make your little heart happy."

She didn't reply. Quietly she translated all of it to Chief Washakie, who eyed the soldiers soberly. Without a word he led the villagers northwest toward the riverbank they'd occupy.

*Shoot Jawbone.* Mary's mind whirled. She wondered how it had happened. Jawbone could be terrible. She'd never approached the horse without a pang.

"I gotta find the damned horse," Victoria muttered in English. "Or tell that sonofabitch Skye. They can kill Skye if they want, but not Jawbone."

Victoria's angry attacks on Mister Skye never failed to dismay Mary.

"He must have taken Jawbone away," she said.

"I know where," Victoria muttered, but she would say no more.

"Where?"

"I ain't saying. They'll get you drunk and find out. And then go kill him."

Mary cringed. A raw hurt lay between the former wives of Mister Skye.

The village reached the riverbank cottonwoods and began to raise lodges. They had the best place because they'd arrived first. The other tribes would camp in less shade.

Mary helped her mother set the tripod and drop in the lodgepoles. Then they hoisted the heavy cowhide cover and fastened it together with willow pegs. Victoria stood aside, muttering to herself in angry bursts. Mary unloaded parfleches from travois and toted her parents' things into the cool shade of the lodge. She was about to carry Victoria's baggage inside but the old woman snarled her away. It shocked Mary. In all her years with the old Crow woman she'd never suffered a harsh word. Mary slumped silently, hoping the older woman would put on a new face. Instead, she burrowed through the parfleches, extracting handfuls of jerky, some pemmican, a powder horn and some cast-lead bullets.

Wordlessly Victoria packed these things onto one of the Skye packhorses. Then she climbed up on her mare. "I'm gonna go away. You translate. You tell your Snake people what the white men want. I'm going to find the Absaroka and help them."

Mary was dumfounded. "You're leaving us?"

"Damn right."

"But Victoria—don't leave me. You're my sister and we've a boy to raise—"

"I don't want nothing to do with any son of the sonofabitch Skye."

Victoria turned her mare.

"Come back!" Mary cried.

But Victoria didn't. The old Crow woman resolutely steered her mare into the Wind River, tugging the packhorse behind. Water lapped her mare's belly as it foundered in the swift current but then it bounded up the north bank and shook itself while the Crow woman hung on. After her horses had shaken off the water she pointed them north.

Mary watched until Victoria was out of sight, feeling a stone in her bosom. Mister Skye's lodge had sundered every way it could.

# Chapter 24

Lieutenant Truscott discovered Big Pope camped south of the Wind River on the Little Wind, and the Shoshones camped a mile northwest in a choice cottonwood forest. Sergeant Pope's locale was as good as any, with excellent grass and ample firewood. The sergeant had seen to that detail: a heap of dry wood lay ready for use.

Behind Truscott, the dragoons rode in, followed by the Indian Bureau caravan.

"Sergeant, show the men where to bivouac and tell the Bureau people to set up camp south of us along the river. Then we have some private business."

Truscott watched the sergeant barking orders and the dragoons hastening to obey. Some way off, Victorious Cummings was stepping down from his groaning carriage and peering at the distant mountains that compassed the vast flats. It had been a boiling day but the waning sun had lost its ferocity. The evening would be pleasant. Truscott noticed a stir in the Shoshone village and supposed that soon he'd be visited by some chief or other.

"All right, Pope. Tell me what happened. Did you do it?"

The sergeant looked uncomfortable. "We found his trail, sir, and almost caught him."

"Almost? Almost, Pope?"

"He gave us the slip, sir."

"You failed? You found him and still failed?"

"He went into rough country, sir. We lost one horse—broken leg, shot it—and lamed another."

"Pope. I can't believe it. I picked the six best dragoons in the troop. You picked the six best saddle horses and the best packhorses. You were armed with the best carbines we have. You have the advantage of decades in the Army. And he gave you the slip. And you wrecked two horses."

"The lame one'll be fine in a few days, sir. The horses—they weren't familiar with rough ground."

Truscott remembered Cummings's scorn of the troops' mounts, and raged. "You're telling me an outlaw horse, a mustang with bad blood and worse conformation, outran you."

"Sir, he knew the country—"

"No excuses, Sergeant. You're a disgrace. I ought to tear your stripes off. And flog every incompetent you had with you."

The sergeant stood mute.

"Write up your report, Sergeant. I'm going to have to submit it to headquarters. You failed."

Pope stared at the grass.

"Pope. Did Skye shoot at you?"

"No, sir. He just slipped out."

"He has a big Sharps. Wouldn't you say you heard it, and the long-range shooting kept you from getting close enough to use your carbines?"

"Well, sir, we didn't hear it."

"Wouldn't you say that Skye resisted military arrest?"

The sergeant seemed puzzled. "Whatever you say, sir."

"Didn't Skye's shooting kill a cavalry mount?"

Sergeant Pope stood silent.

"Write it up, Sergeant, exactly as it happened: Skye kept you at bay with his big rifle; he killed a mount; he resisted your order to surrender. He's an outlaw with a killer horse."

Big Pope smiled faintly. "That's exactly the way it went, sir."

"Have your men sign the report."

"None of them can read, sir."

"I want their names on that report and an X from each of them, agreeing to what happened."

Pope nodded.

Truscott raged. The border ruffian had escaped—for the moment. But before it was over he'd have Skye in irons and the horse would be cold meat.

"I did find out something, sir. That village over there—both of Skye's wives are in it. I sent my men to look but they couldn't find any white men. Skye's not there."

"His wives? They'll know where he is. I want them watched."

"They said they're no longer his women now."

"Watch them anyway. Pope, you can't redeem yourself—you're stupid beyond description—but you can make things easier for yourself if you have men wander through that village several times a day. And every evening."

"Yes, sir."

"One more thing: send out three two-man details all day every day. They're going to watch for Skye. Keep men out there, and have them report immediately if Skye comes in. Now go write that report and bring it to me."

"Yes, sah."

Anthony Truscott was in an ugly mood and the sight of that fat ball of black cloth, Victorious Cummings, coming at him with that miserable clerk McGinty at his side made him all the madder.

Superintendent Cummings halted, leaned into his gold-knobbed walking stick, and surveyed Truscott as if he were an ant. "You've been talking to Sergeant Pope, Lieutenant. Did your assassination crew succeed?"

"What are you talking about?"

"Sergeant Pope's Jawbone execution detail."

"No."

A faint joy built in the face of the fatman. "Ah. Did they encounter Skye at all?"

"Yes."

"And failed. Ah, yes. Skye and his ugly mustang got away. That's what I meant about pretty mounts, Lieutenant."

Stung, Truscott retorted hotly: "He's not here, Cummings. He deserted just as I told you he would."

Cummings sighed. "Deserting is one thing; escaping is quite something else, Lieutenant. I will supply you with Noah Webster's authority. And I remind you, I told him to go. Even so, he's bound to return. One thing about Skye—he's a man of honor. He'll be here."

"A man of honor. Is that what you call him? I'll have him put under guard the moment he arrives—if he arrives. You can forget using him as a translator. He's a fugitive from the United States Army."

"A fugitive, is he? Now what did he do?"

"Shot a cavalry mount and resisted arrest."

"Tut tut, Lieutenant. He didn't shoot a cavalry mount; he didn't have to."

"Are you calling Pope a liar?"

"Ah, Lieutenant. I was an officer for many, many years. None of the little schemes of my honorable colleagues, or upright noncoms, or sterling enlisted men, are unfamiliar to me."

What was it about Cummings? Truscott wilted before the man and hated himself for it.

McGinty seemed uncommonly attentive. Truscott wondered what went through the skull of that wiry reprobate. Nothing savory.

"Pope'll have a report signed by all his men."

"Very good, Lieutenant. Now would you review for me, again, just what Mister Skye has done to you?"

"You know as well as I do what kind of man he is."

"Ah, evasion. Yes, I know what kind of man Skye is. And you do, too." The fatman smiled in a way almost beatific. "A man who hates another without cause is a man who hates something in himself."

Truscott swallowed back rage. "Cummings. If Skye comes in, he's mine. There's nothing you can do about it. I have sixty armed dragoons."

There followed a pregnant pause and then Cummings laughed politely, his vast circumference ballooning and heaving. "Have it your way; but just what're you going to tell them back at Fort Leavenworth if these costly and important negotiations fall apart because Skye wasn't there?"

"I have nothing more to say to you."

"Say, Looie, is there anything I can do to help?" asked McGinty. "I got me clerks to help out and lots of goodies for the Injuns." The clerk beamed with guileless goodwill.

"I want word of Skye. Some redskin'll know."

"I'll expedite it."

Cummings turned on his chief clerk. "I'll have a word with you later, Mister McGinty."

But McGinty winked at the lieutenant when the fatman turned away.

Truscott wondered why he loathed Cummings as much as he did Skye. Maybe with some artful maneuvering he could restore the Indian Bureau to the Army where it belonged. His superiors would relish that. It'd even be worth a brevet promotion.

# Chapter 25

Victoria found her Absaroka people a long day's journey north of the treaty grounds. She spotted them from a high ridge in the Owl Creek Mountains and the sight of them filled her with eagerness. Soon she would see Many Coups. Soon she would be talking in her own tongue instead of Skye's impossible English, or Mary's strange Shoshone.

She knew at once where they would camp that night: the verdant bottoms of Red Canyon Creek. She heeled her little mare down the ridge toward the place far below, but even before she arrived the Lumpwood Society warriors policing this band found her. She hailed them in her tongue, joyous with the sound of Absaroka words spilling from her lips.

"Many Quill Woman!" they cried. She relished the sound of her Absaroka name. The three heeled their ponies closer for news.

"What band is this?" she asked a fine, bronzed young man with heavy cheekbones and a proud stare.

"Most are Kicked-in-the-Bellies. Many Coups is coming, along with most of the chiefs and headmen of the people. And many lodges. The rest of your people are on the Yellowstone near Arrow Creek. I am Pretty Bird of the Otter Clan."

"Ah! My clan, too."

"Many Quill Woman! You give us honor as the woman of Mister Skye. Only yesterday we found him at the hot springs and he got a horse from Many Coups."

"He's not my man anymore," she replied shortly.

The three young warriors absorbed that quietly, reluctant to ask any further questions.

"Was he on his medicine horse?"

"Yes. He rode the great horse. What a horse it is!"

"Where was he going?"

"North, away from the treaty grounds. Many of the People talked about it."

The news confirmed what she'd suspected. She knew where he was going and what would become of Jawbone. A tension within her relaxed. The horse would be safe in the mountains close to her people.

Soon the great Absaroka delegation rode into the cottonwooded bottom. Her people were gaily dressed in bright calicoes, and she loved the sight of them. It stirred a pride beyond words to see the young men sit their ponies. Many were wearing their festival clothing. Tomorrow when they arrived at the treaty grounds, every Absaroka, man, woman, and child, would be dressed for the occasion in great bonnets, buffalo-horn headdresses, eagle feathers, bold-colored shirts, gaudy German-silver jewelry, quilled and beaded leggins and vests. They would shine, and their glory would be noted by every other tribe.

She waited patiently for her people to make camp. No one erected a lodge, though she saw several on the travois. It would not rain this night. But there were meals to begin, robes to be untied, beds to be readied and horses to be grazed and picketed. Later she would greet many of them, and they would gossip until the stars failed.

Many Coups sought her out after he had examined the camp. He had always been a cautious and careful leader, examining the defensive possibilities of a site before he settled down. He found her near the creek, where her mare was chomping lush grasses.

"Many Quill Woman," he said. He beckoned her to walk with him along the creek, apart from the rest.

"Ah, my chief, my spirit lifts to see you again."

"And we welcome you to the band. I am glad to find you. We have many things to talk about."

"I am a simple woman. I have no good counsel for a chief."

He turned to her. "You know the white men. I don't—except for Skye."

"He's not my man anymore," she said crossly.

He nodded. "That is what I am told."

"The sonofabitch—" She realized she was cussing in English, which she was wont to do. Nothing pleasured her more than white men's cussing. "His spirit died away all winter," she continued in her own tongue, "and I knew he had to go to his white people. He didn't deny it."

"He is our friend. His medicine helped the People."

"He still is our friend."

"But soon he'll be gone."

She sighed. "What did he tell you?"

"He told me—away from the ears of others—that Jawbone killed a blue-shirt. Now the blue-shirts want to kill the horse. They chased him for many days. He told me where he will hide the medicine horse and asked me not to tell anyone. I do not even tell you. It will never be named."

"Ah! I know. Once Mister Skye told me where he would take Jawbone when Jawbone was old or lame.

He wants Jawbone to make many strong colts and be happy before his spirit leaves him."

"Then we both know. We will guard our secret. Some of our men will find out when they go to trap horses but the Absaroka people will protect the medicine horse for as long as he lives."

Victoria breathed in the chief's words like sweet mountain air. All her people would protect that great horse, sing many songs about it, and bless the First Maker for this friend of the Absaroka. There would be no need for her to continue her journey north to warn Skye.

"I will be with the Kicked-in-the-Bellies the rest of my days and I will guard the medicine horse," she said softly. "I will go to see him there." She was afraid to name the place, lest the spirits carry the word to waiting ears. "I will make him comfortable when he is old. I will take cottonwood bark to him when the Cold Maker roars and the snow is deep. I will steer away the soldiers and the enemies. I will spend the rest of my life watching over him. We will never be far from him. He is worthy of our nation."

They walked quietly through a velvet evening.

"Many Quill Woman, we are pleased you will be with us. You can help us. I know little about white men and what they want. You are wise in their ways and can help me to understand. They are powerful and I fear them even though we have been friends with white men ever since the trappers came."

"Damned sonsofbitches," she muttered. Cussing was the only good thing she'd ever gotten from white men. She wished there were forbidden words in her own language, words that she wouldn't say in front of a medicine man; words she could use when she was angry. Why didn't the Absaroka have any good anger-words? Then, in her tongue, she addressed Many Coups again: "I will go back with you to the council. The white grandfathers wanted the wives of Skye to translate. But we left. Now I can tell you what they want and I am not beholden to them or to Mister Skye. All this is good."

"Ah, Many Quill Woman. You are the medicine we need. The Above Spirits are looking after us! You will tell the white grandfathers what we want."

She sighed. "I can tell them but it won't change anything. They are coming to take our freedom from us and put the Absaroka nation into a little place." She waved an arm from horizon to horizon. "They say they own all this land from the big waters in the west to the big waters in the east, even the blessed earth under the feet of the people. If we don't give them what they want they'll say we are hostile, and make war on us."

"But the Absaroka have always been friends of white men."

"It doesn't matter," she muttered. "What they want, they'll take, and the past doesn't matter."

The chief walked in silence through the thickening dusk. "I am glad I am old," he muttered.

"We can slow them down," she said. That was the only hope she'd give him. "But we can't stop them."

"Show me how to slow them down, then," he said. "Show me how to resist without destroying my people—and we will resist. Many Quill Woman, it's up to you. Tell me what to say to the grandfathers from the east and I will say it."

"Will you?" She peered at him sharply. "They will give many gifts—after the chiefs make their mark on the paper. They will stack the good things in a heap for all to see—rifles, axes, pots, blankets . . ."

The chief nodded, emboldening her. "When the young men want eagle feathers for their bonnets and their hair," she said softly, "they dig a pit and cover it with limbs and grasses—except for a small hole. They lay the bait, a dead rabbit or dog, across the cover and wait quietly, concealed inside the hole. When the eagle comes to eat, they reach up from the pit and grab its legs and kill it, and take the eagle feathers. That is how it is with white men's good things. We are the wild eagles and the gifts are the bait."

"Yes, Many Quill Woman, that is how it is."

# Chapter 26

The young buckskin Skye rode lacked manners and at first Skye had his hands full. The horse shied and sidled at anything, and didn't much respond to the hackamore. But after a day on the trail the horse settled into an easy walk. He would do, Skye thought.

No matter how he tried, Skye couldn't put Jawbone out of mind. The great horse had probably picked a fight with that stallion and claimed the mares. Or maybe not. Maybe the great horse would go through a period of confusion, like a boy leaving home to enter the adult world.

And win the mares. Skye smiled. Jawbone's instincts would triumph soon enough. But he'd find that mares could kick and fight and act mean; that each band would have a lead mare who'd decide where they all would go, when to stop, when to run, what was dangerous and what wasn't. A great stallion Jawbone might be, but the dominant mare would make the decisions.

It didn't comfort Skye to think about it. This had been a hellish half year and leaving Jawbone had torn something inside Skye so badly he thought it could never heal. In the East he might find a white woman who'd help him forget his two red women but he'd never see another horse like Jawbone.

For two days he rode up the Bighorn River. He discovered signs of passage everywhere: large villages moving south, no doubt Crows heading for the peace council. But they were all ahead of him by a few days, so he rode alone with a strange horse for company.

He made camp well before dark the second day because he needed to hunt. He picketed the buckskin and stalked the river brush looking for meat. He saw a pair of antelope on the distant bluffs across the river, and let them go. A rabbit bolted off too fast for him to swing his rifle around. Something skittered into the river and vanished. He spotted some ducks bobbing in a place where the water eddied beside a current. If he shot one it'd likely be swept downstream.

He passed a swampy area full of arrowhead, whose roots developed an edible tuber in the fall. But it was too soon to get a meal from them. There was always the starchy cattail root and if all else failed he'd eat the miserable stuff. He eyed the chokecherries but it was much too soon to pluck the fruit.

At dusk he pulled an armload of cattails from a slough. He didn't mind. Nature would provide. That was an understanding that separated him from the greenhorns who came west. He could always survive on one thing or another. It struck him that all the years he'd been with the fur brigades he'd scarcely known a thing about nature's bounty. His red wives had taught him and nourished him.

In camp, as shadows lengthened, he cut the rootstock, mashed it and masticated it slowly, making a foul meal.

He heard the rattle of galloping horses long before

he saw any. A war party! He snatched his gear and dove into a willow thicket but it was too late to do anything about his buckskin; the horse lifted his head and whinnied, tugging at his picket line.

The horses were thundering straight toward him, wheeling around copses of trees and brush, following the islands of grass in the bottoms. He saw the first horses closing in, veering suddenly when they spotted his own mount. They carried no riders. They neighed and screeched but never slowed. They looked wild, their manes thick with burrs, their tails matted and long, their flanks scarred.

Then he heard an unmistakable screech. Jawbone! Off to the right against the bluffs, driving these horses—driving his harem. Jawbone snarled, and a moment later the blue roan bulled into Skye's hiding place, his wet sides heaving, his eyes wild and mean. He honked and trumpeted, lifting his head, curling his lips, and bugling orders to his mares. They slowed and finally stopped, but at a long, safe distance from Skye.

Jawbone! Sheepishly Skye clambered out of his willow nest and stared at the horse. Jawbone reared, pawed air, and settled gently to earth, mad with delight.

Jawbone and his harem! The stallion stood there looking mighty pleased with himself. Skye counted eleven mares standing upstream a quarter of a mile, a gray mare off to one side and waiting for Jawbone's command.

"You old devil! Haw!"

Jawbone nickered. He edged closer and stole Skye's top hat and waved it up and down. Usually Jawbone let Skye retrieve it, but this time the horse danced ahead of Skye, never surrendering the hat, edging toward the nervous wild mares. Jawbone led him along the river a hundred yards but then the lead mare had enough: she bolted for the bluffs with her sisters swarming behind her, and vanished into the blue. Jawbone dropped Skye's hat and sprang after them. He took the bluff in giant bounds and disappeared while Skye watched, too flabbergasted to think.

A while later, just at dusk, Jawbone herded the mares down the bluffs and settled them on the lush bottom grasses a few hundred yards from Skye, bellowing threats and snorting love songs to the frightened ladies. This time Skye noticed that three of the eleven were yearlings and there were four foals he'd missed before.

Jawbone's family. Which the stallion intended to share with Skye forevermore.

"Haw!"

Jawbone snorted.

"Who's the greatest horse of all?"

Jawbone screeched.

"Who's the terror of the universe? The lord of all horses?"

Jawbone lifted his snout toward the stars and bugled.

"Who's the king stud?"

Jawbone growled.

"Who's the catamount and grizzly and lion of horses?"

Jawbone plucked grass.

Skye laughed until tears welled in his eyes.

"We're a pair," he said. "We're a pair."

He walked back to his camp and found the buckskin gone. The young stallion had yanked his picket pin loose and fled. Skye hunted through the brush in the thickening dark but found nothing. Jawbone had terrorized him. Maybe the horse would show up at dawn.

The thought sobered him. Tomorrow he would continue his journey to the treaty council where sixty men in blue shirts waited to murder Jawbone. He had no

way to turn Jawbone back. Jawbone wanted no part of
the Pryor Mountains if Skye wasn't there with him.

Skye sat down beside his bedroll, his mind aching
for solutions. He wondered if Jawbone could be hidden amid the great herds of the tribes at the council—
and knew he couldn't. Wherever Jawbone went, so did
a large circle of space. No horse dared to come within
ten yards of him. He'd be an island in the midst of the
herds, easily spotted by cavalrymen—who would instantly kill him. If Skye proceeded to the Wind River
he'd take Jawbone to his doom.

As the night deepened, Skye wrestled with it: he
could ditch the council altogether—against his word
and in violation of his honor. But he would not do
that. He had received a large sum, to translate and to
make the treaty understood. Even if he gave the
money back he would have failed to keep his word.

In anguish he paced through the night, Jawbone
snorted softly beside him, never letting Skye stray far,
as if to say to Skye that this separation would never
happen again and they were a pair for as long as
blood flowed in their veins.

Skye knew that if Truscott succeeded there would be
two deaths: Jawbone's and his own. There were some
things too great for a man to bear: tragedies that murdered the human spirit and then the flesh.

He could think of only one thing to do: he had to
find Victoria. Find his angry and estranged woman.
He didn't know whether she would be at the council
or with her people on the Yellowstone or with Mary's
people. But he had to find her. She was the only other
person on earth Jawbone would mind. She could keep
Jawbone and his mares far away in some safe sweet
place. But where was she? And would she do it?

# Chapter 27

Shortly after the Crows arrived at the council ground the Bannocks came in. Then the Northern Arapaho rode in from the plains to the south and settled along the Wind River. A small delegation of Northern Cheyenne also came to observe, though the Indian Bureau planned to treat with them and the Sioux at a later date. Here at least, all these enemies met in peace. The delegations were composed of impromptu villages containing the principal chiefs and headmen, their families, and various interested warriors and their families. For several days they had been busily visiting each other and hosting feasts. It was all good.

Victorious Bonaparte Cummings estimated that more than three thousand Indians were camping there and several thousand horses were devouring the grasses of the great plain. The council would have to meet quickly or the horses would drift away.

The superintendent and his minions were ready; but they lacked the key man, the translator Mister Skye.

Restlessly Cummings inquired of the chiefs and head-men whether they'd seen Skye. Only the Crows reported seeing him, and that had been long ago. Finally Cummings could wait no longer: the Indian delegations had only so much food; firewood and grass were vanishing at an astounding rate; and the Arapaho were threatening to pull out.

Maybe he'd misjudged his man after all. Maybe Skye had deserted—just as Truscott had said he would. The thought saddened him. In all his life he'd encountered no other man like Skye, a natural-born duke of the wilds, living by a rough code of honor formed in part by his English roots but tempered by the laws of survival.

The treaty hung in the balance. Without Skye they still might negotiate one but it would be more difficult. By a good stroke of fortune Skye's former women were present. That would take care of most of the translation; no doubt within the tribes there were others who could help convey the essentials to the Arapaho and Cheyenne. Still . . . the absence of Skye could collapse the whole affair.

Grimly, Cummings steered his portly self toward Chief Clerk McGinty, who seemed to be the fountain of information for the Indian Bureau.

"No Mister Skye, eh?"

"I'm afraid not, sir. It's the soldiers keeping him away. Me clerks, they see the soldiers patrolling two by two all over the flats. Never an hour goes by but a mess of blue-shirts aren't wandering through those pony herds of the savages. The looie, he's got men posted on yonder hillock with spyglasses, just lookin' for the guide. He's got 'em poking around the villages hunting for the man. He's got that sergeant out there with gewgaws—knives, powder, plug tobacco, vermilion—trying to butter up the chiefs and get the goods on Skye. He's running a reg'lar espionage, me boy."

"All that, eh? I'll put a stop to it. For the sake of

shooting a horse Truscott's sabotaging the entire treaty negotiation. He'll stop it or he'll discover he's in trouble."

"Mister Skye's that important, is he?"

"Everything depends on him, Mister McGinty."

"I thought so. I put me boys out to look for him but I haven't a scrap of news. Say, if the treaty fails, do we have to haul all those annuity goods back agin?"

"I'm afraid so."

"We can't have that!" McGinty seemed agitated. "Me and me boys, we'll put our minds to it."

"There's not much you can do, Mister McGinty."

"Ah, me friend, there's never a trick where we can't get a lick. Me and me friends, we'll have a little talk with the soldier boys."

"No, no, I'm afraid they might do something regrettable." He peered sharply at McGinty. "Like bribing dragoons. You wouldn't do anything like that, would you, Mister McGinty? Of course not. The Indian Bureau wouldn't corrupt the dragoons, would it?"

"The word's new to me, Superintendent. Whatever does 'corrupt' mean?" McGinty smiled beatifically.

"You're a man of many accomplishments, Mister McGinty, doing things whose names you don't know. Leave the soldiers alone. It's the Indians we must speak to. They'll know where to find our missing man."

"Which ones, sir?"

"The Crows, I'll wager. Tell the sergeant to have my carriage harnessed, if you will . . . No, I'll do it. It's time to have it out with Truscott anyway. I must deal with him now—before the whole business perishes."

"Perishes?"

"Skye's that important. Haven't you figured that out? Because of you, we nearly lost him back at Fort Laramie. You might ponder that before entering the confessional next time, Mister McGinty."

The chief clerk cackled cheerfully. "That's why

there's the sacrament of reconciliation, me boy. Your faithful, humble, industrious clerk'll produce Mister Skye."

"I'd rather you didn't."

Superintendent Cummings made his way toward the bivouac, which had been all but deserted for several days because Truscott had sent out his snoops to look for a horse to shoot. Cummings waved his walking stick and sighed. July sun heated his black broadcloth suit but he didn't mind. That somber suit, draped over his vast person, created a certain authority which he found useful.

Victorious Cummings found exactly six dragoons on hand to protect the Indian Bureau and its wagons filled with valuables. Truscott had retreated to his tent for a siesta. Cummings rapped sharply on the tent pole with his walking stick until Truscott poked his head out.

"There you are, having a snooze, Lieutenant. There are six men here, three thousand Indians, and wagons filled with valuables. Where are your men?"

Truscott yawned. "Patrolling."

"Looking for a horse you wish to shoot. Mister Truscott, has it occurred to you that this silly business is sabotaging the entire treaty council? A business that has cost the government tens of thousands of dollars as well as half a year of work by my entire bureau? Not to mention thousands of dollars of Army expense? Will you have it on record that your, ah, obsession with murdering a horse will cost the government upwards of forty thousand dollars and ruin its Indian diplomacy for years to come?"

Truscott yawned again, deliberately. "Go start your council. Nothing's stopping you."

Cummings rapped sharply on the tent pole again. His walking stick had always been an attention-getter and he knew how to employ it. This time it sounded like a fusillade. "The absence of Mister Skye is stopping me."

Truscott started to say something—obviously disparaging Skye—but caught himself.

"On reflection, Mister Truscott, you might consider calling in your dragoons. And instructing your men to leave the horse and Mister Skye alone. You might also consider asking them to welcome Skye and see to his comforts because he is essential to the United States Government now."

"Thank you for your counsel, Superintendent."

"You might also post your men closer at hand."

"You tell them."

Truscott's quills were up; that was plain. Cummings realized that Truscott wouldn't give an inch and this would only resolve itself back in Washington City months from now. "Very well, I will. Bring them in, Mister Truscott, and I'll address them."

"Catch them if you can, Superintendent." Truscott's pout had given way to a smirk.

Cummings measured his words. "I have choices to make. I can proceed and probably fail or go back to Washington without treating with the Indians. In either case, United States Indian diplomacy will suffer a disaster and set back peace on the Plains for a decade. I will let you know this evening. Be prepared to escort us back to Fort Laramie tomorrow. We will each explain the matter to our superiors—in my case to the President and the Secretary of the Interior—and we'll be prepared to take the consequences."

That, at last, wiped the pout off Truscott's face.

"Mister Truscott, I'd like my carriage and a driver as soon as possible."

A half hour later Superintendent Cummings stepped down from the groaning carriage and walked slowly to the great, painted lodge of Chief Many Coups of the Crows. They'd seen the carriage coming across the sagebrush flats and the chief stood waiting for his guest. Beside him stood a graying hawk of a woman. Cummings guessed that she was probably the former Mrs. Skye, and that proved to be the case.

"The chief, he says he's glad you're here. White men and the Absaroka, they're old friends."

"Tell the good and honored head chief of the Crows that I am delighted to be here and I have brought him a small token of my esteem."

He handed the traditional tobacco twist to Many Coups, who accepted it amiably.

"The chief says to sit down and have a smoke."

"Ah, tell him I shall stand."

"The chief says, very well, he'll stand, too. He says your body does you great honor and he wishes his wives were as honorable as you."

"Ah, tell him I appreciate his kindness." Cummings leaned into his black walking stick, wanting to get past ceremony and down to business. "If it is not impolite, tell him we might dispense with the smoke medicine because we are already friends. I came merely to inquire whether he has talked with our translator, Mister Skye."

"He says a few days ago."

"Was Mister Skye planning to come here to translate?"

"The chief says yes."

"That's all I need to know. Thank you, madam. And thank your chief for me also."

Many Coups nodded.

Victorious Cummings made his slow way back to his carriage, thinking about Barnaby Skye. Mister Skye wasn't deserting; he was trying to hide Jawbone from those lethal dragoons. Cummings decided to wait another day or two.

# Chapter 28

The pain that seared Victoria's chest felt so terrible she wondered whether her heart would stop. It clawed down her arms, up her neck, and ate into her belly. But she knew it wasn't her heart. It rose out of her anguish and her fear, and it possessed her body the way the under-earth spirits possess mad people. She could not sit or stand, and could scarcely breathe.

For days, the cocky blue-shirts had patrolled through the villages, not only her people's, but all the others, probing and poking, peering into lodges. Even more of them strolled through the vast herds, examining every horse of gray hue, studying the animals one by one, frightening the herd boys. And still others pushed out beyond the council grounds, manning ridges where they peered at all below them with field glasses.

The blue-shirts were looking for Jawbone. They were going to kill Jawbone. They would not give Skye the slightest chance, but would kill the horse on sight.

They'd shoot him from under Skye if that was required. They hated that horse as if he were the white man's Devil; as if their world could not be made right until Jawbone lay dead. She saw it in their eyes, the deadly alertness, the stares that missed nothing. No lodge or brush arbor escaped their relentless study; no Indian man who looked remotely white remained unobserved. If they saw Jawbone, they would unsheathe their big dragoon revolvers and empty the cylinders, reload and empty them again, and then slit Jawbone's throat to make sure.

Which is why she ached with a pain she could not endure. Many Coups had privately told her what had happened: Jawbone had killed a blue-shirt and the mankilling horse must die.

From Many Coups she had learned something else: the fat Indian Bureau grandfather who had told Skye to flee had also told him it all would blow over in a few days. Then Jawbone would be safe. Maybe Mister Skye would believe it and return with Jawbone instead of hiding him in the Pryor Mountains.

She had to act before the bands of iron clutching her chest squeezed her to death. Night had settled. Some of her people were rolling themselves in buffalo robes. She could not sleep, not with the pain eating her heart out. She slid away from the Crow village, scarcely knowing what to do, a small wraith of a woman padding silently across the open flat. A moon cast cold light, making her route easy. She headed toward the camp of the blue-shirts, straight toward a large wall tent she knew was the lieutenant's. He often sat there evenings, letting the supper fire die, playing with his long golden hair or combing his beard or making the magic signs on paper.

The soldier camp was always well guarded at night. Two pairs of armed sentries patrolled its perimeter, back and forth, from the Little Wind around and back. Nothing could get through unobserved. She located the lieutenant's tent, the smaller one near it that belonged to the sergeant, and another that belonged to the lieutenant's bugler and aide-de-camp. She sat on the hot ground and waited, watching the sentries patrol. She knew she looked like a stump or sagebrush to them. She watched, and found a time in their rhythm when both pairs of guards were walking with their backs turned. She padded through with no trouble at all and froze in the shadow of the officer's tent.

He had abandoned his camp chair and gone inside. Good. She would go inside, too. She listened to the quiet camp and studied the way the men rested, most of them in bedrolls on open ground. Many had not yet fallen asleep. Some were talking quietly. Good. Ah, she would talk to the sonofabitch!

She slid around to the front. He was sitting on a cot and unlacing his boots, his back partly turned. Softer than an owl's glide, she settled to the earth just within the door and waited, her hands primly in her lap. His feet didn't smell the way Skye's did. Everything about him was washed and trimmed.

He discovered her a moment later, his gaze frozen with incredulity.

She lifted a finger to her lips. "Shhh!" she said.

But he didn't. "Guard! Pope!" he snarled. "Sergeant!"

She wondered at that. Skye would have landed all over a silent intruder. She heard a stirring outside. "If you kill Skye's horse, you die," she said calmly. He stared. "You kill Jawbone, you die. So does anyone that hurts him."

Sergeant Pope boomed in and instantly clamped her in massive paws, as if she were a doll. She didn't mind. Already the pain had gone away from her heart.

The lieutenant bounded up and pushed past her and Pope into the moonlit night. "How'd she get here? How'd she get past our perimeter? Listen now, Pope, get their names. I want their names. They're going to do hard time the rest of this trip. They're going to be busted. They're going to learn that guarding a bivouac's important business!"

"I know who's on, sah."

"And where the hell were you, Pope? This little squaw just wandered into my tent. What do I have dragoons for?"

"No one saw her, sah."

"You're damned right! A moonlit night. A quiet camp. No distractions. But she waltzed right in. If it ever happens again I'm pulling your stripes right off your arm. I'll bust every man in this troop."

She felt Pope wince. He pushed her out into the moonlight.

"Maybe you're gonna die, eh?" she said, so softly her words slid under his shouting. Around the camp men sat up, peered at the shouting officer. Some way off, where the Indian Bureau people made their camp, she saw men standing up.

"How'd you get in?" he demanded of her.

She shrugged.

"Are you Skye's squaw?"

She shrugged.

"Answer me—or you'll wish you did."

"I was," she said. "No more now. He got tired of red women."

The officer seemed wild in the eye. Frightened and trying not to show it. Good. Good.

"What did you come here for?"

"I already told you."

"You don't scare me and you don't scare any soldier in this camp. This is the Army, squaw."

She shrugged.

"We're going to kill that outlaw horse. I'm not going back east and report a dead corporal, killed by a rank horse, and I didn't do a damned thing about it. The cavalry knows how to deal with rank horses."

"You gonna die."

The moonlight caught a frenzy in his eyes and she thought for a moment he'd batter her. Instead, he reached into his tent and withdrew his cavalry saber, and slid it out, the scrape of metal shivery in the silence. It looked silvery and deadly in the white light. Armed, he became a different man. The shock of terror slid away from him and contempt filled his smoldering eyes. He swung the saber ever closer, its blade whirring by, feathering past her doeskin dress, slicing it. She stood calmly, intuiting that the man would not hurt her.

He paused suddenly and thrust the blade at her belly. She felt its point sharp against her dress but it did not penetrate. His face lit with wry pleasure. "This is what we do to squaws that sneak into camp. We kill first and ask questions later. You got that? Any redskin comes into camp after this—we shoot first."

"You hurt Jawbone, you gonna die," she said calmly.

A wildness kindled in him but she knew he wouldn't thrust that sword—and ruin the treaty council and himself.

"Your blue-shirts—they don't stop no little squaw coming to kill you. You hurt Jawbone and lots of things happen. Maybe a silent arrow comes in the night, eh? Right through the tent. Lots of arrows until you look like a porcupine. Maybe a knife through the air. Maybe a bullet. Maybe anything. Maybe a little old squaw woman with a hatchet. How many blue-shirts you got, eh? The chiefs say sixty. It ain't enough. A hundred ain't enough. Two hundred ain't enough. Hell's bells, your blue-shirts can't do nothing to stop me. You don't touch Jawbone—and no one touches you."

He slapped her. She felt the smack of his hand, felt her head jerk sideways. It stung. Her teeth had cut her inner cheek and she spat out blood.

"Pretty brave warrior, slap old squaws around."

He peered wildly around him, saw soldiers and Indian Bureau clerks staring; saw Victorious Cummings in a huge white nightshirt watching intently. Something within him shrank. "Get her out of here," he snarled. "Report to me in the morning."

Sergeant Pope manhandled her toward the edge of camp and dragged her until she was a long way away. Then he let her loose.

"It don't matter none if we kill redskins," he said. "Jist as soon cut your guts out as leave you here alive. Same goes for Skye. Don't matter none if we cut his gizzard out and feed him to the buzzards. He ain't but some outlaw."

"Him you do what you feel like," she replied, tasting blood in her mouth. "But you touch that horse and I come after you. I come all the way back to Leavenworth after you. I go east after you. I track you summer and winter, spring and fall, rain, snow, heat, dry, wet—and you die for killing the medicine horse."

Big Pope laughed but she heard the wariness in it.

"After the treaty crap's over, watch out," he said.

# Chapter 29

Yesterday Mister Skye had laughed, and felt the convulsions of his belly loosen the stranglehold of his melancholia. This morning he felt crabby after a sleepless night. Jawbone had kept him awake. The medicine horse had oscillated between his usual sentinel duty over Skye's recumbent form and his mares on the bluffs, which were ready to bolt. Just when Skye drifted off, Jawbone's shriek split the quiet, and off the stallion went to round up his unruly harem. Not even Jawbone could induce them to come down off the bluffs a half mile from Skye.

He stared at the weary stallion in the lemon light of dawn and saw an exhausted horse. Jawbone propped himself up on locked legs and tried to recover his wind before the mares decided to ditch him again. Dried sweat rimed his flanks and buttocks, and his head hung low.

Skye eyed the great horse wryly, knowing that the animal's instincts tore at everything Jawbone had

learned from the day of his birth. Jawbone yawned,
clacked his teeth, and eyed Skye patiently, forgiving
his reprobate master. Skye clambered to his feet, feeling the ache in his bones. A night without sleep always made him old.

Far off on the west bluff stood the wild mares, their
sides gleaming in the mellow light. He could not see
the buckskin anywhere and knew that Jawbone had
driven him off. All he had to ride now was
Jawbone—if Jawbone would let him, with a harem to
look after.

"Well, what're you going to do?" he asked the
horse.

Jawbone chewed vacantly. There were moments
when he looked like the dumbest horse in creation, his
narrow-set eyes heavy-lidded, his expression stupid.
Jawbone yawned, baring stained teeth, and snorted
softly at Skye.

Skye's movement stirred up the wary mares. The
lead mare whinnied and raced out of sight back of the
bluffs. The rest followed. Once again Jawbone thundered after them, showing his teeth and threatening
murder. Skye watched, wondering if he'd see Jawbone
again. If the horse stuck with his harem this time,
Skye's own agony would resolve itself. Jawbone assaulted the grassy bluffs with a series of incredible
bounds and vanished over the western skyline.

"Families put the harness on a man, Jawbone," Skye
said. "Now you've got burdens and a lot of trouble,
you bloody rascal."

It'd be a long walk to the council grounds. Skye
eyed a tree where he could cache his saddle up on a
high limb and wondered what else to leave. He felt
hungry and he wanted meat—good, juicy, red meat
and lots of it.

Skye felt a weariness in his bones that sprang from
anguish as well as his sleepless night. If Jawbone returned, Skye would have to choose between love and

honor. For honor's sake he could saddle Jawbone and ride to the treaty ground—and see an innocent animal slaughtered. Or for love's sake he could ride Jawbone away from danger and call himself a deserter after all. Even as he considered these bitter choices he knew what he would do: if it came to all that, he'd ride Jawbone to safety and sacrifice his word and his honor. He could live without honor—somehow. He'd be a lonely fugitive ghosting through the farthest corners of this wild continent. But he couldn't live with the act of riding Jawbone to his doom.

He extracted a battered tin cup—his sole utensil— from his saddlebags, and mauled some precious coffee beans in the bottom of it. A while later he sipped hot coffee, which restored him to his senses.

The coffee changed his view, as coffee often did. Long ago he'd discovered that coffee is magic: it fosters optimism. A better outlook began to build in him, and along with it the realization that he'd been despairing without knowing the facts. He didn't really know what the dragoons would do. Perhaps he could ride right in and begin his translating with no trouble at all. He doubted it, but he had to admit, as he sipped the hot brew, that he didn't have anything to go on. Maybe Truscott and the dragoons had forgotten the whole tragedy.

A while later Jawbone appeared on the skyline, an apparition lit orange by the low sun. Jawbone stood undecided, his gaze off somewhere to the north, then turned toward Skye and nickered, the sound soft and tender in the hush. Jawbone stood stock-still, torn in two, a ghostly presence far above; then the horse bounded gently down the slope, flowing like quicksilver, drawing from some infinite reserve of courage and energy, and didn't stop until he stood before Skye. He whickered softly, honked, and snorted. Skye lifted his top hat in salute.

"You bloody nitwit, you like your bloomin' master

better than your beeyootiful girls," Skye muttered. "Shame on you, you dumb idjit."

The horse lowered his head and pressed his brow into Skye's chest. A lump filled Skye's throat and he couldn't speak.

A half hour later Skye was ready to leave. He lifted Jawbone's hooves one by one and decided the horse could travel barefoot without trouble. Then they headed up the Bighorn River, passing through a lonely land that put dark thoughts into Skye's mind. They reached the hot spring that night and Skye tugged the weary horse into a larger pool. Jawbone eyed the hot water distrustfully, and then, slowly, relaxed.

Skye didn't sleep that night either. Dark and ominous dreams terrorized him until he crawled out of his buffalo robe and slid into a hot pond in the blackness, seeking the peace that eluded him. By dusk the next day he could reach the treaty ground. But he intended to approach cautiously and feel his way along, ready for trouble. He wanted Jawbone rested and ready to run if running was what they had to do.

He awakened ravenous, but there would be no breakfast: Indian women had stripped anything edible for miles around the famous hot pools. He'd have to wait until he could find something along the way.

At least Jawbone seemed refreshed. The horse had wandered far in the night to rustle some food; Skye had sensed long absences. Skye steered Jawbone up the Owl Creek Mountain trail and paused at its crest, where he could see the treaty grounds off in the distance. They shimmered pleasantly far ahead, as if nothing there could possibly cause harm.

Jawbone stirred up a tan prairie rattler as they headed downslope, and Skye was tempted to kill and eat it. He'd eaten rattlesnake meat once or twice, but in rougher times than this. He chose not to: there'd be good chow at the end of this day's ride. But he would have to fight off the torture of his hunger the rest of the burning day.

He felt Jawbone slow, and decided to rest the horse. He slid off and led Jawbone for a half hour, making his own legs work. When they reached the bottom of the Owl Creeks, Skye mounted Jawbone again and rode across flat plains toward the distant meeting of the waters, passing through a hot and golden summer afternoon. He wanted to sleep so badly he was tempted to step down and snooze. Jawbone wanted to stop every few yards and occasionally paused to nip grass. Skye let him, and chewed on some bunchgrass himself to raise some saliva.

From a slight rise he studied the whole distant encampment. The tribes had come in. Perhaps the peace conference was already under way. Great masses of horses grazed in bunches, herded by boys too distant to see. He felt a quickening of fear and resolved to overcome his weariness. The next miles would require an alertness he no longer possessed. He slid a hand under Jawbone's mane, an ancient signal and bond between this man and this horse.

"There's maybe some dragoons have an eye to kill you," he muttered. Jawbone's battered ears cupped back to listen. "Maybe it's Truscott's orders, maybe just some friends of the dead corporal. Maybe there's nothing; it's all blown over like Cummings thought. But you shape up and keep your eye peeled, you bloody blue beast."

Jawbone's gait lifted into a springy walk. The ugly roan had taken a notion to show off, and he arched his neck and cocked his tail. A bounce lifted Skye gently from his seat.

The old cocksure devil!

Skye forged ahead warily, ready to wheel Jawbone and run. But he saw nothing menacing. Only the Crow village. Off to the left, two huge herds of horses; ahead on the right, a low hump, rising scarcely ten feet above the plain. He studied it closely, his gaze working along its outlines. Nothing. Even so, out of ancient habit, he left the worn trail and steered far left of the innocuous hillock.

He rode past, only to see dragoons spreading out behind him, blocking his retreat. Ahead, more of them poured from a Crow medicine lodge set apart from the village, occupied only by a sacred medicine bundle suspended from the lodgepoles. Smartly, these troopers closed the circle. Then, revolvers in hand, twelve blue-shirted soldiers closed in.

"Get off that horse, Skye, or we'll shoot it out from under you," yelled one.

Ambushed by professionals. Jawbone would die after all.

# Chapter 30

A heaviness filled Skye. Jawbone would die.

A dozen dragoons closed the circle, edging into point-blank revolver range, where they could murder the horse but not hit Skye. They were eager and full of bravado, grinning in triumph, death in their eyes, fingers itchy on the triggers of their drawn Colt revolvers. Seconds remained.

Almost casually, Skye slid his slant-breech Sharps from its saddle sheath, cocked and aimed it at the corporal who was running this execution.

"You first," Skye said.

The corporal's face whitened. The others paused, realizing that the death of the horse would result in the death of a soldier.

"I'll shoot to kill. You'll get me—but not before you die."

"They's some that'd shoot you in the back, Skye."

"I'll still get you."

The threat wasn't working. Skye could see the dragoons edging closer, taking aim at Jawbone's chest. Time stopped. His pulse stopped. The knowledge of his own doom stole through him.

Then a dragoon screamed. He dropped his revolver. An arrow poked clear through the flesh of his upper arm, its hoop-iron point red with blood. Skye's own gaze at the corporal never wavered. He knew Victoria had shot that arrow and that she already had another nocked. She had a way of coming out of nowhere, an invisible wraith.

Some of the dragoons swung their revolvers toward her.

"Who wants to die?" Skye asked. "I'm ready. She's ready."

The wounded soldier writhed on the ground, sobbing, clutching his sleeve, which had bloomed red and was dripping blood.

"He needs help," Skye said.

Jawbone shrieked, a shivering, eerie howl that sounded like something from the caverns of hell, the chilling taunt of a killer horse that would fight to its last breath. Dragoons tumbled back a step.

Then something changed. Soldiers peered toward the Crow encampment and muttered. Skye risked a glance and saw an array of Crow headmen and chiefs, armed with bows or rifles, running to help out. Swiftly the Crows surrounded the cavalrymen. Twenty at first, then thirty, and finally a hundred.

Chief Many Coups walked boldly into the inner circle but stayed well away from the wild-eyed horse. He addressed the dragoons harshly in his own tongue. Skye translated.

"This medicine horse is sacred to my people. You kill it and all of you will die. That is all I have to say."

The prospect of imminent death persuaded the dragoons. They studied the bristling arrows and rifle muzzles, and gave up. Each of them slowly slid his service revolver into its holster.

"Take care of the injured man," Many Coups said. Several of the dragoons gathered around the fallen man and applied a belt tourniquet and began stanching the blood. The man sobbed.

"The Absaroka People do not want a peace treaty now," Many Coups said. "Tell that to the grandfathers."

Skye translated, wondering what would happen. Frantic activity in the Crow encampment gave him his answer. Women were dismantling lodges. Young men were snatching horses from the herd and saddling them. The Crows were leaving. But the warriors stood immobile, guarding Skye and Jawbone, their arrows and guns relentlessly following every move of every dragoon.

In fifteen minutes, even before the rest of the great council knew what was happening, the Crows were pulling out. Women and boys brought saddled horses for the warriors and headmen. Lodges lay upon travois. Many Coups motioned to Skye, who rode out of the deadly circle while the dragoons watched helplessly. Then warriors began collecting the dragoon revolvers until the blue-shirts were disarmed. They kept every revolver and all the cartridges they could find.

Skye found himself riding along with the Crows, heading toward the Owl Creek Mountains once again through the fading evening. Armed Crow chiefs and headmen guarded their rear, ready to fight a troop of dragoons if they had to. Within an hour dusk settled over the Crow procession and by the time it reached the mountains, night obscured the trail. He scarcely knew who was beside him. He hung on to the pommel, thirsty and weary, knowing only that somehow Jawbone lived and he was among old friends, Victoria's people. Little by little his terror slackened until he slumped in his saddle, feeling wave upon wave of grief and joy. Somewhere in the procession rode Victoria. She'd saved Jawbone's life with her quick and deadly arrow. But now the Army would want her, and her life would never be the same. They'd catch her and she'd vanish from the earth. And no white man would ever care.

Jawbone settled down, too. At first the horse had walked on stilts, neck arched, the murder in him terrorizing Crow ponies. Jawbone's own rage burned hot into the evening. But then, as night thickened, the stallion relaxed. Gratefully, Skye ran his hand under Jawbone's mane, feeling the sweetness of life pulsing in the horse's neck. Skye lifted his eyes to the stars, to the Great Mystery, and thanked God for this unexpected salvation. Once again something miraculous had watched over Skye and the horse.

They stopped at a spring-fed mountain meadow and the whole village waited while Skye and Jawbone drank. They were paying Jawbone honor. Skye was glad the darkness concealed his face and eyes from them. The women didn't erect the lodges. Everything remained loaded, ready for a quick getaway. Even the ponies remained saddled while they plucked bunchgrass. There would be plenty of night-herders this time.

"Mister Skye, our hearts are glad because the blue-shirts did not kill the medicine horse," said Many Coups. "Many times, you and the great horse have fought beside us, and given us victories."

"You saved him," Skye said.

"Many Quill Woman did. The blue-shirt was about to shoot."

"Is she here?"

The chief ignored the question. "Will they come after us?"

"Not if the grandfathers can stop it. This was supposed to be a peace council."

"But the blue-shirts might come?"

Skye sighed. "Keep a good guard. We're not safe. And Jawbone's not safe yet. They might sneak in."

"I don't like blue-shirts. I don't want a treaty. What will happen now?"

"They'll call you back."

"I will talk to the elders about it. Maybe we won't go. Will you help us?"

"Any way I can. Maybe you should go back there. You'd get a home for your people."

"The elders will talk about it."

"I owe you two lives."

"You are a friend of the People. Get a good rest and we will talk in the morning. We will stand guard."

Skye nodded, and untied his bedroll from behind the cantle. He stumbled gratefully into the friendly earth, not noticing how hard it was. Jawbone loomed over him, doing his usual sentry duty.

He could not sleep. The terror of the day haunted him.

Jawbone nickered softly, and Skye saw, in the starlight, a slender woman sliding her hands over him, scratching under his jaw. The woman muttered things softly, a terrible tenderness in her voice, her Crow words a love song and lullaby. Jawbone sighed.

Then she loomed over Skye. "You no-good, cussed, dirty, bad-smelling, drunken, stupid, rotten, disgusting, crazy white-man sonofabitch," she said.

She spread a blanket a dozen feet from Skye, and settled into it, her back to him.

Barnaby Skye stared at her small back and didn't know what to do.

# Chapter 31

Lieutenant Truscott listened impatiently to his corporal, Sandy McIver, who was describing the confrontation with Skye.

"McIver, I've got an injured man and a dead one. I've never seen such a bungled job. Skye was bluffing. All you had to do was shoot the damned horse."

"Beg pardon, but he warn't bluffing, sir. And that squaw, she saved me life with that arrow. If Luke'd fired his revolver—I'd not be here to report to you."

"Where'd she come from?"

"No one saw her. She just upped and laid an arrow in."

"McIver, this is flat plains."

"Beg pardon, sir, no one seen her."

"A great bunch of soldiers I've got in F Troop. A squaw walks up and no one sees her. I don't suppose it was Skye's wife, was it?"

"Wouldn't know, sir. No one seen her before."

"You're a veteran of, what? Half a dozen Indian fights?"

"Yessir."

"And I suppose you all just stood around when the Crow warriors came on. You had time enough to shoot a dozen horses and set up a defense against the savages."

"He never taken that Sharps off me, sir. And she never stopped pointing that bow."

"You told me several of your men had revolvers on her."

"That didn't slow her none."

"What about Luke?"

"He's still bleeding bad. Hit an artery. Can't get that arrow out, he screams so bad and bleeds like a stuck shoat."

"Cut off the point, hold him down and pull. If he's still bleeding, cauterize the holes."

"We're fixing to, sir. The sergeant's got men on it."

Truscott was peeved. "Fine bunch of dragoons I've got. Did anyone see all this? Anyone else know why the Crows were fleeing?"

"After a bit some other savages come by and stared."

"Stared, *sir.*"

"Yessir. Sir."

"But no white men? No Indian Bureau people?"

"None o' them, sir. Some dragoons run in afterward, sir."

"All right. This is our own business. You go tell every man in this command that this is no one's business but ours. Not a word to the Indian Bureau, and that's an order. Now, on the double."

"Yessir!"

Truscott watched McIver trot off and wondered why all his plans ran into rotten luck, as if he were ill-starred. Or ran into the Skyes. The Crows were gone and maybe the conference would collapse without them. That might not be so bad; the brass would enjoy anything that proved the corruption and incompetence of the Indian Bureau. Obviously, there would be two versions of this event told back east: the Bureau's version and the Army's. Maybe, if he worked things right ...

He didn't have time to work it out. Rolling toward him was the vast black globe of Victorious Cummings, along with Chief Clerk McGinty and the Reverend Wellington Waterloo Cummings. Obviously a plenary delegation. The thought suddenly amused him.

The superintendent halted before Truscott's tent and leaned into his walking stick. "Lieutenant, you've a man with an arrow in his arm, and the Crows have vanished. What happened?"

"I'm trying to ascertain the facts, sir."

"What facts do you know?"

"There seems to have been an altercation."

Cummings looked annoyed. "Enough of one to send the Crows fleeing. What happened?"

"I'll report to you after I finish the investigation."

"Did it have anything to do with Skye?"

"I'll report later."

"Did Skye return?"

Truscott smiled. "It's an Army matter and the Army will take care of it."

"Did this involve that horse?"

Truscott shrugged, and yawned deliberately.

"You're evading me, Lieutenant. We've lost the Crows and maybe the treaty. I don't know why, though I have my suspicions. Is the horse alive?"

Truscott felt elated. The Indian Bureau had no idea just what had happened at the Crow camp.

"I'm going to have to tell the other tribes what happened. What shall I tell them, Mister Truscott?"

"Maybe the Crows didn't want a treaty."

Victorious Cummings stared long and hard but Truscott refused to wilt under the glare. He'd learned that at West Point: never wilt, never retreat, never admit error, never leave a chink in his armor. Audacity would smooth over anything, anything at all. He'd learned a lot of things at West Point and even more since then. The Army would not only protect its own against civilians but would promote anyone who boldly fostered Army interests, especially in a rivalry with some other part of the government. He counted on some promotions. The ladies who scorned captains loved colonels. The ladies who scorned colonels loved generals. He'd have an adoring lover soon if he played it right. He wanted her to mirror his glory, need him, give to him, be so beautiful that all of American manhood from the generals on down would envy him and secretly wish they had what he had. Somehow, he would turn all this into a promotion, maybe a brevet to major.

"I'm expecting a full report, Lieutenant."

The white flag. Truscott smiled warmly. "You'll have one when I complete the questioning, Superintendent. I may have to rebuke a man or two if he riled up the Crows."

Cummings continued to direct his penetrating gaze into Truscott, but Truscott had experienced worse. "Mister Truscott, the truth of these things can't be hidden long. The other chiefs will soon know. They will tell us. They'll hear it from the Crows. If Skye was involved we'll hear it from him."

"Not very reliable sources, sir. Redskins are congenital liars and that outlaw Skye—well . . ." He shrugged. "You'll soon have the official, witnessed, Army report, and it'll be unimpeachable."

"I will await it breathlessly. Meanwhile, Lieutenant, have my driver bring my carriage around. I must visit each tribe immediately or we'll lose them . . . Perhaps that's what you want."

"I'm here to serve you, sir. Of course the Army would prefer to handle Indian affairs—it's usually a matter of war, after all, dealing with hostiles—but my duty's to serve you and obey the will of Congress."

"Adroitly put, Lieutenant. Now, my carriage, please."

Truscott nodded at Sergeant Pope, who trotted off.

In the distance, chiefs and headmen were gathering and debating, and Truscott realized that an envoy from the tribes would arrive even before Cummings got his carriage. All the better, he thought. He could keep track of things.

Chief Washakie and his Shoshones arrived first but other chiefs were converging from all directions. With Washakie was a lush and striking young woman who caught Truscott's eye. Her jet hair had been parted and hung in two braids; her figure was tall and lithe, her facial features sharply chiseled, her black eyes large and intelligent. She wore a red calico blouse, a fringed doeskin skirt, and quilled summer moccasins. The very sight of her built tumults in Truscott. He felt like iron filings drawn to a magnet. His eyes raked her, absorbing every curve, and he knew he must have her!

She turned out to be the translator, talking an accented English in a soft, low, careful voice. Impatiently he listened while Washakie droned on and she turned his words into English for Cummings. There had been many Shoshones in the Crow village being feasted by their old friends. They had seen Skye ride in; the ambush; the defense by Skye's woman Victoria—the very same hag who'd slid into Truscott's tent!—and the rush of Crow warriors. In short, exactly the story McIver and the men had told him.

Even as Washakie spoke his headmen translated to the other chiefs—Truscott spotted Bannocks, Cheyenne, and Arapaho in the expanding crowd—with sign language. One Shoshone translated directly to his ancient enemies, the Arapaho. Truscott learned that the Crows were also feasting others, some of them traditional enemies. Members of every tribe had witnessed the arrival and ambush of Skye. What's more, there had been Crows visiting the other tribes and at the first sign of trouble they'd raced to their people and gotten the story. Some of them had shared it with other tribesmen.

Superintendent Cummings listened intently along with the chief clerk and the reverend, absorbing all this as fast as the young Shoshone woman could translate it. But Truscott stood bewitched, scarcely considering what he heard, his desire for the red woman thundering through his mind like a tornado.

"My chief wants to know what will happen now. Will the blue-shirts punish the Crows? Is this council over now?"

"No, Mrs. Skye. I want the Crows to return and I'll send messengers at once. What happened was the fault of our soldiers, not them. We will continue."

Mrs. Skye! A spasm rocked Truscott. Skye's other wife! He knew instantly he would have her, he would force the issue, he'd keep her and flaunt her and rub it in, and if the guide slunk back in, so much the better.

"Mister Truscott, we seem to have the story. All the chiefs agree on it. It seems the man you called a deserter kept his word after all—at great risk."

Truscott nodded irritably, his gaze riveted on the bewitching young woman beside Washakie.

"Truscott—you're not paying attention."

Truscott forced himself to listen to the fatman, and forced his mind away from the fantasies that were tickling his loins.

"You and your horse-killers may have cost us a treaty. I'm sending a runner after the Crows—Mrs. Skye, if she'll go. She can persuade them, speak to Skye."

"I will go," she said solemnly.

"No, no, I'll send a soldier! We need her to translate."

"That would not be wise, Lieutenant." Something in Cummings's voice riled Truscott. "Before I send her, I want your promise, given as an officer and a gentleman, that Mister Skye and his horse will be kept from all harm. They won't come in otherwise."

"I will tell them to go away," said Mrs. Skye, who stood solemnly. "Jawbone is a medicine horse, greatly honored by all the tribes. If you do not do this, I will tell them not to come."

"Maybe just for you, my lovely lady."

She stared coldly at him. It didn't deter him in the slightest. "Sergeant Pope, I order the men to leave the horse and Skye strictly alone or answer to me for it. Tell them."

"Yassir." Pope vanished again.

"There now, my lady, I've done it."

She said something to Chief Washakie, and Truscott wished he knew what it was.

"I have told my chief not to trust you," she said coldly.

# Chapter 32

Mary left her son with Rising Crow and Lodge Maker and rode north, feeling a heavy burden on her small shoulders. She was going to find the Absaroka, not because the white grandfathers wanted her to, but because her chief did. The white men and the other chiefs agreed: only she, the former woman of Skye, would be believed and could bring back Many Coups and his fleeing people. In the end she was glad: she hadn't liked the smoldering look of the lieutenant, all his lusts and hungers naked before her eyes. He looked like one who might force himself on her without respecting her will.

Unlike Victoria, Mary still longed for Skye. She loved him. She ached for their boy, who would never see his father again. She'd felt rejected, cast aside. But she'd never stopped hoping that he would find room in his heart again for a red woman. She dreaded seeing him again but steeled herself to do it. If the chiefs and grandfathers wanted him back she would tell him. But she also intended to repeat what she had told Washakie—she didn't trust the soldiers, especially the lieutenant.

She knew what she would tell Mister Skye and Victoria and Many Coups: don't bring Jawbone to the council because they would kill the spirit horse in spite of their promises. Gradually, as she rode into the evening, only a few hours behind the village, a plan formed in her mind: she and Victoria would stay away from the council and hide Jawbone in some secret grassy haven while Skye and the Absaroka returned to make the treaty. Each day and night she and Victoria would watch for soldiers, and flee with Jawbone if they approached. No soldier would ever kill the spirit horse if she could help it!

The signs of passage of the Absaroka village were unmistakable and she followed them over the Owl Creek Mountains even after dark had settled, the smell of manure sharp in her nostrils. She rode into the night, letting her sturdy mare pick her way down the long dry slopes. In the hush before early summer dawn she found the village slumbering west of the hot springs. She halted and let the camp police discover her. In Victoria's tongue she identified herself, and the Kit Fox Society warriors guarding the mixed village that night led her swiftly to Skye.

Jawbone lifted his ugly snout and whickered softly. The sound sent a thrill of joy through her. The spirit horse was welcoming her.

"Well, dammit," muttered Victoria, but Skye slumbered on, some significant distance from her.

"Oh! Victoria!" Mary cried, sliding off her pony and running to the older woman. The Kit Fox warriors dissolved into the darkness as she hugged Victoria fiercely.

"That sonofabitch got Jawbone out of it," the woman whispered.

"No, you did!"

"I did it for the medicine horse, not for that bastard."

Mary giggled, and the old Absaroka woman glared.

Jawbone loomed over them and snorted, his breath hot. Then he bit Mary.

"Oww!"

"He's telling you not to go away no more. He don't like having the lodge all busted up."

Mary rubbed his velvety muzzle and the horse let go of her forearm, which had been clamped by his grass-stained teeth.

Jawbone clacked his teeth crazily. Skye rolled over and she smelled the awesome odor of his feet. Sometimes Victoria had called the Skye lodge the stink house. But Mary had never minded.

She peered at Skye's recumbent form in the dark and her heart left her. She wanted him. She wanted to crawl into his robe beside him. She wanted everything to be all right again, the Skye lodge back together, her boy playing with his father. She wanted his strength and courage, and his strange white men's ways. She wanted his rough hands gently caressing her. She stood so close to the man she loved, so close . . . and so far away.

"How come you're here, eh?" Victoria growled. "Dammit, you gonna tell me something bad."

"I was sent. Chief Washakie sent me. The grandfathers sent me with a message. They said the Absaroka would believe me. They want your people to come back. They want Many Coups to be at the peace council. They want Mister Skye, too. The lieutenant says it is safe now; he will not harm the spirit horse. The fat grandfather, he makes the lieutenant say it."

Victoria hissed, disbelieving.

Jawbone poked his powerful muzzle into Skye's robe and flipped Skye over. Skye sat up instantly, his hand reaching for his Sharps and his other clamping his top hat to his head. Jawbone snorted gleefully.

Skye peered into the grudging moonlight and discovered both of his former wives.

"Har," he muttered. He stood and stretched, furtively eyeing the women as he drove his sleep away. "You got something to tell me?"

Mary watched him with fear and longing. "The grandfathers sent me. They want you to come back. The soldier-chief promises that no harm will come to the spirit horse. They want Chief Many Coups to bring back his people and make the treaty."

Skye sighed. "They had their chance. Don't know why I should. Don't trust Truscott, bloody rotter."

"My chief asked me to tell you he wants a treaty. My people need it. He wants you to do this favor for him."

Skye yawned, not fully awake. "Talk it over with the Crow chiefs in the morning," he said. "This rotten horse keeps waking me up."

Jawbone yanked Skye's top hat from him and flapped it up and down.

"Avast!" Skye roared, half waking up the whole camp. But it settled into silence again. Skye returned to his robes, not wanting any more night-talk.

In the middle of the next morning the greatest chiefs of the Crow nation gathered in a circle under a cottonwood to hear Mary. She knew most of them: the proud, hawkish leader of the Whistling Water people, The Big Robber; old Bear's Head; Rottentail, head chief of the River Crows; and Two Face, leader of two hundred lodges. Behind sat innumerable headmen, many of them handsome, hawkish, with prominent, slightly humped noses, receding foreheads, and intelligent eyes.

She felt them study her as she told them she had been sent by the grandfathers as well as her own Chief Washakie, who wanted the treaty badly. They stirred when she told them of Truscott's grudging promise to secure the safety of the spirit horse.

"Do you believe him?" asked old Bear's Head.

"No. He has a hungry look in his face. The soldier-chief is too hungry, always wanting, always making other men small and obedient, always wanting to see himself in the looking glass. No. He will find a way to kill the spirit horse."

Around this circle sat Skye, Victoria, and most of the best men of the Absaroka nation, many of them still dressed in beautiful festival clothing. One fat woman wore an exquisite elk-tooth dress, hundreds of the teeth sewn to the soft white leather of mountain sheep. These blackbird people produced proud and handsome men, Mary thought, and shapeless women.

A deep silence filled the camp, broken only by the quiet deliberations of the chiefs as they spoke in turn, never interrupting one another. They asked her no more questions; the decisions would now rest on their wisdom and that of the several shamans among them.

"A treaty would be good," said Many Coups. "We are a small nation with few lodges. There are four winds. Upon the north wind are more Siksika than we can count, always threatening to drive us away from our good land. And also the Cree and Assiniboin and the Atsina. We face them all. Upon the east wind are the Lakota, many times more than all the Absaroka, powerful and deadly, wanting our good hunting lands, taking our horses and women and children. Upon the south wind are more who want our home, the Cut-Arm People.

"We have survived because we opened our villages to the white men who came to trap beaver. They traded guns and fought beside us—like our friend here, Mister Skye. We have always been friends with these pale people who trade guns and powder and the soft metal for our pelts. This is our ancient policy. We are strong and brave but we are outnumbered many times over. We must make a friendship treaty with the grandfathers. They will then help us hold our good land forever."

Slowly they talked. Bear's Head worried about the soldiers. Two Face wondered whether the treaty was needed after all. The Big Robber raised the question of Skye and the medicine horse, who would be thrust into danger once again, for no one believed the word of the soldier-chief with the hungry eyes.

But eventually, when the sun stood high overhead, the great ones of Victoria's people had come to two decisions. Many Coups, wearing his bonnet of authority, stood serenely, gazing over the sinewy throng of his nation, and addressed Mary.

"Here is what to tell the grandfathers and what you must also tell the soldier-chief to his face: the Absaroka are a strong nation, well armed and proud. We will make a treaty with the grandfathers so that we may be friends and the grandfathers will help us to keep our land. Tell them the Absaroka will return and make the friendship treaty . . ."

He paused. "Tell Chief Washakie that we will come to make the treaty; that we need one just as his people—your people—need one.

"And tell all of them this: we will invite Mister Skye to join us and translate and take our words and thoughts to the grandfathers. We will guard him with our lives. We will guard the medicine horse day and night and not permit any blue-shirt even to come close. The soldiers must no longer wander through our villages or our herds. And if they try to harm the medicine horse the Absaroka people will be instantly at war, and none of the blue-shirts will see the sun set. They are few; we are many and well armed. We are at peace; but any attempt to harm the spirit horse will be taken as war and we will fight."

Mary nodded. "I will tell them all this. I will tell the soldier-chief myself. I will tell him that his few soldiers will not see the sun set if they harm the spirit horse."

From outside the council circle, Mister Skye stood. "Tell 'em I'm coming in, Mary. I'll finish the bloody job."

Mary nodded. Skye looked forlorn, as sad and alone as he had all winter and spring. Minutes later she rode south, the messages engraved upon her soul.

# Chapter 33

Somberly, Mary steered her mare toward the camp of the soldiers and grandfathers. They'd spotted her from far off and were gathering around the lieutenant's tent. She could see Superintendent Cummings hastening there along with the medicine preacher, and the clerk McGinty.

Good. She would give them her message and then ride to her own people and tell Washakie the Absaroka were returning. There would be a treaty. Her chief would be glad but she wasn't so sure she would be. She'd been around the white men a lot more than he.

She reined up before them. The lieutenant's gaze raked her as it had before. She peered into his eyes and found them filled with that strange pain and conceit and lust she'd seen earlier. His sergeant, Pope, was there, and others of his command. The superintendent leaned into his walking stick like a propped-up ball, while the chief clerk danced from one foot to another, some strange energy animating the dapper man.

She chose to address Victorious Cummings as a way of slighting the lieutenant. Slowly she dismounted, concealing her calves as best she could from that obsessive stare, and then faced the black-clad grandfather.

"I have a message from Many Coups. The Absaroka people will return tomorrow and talk about a treaty with the grandfathers. With them will be Mister Skye and the medicine horse. The warriors will protect the horse night and day. The blue-shirts are not to enter the village or walk through the herds—not ever. Many Coups says to tell you that any attempt to harm the medicine horse will be an act of war against the Absaroka nation. If that should happen no blue-shirt would leave here alive."

The lieutenant smirked. "I don't think the cavalry has much to worry about."

She faced him. "If you kill the medicine horse you will pay with your life."

"A death threat. How pretty."

"Lieutenant. I will stalk you myself, and you will not escape."

Truscott laughed. "First his old squaw creeps in and threatens my life. And now this Shoshone wench is at it, too."

"I don't see it as a death threat, Lieutenant," said Victorious Cummings. "These are promises to retaliate. Your fate is in your own hands: leave the horse alone and they'll leave you alone."

Truscott seemed offended. "I should listen to a pair of squaws?" He laughed. "This is the cavalry, Major Cummings."

"And they are the Skyes, Mister Truscott."

"They were, you mean. He's pitched them out. Typical squaw-man. Uses them and discards them."

Mary refused to let a trace of feeling etch her face. She stood quietly, strong and lithe, absorbing all she could. Maybe she could learn things.

"This is a most magnificent thing," said Wellington Cummings. "Imagine! We'll have a treaty. Peace has returned. Young lady, you have blessed us. And you've blessed the tribes."

"I went because my chief asked me. I do not approve of this treaty."

"Well, Mister Truscott?" Superintendent Cummings was obviously waiting for some affirmation from the soldier-chief.

"I'm at your service, gentlemen. We wouldn't want the whole Crow nation to descend on us, would we?" She discovered mockery in his eyes.

"I don't sense that you are taking Many Coups' diplomacy seriously, Lieutenant."

"Look, Major. Everything we know about fighting Indians is that they'll break and run when confronted with massed fire and disciplined troops. My sixty dragoons and I could cut a path through the Crow nation clear to the Canadian border."

"Fifty-eight dragoons."

"Yes, and you're preventing the cavalry from retaliating for a death and an injury. Maybe ..." He stopped suddenly, shrugged and smiled. "It's a peace council."

"Maybe what?" Mary asked.

He smiled at her. "Maybe you take life too seriously."

"Lieutenant," said Victorious Cummings, "I want the conference to begin as soon as the Crows return. Grass is already short. Set up the treaty grounds this afternoon. Put the chairs and tables out. Raise the sun shelter. Anything you can do to expedite matters— including keeping your troops away from the villages and herds."

"Far be it from the Army to oppose a peace treaty, Major."

"Very well. I will take you at your word." The grandfather turned to Mary. "Thank you, Mrs. Skye. You've done invaluable service for us and for your good chief. Please send my warmest regards to Washakie and tell him we'll see him and his people tomorrow when the talks begin."

She nodded. Something about the vast man in the black suit appealed to her. His spirit was as large as his body. She watched the grandfather walk back to the Indian Bureau camp, followed by the others. They were friends, of a sort, to the tribes. She turned and mounted her mare only to find the lieutenant holding its reins.

"I will go to my people now," she said.

"No, sweetheart. We'll have a little powwow."

"I have nothing to say to you."

"Oh, but you do. You've threatened my life. You've carried a message from Many Coups threatening to annihilate my command and me. I find that rather enchanting. I've never wooed a dusky maiden. You'll have to show me how."

"Let go of my horse."

"I will when I'm ready."

She sat silent. From a distance the sergeant was grinning.

"What is your Shoshone name? Not the name Skye gave you."

She saw no need to answer him.

"Ah, the silent savage. I'm going to have you, you know. I want Skye's woman."

She understood something about him now. She let herself become very still inside, so inert that she felt a coldness creep through her.

"Oh, don't you worry. I'm going to woo you. I'm going to meet your son, Skye's son. He'll like me. What's his name?"

The coldness in her deepened.

"Ah, a half-breed boy. Now there's the way to deal with Skye. Tit for tat, shall we say? But I don't make threats."

She would hide Dirk. The white man wanted to hurt Skye. He hated Skye so much he'd kill Skye's son— and take her.

"Yes, I shall find him and find you. I'll just have a stroll over to Washakie's village. I'll meet your family. I'll meet Skye's boy. I have so much to offer. White women find me irresistible and dangerous. When they come to me they know they're taking great risks. I invite them and they accept! They can't refuse. They love it even if it might result in a scandal. That's because what I give them is more exciting than anything they've ever known. I'll show you things you never knew about. They'll tickle your fancy, and you'll want more."

He did not clothe the nakedness of his purposes, she thought. She'd seen something of it from the first, something in his hurt and lustful eyes, his odd smirk, his conceit, and his unreasoning hatred of a greater man than he and a spirit horse that put all his cavalry mounts to shame. So . . . it was not over. Now she knew. She would give Dirk to Victoria and the Absaroka would keep him. They were armed and ready; they would permit no blue-shirts in their village.

"Ah, still the silent woman, eh? Well, soon you'll be squealing with joy."

Suddenly he let go of the reins. She was free to go. He expected her to kick her mare and race away.

"People can do good or they can do evil," she said quietly. "Even white men have their laws. Mister Skye told us that lust and envy were sins among the white men and that the great rule among your people is to treat others as they would wish to be treated. These are very good. I've talked to medicine-givers about these ideas. The medicine-givers say these are good rules for the Shoshone. Lieutenant, is this not one of your teachings?"

Truscott hadn't expected that. He'd expected another threat from her. It seemed to deflate him. But then he smiled.

"You'll find I'm irresistible," he repeated.

# Chapter 34

It was time to do some expediting. The Crows would return and the council was on. Alphonse McGinty decided he'd start with the detail guarding the wagons.

But first he had to find one of his clerks, Patriot Jones, who could be relied upon to follow instructions. The young man was as loyal to clerkdom as anyone McGinty had ever run across. He found Patriot gutting a rattlesnake.

"Pat, me boy, I've a job for you."

"I'm not Pat. I have no nickname. I'm Patriot. It's a sacred name to live up to."

That's how it always began with Jones. McGinty waited for the skinny Adam's apple to stop bobbing. "Pat, me boy, it's time to do a little expediting. We're gonna expedite a treaty with the redskins and we're gonna expedite some good times for the soldier boys—keep 'em happy and not thinkin' about Skye's horse. And of course, there's gain in it."

Patriot Jones perked up. Gain always caught his attention.

"I'll be sendin' the dragoons to you, me boy, and you supply the dainties, jist like we talked about. And remember. Don't give out none of them cast-iron axheads. Two whacks and they're blunted. And none of them knives either—the blades bend. But you git out the lady stuff, makes the squaws dance. Git ready now and deal out of the last wagon, farthest from the mucketymucks and do it quiet."

Patriot nodded solemnly. "What does this expediting fetch me, Mr. McGinty?"

"Ten percent."

"I'll take twenty."

"I'll think on it." McGinty wasn't about to make promises. Expediting was grubby work. Patriot was showing signs of greed but no one else was quite as reliable.

The clerk vanished toward the rear wagon to open the store while McGinty eyed the two dragoon wagon guards, finally selecting the younger one, who probably hadn't a penny in his britches.

"Aye, lad, and it's a fair day. What's your name?"

The dragoon lowered the butt of his carbine. "Wilson, sah."

"Think of it, Wilson, old son. All them savage women jist lusting for some gewgaws from the wagons. I hear tell they'll make any soldier boy happy for a hank of ribbon."

"I heard better'n that. You can deal if you got something they want. They like to horse around and the bucks let 'em."

"Depends on the tribe, Wilson. Them Crow women—they're enough to make a soldier blush, but the Cheyenne, they don't fool around."

"Yeah, me and my friends, we got it figgered out. But we're on duty all the time, and anyways we're mostly broke. Eight a month don't go far—even when it comes, which it usually don't."

"That's the trouble, me boy. You gamble it all away. I imagine there's a few old boys in your outfit that've got a wad of greenbacks they lifted from you all. Euchre? Monte?"

Wilson laughed. "There's one that cleans us out every payroll and the none of us ever beats him."

"Ah, me boy, a pity. Me and my clerks, we like to see happiness flowing like ale. We'd sell the boys a yard of calico or two if they had a few pennies. Then you'd all go find yerselves a good-lookin' savage lady and have some fun in the bushes. Wish we could give it away but it's govermint stuff."

"I don't got a cent. Hardly nobody has a cent."

"Maybe him that has the wad'll give you a chit. Ever think of that? He'll give you six bits and you can pay him next payday, and you can go make the squaws happy. I seen some real pretty ones sashaying around, especially the curvy Arapaho ladies. And some pretty Shoshone, too. Now them Crow women, I never seen such a bulky lot. Crows, they're not letting no soldier boys near the camp nohow."

"Yeah," said Wilson. "I don't want to chase Crow squaws. I ain't got a nickel, anyway. I could sure use some real live squaw company, though."

McGinty eyed his man thoughtfully. "Well, Wilson me boy, maybe I can hire you."

Wilson stared.

"I need a soldier boy to tell the rest that the Indian Bureau clerks are expediting a bit. We'll sell yards of calico cheap, and if some old boy really wants to woo a savage lover we got some copper kettles, hanks of beads, and the like. But that stuff, it costs more. Now, Wilson. You start gitting the word out, work real hard at it, and I'll give you a couple of yards to do your wooin' with."

"Who, me?"

"Well, if you ain't up to it, I'll hire someone else."

"You figger two yards'll buy a trip to the bushes?"

McGinty shrugged. "Might buy ten trips for all I know. You got to negotiate."

"Yeah, I'll do it."

"Now tell me, lad—who's the moneybags? Maybe I can jist tell him how to do a little business with them that wants a little gewgaw for a squaw."

"It's old Tim Porter, yonder, oldest private in the dragoons, him that knows the fast shuffle. No sooner the paymaster comes than he's got it all."

"All right, me boy. I'll have a talk. And I'll tell Patriot Jones, the clerk at the last wagon, to open up his store and give you a couple of yards of real purty squaw-catcher stuff soon as dusk comes."

"I'll be there! I'm gittin' off in half a hour and I'll tell the boys you're takin' pity on some dragoons who ain't seen no town in months."

Chief Clerk McGinty had no trouble finding Porter. The man looked like an old sergeant and probably had been one before getting busted. Porter had disassembled his Hall-North carbine and was cleaning it.

"Porter, me boy, that looks like hard work."

The private squinted up at McGinty, suspicion in him.

"Be more fun chasin' pretty young redskin ladies, I imagine."

Porter picked at a fouled nipple. "They don't want nothing to do with blue-shirts, McGinty. We got nothing they want anyway."

"You could try a penny, me boy."

Porter snorted. "Money. They never seen it and don't need it."

"Ah, we were thinkin' on that, me and the clerks. We think it'd git the redskins in a proper frame of mind to see a few white men's trinkets. You know—awls, cloth, pots, beads. We thought we'd pass out a little to our soldier boys but it seems no one's got a dime to pay back the Bureau."

"I could buy and sell a whole wagonload."

"Well, why don't you, me boy?" McGinty watched the light turn on in Porter's eyes. "How much you got to lend them others?"

"About three payrolls' worth."

"I figure maybe you could turn it into five or six payrolls, Porter."

Porter squinted up at him. "You're jist cleaning out the dragoons, McGinty."

The chief clerk shrugged. "I'm in the expediting business. People want something and I go get it. Boys want to go squaw-chasing, I'm not against it. I git my price. That's how the world works."

"When does this here store open, McGinty?"

"Soon's it's dusky. Runs maybe to midnight. Every night from now on until the chiefs put their X on the treaty. Then we got to pass the stuff out."

"It's a gouge. Them's govermint goods. I don't like it."

"No man comes to the store but's willing to buy at the price, Porter. You don't like it, you jist stay away."

"Oh, I reckon I'll git into it, damn youse. Save some yardgoods for me, McGinty. Twenty yards and a few kettles. Naw, twenty yards calico, five kettles, buncha beads, mess of knives, a dozen hatchets—I'll cut a swath through the pretty Shoshones first and save all the juice I got left for the Cheyenne lovelies."

McGinty laughed appreciatively and left the private to the cleaning of his shooter. The result of this little tour among the dragoons would be a couple of hundred dollars—a clerk's annual salary. But of course it would have to be divided a little.

There was poetry in expediting, he thought. All he did was make the world happy. Porter would make a bundle when the next payrolls came around and he collected his chits. A whole troop of dragoons would have themselves a frolic for a few nights—if the squaws were willing. And he'd heard tell they often were, and if they weren't the bucks sold 'em anyways. That's how it'd been at all them old rendezvous of the trappers. The squaws, they'd get some white men's fancies, beads and cloth, pots and pans, frills and fripperies enough to gladden some old redskin.

But the poetry didn't stop there, oh, no! A little expediting would quiet these dragoons, upset about the dead and wounded, itching for revenge. A little skirt-chasing would work better than a jug of spirits. They'd forget all about the guide and his horse, not even think about the Skyes until the council was over and the treaty was in the bag.

And then the final poetry: the clerks would distribute all those goods, pour 'em out the rear of their wagons to all the chiefs and headmen, warriors and squaws, medicine men and children that lined up. And all them cast-iron axheads, all them knives that bent, and all the shabby yardgoods that'd fall apart next week—the inspectors would never see. And no one would ever know. Expediting this council had earned McGinty $5,000 and another $1,000 to share with the clerks. And that was the sweetest poetry of all.

McGinty plucked up a daisy and stuck it in his lapel as a token of life's beauty.

# Chapter 35

Victorious Cummings sat tensely in the shade of the arbor the soldiers had erected while the tribes gathered. Before him, the greatest chiefs were settling into a semicircle. Directly behind sat the lesser chiefs, headmen, and shamans of each tribe, and in the next row the principal warriors, clan and society leaders. Beyond, in succeeding rows, the lesser members of the tribes were sitting down, a vast throng that stretched a hundred yards or so in a great arc. For the moment, at least, old enemies sat shoulder to shoulder. But the smallest incident might scatter these proud and wild people. Or worse: a bad twist could start a bloodbath.

At last! he thought. The Crows had returned that morning and swiftly made camp, along with them Skye and his older wife. Cummings had summoned them all at once: three thousand Indians, a hundred white men, and ten thousand horses would soon foul this place. He hoped to conclude the treaty before the whole council was forced to move to a new site.

Beside him in the pleasant shade of the canvas-covered arbor sat Wellington, McGinty, and various clerks and recorders. Also beside him in a camp chair sat Lieutenant Truscott in dress uniform. Outside the arbor a contingent of soldiers had settled into the grass, while the remainder garrisoned the camp and wagons. Cummings had sternly ordered Truscott that no soldier was to appear at the peace council armed in any fashion, but in spite of that Truscott himself wore his ornately sheathed saber, which glinted whenever the sun caught it. A small but significant lapse, Cummings thought. If this gathering were to explode like a bomb, Truscott would surely be the fuse.

None of the tribesmen before him was armed, though Cummings wondered what lay beneath the blankets that some of the warriors in the farther ranks insisted on wearing this hot day. The chiefs wore their grandest ceremonial attire: eagle-feather bonnets with ermine or weasel pendants, elaborate bracelets, necklaces and medicine bundles; fringed leggins or breechcloths, beaded and quilled moccasins; ceremonial staffs of office, from which dangled eagle or crow feathers. The tradecloth and beads and German-silver conchae added a riot of red and blue and yellow to the natural hide and bone and feather tones.

Great proud nations, sovereign and free—until now. Before him sat Many Coups and The Big Robber of the Crows; Washakie and Dancer of the Shoshones; Walking Coyote and White Horse of the Cheyenne, and thirty more distinguished leaders who would listen to him, debate privately within their own tribal councils, and then accept or reject the proposed treaty. The Cheyenne had brought their own translator, a squaw-man named Christopher Ravina. That would help Skye. His former women would translate to the Shoshones and Bannocks and Crows; Skye himself would help with the Crows and talk to the Arapaho.

There'd been no trouble with the Crows. An honor

guard of their Kit Fox warriors stood watch over Skye's horse, and access to their village was forbidden any white man other than Skye. That amazing warhorse was entirely invisible, kept in the center of a vast herd. Skye himself, his older woman Victoria, and Many Coups stared long and hard at Truscott as if to warn the man that his every act would have deadly consequences. Truscott had met the stares evenly, unintimidated and silent. Cummings thought the situation needed watching.

He saw that the great assemblage was ready. Three thousand Indians sat before him in eerie silence. He stood slowly, extracting his pince-nez from his commodious black suit, along with some notes for his opening address.

"Gentlemen, we shall begin," he said to his staff. And then, to the multitudes: "We will begin now with a prayer to the Great Spirit, father of us all."

The Reverend Mister Wellington Cummings had drafted a simple prayer to the Great Spirit. Both the brothers knew that white men's religion fascinated the Indians, and any white divine had their immediate and serious respect.

Joyously, Wellington lifted his arms. "One Above, Great Spirit, First Maker," he began, while the translators followed, "bless your many peoples and nations gathered here to make an everlasting peace. Fill our hearts with brotherhood and friendship as we begin our work. Help us to define the boundaries of nations justly and fairly; help us to heal old wounds and forgive old wrongs. Help us, One Above, to begin a time of peace and joy."

Good! That was a fine beginning. The translators finished, and the great throng absorbed it all as silently as corpses watching someone walk over their graves. It was not a prayer that would please young warriors eager to count coups, steal horses and women, and rise to high office within their tribes, he thought. The ambitious young warriors would be a problem for the peace chiefs.

It was time for the opening address. Cummings made his way out into the sun so that he might be seen by the farthest ranks. He fumbled open his draft. "My chiefs, headmen, medicine men, and friends of many nations, welcome," he began, pausing to permit his translators to turn his words into different tongues. "The grandfathers in the East have gathered you together to bring a new time, a new spirit, to the people of the Great Plains. We want to give each Indian nation a homeland to have and to hold forever; to stop war and stealing; to teach you farming and stock-growing so that you may have a constant supply of good food; to teach you how to live as white men do, with schools to help you learn how to write and read, as well as how to work metal at forges, plow the land, plant seeds, harvest food, make cloth, and live securely."

He wondered whether all that was translatable. Most of these people had only the vaguest notion of what farming entailed or what a school or mill or blacksmith shop was. How did one turn hunters and warriors and gatherers into a different people?

"A time of change is coming. The buffalo will not last, but you will have white men's cattle to replace it. The cattle are easy to herd and the meat is better than the tough meat of the buffalo. You will learn to live the way white men do, on farms, in peace with our neighbors. You will be able to grow and store food against the winters. You will learn all of our secrets and apply them for your own good. We will teach you as much as you want to learn.

"If you do these things, and settle on your own lands, and stay at peace with the other tribes, the white grandfathers in the East will be very pleased with their red children and will send you many gifts and tools to help you farm and herd stock. Your white grandfathers will send you seed and cattle, plows and rakes and scythes, and you will be able to harvest hay to feed your cattle in the winter, and corn to feed yourselves.

"But if you do not do these things or make a good treaty, the white grandfathers will be displeased with their unruly red children and will not send gifts or tools. And if you make war on white men passing through, your grandfathers will be forced to send soldiers to punish those who make war, and you will not like that. So, my good children, we will make a good peace. We will give each nation its own lands to hold forever. And we will extend the hand of friendship to all, and hope that you will do the same."

The superintendent waited while the translators finished, and then sat down, glad to take the weight off his suffering feet. He mopped his sweating face. Even in the shade of the canvas arbor the oppressive heat was numbing his senses.

"That was a dandy, Victorious," whispered Wellington. "The carrot and the stick. They can cooperate or face the music."

"The cavalry is the music," said Truscott. "And they will march to it."

"They know they must abandon the old," Wellington said. "They've been around the fur posts and forts enough to know the future. They've no choice."

"They won't understand the half of what we're asking," Victorious replied. "We'll have to explain everything."

Skye approached him. "Now what, mates?" He didn't seem particularly happy.

"Why, if it's in their tradition to welcome us to this place, now's the time, Mister Skye."

The translator wheeled silently and addressed the assembled chiefs, switching from one tongue to another and using sign language. He lifted his right

hand to his mouth, palm up, and moved it outward
and back a few times, an obvious sign for talk.

Chief Washakie rose, surveyed the crowd serenely,
and then the white men. This would take time, Cummings thought: the Plains Indian chiefs were long-
winded, and it would need to be translated. But the
chief's fingers flew along as he spoke, and the other
chiefs were picking it up.

"We welcome the white grandfathers to the lands of
our ancestors," the Shoshone began. "And we welcome our friends also to the lands of the Sheep Eater
people." He held his right hand in front of his neck,
palm out, his index and second fingers extending upward. Then he raised his hand until the fingertips
were as high as his head.

"Probably the friend sign," Wellington whispered.

"We like what the white grandfather says,"
Washakie continued, while Skye's younger squaw put
it into softly accented English. "We want to learn your
ways. My people are hungry because the white men
have shot the buffalo, and now they all stay far away
and our hunters see none. We need the food and gifts
and the tools and the cattle. We want the white
men and the wagons to respect our land, and when
the grandfathers draw the medicine lines around our
land, then the white men will not enter it."

He sat down again. None of the other chiefs rose,
and some of them looked hostile. Cummings hoped
Many Coups would rise to welcome the white delegation, but the Crow chief sat quietly, a scowl on his
face. Only Washakie was clearly in his camp.

Cummings knew it was time to begin reading the
treaty draft and explaining each of its fifteen articles.
That would take a day or two. He didn't much like the
silence he was encountering or the wariness that
seemed to emanate from the assemblage. Truscott and
his dragoons had already damaged the council, perhaps beyond repair. But that's what he had Skye for.

The success of this council seemed to depend more and more upon that rough old Briton with the savage horse.

The afternoon, was fading. "Tomorrow we will discuss the treaty," he said, and the translators spoke into a great silence.

Many Coups rose: "That is acceptable. The Absaroka will be here. But first we want the soldier-chief to give us his word that no harm will come to the medicine horse or to the Skyes." The chief spoke but the English came from Victoria Skye.

Cummings turned to Truscott, who slowly rose to his feet.

"The United States Cavalry will do whatever it takes to make the council a success," he said.

Truscott's face mocked Cummings, while Victoria translated.

"Tell the sonofabitch that Many Coups wants a straight no-crap answer," she snapped.

# Chapter 36

An arrow! Lieutenant Truscott peered up from his bedroll at an arrow that had pierced halfway through the sloping duckcloth of his tent. An arrow of Indian manufacture. The haft of the iron point was anchored to the shaft with sinew.

It appalled him. Was an officer not safe in his own tent, surrounded by dragoon guards? He reached up and pulled the arrow a few inches into the tent, discovering that it had been inserted into an incision in the canvas, probably made with a sharp knife. Someone had sneaked into the camp and done this thing. He had little doubt who, or why.

He sprang up and pushed into the dawn light, still in his longjohns. "Pope!" he bellowed. "Pope!"

Big Pope crawled from his tent nearby, blinking back sleep.

"Sergeant, look at this."

Pope scratched at the crotch of his Army-issue underwear and studied the gray feathers bound by glue and sinew to a chokecherry shaft. "Some savage shot an arrow," he muttered.

"No, Pope. No! Some savage slid past your guards, cut a slit in my tent, and stabbed this through. She got away without being seen even though you said you'd strengthened the night guard."

Pope blinked. "I added a man, all right. Musta been a dark night."

"Dark nights are what extra guards are for, Pope. The fact is, she could have killed me if she'd felt like it."

"She?"

"That old hag of a Crow woman. Skye's old wife. The one that sneaked in before."

"It's *Mister* Skye, sah."

"This is no time for jokes! Who were on guard?"

"Which watch, sah? First or second?"

"Oh, never mind. Write me a list. They'll face a court-martial, every one of them. And I'm pulling a stripe. You're a corporal, Pope. Maybe that'll teach you to take our security seriously."

"Ah, ah, yes, sah."

"A squaw can kill as well as a buck, Corporal."

"Yes, sah."

"I'll find out how she slid in here. She's laughing at me. When I see her today I'm going to teach her that I can do whatever I want to her—anytime I choose. Not just her, either. I can do whatever I want to Skye, the young wife, the brat, and the horse."

"Yes, sah. The whole Crow nation, sah."

Truscott looked sharply at Big Pope. "That, too, if we have to. Let them face sixty breech-loading carbines if they will. They'll scatter like hens." He yanked the arrow out of the rent in the cloth and inspected it. "This'll be Crow. They all have their different ways and different dyes and marks, you know."

"Guess she wants to be found out, sah."

"Of course she does. It's her little threat. We could march into that herd of theirs and kill that horse and they couldn't do a thing about it. She knows it." He eyed the disgraced sergeant levelly. "Only we won't. A shrewd commander chooses his own time and place to strike. He waits patiently for the right moment. The right moment won't be here. It won't be until the council is over and Cummings has a signed treaty in his pocket. Then, by God, Pope, you'll see some things. The United States Dragoons won't be trifled with. Not by squaws and outlaws."

Pope grinned.

"Wake up every man that was on the first watch and have them report to me on the double."

"Yes, sah!"

Truscott buttoned his shirt, drew up his blue britches, and hooked the galluses over his shoulders. He trimmed his blond beard before a dangling looking glass and slid on his freshly blacked boots, while listening to the men collect just outside his tent flaps.

He emerged from his tent into a chill dawn. Six dragoons saluted. He studied them: Higgins, Thwaite, Cordova, Makous, Zastrow, Hinkle, looking frightened. He'd show them something to be afraid of. He waved the arrow at them.

"This was poking through my shelter. It wasn't shot from a bow out there. It was stuffed in a cut by someone who penetrated this camp and escaped. You've failed every man in camp that entrusts his safety to you while he sleeps. You'll all face charges when we get to Leavenworth. Dismissed."

They stood in the gray light, uncertain.

"Go to bed. First Call's in an hour."

"Sir? Permission to speak?"

It was Higgins, a Tennessee boy. Truscott nodded.

"Sir, I ain't trying to get us off the hook. I jist want to explain—"

"Save your explanations for the trial."

"—about all the coming and going all night, sir."

"Coming and going?"

Higgins looked uncomfortable. "Yeah, half the camp in and out, and we were checking all the time. This here intruder jist got by whiles we was checking."

"Checking, Higgins. What're you babbling about?"

"They's still a bunch out, sir. Maybe a dozen. They'll be in by First Call, I figure, sir."

"Out where?"

"In the villages, sir. They was looking for a little, ah, fun."

"Fun, Higgins?"

"You know, sir. They taken the stuff, stuff the squaws like, and went hunting for some fun."

"Higgins, quit beating around the bush and explain."

Higgins reddened. "They was out looking for women, sir. You know. They've been wanting to try out the squaws, real pretty ones they've seen in every village, all prettied up, smooth and young, all prettied up in doeskin dresses and beads and feathers."

"They sure like the soldier boys," volunteered Thwaite. "They start smiling and pawing through the stuff."

"Speak only when I give you permission, Private. Now tell me what stuff. I'm not quite getting all this."

"The stuff the Bureau clerk's selling. Calico, beads, ribbons."

"Selling? You mean the annuity goods? The stuff the Indian Bureau's going to distribute?"

"The same, sir. Only, the clerks, they tell us we can have a little first, for fun."

"Let me get this straight, Thwaite. The clerks are selling government property to my men?"

"Jist one, sir. Patriot Jones, him with the big Adam's apple. After dark, for a couple of hours is all, off the rear wagon."

"And just where did the money come from? You're all broke."

"Tim Porter, he lent it, sir. He's always got a bundle."

"At what? Double next payday?"

"Triple, sir. But it don't take much to git some gew-gaws for them squaws. A ribbon, it's like a double ea-gle for them. They jist take it and let themselves get led into the brush, like that, all night."

"How many were out last night?"

"Most everybody, sir. We had us a time checking who's what and when. That's why—"

"No excuses, Higgins! You failed."

The men looked crestfallen, but Truscott wouldn't relent. Not after finding a death threat poking through his tent. "All right, dismissed," he snapped. "And get up at First Call."

He watched them file back to their shelters.

Graft! Now he had proof of it. The night had had its rewards after all. Graft! Clerks selling government property so dragoons could go whoring. Lining their pockets. Getting rich. Subverting federal policy. Cor-rupting the savages. One might be doing the selling, but they were all in on it. Now at last he had some-thing on Cummings and the whole lot. Maybe the Army would get the corrupt Indian Bureau back after all, once his superiors found out. He'd need written testimony: affidavits from every man who could write, which amounted to eleven. And he'd take testimony from the rest and have them put their mark on each document. Joy blossomed through him: this was the stuff of brevets.

"Pope!" he roared. "Check each shelter and find out who's missing. If they're not in by First Call put them on report. And Pope—find out all you can about this. Keep it quiet. I want to fry Cummings in his own fat."

"Them 'Rapaho girls is sure sweet and eager, sir," Pope said. "You want some yeller ribbon for yourself?"

It put him in mind of Skye's younger squaw. He wouldn't need ribbon.

# Chapter 37

Victorious Bonaparte Cummings sensed the skeptical mood of the throng that had gathered on the treaty grounds, and worried about it. Yesterday the council had started on a sour note thanks to the conduct of Lieutenant Truscott and his dragoons.

A great deal of thought had gone into the preparation of this treaty but now it all might come to naught. Skye and his horse had become a disruptive force that threatened to shatter two years of planning. But he knew that the fault did not lie with Skye; the real problem was young Truscott, ambitious and wounded and vain.

He glared at the dragoon lieutenant, who was wearing his saber once again, the only weapon visible in a peace council involving thousands. The man looked uncommonly smug. Cummings wished he'd been assigned a senior officer with some sense instead of this shavetail fresh from West Point. He'd have to make the best of it.

This hot July day he and Wellington would read the articles of the draft treaty to the assemblage. It would go slowly, requiring a lot of translating and a large map he had prepared of the mountains and rivers in the whole area. Article I and Article II would be easy for the chiefs to grasp: they declared perpetual peace between the United States and the tribes, and perpetual peace among the tribes. But after that, he would plunge them into controversy. Article III described common hunting grounds, strategically located to cover areas contested by the different nations and to provide access to the buffalo herds for mountain tribes such as the Bannocks.

Article IV would be the stickiest one of all. It described the territories of each nation and the sites of proposed agencies for each tribe. It would settle the Crows along the Yellowstone, with an agency on that river; the Wind River Shoshones right where the council was meeting, with an agency there; the Bannocks on the Snake, with an agency at the old Hudson's Bay Company post, Fort Hall; and the Arapaho on the South Platte, with an agency on that stream.

The Cheyenne, who were observers at this time, would be settled to the east along with their friends the Sioux at a later council. There would have to be other treaties to complete what was begun here: one with the Utes and another with the Western and Northern Shoshones, whom the Bureau hoped to settle on the Snake along with the Bannocks. If the Bureau's designs prevailed, the Bighorn basin, the Three Forks area of the Missouri, and a stretch east of the Bighorn Mountains would all become common buffalo-hunting grounds. These were not only prime hunting grounds but also major travel routes best left untenanted.

"Are we ready?" asked Wellington, surveying the quiet throng.

"We lack the Bannocks."

"They take their time, don't they? My timepiece says ten-thirty."

"My bladder says noon. Wellington, I'm going to ask you to do most of the reading. I'll spell you and answer questions. I'd just as soon we don't have our military friend do any of it."

They waited on while Victorious reviewed the draft. The remaining articles permitted United States citizens to pass unmolested through Indian lands and protected Indians from unlawful acts by whites; gave the United States the right to build roads, railroads, and telegraph lines through Indian territory, as well as military posts, missions, agency buildings, and farms; provided annuities of useful goods and food for each tribe for a period of twenty years, and an annual sum of $15,000 for education and the teaching of vocations. Other articles dealt with compensations for damages, and for exclusion of ardent spirits from Indian lands. The final article said the treaty would be binding on all parties upon its ratification by the Senate.

It would be a tall order to convey all that to tribesmen unfamiliar with many of the concepts, and Victorious hoped the Skyes would be up to it. Victorious didn't doubt that Skye would oppose some of what he would convey. But maybe Skye's darkness could be laid at the feet of Truscott.

As the Bannock chiefs settled to the ground, Wellington rose. After some introductory remarks he began reading. When he came to the ticklish area of tribal boundaries, Victorious rose and pointed to lines on the map with his black walking stick. He had no idea how any of this was being accepted. The chiefs and headmen studied his map impassively. Wellington droned on, pausing frequently for the translators. Skye and the two former wives translated loudly, along with the Cheyenne squawman, Ravina.

"Mister Skye, would you inquire of the chiefs

whether they grasp the boundaries we're proposing?"
Victorious asked during a pause.

Skye reported that the chiefs wanted the whole
thing described again, so the brothers Cummings repeated the boundary clauses. Victorious could not
fathom what the chiefs thought, but he didn't doubt
that he'd soon find out.

By early afternoon all sixteen articles had been read.
Cummings called a break until "the sun is lower in the
sky." He hoped that would mean around five o'clock
to the red men. "Then we will listen to you," he said.
"Perhaps you have thoughts to give to the grandfathers."

The throng slid back to the villages, although some
of the chiefs and headmen gathered into knots and argued the treaty intensely among themselves.

"Have you any idea, Mister Skye, how they're taking this?"

"No, sir. All I can say is, it's too much for them to
grasp all at once. It's outside their experience. You'll
want to take this piece by piece."

"Do they not understand?"

"White men are mysteries, mate."

"Are you personally unhappy with the Bureau's
proposals, Mister Skye?"

Skye shrugged. "I won't be here to see the results.
But I can tell you—some of it's unworkable. Until the
buffalo are gone, young men'll live the way they
have—raiding for horses, attacking their bloody enemies, looking for coups and war honors that'll make
them great men in their villages. You're really asking
them to start doing women's work. That's what farming and stock-raising are to them. A treaty like this attacks their pride. You're pouring shame over their
heads. The women won't stand for it either; they want
their men to do men's work—hunting and warring."

The Reverend Mister Cummings sighed. "You paint
a desolating image, Mister Skye. It's been my dream to

bring gentleness and industry to them; settle them on farms; teach them our mechanics and arts, and especially our sublime religion. But now you dash my dreams."

"Maybe we should kill the buffalo," Victorious said. "Put the tribes in a corner."

Skye lifted his battered hat and settled it again. "Suppose, mate, that the shoe was on the other foot, and the powerful tribes had conquered your East. Suppose they were asking you to live as they do, give up your Christian beliefs, your faith in republican government; stop preaching peace and go to war like any proper red man."

Victorious thought the proposition was amusing but his reverend brother took it seriously:

"You make it graphic, sir. But for God's sake I beg of you, give it your best even if you're a skeptic. Talk to them. Plead with them. Let them know how earnestly we wish for their happiness and well-being and comfort. Ah, sir, they have their choice—they can have us or the Army."

Even as he spoke, Truscott joined them. "You're right," he said, looking oddly indulgent. "After the tribes resist another twenty years and murder another ten thousand white men and twice as many redskins, it'll be up to the War Department to finish up the job."

The young man was goading them but Victorious refused to grasp the nettle.

Skye stared at the young officer. "It's time for us to pull together," he said quietly. "We've a job to do. Your government wants a treaty and it's up to us to set aside our differences and see that the job's done. I'm willing." He offered his hand to Truscott.

Victorious watched hopefully, but Truscott did not acknowledge Skye's outstretched hand. Solemnly, Skye withdrew his hand, lifted and settled his old top hat, and stared at the horizons. Victorious Cummings itched to know what thoughts were forming behind those squinting blue eyes.

"Well, Skye," Truscott said. "We'll have progress one way or another. As law and order advances, the rebels and misfits and outlaws must die, and all their kith and kin."

"It's Mister Skye, sir," the guide said.

# Chapter 38

Mister Skye had been so long away from chairs he could hardly remember what it was like to sit down in one. For all his years in the wilderness, his couch had been the cast-iron earth or a scratchy tree trunk or a cold saddle. He slumped into the roots of a cottonwood, watching the moths, absorbing the amber quiet of twilight.

He had slid back into melancholia and an inchoate yearning for a more civilized life. He felt a terrible weariness: in all the years of wrestling the wilds he'd known only scattered moments of ease and peace, usually with Victoria's or Mary's people. The rest had been heat, cold, wet, pain, terror, anger, flight, war, and desperation. More than ever he wanted to abandon the borders and live quietly in some stout city where there were constables.

But plainly, he would have to wait. For reasons unfathomable to Skye, Truscott thirsted to ruin him. Skye didn't doubt that the lieutenant was hatching something, choosing his own deadly time and place.

All through the afternoon the various chiefs had risen like prairie dogs beside their holes, asked questions, sought understanding. Young Washakie had wanted to know what ratification by the Senate was all about. It was hard to explain to people with no knowledge of how the Yank government worked. The Big Robber of the Crows had wondered whether he would have the right to recover stolen horses. Cummings had replied that the matter would be handled by the Indian Agent who'd be appointed for them.

And so it had gone until early evening, when Cummings called a halt. Nothing had been decided. Some boundary disputes had arisen and needed to be hashed out. There'd be more of the same the next morning. Maybe by the next afternoon the chiefs would decide to put their X's on the fated parchment.

The sour odor on the night breeze reminded Skye that soon the Crows would need a new campsite. And so would the rest of the villages. Time was running out.

Victoria and Mary worked quietly a few yards distant, but miles from him in other ways. Jawbone grazed yellow grass out in the herd, chewing on borrowed time. Danger had brought his former family together after a fashion. The women seemed as dour as he, and even the boy seemed unusually silent, as if this were a meeting of old enemies—which perhaps it was. They'd gathered to protect themselves and Jawbone in the one village forbidden the soldiers. Maybe they were all living on borrowed time.

Something brittle in Skye dissolved at the sight of them around a small fire, roasting antelope that Many Coups had provided. They were refugees here. Copper-skinned Victoria muttered and fumed, a familiar bundle of energy and shrewdness, her fierce loyal-

ties shattered and divided now. She would defend
Jawbone to the death. She would kill soldiers if that
was her only option. Skye caught her glancing at him,
pretending not to see him. But he'd lived with her too
long not to know her moods. Something lay broken
and hurt within her. She labored over her fire with an
empty ferocity that concealed nothing.

They had loved. He remembered when they'd both
been young. How they'd laughed. How the sweet wild
days flew. She had turned herself into a warrior
woman as lithe as a cougar. He remembered how
she'd wanted him to take another wife so she'd have
female company and some help with the lodge duties.
So he'd found sweet Mary and she had come to him
shy and eager, proud to be a bride of the lord of the
wilds.

They'd never ceased loving him, caring for him,
comforting him. Even now they were cooking food for
him as if from habit. The hurt etched in Mary's face
was nothing she could hide. She never looked at him
with those choked eyes. She averted her gaze, turned
her back, as if afraid that if their gazes met she might
weep. They'd clung to each other in the soaring
depths of the nights; conceived their son in joy, shared
cold and wet, danger and death so many times he
couldn't count them.

He watched them toil in this counterfeit intimacy,
and felt a stab of pain. These two women could not
provide him with the things he hungered for; they
could not enter his world. He needed that world again
as a whale needed to surface for air.

But there they were, two remarkable women who'd
given themselves to him only to see him turn his back
upon them. He sighed, feeling the bitter amalgam of
ancient love with the hungers that had tormented him
into leaving these wild borders forever.

"Here's your food," said Victoria, handing him a

stick with sizzling meat. "I hope the sonofabitch is burned to a crisp."

"Victoria—"

She waited, her eyes as hard as agates in the firelight.

"Thank you," he muttered.

"Don't thank me, you rotten fish. I ain't done nothing. Thank Many Coups. He's taken care of you."

"Victoria—"

She stopped her muttering and waited for him to unburden himself. He lifted his top hat and settled it into his gummy hair.

"You and Mary and Dirk, you come sit here."

"We're not here because of you, you big drunk. We're here because of Jawbone. That horse, he's worth twenty Skyes."

Skye nodded. He deserved that. Mary stared at him as she squatted beside the fire. "We should talk about that," he muttered.

Victoria squinted at him as if making up her mind were the hardest act she'd ever done. At last she sliced some dripping meat from the haunch and settled close to him. Mary joined them, her face haunted and fearful. Dirk eyed his father solemnly and clung to Mary, afraid of the stranger his father had become. Skye sighed, torn anew.

They ate silently, the walls of hurt between them deafening. Skye ached to say something, anything, but he knew Victoria would mock his words and spit them back at him. Mary toyed with her meat. She'd lost weight. In fact, she'd become gaunt. It puzzled him.

He finished and wiped his fingers in the trampled grass. "Truscott's not done with us. In fact, he's hardly begun," he said. It was the first any of them had spoken in minutes.

"How come the medicine horse is here?" Victoria asked. "You getting dumber in your old age?"

"He wouldn't stay in the Pryors. That's where I took

him. That's where I'll leave him—someday. Likes me
more than the mares." He smiled faintly. "Brought a
whole harem—a bunch of mares—with him, but he
couldn't keep 'em."

Victoria cackled. The Absaroka loved to talk about
anything to do with mating. Mary remained solemn
and hurt, reminded anew of her own wounds.

"I let that pea-brained, cock-rooster sonofabitch
know I'll git him," Victoria said.

"It doesn't work. Truscott doesn't believe anything'll
happen to him. He thinks of his sixty carbines."

"You tell him, I tell him, Many Coups, he tell him,
but he don't hear?"

"Oh, he hears. But he doesn't believe. He thinks he's
bulletproof."

"What you ever do to him, eh? Holy cow! You beat
on him? You poke your smelly feet under his nose?"

"Nothing! But Jawbone killed a bloody fool idiot
corporal that was trying to wreck him."

"You musta done something to this here lieutenant."

"Yes, I suppose I did. I'd guess I held up a looking
glass and he didn't like what he saw."

"You talkin' crazy dumb white man stuff."

"He saw an old wilderness coon, and after that he
had to prove himself. When the beaver days were over
a lot of the old coons went back east to the settle-
ments. I hear there was always a bunch of wharf rats
and pilgrims and pork-eaters pickin' on them, itching
for a fight, itching to prove something to someone
who'd been up the tall Missouri to the shining mountains. We used to call this the Rocky Mountain College
and if you passed you lived and if you flunked you
died. I guess the strutting popinjay over in that mosquito bog of a bivouac is like that. He can't stand this
old child."

"He touches Jawbone and he ain't gonna be a ladies'
man no more. He don't have enough to cut, but I'll cut
it."

"He'll try. I've got to take the outfit back to Laramie. It's in the contract. He's gonna try then."

"I'll take Jawbone back up to the mountains. I'll keep him safe. I'll—"

"He won't stay, Victoria."

That's when Jawbone loomed out of the night and squealed his anger and joy. The Skyes were all together again. Jawbone snorted, grabbed Skye's topper and made off with it, and whinnied, parading around like a scalp dancer. Around them the Crows peered at the Skyes and at the ghostly horse. Jawbone lifted his head, bared his yellow teeth, and screeched at the moon.

"Put out the fire, Mary," Skye said.

But the golden, glowing woman who'd been his younger wife had buried her face in her hands.

# Chapter 39

When the council reconvened the next morning, Chief Washakie summoned Mary. She felt drained. She had spent the hard night in the Crow camp wrestling with her feelings about Mister Skye. For that one night, at least, the whole family had come back together. But they weren't really together at all.

Her rawboned clan-brother greeted her affectionately. "This morning, Blue Dawn, I will make a great speech to the white grandfathers and they will listen like caught doves. We want this treaty with them but we've many doubts. We wish we knew all the things in their heads. They are like the ones who catch beaver. Make sure our words are given to the grandfathers just as we mean them and if you think they are not understanding, stop me and I will use different words."

"I will do that, Chief Washakie. Mister Skye will be listening, too."

The chief nodded. "These are important matters," he

said. "We are talking about the future of the Snake people."

Slowly the Plains nations drifted to the treaty grounds, all wearing their brightest ceremonial costumes. The greatest chiefs settled themselves in the first semicircle around the white men's canvas-covered arbor; then the headmen and lesser chiefs. Beyond them hundreds of others seated themselves.

The superintendent finally rose. "I will call this council to order," he began. "This is the second day. On the first day we read the treaty to you and explained it. We urged you to discuss it carefully among yourselves. On this day we will hear from you. We will consider any changes you propose."

Swiftly, Mary translated this.

"Tell him I will begin," Washakie said. "I want this treaty and I have things to say." The chief of the Wind River Shoshones waited while Mary conveyed this.

Washakie stepped into the trampled space between the white men and the greatest chiefs. He looked proud, Mary thought. Young and strong, with the face of a hawk. He would say what he felt to the grandfathers and they would listen. A great pride in her clanbrother welled up in her.

"Grandfathers and fathers, chiefs of great nations, welcome to the Wind River. I will talk about this treaty. My people want a treaty with the white men. We have always been friends of the white men. We have let the white men make a road and travel through our land and we have not made war upon them. We have many friends among the white men. When the trappers came they married our daughters. Our friend Jim Bridger married one of our daughters. Now he trades with us and we are happy he is our friend. From him we get guns and powder and knives and blankets. These are good things that help us against our enemies the Utes."

Washakie paused while Mary conveyed all this to

the grandfathers and the translators turned Washakie's words into the tongues of the Crows, Arapaho, and Cheyenne, who listened intently. Washakie seemed to be voicing matters of common interest to them all.

"The land of the Snake people is a great land, grandfathers. To the north it runs to the Snake River country and the Pryor Mountains and the land of the Crows. To the west it runs beyond the Salt Lake. To the east it runs to the Bighorns. To the south it runs to the Uinta and Medicine Bow mountains. This is our home and we have held it for a long time. But now the grandfathers want to make some of our land into a common hunting ground. And take away our hot springs just beyond those mountains. We don't like this but we will agree to it if we must. We are concerned because you have cut off much of our land to the west; everything west of the Green River we must give to our enemies the Utes. We would have to cross Ute lands to go to Fort Bridger, where we trade. We do not want this. We're concerned because the Utes are not here to talk about this. We will make an agreement that we must not fight any other nation—but what if the Utes attack us? They are not here to sign this treaty."

While Mary translated, Victorious Cummings made notes on foolscap.

"We don't want the Green River to be the western boundary of the Wind River Shoshones. That is not good, grandfathers. We want the lands of our people to reach to the Salt Lake, where the many-wives white men are. We are friends of the many-wives whites and we trade with them."

Cummings nodded, and scribbled something.

"Now, grandfathers, my people are very hungry. We have no buffalo. The children cry. Many years ago the white men made a wagon road through our land and many wagons and white men went to Oregon. We didn't mind even though they used our grass and wood and killed many buffalo. They were many but we traded with them and made friends."

Washakie paused, letting the grandfathers and chiefs absorb all that. When he spoke again a hardness filled his words, and Mary tried to convey it.

"But then came the great rush to dig the yellow metal of California, and the road through our land was filled with wagons as far as the eye could see, always more wagons all day, all summer. These gold-hungry white men were different. They didn't trade with us and often they shot at us. Grandfathers, they used up our grass and they killed so many buffalo that none were left for us. And their road is so big and crowded that none of the herds would cross it. So the road cut the buffalo herds in two. Some are far to the south; some far to the north. The herds won't come near the Big Road. Grandfathers—my people starve. Babies are hungry. Mothers weep because they have no food for their children. The hunters come back with nothing. We are very sad. The seers sing but the buffalo do not come."

This created a stir among the chiefs. The other nations had experienced much the same thing. The Cheyenne especially listened with approval, nodding to Washakie's words.

"Grandfathers, it's very hard to keep our young men from attacking the wagons. They are angry. Their bellies are empty. But we have always been friends of the white men and I have counseled patience. I have said to them that someday soon our friends the grandfathers will help us. Now you have come and we are pleased to know that you have heard us. But grandfathers, we see nothing in this treaty that brings the buffalo to us or controls the wagons on the Big Road or gives us our grass.

"Your treaty says we will be taught to scratch the earth and plant like white men, and that is good. We must learn these things even if we don't like it. And your treaty says you will give us two hundred of the white men's cattle. We don't like this meat. It is too soft and has no strength in it. We will eat it if we must but it is bad meat. A few of these cows won't help us. We need many thousands to replace the buffalo or we will starve. And if we starve we will become beggars. And if we beg, then there will be nothing left of the Snake people."

This, too, created a stir among the other nations. The superintendent scribbled on his foolscap again.

"Grandfathers," Washakie continued, "this treaty says that your soldiers will protect us from white men. Is this really true? I think the soldiers will protect only the wagons and whites, and not us. We can't control the young men; no chief can. If they are hungry and angry enough, grandfathers, they will not be peaceful no matter what their elders say. Think on this: if we must have the blue-shirts we want them to control the white men and the wagons; keep them close to the medicine road; keep them off our grass; keep them from chopping all our wood. But we would rather not have the blue-shirts on our land. We think the blue-shirts are not going to help us."

Washakie paused. He had addressed the assemblage eloquently, with a voice that carried far out to the crowd. "Grandfathers," he continued quietly, "we want this treaty if it will repay us for all that was taken. We want this treaty if we can learn how to farm and feed ourselves. But if this treaty takes away lands and doesn't pay us we don't want it.

"There is something else we must know: do the soldiers and the grandfathers follow the same path? You grandfathers tell us we are your children and you will care for us. But what of the soldiers? Are the soldiers for us or against us? The treaty says they will defend us from evil white men—but will they? We must know these things."

Washakie paused amid the utter silence, and then

walked swiftly to his place in the circle of the chiefs.
Mary saw the glow pouring out of him. This young
chief shone like the sun at dawn. After the translators
had finished no one spoke. The great question hung
heavily in the furnace air: would the soldiers enforce
the treaty against their own kind?

Mary was proud of her clan-brother; he had been
wise and strong, thoughtful and friendly. She smiled
at him, her heart filled with excitement.

Victorious Cummings arose slowly from his groaning camp chair and made his stately way into the sunlight. "We will address these matters after we have
heard from the other chiefs. Our friend Chief Washakie has raised important points and we appreciate his
spirited talk. Now then, may we hear from any other
who wishes to speak for or against the treaty?"

Mary studied the silent chiefs, who all seemed to be
waiting for something. Then, quietly, Many Coups of
the Absaroka people walked proudly into the no-
man's-land before the white men's arbor. He looked
strong and powerful. He had an aura, a bear medicine
about him that made him look like a grizzly. Victoria's
bird-people were a great nation. And what he said
would be important to them all: everyone knew that
this treaty hinged upon the Absaroka people. If these
old friends of the whites would sign it then the others
would, too.

"Grandfathers," he said in a roaring voice. "And
great chiefs of great nations. Hear my words."

# Chapter 40

The Crow leader was barrel-chested, bandy-legged, and much older than the Shoshone chief. Many Coups' voice was harsher, too, Lieutenant Truscott thought. The powerful Crow spoke in staccato bursts. Skye's woman caught the angry thread in her translation. The chief probably had a scalp shirt with twenty or thirty locks dangling from it.

"The Absaroka people have always called the Bighorn basin our own," he was saying. "And now we are asked to share this country. We don't want to share it. Many deer and antelope and buffalo live there. But we heard our brother Washakie say that he will let go of it, so the Absaroka people will let go also—as long as we can hunt there."

He paused, letting fat Cummings make a note.

"Now, we don't like this part of the treaty that says we will have forts and soldiers on our lands. On the one hand this treaty says this will be our land forever and no one else's. But another part of this treaty says we must let white men come through and let them build roads and railroads. I have never seen a railroad but I am told it is like the fireboats crawling over the land. Ah! We don't want this! We don't want the soldier forts on our land. The treaty says this is to protect us from white men. Haiyah! The forts and soldiers are not going to protect the Absaroka people!"

Skye's old woman seemed to enjoy that. She snapped out Many Coups' thoughts in volleys, catching all his savage rage, dancing as she spoke. It amused Truscott.

"We do not know about this treaty. My chiefs have talked and talked but we do not know. We are blind! Like Washakie, we wonder what the soldiers think about the Indians. Do they look down the barrels of guns at us? We have talked this over and we have decided what to do: this evening we will invite the young soldier-chief to feast with us and we will talk with him. We will ask him what the soldiers plan to do. We will find out if the soldiers will protect us from bad white men."

Many Coups was addressing Truscott. The lieutenant discovered that he was being scrutinized by countless eyes. A banquet squatting on the grass with savages stinking of bear grease tonight. The thought annoyed him. He'd had his eyes on Skye's younger squaw all morning and he'd planned to have her tonight. Last night, damn her, she'd stayed in the Crow village where he couldn't get at her. But tonight! He'd push that white doeskin dress up her golden legs and grasp a fistful of that straight blue-black hair to hold her to the earth ... He sighed, irritated. No, tonight he'd be sitting at a savage banquet munching on dog and watching the chiefs pluck graybacks from their grease-slicked hair and eat them. Then he'd have to answer stupid questions.

"We want this treaty with the white men. We aren't as many lodges as the Siksika or the Lakota so we need guns. But that is another problem. If they attack us or steal our horses what are the Absaroka to do? If they kill our men and take our women and children shall we let them because we have agreed to this treaty? Haiyah! The grandfathers have no treaty with the Siksika so they can do whatever they want to us. Is this right? The white men's treaty with the Lakota hasn't stopped them from attacking us. The soldiers don't stop the Lakota, even though the Lakota have made the peace treaty. Is that right? We wonder about this treaty.

"We will stop making war—except maybe the young men. No one can stop the young men. But we want to know what the soldiers will do and why they will build forts in our land. Maybe we will all become slaves.

"So we will question this young soldier-chief tonight and when the sun comes we will decide whether we want this treaty."

Victoria finished up as the powerful chief returned to his seat in the circle of head chiefs, and waited.

Truscott smiled tightly. Maybe he could make something of this if he put his mind to it. He'd never been to a savage feast before. Maybe they'd serve him some of those loose Crow women.

"Lieutenant Truscott," Cummings whispered privately, "we'll expect you to be on your mettle."

"I'll go," Truscott said, pulling out of his reverie. "Squaw, tell the big famous magnificent noble chief I'll be there."

Victoria stared long at him and then translated.

Many Coups nodded curtly. Then the fatman prattled on again:

"My chiefs, we have yet to hear from the Arapaho and the Bannocks. And of course we are interested in the views of the Cheyenne. When we have heard all your requests we shall consider changes. But the grandfathers have drawn this treaty very carefully to ensure fairness. We won't make many changes but we will consider each of these things. We urge you to accept what we have offered. Then the grandfathers will be happy with you and shower you with many good gifts. If you do not sign the treaty, your grandfathers will be very angry with you and will not give you the many gifts that were brought here."

Truscott listened irritably for another hour. The oratory of that windbag Cummings was getting more laborious than the famous oratory of the chiefs. Truscott's gaze fell upon Mary. He admired the slenderness of her calves, the lushness of her hips and breasts, and her honey flesh and berry eyes. The Bannocks, she was saying, wanted more treaty goods and a larger home with better access to the buffalo prairies. Truscott yawned. The Northern Arapaho liked their proposed grassy homeland but were worried about white migration along the South Platte, and wanted it forbidden. "White men, the puppy-dog-eaters don't want you!" Truscott laughed softly as he listened to the translation.

His gaze never strayed from Mary. She bewitched him. He'd never had a savage before and he suspected she would be mad with delight. The white women he'd seduced had all possessed banked fires. Now he'd try a savage, raised as nature intended, without all the restraints of civilization to inhibit her. No wonder Skye had taken her; she was a woman made for only one thing. Truscott wanted her all the more because she had been Skye's. To take her would be like gelding the old rogue.

Cummings was calling an end to this session, and just in time. The treaty ground had turned into a frying pan and the stink of sweat permeated the air. "In the morning we will meet. Maybe we will all sign the treaty. Talk it over in your councils now. The grandfathers will consider your changes. Tomorrow, after we sign, we will give you all the gifts we brought in the wagons: rifles and powder, pots and pans, knives, awls, blankets, beads, cloth—all yours tomorrow."

Cummings mopped his brow. Sweat had wilted and begrimed his starched collar. He nodded to his Indian Bureau people and they headed for the shade of some riverbank box elders, to redraft the document. "Lieutenant, you'd better join us. We've things to discuss."

"That's right. Do squaws wear underwear?"

Cummings paused, gazed soberly at the lieutenant, and lumbered to his waiting carriage.

Skye and the old hag wandered off with the Crows; Skye's young squaw joined the Shoshones, a good sign. Truscott watched her as she walked beside the chiefs, talking animatedly with them. Good. She'd be in her own village tonight. A village where soldiers were welcome. He knew the lodge: he'd ferreted that out. Her father lived there with a pair of lusty old sluts.

Truscott walked across the trampled flat toward his bivouac, feeling the brass sun wring sweat from him. He wanted some time to himself.

He plunged into his hot tent, the smell of heated canvas rank in the dead air. He pulled off his shirt and scratched at mosquito bites. The stupid Pope had bivouacked at the edge of a slough that bred the pests. He flopped into his canvas cot and contemplated the banquet. He'd swallow a little coyote, munch some bitter weeds, devour some rancid buffalo fat, and make history. Tonight a shavetail lieutenant would advance his career several notches. They didn't drop their drawers for lieutenants. Captain didn't mean much except hardship; major was the ultimate rank of benchwarmers and incompetents. But colonel . . . colonel was the aphrodisiac rank.

# Chapter 41

The wind had stopped and the dead air was super-charged with heat. Wellington Waterloo Cummings thought it might storm violently though the sky still seemed as innocent as a baby's eyes. He had abandoned his clerical collar. It was hard enough to subsist in this inferno in a black cotton shirt.

He walked past soldiers hiding from the brassy sun and paused at last before Truscott's wall tent. The cream and scarlet regimental and company guidons dangled lifelessly from a staff before it.

"Ah, Mister Truscott."

Nearby, Pope sat up and then settled himself again.

Truscott stirred and then squinted out at the divine. "Ah. You are here to instruct me."

"Well, no, actually. I thought we might go fishing. There's trout in the Little Wind if I can believe my eyes."

"I'm no sportsman, Cummings."

"A walk, then? There's some shade along the river farther up."

Truscott ran a hand through his silky Vandyke. "You want something. The Indian Bureau has designs. Very well, I'll walk."

"No, the Bureau asks nothing of you."

"I see. You're going to approach this by indirection then. You have designs on me one way or another. Let me get my forage cap."

Wellington waited. Truscott emerged with his cap pinioning his blond locks. They walked silently through the bivouac and past the Indian Bureau's camp.

"We have the advantage of you when it comes to mosquitoes," Wellington said. "Poor Victorious thinks he contributes more than enough flesh to their field of honor."

"Their field of honor?"

"A mosquito approaches flesh in peril of its life, sir. A lily-livered mosquito never draws blood."

"Why have you plucked me from my siesta? Not to theologize, I hope."

"That's my calling. Everything—literally everything—harks back to theology, Truscott."

"It's Mister Truscott, sir."

Wellington laughed. "I wanted to tell you, friend Truscott, what we're going to do. We agree with Washakie that the Green River's a poor boundary line. We're going to eliminate that from the draft and let that boundary remain unsettled, pending a treaty with the Utes. But we're going to stand firm about the forts. The tribes'll just have to get used to it. They're right, of course. The forts'll discourage the tribes from ever warring upon us again. That should please you."

"Why should it? I'm a lowly lieutenant, Reverend. Is this the purpose of this little walk?"

"Actually, the superintendent wanted me to sound you out. He didn't send me to instruct you, if that's what you're worrying about. He knows how little any of us could persuade a strong young man. But he thought perhaps you'd help us come to some understanding of your intent. You're a loyal officer and we don't doubt you'd like to see the Bureau restored to the War Department."

"My intent is to cooperate, sir. My orders are to secure the Indian Bureau personnel, transport them, and assist them in achieving their mission."

Wellington laughed quietly. "Very well, then. I'll convey your honorable intent to the superintendent."

"Are we done with our little walk, Reverend? I've a difficult evening before me among savages who'd as soon scalp me as talk, eating dog soup and grubs, and smelling the excrement of the stinking village. And they'll no doubt have Skye translating. Or that old hag."

"Oh no, let's walk some more. These cottonwoods make a pleasant arbor, I think. You seem to have some sort of antagonism toward the guide."

"Scum of the earth. I'd as soon see him behind bars."

"Because he jumped a British ship?"

"That and his arrogance and crookedness and incompetence."

"You must see things in him others don't. You know, they esteem him at Fort Laramie. Colonel Hoffman says he's the best man around. Chouteau down in St. Louis—they employed him for years—says there's none finer. That's how the Bureau got him. A dozen good men spoke for him—Robert Campbell, the fur man. Tom Fitzpatrick, another fur man who's with the Bureau now. Old Bridger. Well, Lieutenant, what do you see in him the others don't? Or what do they see in him that you're missing?"

Truscott scowled at him. "I'm just a young officer, and I know my views have no weight compared to such distinguished—"

"No, no, they count. We want to know what you think. You've a personal grievance of some sort against Skye and we've never grasped what it is. It's important to us because he's bound up with the tribes and our success or failure here. You've some sort of design on the man and his horse, and it affects us."

"I knew there was a reason for this stupid walk."

"Well, sit then. There's a log ahead. We can sit and watch the river."

They sat beside the Little Wind, a cold stream rushing its burdens out of the mountains. Truscott had drawn into himself and stared sullenly at the river as if performing a duty. Wellington waited, hoping the young man would talk about Skye, even a little. But Truscott sat rigidly, those wounded eyes gazing forward, a nervous tic spasming the muscles of his cheek.

"My father named me for the Great Duke and the great battle he'd won," Wellington said. "It was a good choice. Not because I emulate the Iron Duke—the man was a bullheaded tyrant. But because of something the man said that haunted me and turned me toward the seminary. His Waterloo dispatch said—now consider this—it said, 'Nothing except a battle lost can be half so melancholy as a battle won.' Think on it."

"That's an excuse never to strive."

"Do I seem to be a man who's never strived, Truscott? No, no, it's about prices. Prices and consequences for our every act. All our acts, but especially those we might define as battles. Every victory is a tragedy, except divine victories. Do you think no man regrets what he did to succeed? Ah, the deathbed remorse, the confessions I've heard—"

"There you go, theologizing."

"Ah, Truscott. A young man sets his sights on a mountaintop and races toward it scarcely knowing who's hurt along the way. He sets his cap for a lady scarcely knowing what other young ladies and gentlemen are hurt."

"I don't like your defeatist philosophy, Reverend. I'll

have what I want; I do what I set out to do and never mind the consequences."

"I'll tell you a paradox, Truscott. That'll get you less far upon the path of life than ordinary prudence would fetch you. It's a delusion of the young. I'll tell you what life's about. It's about shaping our character, refining the dross from our nature. Controlling our weaknesses and vices, strengthening our virtues and employing them. That's the only purpose of living. Every other goal is melancholy in the end, as Wellesley—ah, Wellington—perceived after his victory. Wealth, power, fame, advancement—those are melancholy goals. A man can choose higher purposes and end up happier."

"Are you done?" Truscott stood impatiently.

"No, not really. I've digressed. We want to know what your intent is. Skye, I mean. The horse. It's critical to us."

"You'll have your treaty, Reverend."

"And after the treaty?"

"I'm at your service."

"You don't answer."

"I'm tired of being grilled like a common private."

Petulantly the lieutenant marched back toward camp, letting the reverend trail behind. Truscott stalked the riverbank, scarcely noticing the glory of the wilderness, the sweetwater creek tumbling toward the Gulf of Mexico; the thick chokecherry brush with its still-green fruit, the dart of the saucy magpies. He passed through robust and healthy land like a lethal disease, a shadow hiding the sun, a cold caldron of vices passing through an innocent place, leaving a chill in the air. Odd how the man exuded sickness, an oppressed spirit, dark and hungry design.

Truscott's hatred of Skye seemed as unfathomable as ever. Neither Victorious nor Wellington could penetrate to its roots. Wellington wondered whether the darkness sprang from something bleak and cruel lurking beneath the young man's veneer like a blotch on the soul. The young man would have his terrible victory over Skye. And little did he grasp what a melancholy victory it would be. A man so secretive and obsessed would be hard to stop. Not even Skye, with all his wilderness wiles, could defend himself.

# Chapter 42

A Kit Fox Society warrior led Truscott into view. Skye sighed. The lieutenant had indiscreetly worn a holstered revolver and a saber, deliberately gauding himself with instruments of war.

The great chiefs of the Absaroka people had seated themselves in a circle well away from the village, in a grass park among the ancient cottonwoods along the Wind River. Beside them a haunch of buffalo boss ribs sizzled on a spit, tended by several women. The chiefs wore their badges of office because this amounted to a state dinner.

Skye watched Truscott's progress with the tiniest worm of fear building in him. One shot from that revolver, one thrust of the saber could kill him. The man would be mad to attempt it, but reason did nothing to comfort Skye's gnawing worry. The Kit Fox warrior stopped short of the circle, and Truscott advanced primly.

"Have a seat, Lieutenant," Skye said. "We've a treat. Some of the hunters found a few buffler up a valley."

"Better than grubs and boiled dog," Truscott said. He lowered himself to the grass in a gap in the circle obviously meant for him, wrestling his saber until it poked out behind like a silver tail.

Rottentail's eyes asked Skye for a translation and Skye diplomatically said that the young warrior chief preferred buffalo to other things. But Many Coups was scowling faintly: the chief passably understood English even though he never spoke it.

The sizzle and smoke of the roasting meat drifted among them, building hunger in Skye's belly. He'd get a fine feast out of this anyway. The last thing he'd wanted was to translate but Many Coups had insisted. Victoria, distrustful as ever, had filtered into the twilight to guard Jawbone. She'd muttered that it would be just like Truscott to plot something that would happen while he dined with Absaroka chiefs.

Truscott was a pretty man, Skye thought, privately echoing Cummings's thoughts. A pretty man with pretty horses. The lieutenant looked dashing. The late light lit his silky Vandyke, vanished into his troubled eyes, and caught his proud, pursed lips, the cant of his head, and the poses. Now that Skye studied Truscott he grew aware of the poses, the theatrical postures, the stiffness of a body held in a way to make impressions, to turn young ladies into idolators and men into grubs. Truscott was like an actor playing Caesar.

The posing explained a lot about the man. Truscott was simply self-obsessed. His career, his quarters, his conquests, were all a shrine to himself. Skye began to fathom just what his own offense was: he was real.

"I don't believe you've met these chiefs," Skye said. "On my right is Many Coups, who's your host tonight. Next to him is The Big Robber of the Whistling Water band, perhaps the greatest of the Absaroka chiefs. These people have no hierarchy; a chief's wisdom and medicine and gift-giving make him important."

The Big Robber knew he was being introduced and

nodded. He wore for this occasion a single eagle feather, white with a black tip, tucked into a hairknot at the back of his head. He wore a large medicine bundle on his coppery chest. A terrible scar ridged and puckered over his left shoulder.

Swiftly Skye introduced Truscott to Bear's Head, wrinkled and gray, the oldest of the great chiefs; and to Rottentail, whose single braid, gauded with German-silver conchae, fell behind him to the grass; and then to young and energetic Two Face, who had a high receding forehead and a sharp, disconcerting gaze.

Many Coups rose, spoke swiftly, and clapped hands. Instantly squaws began sawing off succulent, steaming chunks of tender hump heat from the boss ribs of the young cow.

"He says welcome, soldier-chief. Eat now, and then the Absaroka will ask you many things. That's humpmeat, mate, and this child thinks it's prime."

Swiftly the plainly dressed women, most in shapeless calico, loaded wooden trenchers with steaming slabs of pink-and-brown meat, which stabbed dizzying odors into the quiet air. Then they added strips of buffalo backfat that had been roasted until it was crisp and buttery. Using horn ladles, they dished out a soup of buffalo fat, prairie turnips, and greens from a black iron kettle into sheep's-horn bowls and handed them out. Truscott accepted his daintily, and set it on the earth, wiping his smooth, slender fingers in the grass.

"It sure looks pretty," said Skye. "Eat up, mate. Stab the meat with your sticker or use your digits."

The chiefs beamed and laughed among themselves. No Absaroka failed to enjoy a feast, especially one featuring the best parts of a buffalo cow. "See how he eats," said Rottentail in his own tongue as he popped succulent pink meat between his teeth, using his fingers.

"Like a butterfly," Two Face said.

"They're talking about me, Skye?"

"They admire your manners, Lieutenant."

Truscott lacked a knife so he hunched forward, gnawing off juicy tidbits, trying not to let them drip onto his britches.

Skye belched happily, feeling his gut swell with good meat. A buffalo roast was as good as any way to promote peace, he thought. The chiefs obviously did, too, nattering among themselves and largely ignoring their guest. Truscott didn't ask for a translation, and just as well. But at last, all the chiefs, red and white, had had their fill. They wiped greasy fingers in the bunchgrass, tossed gristle to the whining camp dogs, and settled into a quietness.

Many Coups addressed Skye, and Skye translated. "He wants to know where white men keep their women," Skye said. "They've seen a heap of white men but no ladies."

"The women enjoy the comforts of cities," Truscott said. "They'll come along when we build cities—big villages."

"Ah, they are going to build big villages here!" exclaimed Rottentail. "Then we'll see women. Now we lend them ours."

The chiefs wheezed cheerfully.

"Yes, the soldiers come with ribbons and our squaws desert us and go to the bushes," said Bear's Head. "This is a good thing. When the white women come we'll try them out. Maybe they'll like us better."

Skye translated patiently to the purse-lipped lieutenant.

"Tell them that they won't have white women; white women won't have them," Truscott said.

Skye paused, and translated carefully.

The chiefs smiled. The Big Robber said, "Ah, wait until we play the love flutes. Then we'll see."

But even as they chortled, Many Coups redirected

the talk. "Ask the young chief why the white men want to build forts in our nation."

Truscott answered smoothly: "To keep you peaceful. The soldiers will see to it that no Indian tribes wage war upon white men."

Skye translated, thinking the answer was candid. The chiefs listened amiably.

"Now that makes sense," The Big Robber said. "I can understand that. There's not much about white men I understand, but I understand their war."

"Are the People the enemies of the white soldiers?" asked Many Coups.

"When they kill or rob whites. Then we punish them."

"Well, that's what we do," said Two Face. "We revenge ourselves, and satisfy honor."

"We used to talk with the soldier-chiefs. Now we talk to these grandfathers in black clothing. Which are better for us? The soldier-chiefs or the grandfathers?"

Skye quietly translated. Truscott was fielding tough, penetrating questions. The Absaroka had a canny grasp on the nature of white men, he thought. Far better than Truscott's grasp of Indians.

"The soldier-chiefs," Truscott said at once, after hearing Skye. "The grandfathers will not give you what my government wants you to have. Their clerks sell stuff to my men, and my men use it to buy the favors of your women. But my government wants you to have these things as gifts. No, the grandfathers are not good for you. I wish Congress hadn't taken the Bureau—" He stared helplessly at Skye. "Tell them the clerks are grafters; that they're better off when the Indian Bureau is run by the War Department."

Skye did, having trouble conveying these ideas to the chiefs. But Many Coups, at least, nodded. He and Skye had had many a talk about the white men in the East.

"When the white people come and kill our buffalo

will the soldiers come and chase us away, or chase them away?"

"The soldiers'll chase you away because they'll always side with white men," Truscott replied. "The white people will expect the soldiers to help them when they come."

"That's what we thought. Aah! We don't believe this treaty that says the blue-shirts will protect us from white men," muttered The Big Robber. "It makes no sense. The grandfathers are fooling us. We know that."

Truscott smiled faintly, relieving his pout for the first time. "I am more honest with you. I'm a soldier-chief."

"Ah, yes. A chief. What are your war honors?" asked Bear's Head. "What enemies have you fought? Pawnee? French? How many have you killed? You must have killed a hundred to be a chief."

Truscott pursed his lips. His quick, hurt eyes glanced this way and that. "Not a hundred, my friends."

"He says he hasn't killed a hundred," said Skye to the Crows, with faint humor.

The chiefs laughed.

# Chapter 43

Chief Many Coups stood abruptly, and spoke to Skye.

"He says you'll go now, mate. That warrior will take you out of the village."

"That's it? Don't they want to know more?" Truscott asked.

"They just wanted to take a gander at you. They'll talk over what you told 'em. You did your best, didn't you."

"I what?"

"Talked 'em out of signing. It'll get back to the Indian Bureau, you know."

"There you go, Skye, impugning my motives."

"You probably failed. Crow're pinched between Sioux and Blackfeet. They need the forts and soldiers to survive. They figure the blue-shirts'll defend their borders. They like having some soldiers around."

"But—" Truscott thought he'd torpedoed the treaty. "Tell them—" He thought better of it. The chiefs eyed him quietly while Many Coups waited for him to leave. He stared at Skye. "Did you tell them what I said? Obviously you didn't."

"Exactly, mate. Anyway, Many Coups understands English well enough."

Many Coups nodded. "I talk it," he said, staring at the lieutenant.

Truscott stalked through the lively village, seeing what seemed to be a social hour, tribesmen gathered in cheerful circles while the blue light of evening lingered across the west. Something had gone wrong. The Crows knew they were dealing with the corrupt Indian Bureau but they were still inclined to sign. Maybe Indians were invincibly stupid.

His escort left him out on the plain a hundred yards from the village, a mile from his bivouac. The soft twilight reminded him it wasn't late. He stood in sudden silence, the breeze still, the birdsongs gone for the night, dry grasses mute. Now was the time. He turned toward the Shoshone village up the Wind River, walking lightly, his mind and loins swelling with the thought of luscious Mary. She'd been staring at him at the council; once or twice their eyes had locked, and he'd averted his gaze. She wanted him and now she'd have him.

He walked jauntily past Shoshone night guards, past looming cones of cowhide, their blackened tops jabbing at the first stars. Men and women lounged in the grasses, gossiping and laughing. No one worked much on a fine summer's eve, when the coy cool air eddied out of the mountains. He headed past Washakie's lodge, curiously unheralded by lances, medicine tripods, or other ensigns common among the Plains tribes. Old men watched him. Women averted their eyes. This tribe had one foot on the Plains and one in the mountains, and seemed different somehow, quieter and poorer.

He found her lodge. He had reconnoitered Washakie's village several times and knew she lived on the outermost ring of lodges close to the river. She was staying with an older man and woman who were probably her parents, and some others. He found them all, and a dozen more he'd never seen, squatting in a circle before the lodge. Skye's brat sprawled beside her. Truscott studied the little mixed-breed bastard, seeing the stupidity in its face. Mixed-bloods were all defective. Mary gazed up at him as he loomed over him. They all were curious.

"Ah, I've found you, Mrs. Skye. The grandfathers—ah, they need you. A matter of the translation."

She intuitively translated this to all her relatives and friends before she answered him. "I will come when the sun rises," she said.

"No, the superintendent needs you now."

"Let him come here and talk to Washakie. I will translate."

Stymied. He grinned. "Come along, and we'll talk about things. Like Skye. Or the horse. Maybe we can come to some pleasant understanding. Maybe I'll forget about the horse."

She paused, and then said something to the silent Shoshones. The man Truscott took to be her father stared unblinkingly at him as if to memorize Truscott's face. The lieutenant didn't mind. He'd put much thought and effort into his face. His golden hair hung down, framing his lean countenance. It made him glow, seem somehow magical to the beholder.

She rose, and he watched her lush breasts shift under a loose doeskin dress of clay-whited leather that had been worked as soft as velvet. He felt desire thicken in him.

She joined him wordlessly. The mention of Skye had done it. Skye was the magnet, the fishhook, the snare for any Plains Indian. He led her through the amiable village past a few coals still gnawing at cottonwood, emitting a sour smoke. Past a few quiet men with long lances standing away from the village in the bunch-grass, watching a batch of malformed ponies.

She followed along while he walked briskly into the thickening dark, the heavy throbbing dusk matching the swelling of his loins. All his weight had gathered there, weighing a ton, as if boulders hung from his belly. It was a mile and a half to the bivouac across the long angle of the rivers but he didn't plan to walk that far. There'd be no brush, no canebrake, not even a ditch on the flats to conceal them, but the swift dark that cloaked the animal acts of man and beast would wrap them like a buffalo robe. Not even a cricket needled the silence.

He paused, letting her catch up, feeling the tickle of sensation in his fingers as he anticipated the feel of her heavy breasts. His pulse elevated and the stones below his belly weighed like shot-tower lead in a bag. He had never carried such weight before, cannon balls dragging every muscle of his torso.

"You wished to speak to me about Mister Skye and Jawbone," she said coolly, her lips turned down. "I will listen now."

"Ah yes, Skye. You're better off without him."

She said nothing.

"You need a man. It's obvious from your—condition." He felt her gaze upon him and smiled. "I'm glad you enjoy me. It pleases me."

"What about Jawbone?"

"What about it?"

"You said—maybe something could be agreed, is it so?"

He smiled. "If you want it to be so. It depends on you. Do you like me?"

He stopped walking and faced her. "I always knew you wanted me," he said. "I could see it." He lifted his forage cap, letting his blond hair fall loosely, framing his manly chiseled face.

She stopped, too, facing him. "I will go back now."

He clamped a hand over her smooth wrist, feeling the young flesh his fingers tingled for. His pulse galloped. She didn't struggle but drew a sharp breath and peered around her. Utterly alone. Off on horizons, dim worms of light lit the villages.

"Red women are exciting, full of life," he muttered. "I know what you want."

"Tell me about Jawbone," she said tautly.

"Oh, you won't have to worry anymore. Forget Skye—he's gone. Forget the horse. I'll give you better."

He drew her firmly toward him until he felt her curved hot body press into him, felt the heaviness of her breasts. "I will go now," she said and pulled back, putting coldness between them.

He didn't let go. "You want this. All squaws want it."

"You are a liar, soldier-chief," she whispered. "I thought it was for Jawbone."

"It's me you want, Madame Skye. Admit it. You can have me if you never mention Jawbone again. You must do as I say. There are things I like." He laughed and spun her into him again, feeling the massive weight at the foot of his belly grow to the bursting. She seemed to melt into him and he knew the fight was over. A squaw's lusts couldn't be contained. Happily, he drew her hand toward the clamorous ten-ton weight.

The knee banged hard into him, collapsing him forward into her. He gasped. Heavy pain shot through his loins. Tons and tons of weight vanished even as the pain radiated outward in red shafts. He sputtered and drew her close with one hand while the other clamped his groin. He thought he'd die of pain.

She wrestled with him silently, pulling back, but he hung on, snickering madly while pain sent red streaks through his brain. She lunged forward, surprising him. He staggered back, putting air between them. Her moccasin hit him and the red pain turned white. He gasped, all the weight gone from him. He folded, clawing at his groin with both hands to protect it. He felt another blow but it hit his thigh as he tumbled into the grass.

He sobbed and gasped and hated the tears in his eyes. "Slut! Leading me on," he gasped, both his hands clamped over his manhood.

He felt his head being yanked; her hand clamped his blond hair and twisted. His chin snapped forward. He clawed at her with one hand while the other guarded his glass beads. She was sawing, slicing.

Being scalped! He squirmed, inflaming the caldron below, and groaned. He felt the tug and rip as she worked his hair and then suddenly his head dropped. Cool air eddied about his ears. Scalped. He peered about but she'd vanished into the dark. He lifted a hand to his head expecting to find stinging bone, a circle of ragged flesh, and blood all over his fingers. But he found nothing like that, only the stubs of the hair she'd hacked free. She'd chopped off his hair.

# Chapter 44

Lieutenant Truscott curled in the grass, the heavy pain lancing in all directions. He was going to vomit and crawled up on all fours. His stomach convulsed in cataclysmic heaves but nothing came of it and each spasm drove pain into his skull. He lay back in the grass, panting, and waited for what seemed forever, until it didn't hurt so much. He wanted to walk back to his camp but the slightest movement convulsed him again.

He probed his head, sickened by what he felt. Some of his hair still hung in long waves but elsewhere it had been chopped off at the scalp. She'd slashed and sliced from one ear to the other while he lay crumpled in white agony. His hair! How he'd loved his long hair! Without it he felt baby-weak. She'd hit his private parts twice and barely missed a third time, then stolen his hair like the Devil steals souls.

He clambered to his feet at last, choked down nausea, and walked. Every step tortured him but he con-

tinued gamely until at last he crawled into his wall
tent. He fumbled about until he found his field desk,
extracted a candle, and lit it with a lucifer. He found
his hand mirror and beheld himself. It was worse than
he imagined in the darkness: hair chopped and sliced,
long and short. His face looked lumpy and coarse
without its gilded frame. The pain had wrought
blotches in his flesh and bagged his eyes. He straightened the vagrant strands, his slender fingers gentle as
a nun's hands upon the dying. He would have to scis-
sor the rest off as best he could, even up the carnage
and wait, wait for months to recover his glory. He'd be
back at Leavenworth long before that, to his regret.

He slumped back, hating her. She would pay, not
only for this but for scorning his advances. Few
women ever had, least of all a red slut.

Slowly he trimmed the remaining locks. But he
couldn't bring order to the wreckage, not when the
woman's dull knife had slashed hair right at its roots.
That eliminated one explanation that had been forming in his mind: that he'd chosen to cut it himself. He
couldn't conceal the truth. But yes, he could temper it
a little, keep the enlisted men from laughing up their
sleeves. A story formed: he'd been jumped by half a
dozen warriors—no, make it ten—who'd pinned him
to earth after a brawl and had counted coup with their
skinning knives. Yes, that would do. Shoshones, too.
Ten Shoshones counting coup, seething with hatred for
white men, dancing fiendishly about him.

Tomorrow at dawn he'd slip out there and recover
his shorn hair; he didn't want the savages to find it.

He slept fitfully. His body remembered its hurts
whenever he moved. In milky predawn light he
jammed down his forage cap, marched past a staring
sentry—they'd know soon enough anyway, he
thought—and headed across the empty flat. But he
couldn't find the spot and he couldn't find the hair.
He meandered about, worked in widening circles

through sagebrush and buffalo grass, and found nothing. Defeated, he stalked back to his camp past awakening men who gaped at him. His heartbeat lifted. He would have to say something fast.

"Pope!" he snarled.

The top sergeant crawled from his shelter sleepily.

"Come in here."

Pope, in his fragrant longjohns, followed Truscott into the officer's tent. Awake now, Pope gaped, obviously suppressing amusement.

"I was jumped last night by ten Shoshone bucks. They were counting coup. Wrestled me down and cut it. Tell the men right now, not at roll call. I don't want a snicker out of them. I'll have more instructions later. I can't let this—this insult to the United States Dragoons go unpunished."

"Yassah. You look right handsome, sah. How do you know they were Shoshones?"

"Out!"

The longjohns vanished. Truscott sat on his cot devising punishments for the Shoshones. Now that he'd identified the Shoshones as the culprits he'd have to rebuke them or give the lie to his words.

He had to report the incident to Cummings, too, and warn Cummings that there'd be reprisals. He chose to do that himself. Warily, he crushed his forage cap over his shorn head and walked to the Indian Bureau camp, ignoring the stares.

He found the Cummings brothers and clerks at morning mess. They stared at him solemnly and then stared at their johnnycakes.

"There was an incident. Ten Shoshone bucks caught me last night—and counted coup. I can't let this go unpunished."

"What happened? Try this slower," said Victorious Cummings.

"I was jumped in the dark out on the flats. They

surrounded me, wrestled me down, and—cut the hair."

"You sure it was Shoshones?"

"Of course I am."

"What provoked them?" -

"Their hot savage natures."

Cummings looked doubtful. "Something must have set them off, Lieutenant. Is this the whole story?"

"Are you implying that—"

"No, no, no. But I'd like to talk you out of taking rash actions. We expect to sign a treaty today."

"I'll do what's necessary, Major. If they don't respect the United States Army we're all in trouble."

Cummings rose. "I'm sorry this happened. I'm sure you feel offended and embarrassed. It's an insult to your person. But Lieutenant, take hold of yourself. We've larger matters to attend to, matters of great moment . . . Please ignore this, ah, episode, and we'll complete our business. Four tribes willing to sign, if the whispers coming to my ears are true. A great moment, sir, in our diplomacy with the Plains tribes. You understand."

"No, that's not what is going to happen. The Army'll punish those bucks."

"You say this happened at night? How do you know who they were?"

"I know them. I could point to every one."

Skepticism slid across Cummings's face. "You were thrown to the ground at night, you say. You struggled. Yet you can identify these warriors? I don't think so, Lieutenant."

"I'll know most of them when I see them."

"Mister Truscott—this is a matter for me to take up with Chief Washakie. He'll be able to come up with your assailants easily, and they'll come over here and offer their apologies. That'll be the end of it."

"No, that's not the end of it."

Cummings stared. "I won't have some shorn

hair—no matter how embarrassing that may be to you, sir—disrupt the peace we're creating here. I'd strongly advise you to forget it. No permanent harm done. It'll all grow out."

"No harm done! They counted coup! They'll defy white men now."

Cummings shook his head. "No harm done, sir. A minor incident coming at a historic moment."

"You don't understand. They counted coup. Don't you grasp what that means to the United States Army?"

Hot rage boiled through Truscott. He knew what he was going to do, Cummings or not. He was going to corral ten Shoshone bucks and hang them.

"I'm sorry, Mister Truscott. I must direct that you do nothing. I'm sorry it comes to this. I'll bring the matter to Chief Washakie's attention immediately after the treaty is concluded. I'll hear him out. And then, perhaps, we can withhold some of the treaty gifts we'd allocated for the Shoshones. That'll satisfy your honor, satisfy the Army, and keep it all in perspective. That's the key to it, Lieutenant. Keep this in perspective."

"Is that your order? I respectfully dissent."

"Record it in your log, sir, and let it be settled in the East. As long as I'm in charge, yes, it's my instruction. I want no retaliation of any sort. I'll deal with Washakie."

"He'll invent stories; they all invent stories, whatever suits them." Truscott knew that the Shoshones would have a different version of the episode. He began to sweat.

"Mister Truscott, if some warriors have dishonored the Shoshones, the chief will rebuke them. You don't need to. Just what sort of retaliation do you have in mind, eh?"

"Why—I haven't devised one yet."

Cummings's stare seemed to bore through him. The man was reading him all too well. "Well, don't devise one," he said quietly. "And Lieutenant. Please keep your soldiers away from the council today. This is the crucial hour. They'll tell us whether they'll sign, and if they will, we'll be about it at once. I especially don't want armed soldiers around."

Truscott knew he was in big trouble if Cummings talked to Washakie. He would be in trouble if the Skye squaw started talking. He needed time to think. Time to act.

"Yessir," he said in a choked voice, and stalked away, feeling the stares on his back.

# Chapter 45

Clutching her golden treasure, Mary hurried back to the Shoshone village. Her heart sang. She had big medicine clamped in her fist. She was a great warrior woman, just as Skye had taught her to be. A soldier-chief's hair, the color of gold coins, was bigger medicine even than grizzly-bear claws. Tomorrow all the village would see the hair that shone like the sun, and laugh.

She hadn't laughed in many moons but now her spirit bubbled. She had the soldier-chief's hair! It had been easy to take, too. He had never suspected she would resist him. He had thought he was doing a favor to a red squaw. She bounded into her village and found it dark. Her parents' lodge was dark, too, so she slid quietly inside, laid her golden treasure next to the cowhide wall, and waited for dawn.

Even before Sun awakened from his bed, she quietly rummaged through her parfleche. Dirk stirred over on the men's side of the lodge. She smiled at him. Then she slipped out the lodge door, being careful not to awaken her father, her mothers, and her brothers, and began her work. She would have her necklace done even before the village awakened and when they arose they would see it on her breast. She wet some fine sinew taken from the back of a buffalo cow. Then she divided the golden hair into four piles. It glowed in the dawn light, exuding some mysterious power that made her respectful of it. This golden soldier-chief hair would give her unknown powers. With it she could command the sun to hide or the fleeing doe to stop.

She pinched and twisted the end of one of the piles, making a tuft of it, and then wrapped the wet sinew around it again and again. When the sinew dried it would clamp the yellow hair like glue. She made four tufts, the sacred number, and then anchored each tuft to German-silver conchae Skye had given her once, until a golden tuft dangled from each shining concha, shattering the low sun's orange light. It delighted her. Then she strung the conchae on a necklace of thong, separated by blue wooden beads. Ah! She held up her creation, admiring it.

"What is this, Blue Dawn?"

She turned, discovering her father standing just outside the lodge, preparing to make his sun-prayer. She grinned and held up her handiwork. "The soldier-chief's hair," she said.

He stared darkly at the necklace. "You killed him?"

"No, no. He wanted me for his woman."

Rising Crow digested that, not liking it. "Now you are the woman of the soldier-chief?"

"No," she said. "I wouldn't let him."

"Is this something for the elders to know?"

"Oh yes! I counted coup. When the soldier-chief was lying on the ground holding his man-part, I counted coup."

Rising Crow frowned, but finally caught her joy and laughed. Ah! Here was fun this day. Sun would see lots of Snake people laughing at the white chief this day. "It is a good joke," he said. "But maybe it will bring us trouble."

"It is bigger medicine than a necklace of grizzly claws," she said.

"Maybe bad medicine," he replied. He seemed torn between the humor of it and the worry.

As the village awakened the news scurried like field mice into one lodge after another, and even before anyone ate anything they all paraded by the lodge of Rising Crow, Lodge Maker, and Pretty Doe to see this amazing thing.

As soon as the sinew had dried and shrunk, Mary lifted the medicine necklace to her bodice and tied the thong behind her neck. The golden locks dangled playfully over the swell of her breasts, like Truscott's itching hands. She laughed. Grandmothers and grandfathers, warriors, women, and children stopped to see and laughed, too. Her Skye-son crawled through the lodge door and fondled the necklace, too sleepy to say anything. Ah, the sun shone on the Snake people this day!

Then Washakie came. He squatted down beside her, and studied the necklace solemnly. "Tell me about this," he said unsmiling.

She did, carefully, leaving nothing out, while her family listened discreetly.

"His hair was his medicine," Washakie said. "Often I watched him toss it about like a horse's mane, or run his small white hand through it. Often I saw him strut and pose, letting the sunlight shine off the gold-coin hair so the world might know he was a blessed one. He will not make a joke of this."

"It is no joke to me," she retorted. "He thought no one could resist him. He told me I must do exactly what he said if I wanted to please him. He was going to make me do something—I don't know what. I never liked him. Something bad is in his eyes and heart. He thought I would lie down for him and when I wouldn't, he got mad. He would have disgraced me. I fought the soldier-chief. I have fought other men before and I know where to strike."

Washaki listened quietly. "We will see," he said grimly. "This shining hair worries me. Maybe the People will suffer. I will tell your part of it to the grandfathers and see what they think. Clan-sister, perhaps you did not act wisely."

She felt rebuked. She hadn't thought about acting wisely, and she hadn't thought about the People at all. "Maybe I should not wear this medicine necklace."

"Wear it. It's good. You have great medicine now and you must not betray it. Maybe you have blessed all the Snake people. You cannot take it off or it will work against you."

His words still troubled her. "Maybe I should take it off at the council. Everyone will see his naked head and see his hair on me, and laugh at him. But he will not laugh."

"You must wear it."

"Aiee! I don't know what I fear more, the soldier-chief or the anger of the spirits. I wish Skye would tell me."

"He'll be there, clan-sister."

"He won't care. He wants to go away from here."

He smiled gently. She loved the young chief when he smiled at her like that. He wasn't like other chiefs, who hardly spoke to women. Not this sunny, open Washakie, whose spirit thirsted for the well-being of his people. She met his gaze with adoration and regretted the clan rules that forbade marriage within a clan. The rawboned young chief sensed her feelings and squeezed her hand.

"We must take heart. This will be a good day for the Snake people. We discussed the grandfathers' treaty long into the evening and we decided it is good. Today we will put our mark on it. We heard from the

Absaroka, too. Rottentail and Two Face came to us to talk even while you were stealing the hair-thunder of the soldier-chief. They had asked the lieutenant many things at Many Coups' feast. He didn't want them to sign the treaty. He said bad things about the grandfathers—and maybe these are true. Those who came with the grandfathers are thieves. But after the lieutenant had gone the Absaroka elders decided to sign. It would be better to be children of the grandfathers than children of the soldiers."

"I wish I could ask Mister Skye—"

"Well, ask him! I will, too, just before the council. He's one of them but he cares for us and his word will be good. The Bannocks will follow our lead. I don't know about the Arapaho. They're no friends of the Snake people and we haven't talked with them. I'm telling you this to help you put my thoughts into the tongue of the grandfathers."

A while later, after nibbling pemmican along with some buffalo backfat and greens snatched from the riverbank, she drifted toward the council. All the Shoshones would be there this hot day to see Washakie make the treaty and collect all the gifts the grandfathers had promised, which lay hidden in the white-covered wagons. She wondered what she would receive. A knife maybe. She could use a new ax, some calico, powder for her old flintlock, and a bar of galena.

But her feet dragged and she was filled with foreboding. She shouldn't be wearing the medicine-hair! She felt a thousand frightful spirits tugging at the fringes of her doeskin skirt, and she wanted to turn back. What good was the medicine-hair necklace if it was bad medicine? She stroked the blond hair of one tuft, fine and silky, as soft as rabbit down. It made her fingers tingle and the colors and scents of the earth explode in her mind.

She arrived late at the council. The air shimmered

with heat, making the distant ridges undulate. The covered wagons filled with white men's gifts had been drawn up to the council grounds and Indian Bureau clerks were slowly unloading a rainbow mountain of blankets and bolts of cloth. She saw the Cummings brothers and all their aides sitting in the canvas-covered arbor. She saw Victoria, Mister Skye, and Ravina, the translators. The chiefs of the several nations were seated in their front-row semicircle, with all the headmen, warriors, and people sitting patiently behind, witnesses to the signing of the treaty.

The golden-haired necklace caught the eye of the chiefs, who stared intently at it, as if every yellow strand were a curse. The hair could be none other than the soldier-chief's and their faces registered the knowledge, though nothing was spoken. The grandfathers noticed it, too, and leaned over to whisper to each other. Skye and Victoria noticed, their gazes riveted to the golden tufts dangling from the silvery conchae. She smiled proudly and stood straighter.

But she didn't see the lieutenant in his usual place in the arbor; indeed, she saw none of the familiar blue uniforms of the soldiers. It was as if the white men's army had vanished.

# Chapter 46

The matter required attention. Victorious Cummings rose, poked his burled walking stick into the soft clay, and made his slow way to Mister Skye, who was standing before the Arapaho.

"A word with you, sir, about the former Mrs. Skye?" Skye nodded.

"Those are the lieutenant's locks upon her bosom."

"Medicine," said Skye.

"Counting coup, perhaps?"

"More'n that, mate."

"You don't suppose some warriors gave those locks to her?"

Skye shook his head. "Warriors wouldn't do that. Not any tribe I know. They wouldn't let a squaw touch big medicine."

Superintendent Cummings sighed. "Is it possible that the former Mrs. Skye managed—"

"I'm bloody well thinking it. I taught her how to defend herself. Navy ways."

"But you're only supposing. You've no proof."

"Superintendent, Mary wouldn't make that medicine necklace unless she cut his hair. It'd be cheating—public lying."

"You're certain?"

"Totally."

"You suppose the lieutenant assaulted her?"

Skye sighed. "Anything that is mine, or was mine, seems to obsess Truscott."

"I've a different story from Truscott. He says ten Shoshones jumped him last night and counted coup."

"You'd see ten warriors out there decorated with blond scalplocks this bloody morning." Skye glared at him. "Tell me, Cummings, do ye see the bloody locks on 'em?"

The superintendent didn't.

" 'Twas the bloody lieutenant trying to make himself a man."

Cummings had to agree. "Will this affect this peace conference? We're on the brink now."

Skye lifted that battered top hat. Cummings saw pain in the man's face. "I don't know. Let's get this over with."

"Would it help to confer with Chief Washakie? Surely he'd know what his warriors did or didn't do."

"Don't know, mate." Skye's gaze lanced him. "But I know this. It's not a private matter. The whole tribe's involved."

"I fear it is. Thank you, sir. I regret your suffering," Cummings said, and sailed to shade like a heeling galleon.

There was nothing to do but open the final session and wait. Before him, in a sweeping semicircle, sat the principal chiefs of four nations, as crafty as Balkan princes, and a crowd stretching beyond the throw of his voice. Now all the months of labor and planning and diplomacy would succeed or fail.

Hot again. What was more fierce than the High

Plains sun? Maybe Skye's anger. Cummings sipped cold river water from a sweating tin cup and decided to begin.

He opened the session with a swift review of the treaty; a promise to distribute the annuity goods immediately after the signing; and a plea for a new time of peace and friendship among the tribes and white men. He spoke slowly, letting the translators convey his ideas to that barbarous mob. Not a zephyr stirred. He saw before him intelligent Mongols, cunning warlords, and hadn't the faintest idea what was passing through their minds. He'd discovered here the universal qualities of mankind: wisdom, temperance, forgiveness, realism, as well as frivolity, anger, scorn, and dark threats writ in copperplate flesh like the marks of Cain. He had come here supposing these red men were simple and unsophisticated; he knew better now.

He intended to invite the Crows to speak first; let the white men's tame friends snare the wild hares. Let the Shoshones speak last and least, lest the blond hair on the bosom of Skye's squaw overturn the imperial designs of Washington. But some instinct told him to let nature follow its course.

"Which nation wishes to speak first?" he asked.

For a long moment no chief stood. They all seemed to be waiting for Fate. Then young Washakie walked into the open space where the translators stood, stopping beside Mary. Cummings sighed. He'd made a mistake after all. He'd just thrown away years of preparation and a private dinner at the White House.

The young chief possessed himself as an athlete does. His festival clothing was relatively simple compared to the plumage of some of the other head chiefs. He wore a red cloth band about his head that pinned his jet hair, a small medicine bundle at his breast, a breechclout, fringed leggins, and whited moccasins.

"The Snake people have always been the friends of white men," he began, and waited patiently for translators to convey his thoughts into several tongues. "The grandfathers have promised us many things. They will protect our grass and game from the wagon travelers. Their soldiers will help us keep peace. They will teach us their sign magic so that we may have their wisdom. They will show us how to get metal and make guns. They will show us how to make our own blankets. They will show us how to scratch the earth and get food. They will send us the blackcoats with their sacred books to teach us about the Great Mystery. They will send us an agent to make our voice heard. These things are good. We will learn. We will be safe. We will have plenty of food and never go hungry. For two days and two nights my chiefs and I have talked about this. We will make the mark on the treaty."

Victorious Cummings rose, astonished, and settled down again. In a few simple and eloquent words Washakie had approved. And without a reservation, a negative comment, or a worry. It seemed almost miraculous in the light of Truscott's conduct.

Cummings realized he'd done the right thing after all, letting the invisible strands of High Plains diplomacy play out their own way. He stood as the young chief returned to his people.

"The grandfathers are pleased by the gracious words of Chief Washakie. We will do our utmost to meet our obligations to the Shoshones and to all the nations that join us," Cummings said. "Now who will speak?"

Red Water, a hooknosed lesser chief of the Bannocks known for his oratorical prowess, arose to proclaim that the Bannock cousins of the Shoshones would also put their mark on the paper, and would forever be the allies of the white men. Mary listened intently, translating the unfamiliar dialect of the Shoshone tongue while fresh breezes toyed with the golden tufts of hair upon her breast.

Once again, Cummings felt pleasure steal through him. The Truscott incident seemed to be forgotten, or maybe just ignored. The worst was probably over— unless the Crows bolted. "The grandfathers are pleased that the Bannocks will join us," he said. "Many good gifts await the Bannock people."

By some unspoken order that Cummings couldn't fathom it became the Crows' turn. Many Coups, dressed in fringed elkskins dyed yellow and green, stepped forward to address the Indian Bureau officials while the elder Mrs. Skye translated.

"Grandfathers," he began. "We have debated these things for many days and are divided. Some of my people believe the treaty is a good thing; some don't. Some of us think that a treaty with the soldiers would be better than a treaty with the grandfathers. Others want a treaty with the grandfathers. But we do not have control of these things. The great grandfather far to the east sends whoever he will to us."

He peered about, especially at the Cheyenne. "We are not a large nation and we are surrounded by ene- mies. But we have survived because the trappers and traders have brought us guns and powder and bullet metal and knives. Now we have been promised the protection of the soldiers, too. We will welcome the soldiers if they help us. They will stop the Siksika and the Lakota from stealing our horses and taking our women and children and killing our young men. We are uneasy. We wonder whether the grandfathers will truly do all that they promise us if we make our mark on the treaty. We wonder whether the soldiers will be for us or against us. But I have spoken in favor of the treaty because our friend Mister Skye has never failed to give us wisdom. So we will sign your treaty, my grandfathers."

Cummings rejoiced. Behind him, in the arbor, he heard the happy whispers of his assistants. Skye had been the key. It had all paid off. Without Skye it would have fallen apart. Cummings studied the man, who stood quietly in the bitter sun with some terrible sadness bending him, and he wished he had the means to heal whatever had torn the heart of that man without a country.

The Arapaho followed suit, though somewhat antagonized by it all. The thought of all those gift rifles, axes, knives, and blankets going to the other nations drove them into the fold. After they, too, had consented, Cummings arose.

"The grandfathers are pleased with you all and we have good things for you. Now, we will have you make your marks, the chiefs of one nation at a time."

Swiftly, Alphonse McGinty set up a camp table, unstoppered ink, sharpened quills, spread blotters, and unrolled the treaty parchment, all the while oozing a jaunty joy.

"Mister McGinty, the translators will give you the name and nation of each chief. Write it, leave a blank, and then write 'His Mark' after the blank."

"Yassir, melawd," the man said, with a vast excess of cheer. Cummings believed the Irish were unduly emotional.

It all proceeded smoothly. The headmen of the nations walked to the table in the order of their speaking, the Shoshones first. Washakie waited while McGinty scrawled "Of the Shoshone Nation" at the top, and then wrote "Washakie," left a space, and added "His Mark."

McGinty dipped the quill and handed it to the chief, who slowly drew an X in the blank space, next to McGinty's finger.

And so it went. Thirty-nine chiefs and headmen signed. Alphonse McGinty danced. Skye scowled and studied the distant bivouac.

# Chapter 47

The slithery clerk from the Indian Bureau bore a message for Lieutenant Truscott: Superintendent Cummings requests all available dragoons to help with the distribution of treaty goods. And he requests that Truscott come to the council ground to supervise.

Truscott had expected it. It would take every available man to hand out the goods. He dismissed the clerk irritably. He would soon be seen almost hairless by two thousand savages and a score of clerks. Worse, he'd be seen by Skye, that vicious squaw, and the old squaw, for that matter. But he consoled himself: they might enjoy themselves for now—but not for long.

He smoothed the ragged remains of his locks with gentle fingers, knowing that no barber could conceal the insult to his person. He felt naked. His golden hair had been more precious than stars of gold thread sewn to his epaulets; fair ladies had succumbed to that hair and had strung it through their fingers in moments of passion. But still, he could turn it to good use. How the girls would adore him! These were the red ribbons of war, violence in the night, and swift white man's retaliation. The story had bloomed in him and he was ready to tell it to anyone.

"Pope! Get every man who's free. We're going to hand out the Indian Bureau's stuff to our red brothers."

"Some new kind of soljering," Big Pope muttered, as he marched off to corral his blue-shirted apes. "Kissing the stinking enemy."

In minutes the bawling sergeant had collected more than forty unkempt men, told them to tuck in their blouses, leave their revolvers in camp, and shape themselves into marching order to go wet-nurse the savages. Then he marched them across the burning flats to the distant mob. Truscott followed, wearing his revolver and saber.

They arrived just when Wellington Cummings was handing each chief a good Leman percussion-lock rifle, ammunition, new cavalry saddle, and blanket, while Victorious shook their hands. Off behind the canvas arbor, sweat-stained clerks worked frantically to divide the amassed goods into four heaps. Truscott halted and let them all stare at him. He'd steeled himself for it. The worst of his shearing lay hidden under his forage cap and he looked little different from his own rough-shorn soldiers. He gritted through the moment and then the chiefs were passing by the superintendent again to receive their booty. The visiting Cheyenne chiefs received a saddle apiece.

"Ah, Truscott! We've a treaty!" the superintendent exclaimed. "I'll assign you to Mister McGinty now. We've a task fit for Hercules getting this stuff out. But tomorrow it's all over and we'll go home."

Assigned to McGinty. Truscott's nostrils twitched. The apple-cheeked Irishman in the black bowler bobbed and weaved among his clerks, clucking cheerfully.

"Sergeant Pope. Take your instructions from Mister McGinty," Truscott said.

"Yassir! Yassir. Yassir. Take it from McGinty."

Big Pope glared at him and marched his men toward the clerks, leaving rank sweat in the breeze behind them. The whole council ground stank like a pigpen.

Truscott stood apart, watching frenetic labor. Clerks toted crates and kegs. Headmen and chiefs stood and stretched. Lesser savages stirred and gossiped. Furnace winds sucked them dry. Under the hot canvas the big mucketymucks stood and talked, their beards bobbing in the brown shade.

Inured at last to the frequent stares, Truscott wandered into the distribution area, watching his men tote and haul while their blue shirts blackened. Others crowbarred crates open or loosened bales of blankets. He peered into an open cask of knives and lifted one out. Cheaply made thing, raw wood riveted over a crude hasp. He thumbed the edge and found it dull. He flexed the wrought-iron blade—and it bent. Astonished, Truscott lifted another—this time taking care that no one was watching. Same wrought iron, but it didn't fold when he tried it. Blades of wrought iron—weak, soft, easily machined.

This stuff was not what the United States Bureau of Indian Affairs had contracted for. Graft. His pulse climbed. He peered about wildly, eyeing bolts of printed calico with ends snaking in the wind, mountains of blankets, axes, kettles, hatchets ... Graft! He needed help, fast, before all the evidence vanished into savage hands.

"Big Pope!"

The dripping sergeant wheezed up.

"Pope, damn you, listen hard. I want at least one of everything here. You're going to filch it without being caught. I see some of the men've taken off their blouses. Hide the stuff under the blouses. Get those burlap sacks. Pack it back to my tent and don't get caught. Pope, do that and the Army's won."

"Won, sah?"

"We'll get the Indian Bureau back again. Graft! Get that into your skull and let it pasture between your ears. Do it!"

"Yassir," Pope said, uninterested. "Mucketymuck wars."

Truscott watched the sergeant snatch a blanket, chop off a yard of billowing calico, snitch awls and hatchets and kettles, becoming more and more blatant about it because none of the other busy men had the slightest interest in what he was doing.

Truscott meandered through the chaos. He fingered a blanket, finding it light and porous, so loosely woven it wouldn't keep lovers warm on a steamy night. Ecstatically, he tugged at a bolt of flannel, finding fabric so flimsy it might last a few weeks. Excited, he hefted a red-painted ax with an unhoned blade and swung it at an empty crate. A few whacks later he studied the blade, finding the dull edge gouged. The red paint hid gray-iron axes. These were cast-iron, not good carbon steel. These wouldn't hold an edge and would dull into uselessness in a few months. Junk!

He found tin cups with handles barely riveted on; sacks of flour crawling with mealworms; New Orleans sugar that had been water-soaked; cast-iron frying pans with broken handles—probably manufacturing rejects; and bags of unroasted coffee beans that looked a year old.

Like a placer miner plucking two-ounce nuggets from his gold pan, Truscott collected incriminating samples and slid them into the pockets of his tunic. Big Pope had finished his filching and was industriously stuffing the loot into burlap bags.

"Ah, me lad, what be ye up to?" asked Chief Clerk McGinty, eyeing the sergeant.

Sergeant Pope stammered, stared at Truscott, and

began rocking on his flat feet. "Ah, Clerk McGinty, I have me a terrible taste for wild red ladies, and you've caught an old three-stripe soljer fixin' to go out and woo before the whole kit and caboodle of them skitters away."

McGinty cackled. "It's a man's need," he said. "And old Uncle Sam, he can spare a little. Take enough for the lads to have a spree and think ye kindly on the clerks. We'll come to you for a favor by and by." He turned to Truscott. "Give your stiff old Adam a fling, meboy. You desarve one after losing your golden locks."

Anthony Wayne Truscott stared the man down. McGinty winked and wandered off.

Done, and wondrously simply. Truscott felt like promoting old Pope on the spot. He watched the sergeant heft three sacks of contraband and hike toward the bivouac.

Long lines had formed at each pile, and Truscott watched the clerks hand a blanket, knife, and hatchet to each male, and two yards of calico, an awl, knife, needles and thread, and an ax to each woman. At least the clerks knew who did the drudge work in any Plains Indian village, he thought.

The savages laughed and joked, while berry-eyed children squealed and poked wet fingers into sugar sacks. This was Christmas for them but they didn't know how poorly they were faring. Truscott watched the Arapaho collect their loot, and then he turned to the Crows as they got their stuff.

His real business was with the Shoshones so he drifted that way, past dripping dragoons, feeding white men's junk into the maw like Canaanites feeding Moloch. He wanted her and her brat more than ever.

Hundreds, thousands of coppery Indians wandered, laughed, clustered, exclaimed over their prizes. He'd have to search hard. He pushed through the Shoshones, recognizing their rawboned features and wide faces now.

Then he saw her far off. Skye's younger woman, her back to him, holding her son's hand. Good! He pushed through, past soldiers and clerks, down the line. The Shoshones saw him coming, and their bright joy caught like a stopped clock. Silence swallowed him as he strutted forward.

She turned to see. On her breast hung a medicine necklace made of four tufts of his own yellow hair, giving the lie to the story he'd told all that long hot day.

# Chapter 48

Victoria saw Skye walking toward her. She knew what he wanted. She knew she'd gladly do it no matter how angry she was with him.

All around her laughing and gossiping women were dismantling the Absaroka encampment and soon her people would head toward their separate villages. Women slid the heavy lodgecovers down their lodgepoles and packed them on travois; stuffed parfleches and hoisted them onto packsaddled ponies; chased children away from sacks of sugar. She loved them. She would go with them to her own Kicked-in-the-Bellies band.

He stood before her, solemn, stiff, and uncomfortable.

"I've something to ask," he said.

She nodded, not stopping her own packing.

"Would you take Jawbone north with you?"

She nodded. "I'll ride him."

Apart from Skye she was the only person Jawbone would obey. He'd be safe with the Absaroka.

"Let him go up in the Pryors—just like we talked about." He grinned faintly.

She nodded again. "I'll stay there with him."

"Don't put yourself out."

She flared. "For the medicine horse I'll do anything." He nodded, chastened, and stood there awkwardly. "I'll hitch a ride back in one of the Bureau wagons. That's my contract; take 'em back to Fort Laramie. Then I'll be free."

She stopped packing and squinted up at him. "Then what you do, eh? Sonofabitch."

"I don't know. Go east. Find a city. Find a life . . ."

"Find some damn pale woman and never tell her nothing."

He didn't answer and she read anguish in his eyes.

"I'll take care of Jawbone. Them blue-shirts come after us, they got a war. Many Coups, he's still got guards out at the herds. He thinks maybe that soldier-chief might try now, everyone's packing and busy and looking at their cheap stuff. Bad stuff. Damn Indian Bureau gave us dung. I tell Many Coups that, but he's got a good new rifle and Army saddle so he isn't listening hard." She spat. "Later he'll know and maybe he won't think so good about white men. They all no damn good."

Skye lifted his old topper and didn't argue with her.

"Bad metal," she said.

Skye nodded. "McGinty's doings, I reckon. Bloody crook. I'd forgotten how bloody mean it is. Big cities. People so crooked they don't know straight."

"If that's what you want you can damn well have it. I gotta pack now." She glared at him.

"Victoria—" he faltered. "Victoria. I'm sorry."

"Get the hell outa here."

But he lingered, shifting uneasily from one foot to another. "Take care of Jawbone."

"Damn you. When did I ever not?"

He gripped his top hat and twisted it through his

rough hands. "Take care of Mary and the boy. I'll never see him again."

"You'll never see Mary, neither, but you ain't thinking about that. Just the boy."

"I'll miss her."

"Like hell. You'll be too busy fooling with white women."

"I'll miss my family. I never had a chance to say it last winter. I could hardly talk. Something hit me hard."

In some awkward way he was telling her he loved her, loved Mary and Dirk, and it touched her. "Get out!" she yelled.

She saw the soldiers too late. Four of them approached from the side, revolvers drawn. "Sonofabitch!" she snarled, ducking toward her parfleche, where her old flintlock rested.

"Don't move," said one, the sergeant, Big Pope. "I'll plug you both."

Skye whirled, grabbed for his revolver, and found nothing. Like all the rest at the peace conference he was not armed. He stopped, and surveyed the foursome.

Around them, Victoria's people continued to pack and laugh, oblivious to all this.

"Gotcha, Skye. Take us to the horse. You make a scene and you're dead."

"I guess I'm dead," said Skye. He didn't budge.

"Walk!"

Skye stood.

"We got your Shoshone squaw and the brat. Walk out to that herd and get the killer horse or we'll fix them both."

Skye stood.

Pope obviously didn't like it. Victoria's people busied themselves nearby, their weapons close at hand.

"Where do you have Mary and Dirk?" Skye asked.

"Lieutenant's got 'em in our camp."

"Why?"

"Because he wants them—and you."

"What'll happen to them?"

"I'm not here to answer questions, Skye. Truscott'll do that. Now march."

"No, Sergeant. You're not getting that horse. There's still some guards there."

The other three dragoons looked nervous. The dwindling Absaroka village lay between the blueshirts and the distant bivouac. Pope was discovering it wasn't so easy to jump the Skyes. A wild thrill of death leapt up in Victoria. She'd kill one before she died. She had her knife.

Pope turned to a dragoon. "Go back and tell Truscott to brain the brat."

The soldier wheeled away. Skye didn't move.

"You want your brat killed, Skye?" Pope asked.

"I think Truscott has something like that in mind anyway, Mister Pope. It's in him to destroy us—sooner or later, after the tribes pull out."

"Move your butt."

"I'm not in your Army, Pope."

"Them bucks're staring, Sarge," said one.

Victoria saw Leaps at Night and Running Badger watching. They obviously had seen the drawn revolvers. Running Badger slid toward a knot of Absaroka she didn't know, men from the Whispering Water clan.

Pope cursed melodically and studied the situation, which was obviously clouding with every moment.

"Send Superintendent Cummings and a carriage," Skye said. "We'll go talk—under his flag."

"Who're you to be giving orders, Skye?" The sergeant waved his cocked revolver upward.

"I gather Cummings knows nothing about this," Skye said.

Pope didn't reply. Nervously he eyed the gathering warriors. It'd come to an impasse.

Victoria simply walked away.

"Hey! Stop!" Pope yelled. She didn't. She knew they'd neither shoot nor manhandle her.

Skye followed and they didn't stop him, either, though the three bores of their revolvers followed his every step. He eyed her and admired her feisty courage.

Pope and his men stared, outnumbered, and then wheeled away.

"Guard the medicine horse," she said in Absaroka to Running Badger. "They will kill it. They have the Shoshone woman and the boy Skye."

The warrior nodded and trotted away. This would reach the ears of Many Coups. Around her the encampment was melting away like snow in June. Bear's Head, Rottentail, and Two Face had started north with their people. Far away she saw the Arapaho people and the Shoshones leaving.

She watched the three blue-shirts ebb from sight through the dismantled village and wondered what would come next.

"I don't like white men," she said to Skye. She thought he didn't either. But he was about to go live among them again.

"I'll get Mary and Dirk," he said. "This is all bluff."

She stared, unbelieving. "They'll capture you."

"I can get them. Truscott wouldn't dare. He lacks nerve. All you have to do is face him down. That's why he hates us. He's all front, like a theater set."

"What's this, a theater set?"

"A mask—he's a mask," Skye said.

"Don't go. I see a wildness in Truscott—ever since he loses his rotten, no-good, yellow hair."

"I'll face him down. Get Mary loose. God knows what he'll do to her if he keeps her. He'll use her in bloody ways—" He stopped talking so abruptly she was startled. But she knew how Truscott would use Mary.

"You don't give a damn about her or Dirk. She ain't yours. You quit us, you no-good greasy bum sonofa-bitch. You just care about your medicine. You don't want Truscott to touch what was yours. It's you against him. She don't mean nothing no more. If you free her and Dirk you'll just send her away again."

She saw something crumple in his face, as if he faced the world alone, without a lodge or a tribe or a friend. Then she saw the hurt look in him, and the marks of torment that caught at the corners of his mouth.

"I have to go," he said. "He's got sixty carbines and a weakness of the soul. I can deal."

"That's why you're going. To prove you've more medicine," she shot back.

But he was choking back his feelings. "Tell Many Coups not to leave for a bit. I may need the help of your people," he said. "Good-bye, Victoria. I'm on my way to Laramie."

He loomed beside her and she felt his lips brush hers, shooting lightning through her. Then he wheeled away and she watched his back.

# Chapter 49

Skye hastened angrily down the long angle from the Crow camp to the Indian Bureau camp. Far ahead, he made out Pope and his two men. In the distant bivouac he could see a flurry of horses. The Indians had already vanished. The Arapaho were only a smudge of golden dust to the south; the Shoshones had gone up the Wind River; he couldn't see the Bannocks at all; and most of the Crows were toiling up the benches miles to the north.

All gone. His life, too. He felt oddly like the boy of fifteen, snatched off the streets, who had found himself buried alive on a Royal Navy frigate, frightened and alone, a murderous veil between him and his family in London. Maybe his life was over; maybe he'd rot in the Eastern cities and pine for the scent of sagebrush riding down the wind. Maybe he'd find that this was the clean and nurturing place, that the civilized world was rotten, greedy, and corrupt. He didn't know.

He knew he loved his family. He had thought they

hadn't fulfilled him; he needed the white man's life. Now, as he walked, the possibility of mistake gnawed at him. He sighed. He was almost through. He would back down Truscott—he didn't doubt that the hollow young man would cave in—and take the party back to Laramie, his contract fulfilled. And then ...

Far away he saw the bivouac swallow Pope and his men. Minutes later a great clot of horses erupted from the camp. Mounted riders in blue! Thirty, forty, fifty, trotting straight toward him, the sun glinting off revolvers in hand; Truscott's saber flashing. The lieutenant was leading the whole command. Beyond, he could see the clerks at the Indian Bureau camp watching.

Skye stood stock-still, gauging his chances. He had come too far from the Crows to help them—or Jawbone. But he had to try. He always tried. He wheeled around and lumbered toward the Crow village, feeling his breath rasp his throat as he ran. They were swiftly overtaking him; he wouldn't make it. But he kept on running, feeling his heart pound blood to his limbs. Truscott! A wild rage built in Skye.

They were coming at him—but then they swerved slightly, and rode on by, lifting to a canter as they headed toward the remnant of the Crows. He felt the earth vibrate as their hoofs hammered hard clay; heard the hot breath of the horses; saw the black glint of fifty loaded revolvers, three hundred balls to pump into Jawbone. They swept by, except for Truscott, who steered his handsome horse toward Skye and reined in a few feet away. He was smiling. His saber sliced air, severing sun from wind, and wind from dust; a mad surgeon's tool.

Skye didn't stop. Truscott wheeled the horse between Skye and the Crows, and slashed at him with his saber. The blade severed Skye's buckskin shirt.

"Skye, I could run this through you," Truscott said cheerfully while his flashy horse danced.

Skye paused, seeing no escape. Truscott smiled down from his bay and then watched his command drive straight toward the small Crow herd where Jawbone grazed.

There'd be only two or three guards now. Crow boys. Skye gulped air and waited, dreading what would happen. He felt helpless. Nausea quickened in his belly. Not this. Not this end for Victoria, who'd shoot to kill and be killed; not this end for a great horse. Skye stood, feeling the earth tumble from its orbit beneath his feet.

At that distance, he could see little. The troop plunged into the cottonwoods along the Wind River where the Crow herd grazed. And then there was only silence.

"The whole command's itching to kill your outlaw, Skye. This time they will," said Truscott.

"You never told me what the charges are."

"You're a deserter and a fraud."

"And my wives?"

"Common criminals."

"And my son?"

Truscott smiled. "A breed brat. Too bad about him, Skye."

"And what have you in mind?"

"Shoot you in a few minutes. In front of them. And then them."

"Does Cummings approve?"

Truscott laughed. "He doesn't count. I've got his Indian Bureau by the topknot."

"Graft."

"Congress'll give it back to the War Department. I'll get a couple of brevets. You'll be coyote meat. You can stand there and sum up your life. How does it feel to have lived a worthless life? What have you achieved? Who will remember you? Will anyone care?"

"Yes," said Skye.

# Chapter 50

Victoria saw the blue-shirts boiling toward her, and understood. They were coming to execute Jawbone. The herd grazed in the cottonwood groves nearby.

She could not reach Jawbone in time to ride him to safety. Cursing, she lifted her flintlock, primed it, and fired it to alert the camp. Around her, warriors ran for their weapons. Only twenty or thirty remained in the village. She poured powder from her horn, patched and rammed a ball, poured priming powder into the pan, all the while watching the onslaught of the dragoons, cantering ever closer, revolvers raised. They were heading directly for the herd and would miss the camp by two arrow-lengths.

What chance did she have?

She could kill one. She knelt behind a gray cottonwood log, leveled her longrifle, picked the lead rider— she recognized the sergeant—and fired. The recoil shot pain into her shoulder. Red bloomed upon the sergeant's chest and slowly the blue-shirt slid to earth, his foot caught in the stirrup.

Her shot was answered by a crackle of revolver fire but the dragoons were a hundred yards away. Two Absaroka warriors joined her, firing ineffectively into the rush of blue, and then the dragoons had passed the camp and were penetrating the cottonwood groves. That had slowed the blue-shirts for only a few seconds. Two soldiers caught the sergeant's horse and stepped down to free his foot from the stirrup.

Good! Viciously she rammed another patched ball home and began running lithely, like a shadow through the dappled shade, toward the herd. She heard the bark of revolvers but no return fire from the three boys guarding the remaining ponies. They'd probably run for their lives.

Two Absaroka warriors, Little Finger and Makes Noise, plunged toward the downed sergeant and the two soldiers trying to get him back up on his saddle. Makes Noise shot but missed. Little Finger released an arrow, which pierced the thigh of a blue-shirt. The man screamed. Victoria left them to their private war and ran frantically toward the cottonwoods. Jawbone, Jawbone . . .

Behind her she heard white men's shrieks, and knew one small battle was over: there'd be three new scalps on the lances of the Absaroka this day! Some peace treaty! Aagh!

She saw others of her people gliding through the cottonwoods: warriors who'd grabbed anything at hand, mostly lances and bows and quivers. But it was too late. The dragoons burst into the meadow where the herd grazed. She heard the crackle of revolvers again and Jawbone's terrible shriek.

Run, Jawbone! She prayed to Magpie, her spirit-helper. "Tell the medicine horse to run like the wind."

Jawbone shrieked again, and then she heard the uproar of horses: the whinny and shriek of frightened ponies, the snort of mad animals, the desperate sucking of air, the snap of the revolvers, the yelling of white men, and the occasional whir of a loosed arrow. But she could see little. Pursuers and pursued vanished down the Wind River, leaving only a haze of dust filtering the quiet sun poking into the cottonwood parks.

She didn't follow. Always, Skye had taught her to anticipate the enemy. She didn't know where the herd would lead them but she knew they had to return to their bivouac. She hastened that way, anger filling her old breast, raw hatred climbing her throat like bile.

Off to the left she saw Many Coups clamber onto his pony to direct his handful against this overwhelming enemy. She could tell from the sharp, choppy motions of his arms and hands how furious he was as he directed his few warriors to harass the rear of the dragoons and sent his women and children deep into the bankside brush to protect themselves.

Peace treaty! If she lived through this day she would stalk the lieutenant; she would catch him sooner or later, kill him, scalp him, mutilate him, and leave his spirit to wander the earth, unwelcome at the gatherings of the dead. She had vowed it to him and now she would fulfill her vow.

She slid through the flat where the village had stood, past dark fire pits, past yellowed circles where the lodges had rested, straight toward the soldier-camp. She crouched low, scurrying along little dips that seemed not to conceal a hare, itching to catch the soldier-chief and kill him. He was there somewhere, and she would show him that the word of a Skye woman was true.

The thought caught in her heart. A Skye woman.

Where was Skye? They would have him. They had Mary and Dirk. Only she remained free. She paused, catching her breath behind sagebrush, knowing she was almost invisible to white men. She was still a Skye woman. She would free them all or kill those who harmed any Skye.

# Chapter 51

Muffled thumps rode the wind: the crack of revolvers, the lower whumps of Indian rifles. Lieutenant Truscott's private war. Skye felt his heart stall and a lump ride slowly down his esophagus and stop halfway, burning out his chest.

The hot wind swirled powder smoke at him. Truscott reined his gelding, which chafed at the restraint, wanting to race toward its fellows. Skye watched the delicate hand that held the saber.

"Truscott, if you're half a man you'll spare my women and my son."

He smirked. "Why? Let's say they had the misfortune to be your allies in crime."

Skye swallowed hard. "Truscott, if you harm the horse, you'll die. That goes for my family."

Truscott flicked the saber in reply. The blade whirred through sunlight, fracturing it. "That's an odd thing for a man in your position to say. Bravado. Bluff. Redskin medicine. It sums up your life."

Far away, Indian ponies exploded from the cotton-woods, racing downriver. A blue dot led them. Behind, dragoons pursued, firing occasionally, gaining ground. Skye watched, riveted to the spectacle the way French mobs watched the doomed being led to the guillotine.

The dragoons caught up to the winded Crow ponies, scattering them. Jawbone vanished in brush, emerged as a blue whir, and vanished again behind a low mound. He shrieked suddenly, the sound eerie and faint in the hot breeze, and wheeled out of sight. The dragoons swung after him and vanished into the earth. Skye heard thumps. Then, suddenly, Jawbone appeared, a shining dot beyond the bottoms of the Wind River, sunlight refracting like stars from the water dripping off him. He'd plunged across and was climbing the benches beyond in gigantic leaps. He was gaining ground on all the pretty horses and all the blue men.

Then other dragoons burst into view, flanking Jawbone, closing on him like bear's jaws. Jawbone stopped, whirled, shrieked, and bolted down a rough grade for the river again.

Skye dared to hope. Those flatland horses, even grain-fed, would quit before Jawbone did—if Jawbone escaped the snarling balls that raked his progress. Maybe, maybe—if Jawbone was smart enough to pick out friend from enemy.

"Caught him, Skye. My dragoons outmaneuvered your outlaw."

Skye didn't reply. He watched Truscott gloat.

Then Jawbone exploded from the woods just where the Crow village had been, racing straight for Skye as if the wind had carried the scent of his master to him. Behind, dragoons burst from the cottonwoods also, but they had lost ground. Jawbone stopped and wheeled, lifted his head until it touched the feet of God, and shrieked, a sound so ghastly that it terrorized the pretty horses. Some bucked and pitched; several riders spilled. Others veered away. Still other dragoons dodged around the chaos, and lost more ground.

Truscott laughed. "Looks like I'll have the coup de grace myself," he said. He slid his saber home in its sheath even as he plucked up his revolver.

Jawbone raced straight toward them, bug-eyed, running low and flat, his rough gait awful to behold, his nostrils flared and lips distended. From some wound on his withers he leaked blood. Skye felt shocks of terror course his veins and felt his muscles gather. But Truscott swung his revolver toward Skye.

"Don't try it."

"Stop me."

"One for you; five for it."

It might save the horse. It'd beat a firing squad.

Truscott leveled his revolver at the thundering blue horse. Skye sprang, slamming the withers of Truscott's bay, spoiling the aim as the shot exploded. The man cursed strange oaths.

Truscott pistol-whipped Skye, screaming hate. The barrel cracked into Skye's ear, and again into his skull, shooting white streaks of pain through him. Then Truscott fired again; Jawbone screeched and sailed past. Skye threw himself at the horse again, wrecking another shot. Truscott fired at Skye, the noise deafening, and Skye felt the ball sear his upper left arm.

Jawbone was fast escaping revolver range. Truscott reined his horse around to pursue. Skye hung on to a stirrup, wrecking the maneuver. Truscott snapped a shot at the wild blue horse but Jawbone was gone. Dragoons were closing, riding by in hot pursuit.

Truscott loomed over Skye, and again smacked the revolver barrel over his skull. Skye lost his hold of the stirrup and felt the earth rise and smite him. And that was the last he knew.

# Chapter 52

Victoria reached the crest of a low incline and saw a terrible thing before her: Skye, on foot, a prisoner of the lieutenant, who sat his gray horse and waved his saber. She would kill the lieutenant! But the way was across open meadow, farther than her longrifle could throw a ball. She had to get closer.

But even as her squinting eyes searched out a thread of a ditch, or a patch of high grass, or a faint rise in the open country, she heard the clamor of war along the Wind River, saw Jawbone burst out of the cottonwoods and race straight toward Skye and the lieutenant; saw the officer replace his saber and draw his revolver. And far behind Jawbone the dragoons chased doggedly, on winded horses, losing ground.

She wanted to scream. Cry to the medicine horse. Ah, Magpie, Magpie, spirit-helper, help me! She watched Jawbone running rough, low to the ground, ears flattened, nostrils flared. She watched the officer lift his revolver; saw Skye plunge and upset the horse, saw the officer brain Skye. Jawbone thundered past, still gaining ground on the weary, burdened dragoon horses. She sighed. Skye lay on the ground, still as death; Jawbone was safe—as long as the winds whispered in his ears, and the Above Spirits guided him away, away ...

But then the officer aimed his revolver at her man. She heard nothing. Even at that distance she could see him working the hammer over and over—but he'd discharged all his balls at Jawbone. She waited for the blue-shirts to race by and then sprang forward while he fumbled with his revolver. She had to get into range. But then he holstered the revolver and loosened a picket rope from the cantle of his saddle. He tied one end around Skye's legs, then mounted and slowly dragged Skye, feet first, toward the bivouac. Skye's fringed leggins slid over the grass, but his flannel shirt rode up his chest, and his top hat dropped from his head and lay abandoned, like Skye's spirit lost between worlds.

She squirmed closer but she had no cover, and he was lifting his bay horse into a trot while Skye flopped behind, through prickly pear, over grass and rock, leaving a red trail. She stalked behind, taking risks, progressing in bursts. But it was too late; the soldier-chief dragged Skye into the soldier camp, where three sentries swiftly surrounded her man. She saw no sign of Mary and Dirk. But over in the camp of the Indian Bureau she saw the great figure of Victorious Cummings moving angrily toward the soldiers, followed by a dozen civilians.

Good, let them argue. She would creep up into range and kill the lieutenant. She lay in a tiny hollow in the prairie too small to hide a rabbit, and she couldn't move. The first of the dragoons were drifting

back, some walking limping horses, some on foot.
Some supported a wounded man between them. Some
horses, without riders, wearily followed the rest. Some
came close and kept her pinned to Mother Earth. She
watched them, hated them, vowed to kill the first one
who spotted her. But they weren't looking for enemies
in open plains and their eyes had been sealed shut by
the Above Spirits.

Far to the south she saw the remnants of the
dragoon troop straggling in, defeated. She studied
the distant horizons and saw what they didn't see;
the great medicine horse shimmering in the afternoon light, the horse of all horses, studying all
that lay below. Jawbone had escaped them! She
thanked the Above Spirits for their mercy and Jawbone's own medicine spirit for giving the horse wisdom.

Then her heart hardened. She would soon slide into
the bivouac, and the lieutenant would see the sun no
more. She might die but it would be a good death. She
lay quietly, waiting for night to cover her with safety.
The sun had already fallen almost to the ground and
soon it would be the time to strike. The last of the dragoons drifted in, and she watched them picket the
sweat-blackened horses north of the camp and return
to the campground, where a crowd had gathered
around the soldier-chief and the big man in black.
They were arguing, but the winds brought her none of
the sound.

Then she caught movement along the Wind River
and saw a thing that lifted her heart: Many Coups and
his handful of brave Absaroka warriors were quietly
collecting in the woods there. She knew that Many
Coups also had a vow to fulfill: anyone who attacked
Jawbone would become the enemy of the Absaroka
nation. Then she understood, even without words,
what the chief would do: while the white men argued

into the dusk he would steal their horses and mules, which stood unguarded on their picket lines because the lieutenant had been too interested in Skye to make his camp secure. She exulted.

Just when her warriors stole the white men's herd she would slip in for the kill.

# Chapter 53

Victorious Cummings hastened toward the bivouac, scarcely believing his eyes. He propelled himself along with his black walking stick, which gouged holes in cast-iron clay. Behind him, Wellington and a gaggle of clerks followed.

Ahead, Lieutenant Truscott was dismounting from a winded horse. Skye, who'd been dragged there by his feet, writhed and groaned, semiconscious. His head was a mass of blood. Dragoons drifted in, either on foot or on heaving, sweat-stained mounts.

"Lieutenant! Let that man go."

Truscott ignored him. His attention was on the incoming dragoons. "Rub down and picket your mounts. Keep your carbines at hand."

"Truscott! I'm addressing you. What is this? Attacking a Crow village! And this! This!" He pointed at Skye.

Truscott pretended not to hear, sending Cummings's pulse racing. The lieutenant walked back to Skye, pushed the toe of his boot into the man's ribs, and watched Skye groan.

A corporal reined his winded horse before Truscott. "Corporal Rourke reporting, sir. Three dead—Sergeant Pope, Immel, Patricio. Two other casualties. Two men fell off their mounts, pretty banged up. We didn't get the horse."

"Idiots. I told you to surround the herd first."

"We did, sir, driving in from both flanks. The outlaw's a spooky horse, sir. The guards slowed us. We chased them off."

"And I suppose that bag of bones outran fifty grain-fed cavalry mounts."

The corporal swallowed and said nothing. For a fleeting, sad moment, Cummings exulted.

"What happened to Pope?"

"Him'n Immel and Patricio got caught. Crow fire got Pope and some arrows got the others."

Truscott sighed. "I send a troop of dragoons to kill one horse and you botch it."

"Truscott!" roared Cummings. "You're under arrest. Drop that revolver and unbuckle that saber and go to your tent. I'm your senior officer."

Truscott at last turned to Cummings, with demons dancing in his eyes. "Sorry, old pops," he muttered, chewing on his yellow mustache. He turned again to the dragoons. "Secure the camp. Get rid of these clerks."

Several armed dragoons began pushing clerks back with their carbines. Off a way, at the bank of the Little Wind, other dragoons were wiping down and picketing horses.

Skye had sat up and was holding his head in his bloody hands. "Bind up that man. He's bleeding," Cummings roared.

"Sorry, old boy. We'll be shooting him in ten minutes. Let him bleed. I want the rest of my men here to see what happens to a renegade Indian-lover and traitor. They've been waiting. For a long time."

"Mister Truscott," said Cummings quietly, "I require you to surrender your weapons and report to your tent. You're under arrest. You've probably wrecked months of diplomacy. Made war on a peaceful band of Crows who just signed a peace treaty in good faith. Now you're planning to murder an innocent man."

Truscott smiled again, mad angels dancing in his eyes. "Sorry, my friend. My carbines are in command now. I didn't attack the Crows; I sent men to kill an outlaw horse that needed killing. They attacked us. As for Skye, the sooner he's executed the sooner this country can be civilized. He's a red-loving renegade. He even admitted it from the start."

Cummings stared around him. Half a dozen dragoons with carbines at the ready controlled the area; others were joining them. Off a way, two dragoons were prodding the younger Mrs. Skye and her boy out of a tent. Bunches of dragoons emerged from the pasture where the horses had been picketed.

Truscott watched. "I want her to see the old boy shot. That'll teach her not to hook up with a renegade white man. Then I'll turn her over to the whole command. By tomorrow she'll want to kill herself. It'll be a good lesson."

At a nod from Truscott, two dragoons lifted the befuddled Skye and dragged him to a box elder tree close to the river while Truscott ambled along. They hoisted Skye and tied his bloodied arms behind the trunk. Skye sagged into the tree.

"There. We're about set," Truscott said. "Too bad he's so far gone he won't know what hit him. Some big-medicine big shot he turned out to be."

"Truscott, this is murder. I'll see you court-martialed, convicted, and hanged."

"Oh, no, I don't think so. An Army court-martial board won't see it that way. The War Department ran

the Indian Bureau for the benefit of white citizens—
against red enemies. And we will again, after you
bleeding hearts are ousted. I assure you, executing a
dangerous renegade and rabble-rouser of redskins is
hardly a matter to upset the high command."

Cummings feared that Truscott might be right.
"You—" he said to a passing dragoon. "Any man who
harms Skye is going to hang for murder." He said it
loudly, knowing his voice would carry to the others.

"Don't let him scare, you, Private. You're under orders," Truscott said velvetly.

The private stared uneasily from man to man and
slid away. Truscott looked amused.

"There he is, sir," mumbled the corporal, pointing
east.

Far off on a bench, Jawbone stood proud, lit golden
by the setting sun. He pawed the grass. He lifted his
head and whickered to Skye, the sound keen on the
eddying air.

A soldier hawked and spat.

It gladdened Cummings's heart that at least one
wild thing had escaped this man who had to
dominate—or kill what he couldn't dominate.

"He's a great horse, Mister Truscott."

"We'll get him sooner or later. He'll hang around
and we'll have our chance."

"And when you're done, who will you be?"

Truscott laughed softly. "A brevet major."

"Who'll you be when you examine your soul in the
night? Or when God examines it?"

Truscott snorted. "A brevet major on his way up."

Wellington responded: "Don't offend God, Mister
Truscott."

Cummings felt in the pocket of his commodious
pants for a penknife with which to sever Skye's bonds.
Surely they would not touch him.

"Stop him," said Truscott.

Two dragoons grabbed his arms and steered him away.

Mary and the boy arrived, prodded forward by the carbines of the dragoons. Tears slid down her cheeks. She stared at Skye with love and desolation brimming from her swollen eyes.

"Well, squaw. Now we'll see how you weep. Watch your renegade die. And after that you'll enjoy the company of my men. All of them, if they feel like it."

"You will have to kill me—or I will kill you," she said, a desolate courage rising from her in the soft twilight.

"You won't sound so brave when the night's over."

"You heard me," she said, her voice rising out of some well of invincibility within. "I will come, I will come for you. In the night, in the day, far away, beyond this land. And you will die."

"Stop this terrible business! In the name of God!" Wellington Cummings cried. "In the spirit of Christ I command it!"

Truscott laughed softly. "Corporal, bring me six men armed with carbines. Let's get this over with."

"This is murder, Truscott. Every one of you will hang," Victorious roared.

The corporal pointed at six frightened dragoons, who formed into a firing squad fifty feet from Skye.

"Sir," asked one trembling man. "I wish to be excused."

"Do your duty. Five years in the stockade if you disobey orders. And if you don't aim true I'll put you against the tree."

All the dragoons were back in camp now, watching, waiting.

"Have at it," Truscott said. "Fire at will."

The nervous soldiers delayed.

"I said, shoot the man."

But no one did.

A sudden rush of hooves near the riverbank turned

their heads. There, ghosting in and out among the cottonwoods, box elder, and willows, coppery warriors were driving away the herd of dragoon horses and draft mules. Cummings thought he saw Many Coups himself, low on a pony, riding hotly behind some horses whose picket lines flayed the wind. Then they were gone. A few of the dragoons emptied their carbines into the woods, lacking a target. They listened to the thrum of hooves and the whinnies and shrieks of maddened horses growing fainter and fainter in the dusk.

"Thanks to you, Mister Truscott, we are now afoot," Cummings said.

"Some treaty, Cummings. They promised not to steal horses or attack soldiers."

"Truscott—doesn't it occur to you that you started it?"

Truscott shrugged. "We went to shoot a horse."

Cummings felt helpless; he and his clerks were unarmed in the face of an obsessed lieutenant commanding a whole troop of itchy dragoons.

"Permission to take a squad and collect horses, sir," said Corporal Rourke.

"After the show, Corporal. It can wait a minute. All right. Let's get this business over," said Truscott, turning to enjoy Skye. The guide was alert now, watching his own death proceedings silently.

"Good. You can enjoy your own execution."

"What are the charges?" Skye mumbled.

"Whatever you want. Anything's fine."

"I will present myself to your judges. Take me east."

"Too late, Skye."

"I will not let this happen," said Victorious, walking straight toward Skye.

"Get out of the line of fire!" yelled Truscott.

But Cummings kept walking, his stick biting the ground.

Skye's woman sobbed.

"I warned you!" Truscott screamed. "Ready, aim . . ."

Cummings reached Skye, and turned to shield the guide with his massive body. He stared into the faces of the frightened dragoons, whose carbines pointed straight at him.

"Do not commit murder," he roared at them. "You'll be punished!"

"Fire!" screamed Truscott.

A ragged volley followed.

"For the love of God," Cummings said.

# Chapter 54

Skye felt the contents of his stomach slide back down his esophagus and his frantic pulse slow a little. Before him, Victorious Cummings muttered, rocked, toppled back into Skye, and slid to the earth, sighing.

Three dragoons dropped their carbines and fled; the other three, looking miserable, flopped into the grass and sat there. There were two holes in Cummings's chest.

An awful silence fell upon them all. Skye caught a whiff of burned powder in the eddying air. He tugged at his arms but his wrists were securely bound behind the slender tree. If he could free himself he'd kill Truscott with his bare hands.

"Halt!" Truscott yelled at the fleeing dragoons. "You're in trouble!" He loomed over the three who'd collapsed to the ground. "Get up and reload." He turned to the rest of his men. "Drag him out of there."

No one moved.

Then Wellington raced to Cummings and plunged

to his knees beside him, staring at the ghastly gout of blood spreading across the superintendent's midsection.

"Victorious!" he cried, shaking the body. "Victorious!"

The superintendent sighed and no more sound came from him. Those two shots to the heart had killed the huge man. Skye needed to vomit; instead, he sagged into his bonds, leaking tears. McGinty and other clerks gathered in horror around the mound of black that had been Victorious, while Wellington slowly shut his brother's eyes and slumped over his body.

Skye beheld a martyr. The man had given his own life so that Skye might live. A lump rose in Skye's throat. He didn't deserve it. A giant, a larger-than-life giant, a majestic mortal had given himself up to protect a worthless British salt named Skye. He felt small. What greater love could a mortal give another?

"All right, all right," said Truscott. "Too bad, but he has only himself to blame."

Wellington turned slowly to Truscott. "Lieutenant, my brother is dead."

"I regret it as much as you do," Truscott said defensively. "Now let us get on with our business." He turned to several dragoons. "Help them carry the superintendent."

No one moved.

"Do you want to be put on report, too?"

Still no one moved.

Skye felt the sawing of a knife on his wrist bonds behind the tree. His heart leapt.

"Don't move, dammit," Victoria said. "This sonofabitch takes cutting."

"Victoria!" he breathed.

"You get the hell out. It's so damn dark white men don't see nothing."

Skye felt his hands fall free. They hurt. All of him hurt, especially his lacerated back. His head throbbed.

"What do you want me to do?"

"Wait for darker," she whispered. "Now shut up."

"Who's with you?"

"Mary, Dirk. They got out while the black-robe man prayed."

Something as sad and lonely as vees of ducks flying south in the fall filtered through him.

"Many Coups here," she whispered. "We got the horses. Now we're gonna get that dumb lieutenant. He makes war; he attacks our herd—we fix him good."

"I want him!" Skye growled. He wanted to squeeze Truscott's throat shut with his bare hands. He yearned to spring at the man and pound him into the dirt, pound him so hard he'd never forget it. But fifty armed dragoons crowded the flat.

"Now!" she whispered. The lieutenant's back was turned; a cortege of clerks carried the superintendent's body toward the Indian Bureau camp. The firing squad watched, dejected.

Skye darted around the tree and stumbled into brush, feeling her bony arm catch him and lead him. They crackled through canebrake.

"Here!" she said, gently lowering his top hat over his blood-soaked hair. "I got your medicine hat."

Skye found himself trembling.

They stumbled to the Little Wind and waded across through knee-deep water, plunging into canebrakes on the east side. He discovered half a dozen Absaroka warriors crouched there, armed and waiting. And Mary and Dirk.

Some hot bubble of emotion burst in him and he clutched Victoria, feeling his relief and rage mingle with hers, feeling her gentle hands tender upon his bloodied back. Then he held Mary, feeling her warmth and love; and drew his son to him also, unable to see through the blur in his eyes.

They heard shouting across the water: "Skye's gone! Get him. Shoot to kill."

Hands pushed Skye and his family into the night, guiding them upstream. He didn't want to leave; he wanted to stomp back and thrash Truscott.

Victoria led Skye, her old longrifle in hand, muttering curses at the blue-shirts. Skye heard the spastic cracks of the carbines firing blindly into the river brush; there'd be no targets in the deepening night. The Crows didn't return the fire. Skye ran as well as his shaky legs permitted while his head throbbed and his stomach churned. He stumbled suddenly into another group of warriors beneath some cottonwoods. And something else: a familiar snort and nicker.

"Jawbone!"

The gray ghost pushed into Skye, sniffed blood, snorted, pressed his head down upon Skye's shoulder. Skye's last aplomb deserted him and he wept hotly, wept for the days of his self-exile from those he loved; wept for Jawbone; wept for all that he'd inflicted on Mary and Dirk and Victoria; wept as one lost and broken and remorseful, all the while feeling Mary's arms about him and Dirk's hand in his.

Jawbone bit him on the arm, just as a reminder of his delinquencies, and then butted him in the chest.

The pain felt terrible. "Avast!" Skye muttered. He stood dizzily, too sick to move.

"You must go," said a commanding voice in the Crow tongue. Many Coups was offering him safety. "Your Shoshone woman will mend your wounds up the river. We have horses. Here."

He thrust something at Skye, and Skye felt the hard, cold contours of his Sharps. "When they are all watching your death I send Little Boy for your things, and he got them all. The blacksuits never saw him. Here is your saddle."

Somehow Skye saddled Jawbone, reeling through the old routine. He stuffed paper cartridges for the

Sharps into his battered shirt. The sound of war rose behind him. But as he listened he realized it was one-sided war: he heard the crack of carbines blindly raking the distant brush but he heard no return fire. The dragoons would search the immediate riverbanks and quit because the curtain of night had descended upon them.

He boarded Jawbone and almost fell off as a wave of dizziness and nausea washed over him. He clutched the pommel with both hands as he felt his gorge rise. He couldn't stop the heaving of his gut, so he leaned to the left and vomited, while his angry horse sidestepped and snarled. He wiped away his gorge and sat upright again, so dizzy he could barely stay seated.

He heard the movement of the Crow warriors and Victoria's soft cursing. He knew Mary and Victoria were close by but he couldn't see them. It was all he could manage to hang on. His head throbbed mercilessly with Jawbone's every footstep and his left arm hung limp, its muscles swollen and useless. Still he endured.

After a while he was aware that the Crows were fording a stream, and after that they paused.

"You all right?" Victoria asked crossly.

"Dizzy. Truscott pistol-whipped me several times. Head's busted open. Dragged me a mile." ·

"We gonna stay right here. We just crossed Wind River. Them blue-shirts are on foot; they ain't coming. Many Coups sent runners and soon the Army's got more damned Absaroka than it ever seen before." She laughed harshly.

"I can handle it myself. I'll get him," he said, as he fell off Jawbone.

# Chapter 55

Wellington Cummings drew a blanket over the body of his brother. The clerks drifted into the night, silent and shaken. He realized he was now in command; he was the assistant supervisor, the senior person on this Indian Bureau mission. He would have to set aside grief and shock and somehow deal with the lieutenant. He did not know whether he was up to it. He had always been a contemplative man, focused on life's larger truths, not a commander of men. Yet he could not abdicate, especially to a man so poorly balanced as Truscott.

The two camps lay dark and eerie, unlit by fires. No clerk wished to make himself a target. Over at the dragoon bivouac the men were still poking through river brush, hunting Skye and his family as if they were raccoons.

Wellington drew a breath, straightened his blood-stained black coat, and walked resolutely back to the bivouac, his steps punctuated by the occasional bark of carbines. The soldiers were sniping at anything that whispered in the night.

He found Truscott standing beside the execution tree, barely visible in the moonless gloom, shouting orders at unseen dragoons. "He can't be far. Keep searching! No quarter—I want the whole family, dead or alive."

Wellington choked back his loathing of the man. This would be no time for accusations. "Lieutenant, a word with you."

Truscott turned. "Look, I'm busy. I don't want civilians around here. I've responsibility enough—"

"Lieutenant, I'm assuming the direction of this expedition. I'm the ranking official now. I insist that you recall your men and stop this business."

"You? Giving orders?"

Wellington didn't reply. He didn't need to. The facts spoke for themselves.

Truscott laughed shortly, unable to deny the obvious. "I'll deal with you later," he said at last. "I'm leading a battle and you're in the line of fire."

"I don't see you leading anyone." Immediately, Wellington wished he hadn't said it.

Truscott exploded. "It so happens, Cummings, that I've lost all my noncoms but one corporal. There's no one left to command. I'm here because it's the safest place. There's Crows out there."

It hung there. Wellington coughed, embarrassed for the lieutenant.

"When your men return I wish to speak to them. We've serious problems, including the loss of the livestock. We haven't so much as a mule to pull our wagons back."

"That's a military problem, Cummings. We'll take care of it."

"Very well," he said gently. "Please tell your men that there'll be a graveside service for Superintendent Cummings tomorrow morning. Many of your men loved and honored my brother and will wish to attend."

"I'll think about it," Truscott said, petulance in his voice. "We're under fire."

"I've heard only your carbines."

"They've freed the renegade. Stolen our horses. I would think even a minister would grasp that much."

Wellington nodded mildly and walked back to his camp. Things could wait until the morning. He slid into the wall tent he had shared with his brother and was stricken by grief. His strange, enormous older brother had somehow turned his private affliction into a grandeur that had set him apart and ennobled him.

Outside, the random firing halted. He heard the dragoons returning, heard Truscott post a double guard, and then heard nothing. They obviously hadn't found the Skyes, and for that Wellington breathed a small prayer of thanksgiving.

A bleakness settled over the whole encampment: the superintendent of the Indian Bureau murdered; no horses or draft mules; dead and injured men, some groaning on pallets over there. In the inky darkness of his tent, Wellington Cummings asked his God that he might be given strength to shoulder the burden that had been thrust on him. Then he settled into a sleepless vigil, remembering the remarkable life of his brother.

At first light his clerks began to chisel out a grave, and by nine all was ready. Victorious lay within a shroud cut from wagonsheet beside a shallow trench chopped into caliche. The clerks gathered, and then some of the soldiers and teamsters. Wellington counted more than thirty, a good number given the injured, those on guard duty, and the dozen or so who understood little English. Two of those who had been forced into the firing squad were present, but Wellington knew that these were ones who had aimed high or wide. At the last, Truscott appeared. The officer wore a dress uniform, his saber rattling at his side, his epaulets golden in the sun.

Wellington stood beside the grave, feeling the bitterness of death catch in his throat under his white clerical collar. A breeze toyed with his silk stole.

"Thank you for joining me this morning. This will not be a funeral; I will offer that when I return to Virginia, among my own people. This will be a prayer, the celebration of a good life; and a few words about what Victorious Bonaparte Cummings sought here, through his stewardship of the Indian Bureau."

He read a prayer for the dead, one filled with the hope and promise of a life beyond the grave. Then he began a simple eulogy of his brother's life, while the dragoons stood, forage caps in hand, and the clerks formed an honor guard around the body.

Then Wellington turned to matters more imminent. "Only a few days ago we gathered on this quiet plain to conclude a treaty of perpetual peace with the leaders of four great nations. It was Victorious Cummings's design to settle these nations in generous homelands, help them learn our modern ways and enter peacefully into our nation. The task was always beyond the capability of any official. There had always been rivalry between the War Department and civilian reformers as to who should control the Indian Bureau and whether the Bureau's business should be simply the subjugation of the tribes by force, or whether we had some responsibility toward these fellow mortals. My brother always believed we had heavy obligations to them. We could not stem the tide of immigration—no government could—but we could do whatever was fairest and most honorable."

Truscott said nothing, but his strange, troubled eyes burned with fires.

"Now, his untimely death shocks us into remembering that we have larger and higher obligations. We owe Congress and the people of this country our respect and obedience. They've set national policy. That policy is not the Army's, nor the Indian Bureau's, but the policy of President Pierce's administration and Congress. It's a time to set aside our differences and work together as Victorious Cummings would want us to do. He gave his all with his martyr's death. We owe him the fulfillment of his mission. To subvert it is to dishonor the dead."

Truscott stirred but remained silent. Wellington eyed him quietly, daring him to interrupt a sacred service.

"My brother would be alive today if we had all concentrated on the larger matters . . . instead of the petty. Some among us wanted to kill a fine horse . . . and execute a man who walks to the beat of a different drummer. My brother, a retired officer, wished that the whole cavalry might be mounted on horses so magnificent; and as for that man, my brother believed that his chosen life, bridging the world of red men and white men, was the key to the success of the conference. And so it proved to be. Without Mister Skye and his remarkable family, the policy of Congress and the administration would not have been achieved. But because there were those who wished to destroy both the man and horse, my brother is dead, a martyr to his country, to the red men he respected, and to the will of God. For it is written in the Beatitudes, 'Blessed are the peacemakers, for they shall be called the children of God.' "

Wellington paused, watching Truscott redden and fidget.

"I would remind all you good and true men who bear arms that there's a higher law than that of commanders; that one cannot blindly obey that which is evil. The blue uniform and the soldier's oath will not clothe naked evil. Now we have a duty before us: we must work together as never before, patch the peace if we still can, and return to Fort Laramie by whatever means. It will require cooperation, forgiveness, mercy, and generosity. It will require the virtue of each and every man present.

"At Fort Laramie we will face an exhaustive inquiry into these tragic affairs; and that will be only the beginning. We may expect Congress to examine each participant minutely. Those who are blameless will find honor; those whose judgment was flawed, or suffered moral lapses, will face just punishment. Those who testify truly will be vindicated; those who don't will be caught out. Think on it, and for my brother's sake make right what has gone wrong."

He paused, lifting his arms in benediction. "And now may the grace of the Father, the Son, and the Holy Spirit dwell with the beloved departed and with those here present evermore. Amen."

But even before he finished, and before the body of Victorious Bonaparte Cummings was lowered into its final resting place, an apparition appeared before them.

# Chapter 56

Before them stood Skye. He looked ghastly. He didn't wear his top hat because his head was misshapen from the pistol-whipping. Black flesh circled his eyes. His eyeballs had turned bright red. His left sleeve was caked with blood from the bullet wound, and it hung useless. In his right hand he carried a stick of some sort but otherwise was unarmed. Behind him stood his women, each carrying a nocked bow, and four Crow chiefs.

Anthony Truscott was delighted. The fools had walked right into camp. He surveyed the chiefs, dismissing them. He spotted Many Coups, Bear's Head, Rottentail, Two Face, and several other Crow headmen and warriors.

The clerks and soldiers stared uneasily from beside the grave; the savages and Skye stared back.

"Arrest him!" cried Truscott.

No one moved. His men at graveside were unarmed.

"I order you—arrest him. And the women."

"Hold up, mate," Skye said, "Many Coups wants you to know that there are over six hundred Crow warriors and headmen on the other side of the Wind River. If any harm comes to us no soldier will leave here alive."

"It's a bluff. They've all left!" Truscott yelled. But even as he spoke, Skye's women aimed their bows at him. Panic shot through Truscott.

No soldier moved.

"In the name of God stop your raging, Lieutenant," the reverend snapped. "We're conducting a holy service."

"But this is war."

"We're sorry to interrupt," said Skye.

"Your business must wait, Mister Skye. We are burying my brother."

"The Crows are withdrawing from the treaty, Reverend. But we'll wait—"

Truscott gloated. He'd succeeded in torpedoing the treaty after all.

Cummings looked nonplussed. "But Mister Skye, the treaty's done."

"It hasn't been ratified by your Senate. If your government has the right to reject it, so do the tribes. But we'll wait. We wish to honor your brother."

Many Coups spoke to Skye, who conveyed the message. "Many Coups says that the Crows honor your brother and want to join in the burial. The Crows know that the superintendent was their friend and sought the good of their people. The Crows want you to tell the great grandfather in Washington that they will always honor your brother."

Wellington Cummings nodded, something bordering on tears filling his choked face. He sniffled and then nodded to the clerks. McGinty and all the clerks clustered on both sides of the shrouded body and wrestled it clumsily into the earth. The remains of Victorious Cummings smacked the bottom of the grave with a dismaying thud. Then the two clerks with spades swiftly shoveled the torn clay into the hole. It landed on the canvas with staccato thumps.

A few minutes later a mound of yellow clay rose over the body of the superintendent. Wellington, barely in control of himself, fumbled open his Book of Common Prayer and read a final blessing, commending the soul of Victorious Bonaparte Cummings to God. Then he stepped back and pawed tears from his brimming eyes.

But it was not over. Many Coups stepped to the head of the grave and drove a splendid lance into the earth. A breeze whirled the eagle feathers dangling in bunches from its staff.

"This is a chief's lance," Many Coups said, while Skye softly translated. "Forevermore this place will be sacred to the Absaroka people. This lance will tell all Indians of all tribes that a revered person lies here and no one must profane the place. It is the honor the Crows bestow on a great man of the white people."

Cummings wept. He embraced Many Coups silently, unable to speak.

Truscott watched it all with impatience, his mind devising ways to take advantage of this opportunity. The Skyes had walked straight into his parlor.

"Now then, Mister Skye, we'll discuss the treaty with them," Wellington said.

"Are you sure, sir? My people are willing to wait."

*My people!* The heresy was delicious in Truscott's ears.

"Now is as good a time as any."

"The Crows, sir, want their names scratched from the treaty. No sooner than they signed it, they say, the soldiers started a war, attacked the village and the herd. They can't speak for the other tribes, but they're determined to withdraw."

"I'm terribly sorry. What the Army did was not—"

Many Coups spoke sharply.

"The chief says they won't honor the treaty whether they signed it or not. It's like dirt to them."

Cummings surrendered. "Mister McGinty, bring the treaty and pens and ink."

The chief clerk hurried off to a wagon and soon returned with the rolled-up parchment. He unrolled it on the grass and drew a black line through the names of the Crow chiefs.

Skye said something in the Crow tongue to Many Coups and the chief nodded. "That cancels it," Skye said in English.

"I'm afraid, Mister Skye, that the Senate won't ratify a treaty with the principal tribe scratched off it. The whole treaty's doomed. This trip—all of Victorious's work . . ."

"It can't be helped, sir," said Skye. "The dragoons managed to torpedo it. On purpose, I imagine."

Truscott gloated while McGinty rolled up the treaty and returned it to the wagon.

"Mister Skye, convey to our guests my double grief. Not only is my brother dead but also our hopes for a treaty with their nations. I am stricken almost to death. I'd thought at least to salvage the treaty as a memorial to my good brother's name and purposes. But now . . ." Cummings's voice trailed off.

Quietly Skye translated to the solemn chiefs and warriors. None replied. What was done was done.

Truscott rejoiced. The turn of events impelled him to take the next step.

"Skye, you're under arrest. Come quietly—you and your squaws—or take the consequences."

A few of his men stirred, eyeing the blood-caked man fearfully.

"I have business with you, Truscott," said Skye. "It may as well be now." The man's voice rumbled with doom.

Skye lumbered toward Truscott, his red eyes glowing fiendishly. "What are the charges, Truscott? Tell me the charges once again."

"Stop where you are!" Truscott bawled. He whipped out his saber and slashed air with it.

"There are no charges, Truscott."

The man kept coming at him, straight toward the glinting saber. Skye was berserk. Truscott felt his own wild laughter erupt from him.

"I'm real and you're not," Skye rumbled. "That's what it's all about."

"I don't know what you're talking about." Truscott found himself stepping backward. He couldn't control the impulse to retreat.

"I'm real; you're smoke," said Skye. "And you know it."

"Stop him!" Truscott bellowed. He'd backed into his soldiers beside the grave.

"For the love of God, stop this, Mister Skye. For the sake of my brother," the clergyman implored.

"I think he'd be applauding, mate."

The soldiers gave way for Truscott. He stumbled over Victorious Cummings's grave, toppled, and sprang up again, panic working through him. Skye never stopped.

Panic swept Truscott. He laughed crazily. "I'll kill you, Skye. I've a saber and you're not armed."

Skye kept coming. "I'm armed, Truscott." He waved a hardwood stick. "This is a belaying pin—the weapon of any common seaman. Test me."

Truscott did. He lunged at Skye, his saber slapping and jabbing wildly, seeking quick victory. But Skye parried with his stick. It flared at one end just ahead of a handle, protecting Skye's hand. Truscott's wild saber clacked against hardwood. Skye grinned. Truscott thrust wildly but the belaying pin bashed the thrust aside. Then a stunning blow knocked it out of Truscott's hand. His fingers stung. The saber clattered to earth in two pieces.

"Arrest him!" he shrieked.

Skye kept coming. Truscott backpedaled, dodged, and danced. Skye lumbered toward him.

Truscott turned to run but Skye's massive hand—the one attached to his bad arm—caught Truscott's tunic at the chest. Skye shook Truscott until the officer's teeth rattled. Truscott flailed at Skye with his small hands. He smelled Skye's foul breath, and peered into those blood-red eyes, only inches away. He felt as if he'd been shaken to little pieces.

"You're striking an officer," he shrieked.

Skye laughed, nauseous gases erupting from his belly. He slammed Truscott into a cottonwood tree. "We'll fix that," he roared. His left hand grasped one of Truscott's golden epaulets and wrenched it off the tunic with such violence that Truscott was thrown sideways. Skye yanked the other epaulet off, yanking Truscott in the other direction. The shoulder seams had burst.

"There you are, Truscott. Now you're a private. We can settle it man to man."

"Leave me alone! I'll fix you when I get back."

"Back to Leavenworth, Truscott. Leavenworth. They'll hang you for murder at Leavenworth."

"I was doing my duty—"

"Murder, Truscott. Not even a former lieutenant escapes the gallows."

"I'll escape."

"Into what? The stockade? How about twenty years for wrecking United States diplomacy? Disobeying orders? Subverting the council every way you could? You're done, Truscott. Disgraced. Do you think any officer in Washington City will stand up for you after the facts are out?" Skye laughed heartily, and rattled Truscott's rag-doll body again. Then he let go. Truscott sank to the earth, pawing at his naked shoulders and finding no epaulets there.

Skye turned to Wellington Cummings. "I'm sorry. It had to happen."

# Chapter 57

Skye watched the Crows herd the draft horses and mules into the bivouac, where soldiers swiftly caught them.

Wellington Cummings was astonished. "What is this, Mister Skye? Are they returning the horses?"

"They're turning back the draft horses and mules. Crows want you out of here. They're keeping the dragoon mounts. They figure the saddle horses are the spoils of war, Mister Cummings. There's no treaty stoppin' them either."

"We can leave? We're not trapped here? Praise God!"

"Maybe you'd better praise Many Coups' diplomacy."

Pandemonium reigned. Everywhere, dragoons and teamsters stalked the loose draft animals. Clerks helped, cornering the big horses, throwing harnesses over the backs of giant Army mules.

The sight of the draft animals energized Truscott,

who suddenly lifted himself from the roots of the tree where he had slouched. Skye watched the officer tear toward the milling herd, intent on catching an animal.

"Harness up the animals. We'll leave in an hour," Truscott yelled.

But the soldiers were already doing just that and scarcely heard him.

Skye watched Truscott collect two bridles and stalk a pair of mules. He bridled the mules and led them to his tent and picketed them there. Then he saddled both mules.

Skye sighed, knowing what he was seeing, and walked back to the Indian Bureau camp, where clerks were busily throwing their gear into the wagons.

He found Victoria and Mary watching the hubbub, along with several Crows.

"You beat the crap outa him," Victoria said, her eyes aglow.

"He earned it."

She was smiling at him. "Damn! That was good to see."

"I didn't even strike him. I just shook him and pulled off his shoulderboards."

"The lieutenant boards?"

"His rank's sewn on in gold thread."

"Damn, that was fun!" she said. She touched him and it sent a jolt through him. "You feeling better?" she asked, her gaze intent.

"I hurt so much I can't think."

"I don't mean that, dammit. You got a skull thick as a buffalo's."

He laughed. She laughed, too. Mary's somber face dissolved into laughter.

"I was proud of my—of you," Mary said.

"Where's Dirk?"

"He is with the Crow mothers across the river."

"Wish I could see the rascal."

Mary's face crumpled. "He's not far away, Mister Skye. He—wants to see you."

Skye ran a hand delicately over his lacerated skull. "I have to take them back to Laramie," he said. "Would you keep Jawbone? I don't want him around those dragoons. There's some as would shoot him. They blame a lot of death and injury on him."

"Sonofabitch," she muttered. "I should take him where you want to leave him, yes?" She eyed Skye truculently.

"No, Victoria. Don't take him up to the Pryors."

"Why not?"

"I'm coming back for him. I'm—not going east. I'd hate it in a minute."

"You ain't going?"

"No. My home is here."

"You good-for-nothing sonofabitch," she snapped. "Make up your mind."

"I have, Victoria."

The Skyes stood quietly while clerks threw camp gear into the wagons and dragoons hooked harnessed teams to the wagons. They'd be clearing out in a few minutes. Skye was stabbed by a desire not to go. But he had a contract to fulfill.

Many Coups approached. "The soldier-chief has put saddles on the mules," he said. "I think I know why."

"Watch," said Skye.

They waited a few minutes. Then they spotted Truscott riding along the river on one mule while leading the other, which had been turned into a pack animal. The thick river brush almost hid him. He forded the Little Wind and vanished on the far bank.

"Sonofabitch!" yelled Victoria. She whooped and danced. Mary smiled softly.

None of the busy clerks and dragoons had seen Truscott leave.

"Gone to California," said Skye. Truscott was heading toward the California Trail. In a bit he would spur his mules. By the time anyone went after him he'd be five miles over the hill.

Wellington Cummings approached them, his face still rigid with grief. "Was that the lieutenant I saw riding up the river?" he asked.

"Deserted," said Skye, enjoying himself.

"Deserted!"

"Couldn't stand what was waiting for him at Leavenworth, I guess. Couldn't stand losing his mask."

"I can't believe it. An officer deserting."

"It proves something," Skye said.

"You don't suppose he's racing back to Laramie ahead of us to poison the minds of everyone before we get there?"

Skye smiled. "We'll see, won't we?"

"I've dreaded that above all else—Truscott, with his gilded tongue, back there inventing lies, twisting everything around."

"I wouldn't worry about it," muttered Skye. "He's gone."

Quietly Victoria translated all this to Many Coups.

"Haiyah! That is how we do it. The disgraced man must leave the camp and go somewhere else," Many Coups cried in Crow.

"You know, Mister Skye, we're duty-bound to go after him," said Wellington. "Catch him and turn him over to his superiors."

"His own conscience will punish him. Every soul here knows he's smoke. Every time he peers into the looking glass at his beautiful blond hair he'll see a deserter. I take a certain pleasure in it."

"I understand," said Wellington. "But my conscience rests uneasy."

"There's justice in the universe," said Skye. "It'll

catch up with him sooner or later. He could strike it rich out in the goldfields, yet still hate himself. We can't escape justice."

Corporal Rourke approached. "Sahs, have you seen Lieutenant Truscott? We can't find 'im. He was 'ere only a few minutes ago, saddlin' some mules. Now he's gone and we're about set to go."

"I don't think you'll find him, Corporal," said Wellington.

"He's around, sir. We'll find 'im."

"No, I don't think so ... He's left us."

"Left us, sah? You mean left us?"

"Young man, you're now the ranking soldier. A noncom. I'm putting you in command of the troop. And I'm placing Mister Skye over you until we get to Laramie. Will you heed him?"

Rourke looked from Wellington to Skye. "You mean the lieutenant—"

"Over the hill," said Skye.

"Over the hill, is he now?" Rourke whistled. "Over the bloomin' hill. The act fits the man. Shall we go after him, sah?"

Wellington glanced uneasily at Skye. "Do you think you should, Corporal?"

"It's in the book, sah. But we lack the mounts to git him."

"Let it go, Corporal. The Army'll catch up with him. He's heading for California wearing his uniform. And riding a pair of Army-branded mules."

"I never heard of no officer going over the hill, sah. Pardon my saying, but it's a rotten soul in him made him do it."

"This'll surprise your men, Corporal. You'll have to break the news," Wellington said.

"Yessah. God spare us. I'll tell the men. They won't believe me, sah."

"We'll tell them together. Some of us saw him ride out, Corporal. I did."

Skye led them to the wagons, where the Army teamsters were hitching teams and loading the last of the gear.

"Har, har!" Corporal Rourke yelled. "The guide has something to say to youse."

Slowly the soldiers stopped their toil and waited.

"Lieutenant Truscott has deserted, mates," said Skye. "He saddled a pair of draft mules and took off a while ago. Some of us watched him. He's probably on his way to California."

The men stared unbelievingly at Skye, and then at the empty bivouac. Truscott was not in sight.

A dragoon laughed. "Goes to show the high mucketymucks ain't so fancy."

"The ranking soldier is Corporal Rourke, here. He's a good man and I'm placing him in command," said Wellington.

"Stand for roll call," bellowed Rourke. "I don't want a bloody man of ye taking notions."

The dragoons reluctantly formed into a line. Rourke paraded before them, naming each.

"You're all here, saving for the dead and the poor souls resting hurt in them wagons. Keep it that way. We're marching back to old Leavenworth proud o' the blue. Any man objecting, let him step farward and put up his dukes."

None did. The transfer of authority had gone without a hitch.

"See to your work, now, and be quick about it," Rourke roared.

"The corporal has a way about him. I'll put in a word with Hoffman when we get back there," Wellington said.

"I think we'd better look at Truscott's campsite," Skye said. "See what he took. You'll want to make your report as complete as possible."

Skye and Wellington Cummings walked into the

empty bivouac area and located the rectangle of yellowed grass where Lieutenant Truscott had slept, preened, plotted, and undermined the whole peace expedition.

Three gunnysacks filled with something lay abandoned.

# Chapter 58

Wellington squinted about him. He and Skye were alone in the emptied bivouac. All the rest were clustered around the wagons.

Skye emptied a gunnysack. Annuity items. A skillet, pot, knife, tin cup, some hanks of beads. He emptied a blanket and various ragged pieces of calico and flannels from another. The third sack yielded various staples, coffee beans, flour, sugar, stuffed into Army cartridge cases.

"What's this? Annuity goods. Do you suppose Truscott was stealing this?"

"No, mate." Skye squatted and examined the stuff closely. His big, awkward fingers poked and probed, while Cummings watched, bewildered.

"He was collecting evidence. See here," said Skye. "A handle should be riveted to the skillet, but it's off. This pot lacks a bail. And look at this knife—wrought iron, I'd guess."

He handed a crudely made knife to Wellington.

"You're saying these are defective goods, Mister Skye?"

Skye took the knife. "Feel that blade. Dull edge. Look." He bent the blade and it stayed bent. "That's not steel."

He handed Cummings a red-painted axhead. "Look at this, mate. No machined edge on it. Cast iron, I'd guess." It looked like a useful tool. "If it's cast iron it's almost useless."

A foreboding built in Wellington Cummings.

Skye lifted a blanket and shook it. "Look at this, mate. You can see through it."

Light filtered through the flimsy blanket. Then Skye held up shoddy flannels and calicoes, fabric that wouldn't last a month.

He opened a cartridge case full of wrinkled and mottled coffee beans. He examined some flour, and pointed to the brown mealybugs in it.

"Mister Skye, I don't know what to say. It's our policy to buy top-quality goods. We want the tribes to be well outfitted with things they need. That's not just humane, it's simple diplomacy."

"Some of it's all right," Skye said. "That's a pretty good looking glass. But a lot isn't. I knew it."

"You knew it, sir?"

"Saw the stuff handed to the Crows. Most of it made 'em laugh. They bent the knives, emptied the flour sacks, threw out the coffee beans. I imagine those beans've sat in the back of some Brazil warehouse for years."

He pried open a pasteboard carton of gunpowder and found it caked from some ancient soaking.

"Graft," said Wellington Cummings. "Graft! Mister Skye, the wrath of God will descend on our suppliers. I'll track down every crooked merchant. I'll send them to jail!"

"I'm afraid it's not quite like that, mate."

"Oh, I know it won't be easy. I'll make myself unpopular. I'll step on toes close to the administration. But pity the poor Indians, Mister Skye. They bargained in good faith. It's a wonder the whole lot of them didn't come back and cancel the treaty on the spot."

"Some of it's useful, mate."

"Don't they know quality, Mister Skye? Couldn't they tell?"

"Of course they do. Hudson's Bay always had the advantage over Yank traders because they trade high-quality stuff. The blankets are top-notch. Their trade rifles are solid and last forever. The Indians know exactly what's well made and what isn't."

"And now we've shamed ourselves."

Skye stood and peered uneasily at Wellington. "I don't know how to tell you this, but your trouble's inside of the Bureau. You'd better start with your clerks."

Wellington was aghast. "My clerks? You mean Mister McGinty?"

"Him especially. Didn't he negotiate for the goods? Wasn't it up to him to inspect them, make sure they were up to snuff?"

"Excuse me, Mister Skye, but what possible benefit would Mister McGinty get from it?"

Skye sighed. "He lives high on a clerk's salary, sir. Even a chief clerk's salary."

"Why, so he does. I've always thought the man had a private competence. Why, sir, the Bureau's been cheated."

Wellington felt dizzy and settled into the grass. "My brother's dead—and betrayed. The treaty's doomed. And now this." He felt desolated. "I don't know what to do."

Skye squatted beside him. "You'll have to deal with it."

"Maybe I'm guilty as charged, sir. We knew McGinty was making a bit on the side. The patronage system is something no man can buck, sir. You pay your tribute to the administration, no matter who's in. You pay it or you don't work for the government. McGinty always took some tribute out of everyone's pay for Pierce and Fillmore and the rest. A venal business, but one to endure since there's no cure. But sir, I swear before God that neither Victorious or I had any inkling—"

"Whoa up, mate." Skye's beefy hand steadied Wellington.

"What should I do? I'm a clergyman, not a bureaucrat. I know this—if I make it public, they'll put me out of the Bureau so fast I won't have time to empty my desk. And blacken my name. That's how politicians are, sir. Show them evil in their empire and you're ushered out."

"Mister Cummings, you'll do what's right no matter what price you must pay."

Cummings quieted. "Thank you, Mister Skye. I'll have a devil of a time but I'll do what my conscience requires."

Skye began packing the stuff into the gunnysacks once again.

"I suppose I'd better hide it from the clerks. If they find it they'll get rid of the evidence," Wellington mused.

"I'll give the sacks to Rourke and tell him to put them with the dragoon gear. You can have Rourke turn these over to Colonel Hoffman at Laramie. Hoffman can seal it all in a barrel and send it east on Army transport."

"But won't the Army use it against the Bureau? I'd hate to see Congress turn the the Bureau back to the Army—put the poor Indians in the hands of generals."

"That was Truscott's scheme, mate. But not every officer's like him. I think you'll find allies there, men who'd like a civilian Bureau helping the tribes."

"Yes, thank you." Wellington stood and peered about him. "I'll do what's necessary. Maybe I can clean house myself. But if I can't, I'll find allies. Maybe in Congress."

Skye finished the repacking and hoisted the sacks to his shoulder. "Let's go talk to Rourke," he said.

They walked back to the forming wagon train and Skye dropped the sacks onto the bed of a wagon holding dragoon gear.

"Corporal Rourke, I want those bags protected. Consider them sealed," Wellington said.

Rourke nodded. "Evidence against 'im. Saw youse out there."

"Evidence anyway," Wellington said. "Protect it."

"Certainly, sah. We're ready to go any time, sah."

"Form them up. I'll say good-bye to Many Coups and the Crows, and we'll be off."

He headed for the knot of Crow headmen who stood watching. Skye was standing painfully before his former wives, the three of them solemn.

Wellington studied them for a moment. The Skyes were trying to say good-bye again, and having a bad time of it, locked into their separation.

He decided what he would do and the thought gladdened him. He approached the Skyes, feeling as if he were an intruder upon some private and painful family conference.

"Mister Skye, our work is over. We're going east. There's no need for you to take us back to Fort Laramie. Our Corporal Rourke is a bulldog, and he'll get us there safely. I'm dismissing you here. Of course if you choose to go back—why, ah, we'd welcome your company. But I thought perhaps you and Jawbone might prefer the company of the Crows."

Skye studied him with those alert blue eyes. "You're cashiering me?"

"Not cashiering you, Mister Skye. Releasing you from further service. You've fulfilled your contract. I'll square it with your agent—Colonel Bullock, is it?— and the commander there—Hoffman, I believe it is. Is that acceptable to you? Or, ah, were you planning to go east?"

A strange, almost unfathomable emotion slid across Skye's features.

"No, I'm not planning to go east. Never. The East came to me here, sir. I don't like the East. I like it here—and always will. I didn't know what I had."

"I understand, Mister Skye. You've served us beyond duty, beyond devotion. You've served us with glory, at terrible cost. I will always honor you."

Victoria said, "Tell Bullock the sonofabitch won't be back until spring."

"I will convey the precise message, madam."

As the caravan rolled south, Cummings's last view of the Skyes confirmed his judgment. Skye stood watching, flanked by his wives. His burly arms had encircled the waist of each.

# Chapter 59

Sometimes in the night Mary cried. Not because she felt sad but because the sweetness of life overwhelmed her, and then her eyes overflowed. She lay in the stillness of the lodge and stared at the flinty stars through the smoke hole. A while earlier Mister Skye had come to her and made love, and she had clutched him to her with a strange joy. Now he was asleep, the faint rasp of his breathing rhythmic in the night. He had come to both of his wives many times the past moon.

She could not sleep, so she drew her thick Hudson's Bay blanket about her and slid outdoors. For a moment she admired the creamy new seventeen-skin lodge, still not stained by smoke. It had been the gift of Victoria's Otter Clan sisters. Mary felt as comfortable here among this Kicked-in-the-Bellies village of the Crows as among her own people.

This autumn had been sweeter than any she'd known in her young life, somehow filled with mystery and magic and something more, a sacredness that had scented it. She loved Mister Skye, but that was less important than the other: Mister Skye loved her. She saw it in him the day he fought against Truscott. She had been horrified by his bruised and bloodied body, but the hurt and bewilderment were gone from his eyes. He had gazed on her through eyes as clear as a trout creek, and she had seen his love for her pooled in them, just as it always had been.

The village had meandered through the fall, following the buffalo and finding them plentiful. This night they were on the Musselshell, and tomorrow they'd make more meat from the great herd that grazed at the foot of the Snowy Mountains. Mister Skye's body had swiftly healed and his spirit showed no sign of the strange ordeal that had gripped him for so many moons. He had spent sweet, indolent days showing Dirk how to hunt, fashioning a tiny bow and some arrows for the boy. Mary's son had first stared at his father shyly, something reserved in his small face. But Mister Skye had won his son back and soon his whoops and roars were triggering squeals of joy from this half-white, half-red child. She had watched quietly, saying nothing because nothing needed to be said.

Victoria had never looked happier. She was in her village and would stay there the whole winter. She had her man back. Each day she slid away to gossip with the clan-sisters, jabbering in her own tongue. But she never neglected Mary and often the two gathered roots and berries together. With the frosts the buffalo berries sweetened, and Mister Skye's wives made a good pemmican of them and stuffed the long tubes of it into their parfleches against a time of hunger or winter trouble.

Mary wondered whether Mister Skye still yearned for those things that a red woman could not provide him: the things in books and magazines, the gossip of white men and women, the fancy clothes that white women wore, and whatever those people talked about together in the night when they made love. She saw no sign of it in Mister Skye. He never looked eastward, never even suggested a trip to a trading post. He spoke Crow to Victoria and Shoshone to Mary, but when they were together they all spoke English.

That was why Mary cried. Life was so sweet she could barely endure the sweetness.

Jawbone snorted, and glided up to her, ghostlike. He nudged Mary with his muzzle, and nickered so quietly that no one in the Skye lodge would hear. He yawned, opened wide his terrible jaws, and nipped her shoulder.

"Ow! You are an evil horse," she whispered to him. "I'm glad your medicine is good. We would have given our lives for you if we had to. But your medicine was too strong for them."

The thought of the deadly soldiers marching through the lands of the people chilled her for a moment. But that was a long time ago and maybe they would not come again for a long time.

She crawled back into her lodge, enjoying its leathery fragrance and the peaceful breathing of those she loved. She curled up against Mister Skye and in the darkness his arm drew her close.

# Author's Note

All the Skye's West stories are pure fiction, but they hew closely to actual history. There was no such treaty as the one described here, but the text of this treaty was taken from the actual Treaty of 1855 with the Blackfeet. The 1850s were the decade of treaty-making with the Plains Indians, and by the end of the decade most tribes had been placed in reservations. Through the middle of the nineteenth century reformers contested with the Army for control of the Indian Bureau. Each side had its weaknesses, and no approach ever dealt very well with the dispossession of the Indians.

Washakie was a great Eastern Shoshone chief who was eager to adopt the ways of white men, and led his people in that direction. He became the principal chief of the Eastern Shoshones in 1840 and died in 1900 at an age well over 100. In the 1870s he joined General Crook, with about 150 of his warriors, in the campaign against the Sioux and Cheyenne. He received a military funeral and burial that honored his career in the

Army. He represented his people in the various treaty and cession councils between them and the United States Government. The first of these actually occurred at Fort Bridger in 1863. It defined the boundaries of the Shoshone Reservation, giving the Shoshones a vast territory amounting to 44,672,000 acres. In 1868 the second Fort Bridger council reduced it to 2,774,000 acres in western Wyoming. In 1874 additional gold-bearing areas of the reservation were also ceded.

—RSW

# SKYE'S WEST
## BY RICHARD S. WHEELER

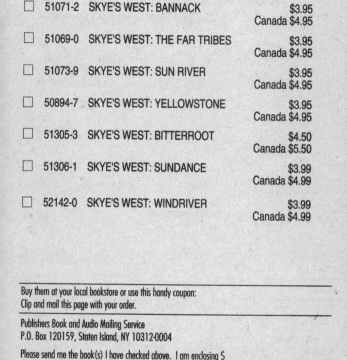

| | | |
|---|---|---|
| ☐ 51071-2 | SKYE'S WEST: BANNACK | $3.95<br>Canada $4.95 |
| ☐ 51069-0 | SKYE'S WEST: THE FAR TRIBES | $3.95<br>Canada $4.95 |
| ☐ 51073-9 | SKYE'S WEST: SUN RIVER | $3.95<br>Canada $4.95 |
| ☐ 50894-7 | SKYE'S WEST: YELLOWSTONE | $3.95<br>Canada $4.95 |
| ☐ 51305-3 | SKYE'S WEST: BITTERROOT | $4.50<br>Canada $5.50 |
| ☐ 51306-1 | SKYE'S WEST: SUNDANCE | $3.99<br>Canada $4.99 |
| ☐ 52142-0 | SKYE'S WEST: WINDRIVER | $3.99<br>Canada $4.99 |

# WESTERN ADVENTURE
# FROM TOR